"What?" He looked confused.

"You haven't even kissed me. On the lips with your lips," she explained, rolling her eyes. "So don't stand there and tell me you—"

He moved so fast she wondered if he had special powers. Before she could even take her next breath, his hands were on her cheeks and he was tilting her head back.

And then his mouth was on hers.

Nikki knew she'd never been kissed like this. There was nothing soft and sweet about this kiss. Oh no, this kiss branded her within seconds. His mouth moved along hers as his fingers played out across her cheeks.

Everything they'd been arguing about slipped away, and it was just him finally, *finally* kissing her. Nikki's body, her heart, and every part of her took over. She wrapped her arms around his neck as she kissed him back.

By Jennifer L. Armentrout

The de Vincent Series

MOONLIGHT SEDUCTION
MOONLIGHT SINS

TILL DEATH
FOREVER WITH YOU
FALL WITH ME

By J. Lynn

STAY WITH ME
BE WITH ME
WAIT FOR YOU

The Covenant Series

DAIMON • HALF-BLOOD
PURE • DEITY
ELIXIR • APOLLYON

The Lux Series

SHADOWS • OBSIDIAN
ONYX • OPAL
ORIGIN • OPPOSITION

Gamble Brothers Series

TEMPTING THE BEST MAN
TEMPTING THE PLAYER
TEMPTING THE BODYGUARD

JENNIFER L. ARMENTROUT

Moonlight Seduction

A de Vincent Novel

AVONBOOKS

An Imprint of HarperCollinsPublishers

MOONLIGHT SEDUCTION. Copyright © 2018 by Jennifer L. Armentrout. All rights reserved. Printed in the United States of America. No part of this book may be used or reproduced in any manner whatsoever without written permission except in the case of brief quotations embodied in critical articles and reviews. For information, address HarperCollins Publishers, 195 Broadway, New York, NY 10007.

First Avon Books mass marketing printing: July 2018

Print Edition ISBN: 978-0-06-267456-2
Digital Edition ISBN: 978-0-06-267454-8

Cover design by Amy Halperin
Cover photograph by Wander Aguiar Photography

Avon, Avon & logo, and Avon Books & logo are registered trademarks of HarperCollins Publishers in the United States of America and other countries.
HarperCollins is a registered trademark of HarperCollins Publishers in the United States of America and other countries.

FIRST EDITION

18 19 20 21 22 QGM 10 9 8 7 6 5 4 3 2 1

For you, the reader

Prologue

Six years ago . . .

*N*icolette Besson was going to *die*.

She was seriously going to drown herself if the de Vincent brothers didn't leave the veranda. Like, hold her own head underwater and never come back up, because there was no way in heck she was going to let them see her in her new bathing suit.

Nope.

She peered over the edge of the pool. There was a good chance the brothers didn't even know she was in the pool since she was on her knees in the shallow end, hiding like an idiot.

What were they even doing over there, all huddled together, whispering? Knowing them, they were probably up to no good whatsoever.

If her daddy knew they were out here, all crowded together like they were, with Lucian, as always, in the middle of the huddle, he'd say they were up to *shenanigans*.

Whatever shenanigans meant.

Devlin was the oldest de Vincent, and Gabriel was the middle one. Lucian was the youngest of the brothers, and he was always in trouble. *Always*. Especially since their momma died and their sister disappeared. Devlin and Gabriel looked just like their father, dark haired and intense, but Lucian and his twin took after their mother.

She really hoped Lucian's friend wasn't with them. Parker Harrington gave her the creeps. He was always . . . *staring* at her. Which was weird, because he wasn't particularly nice to her. Sometimes he stared at her like she wasn't worthy to be sharing the same air as him, and other times, he stared at her like . . .

Nikki shuddered, not wanting to think about that.

She bit down on her lip as the cement edge of the pool practically burned her fingers. When were they going to leave? Her mom would be done in the kitchen soon and she'd have to get out of the pool and then they'd see her and she would *just* die.

Gosh, why in the world did she ever get in this pool? She couldn't even swim, but everything had been so hot and sticky. And she'd been bored sitting in one of the many rooms in the mansion, not touching anything or going anywhere because Mr. de Vincent was home.

Mr. de Vincent didn't like noise of any kind, and all Nikki did was make noise. Lots of it. Sometimes she just got excited and forgot where she was. Sitting quietly was not how she wanted to spend her summer vacation from school. Ugh. They had—

Lucian suddenly threw his head back, laughing wildly. The sound startled her and she felt her lips twitch. Lucian had the *best* laugh. It always sounded like he was seconds away from something crazy happening—something that would most likely upset his father and make her parents shake their heads fondly.

What were they doing?

Her gaze shifted to Devlin. He was standing there, staring at Lucian with a blank face. Gabe was grinning, though, and shaking his head while Lucian made weird gestures with his hands.

Gabe was always grinning.

Nikki wondered if Gabe had brought her any spare wood back from his workshop. He hadn't in a while and her fingers were itching to make use of the new woodcarving set her parents had gotten her for Christmas. She was just learning how to make beads out of the wood, the hollowed-out kind she could force string through to make a necklace or bracelet. She could ask Gabe now, but then he'd see her in the pool, and she couldn't let that happen.

If there was one person she did not want to see her in her bathing suit, it was Gabe.

Inching over the floor of the pool, she was careful and quiet as the water steadily rose around her. A sudden gust of wind rocked the patio umbrella and the scent of roses from the nearby garden surrounded her. The sky was starting to turn gray and mean looking toward the south. A storm was coming. *Great.* Maybe she wouldn't have to drown herself. Maybe she'd get lucky and lightning would take her out.

Because she was not letting them see her in her stupid, too-big one-piece Mom bought from the local Kmart.

No way.

The de Vincents were like three brothers to her—older brothers. Like *waaay* older. Well, Gabe and Lucian treated her like a sister. Not Devlin, though. He acted like she didn't exist, and that was just fine by her, because Devlin didn't like noise either and he never smiled. Like ever.

Even though Nikki had just turned sixteen, she wasn't even sure how she felt about boys other than the fact she found most of them annoying. She heard her momma once telling her daddy that she was a late bloomer. Nikki rolled her eyes. She wasn't a stupid flower or something.

But the de Vincents were different. They weren't *boys* in any real sense of the word. And everyone Nikki knew found them attractive. After all, her best friend's older sister had supposedly hooked up with Lucian and was now totally obsessed with him.

Not that Nikki would ever admit this, but she always thought Gabe was *sooo* hot. It was because of the hair.

He wore it longer than his brothers, to his shoulders, and it looked thick and soft, and made her want to do weird things, like touch it.

Randomly touching his hair would be super weird.

And she super doubted he'd appreciate that.

Nikki flushed as she found herself staring at Gabe. He was wearing a pair of jeans and a white shirt, and he was barefoot even though the pavers had to be steaming hot under his feet.

She kind of thought he had nice feet.

Gabe had a nice laugh, too. He also had a nice smile. One that always made Nikki smile. And he was *kind*. He always sat and asked her how school was or what she and her friends were up to. He showed her how to turn a square piece of wood into something amazing. He was a friend to her despite the fact he probably had a ton of better stuff to do.

The three brothers were very different. Devlin was the cold one. Lucian was the crazy one. And Gabe was just . . .

Nikki bit back a sigh.

He was just, well, *everything*.

Off in the distance, she heard the rumble of the nearing storm and she knew the weather could turn bad quick, but she stayed in the pool, her gaze glued to Gabe.

He never treated her like she was inferior because her parents were the help, like some of their ignorant, snobby friends did whenever they were over at the house throughout the years. Like Parker did. Like Devlin often did whenever he chose to actually acknowledge her.

She knew Gabe had a serious girlfriend when he'd been away at college, because he'd brought her home once, over Christmas a few years ago. Her name was Emma and she was beautiful and nice and Nikki just—she just *hated* her.

Whatever.

Gabe and Emma weren't together anymore.

Nikki smiled to herself.

Continuing to creep along the edge of the pool, she

stopped when she felt the bottom start to dip. The pool got deep quick, so she had to be careful unless she seriously wanted to drown. So she held onto the edge of the pool with her hands, moving further into the pool, closer to the diving board she'd only ever seen Lucian and Gabe use. They'd throw themselves off it, showing no fear.

Nikki wanted to do that. Have no fear like—

The entire world flashed an intense white as lightning struck the ground nearby. A crack of thunder reverberated, sending a chill of fear straight down her spine. She shrieked as the sky ripped open. Heavy rain poured, pounding off the patio surrounding the pool and the water.

Forget staying in the pool!

Scrambling along the side, she started to lift herself up with her arms. Her wide-eyed gaze whipped around as another bolt of lightning struck the ground, not too far from the pool.

The brothers turned right then, just as she managed to get one scrawny leg out of the pool and onto the slippery patio.

Gabe stepped forward, toward the edge of the veranda, where he was all dry and safe. "Nic?"

She gasped as her eyes met his. Oh no. Not only was she in her bathing suit, she looked like a drowned cat trying to climb her way out of the pool! She could seriously just *die*—

Thunder exploded again. It sounded like the sky was falling all around her. Then it happened, so fast that one second her foot was slipping and then the next thing she knew water was swallowing her whole.

Shock robbed her of the ability to think. Too caught off guard to close her mouth, she dragged in mouthfuls of water as she sunk into the pool and the water churned above her.

Her lungs burned and wheezed as she squeezed her eyes tight. Trying to resurface but only seeming to slip further down, panic overtook as she flailed underwater. Her butt hit the bottom of the pool, the impact soft but jarring.

Squeezing her eyes shut, she shook her head frantically as the burn in her chest crawled up her throat and along the back of her skull. She felt weird. Like a thousand fire ants were marching along her skin and—

Hands suddenly grabbed her arms. An arm circled her waist. There was a powerful pushing motion and then she shot straight up. Her head broke the surface. Rain pelted her face as she opened her mouth anyway, trying to get air, but all she could do was cough and spit up water.

Someone dragged her through the pool to the side and then another pair of hands was there, grabbing her and lifting her up out of the water. She fell to her knees, gagging as water splashed up beside her. Arms went around her waist again, lifting her. The world spun as she felt herself being carried under the veranda. Laid down gently, she was immediately rolled onto her side.

A strong whack hit along her back. "Come on, Nic. Spit it up. Come on. Get the water out, Nic."

She recognized the voice—knew who it belonged to because only one person called her *Nic*, but the water was coming up and out as she wheezed and spit out what felt like an ocean's worth of water.

"There you go." The hand on her back was rubbing her now, no longer single-handedly beating the water out of her lungs. "That's it."

Finally able to breathe without choking, Nikki rolled onto her back and found herself staring up into eyes that were the color of the sea off the coast, an endless blue-green.

Gabe.

"You okay?" he asked, concern filling those beautiful eyes with every passing second she was quiet. "You're starting to worry me, sweetheart."

Sweetheart?

He'd never called her *sweetheart* before.

Over his shoulder, Lucian leaned in. "Did she hit her head?"

Someone cussed, causing her to flinch.

"Dev," Lucian sighed, looking behind him at where she guessed Devlin loomed.

Gabe was still staring at her, his hand on her shoulder, and she knew she needed to say something before they went and got her parents. "I . . . I didn't hit my head."

Relief filled Gabe's face. "Thank God." His shoulders lowered, and it was then when she realized his white shirt was soaked and plastered to his skin. There were all kinds of interesting dips and planes under that shirt. "You scared the hell out of me, Nic."

Then the reality of what just happened struck her.

Gabe saved her.

Oh my God, he actually saved her from drowning!

He smiled down at her as he shook his head, sending wet strands of hair into his face. "You're okay, right?"

She nodded, thinking she should probably sit up. "You saved me."

That smile grew. "Does that make me your hero?"

"Yes," she whispered and then nodded just in case he doubted her. It totally made him her hero.

Gabe chuckled.

"Jesus," Devlin grunted, crossing his arms as he moved into her line of sight. "That would be the last thing we need. Her drowning herself in the damn pool. What are you even doing in here? This isn't your pool or your house to use as a damn playground."

Her eyes widened. Tears burned the back of her throat as she shrunk back against the hot stone. He would say something to her parents—to *his* father. Then her parents would get yelled at.

Gabe's head whipped around. "*Devlin.*"

"The little idiot can't even swim," Devlin shot back, and

against her will, she felt tears crawling up her throat. She wasn't an idiot, but he was right. She couldn't even swim. "Christ," he muttered. "Livie and Richard know better than to let her run around like a brat when Father—"

"That's enough. Seriously." Gabe let go of her shoulder as he twisted toward his older brother. "It was an accident. It's over. Nic's fine. So shut up or go somewhere. I don't care where as long as it's anywhere but here."

Lucian's brows flew up and he looked like he was seconds away from bursting into laughter as Nikki sucked in a gasp. She'd never, *ever* heard Gabe speak to Devlin like that.

No one spoke to Devlin like that.

Gabe turned back to her, his shoulders tense. "I guess I'm going to have to teach you how to swim, aren't I?"

It happened.

Right then and there, *it* happened.

Nicolette Besson fell head over heels in love and she knew, just knew in her heart of hearts, that one day she'd marry Gabriel de Vincent and they'd live happily ever after.

She would be his.

Because he was already hers.

Chapter 1

Six years later . . .

It took every ounce of self-control for Gabriel de Vincent to stand back and do nothing. Just stand there and watch him being led away, but that's what he had to do, because that's what he'd promised and Gabe tried to be a man of his word.

Sometimes he failed at that. Failed at that in ways that haunted him late at night, but he wouldn't go back on this.

He'd promised them three uninterrupted months.

That's what he was going to give them.

His jaw ached from how hard he was clenching it as the Rothchilds walked back into the restaurant. He didn't take his eyes off them, not until he couldn't see them anymore. Only then did he look at the slip of paper.

Looking down at the drawing of a puppy on a piece of blue construction paper, he felt the worst mix of emotions. Sadness. Pride. Helplessness. Hope. Fury that he'd never tasted before. He had no idea how one person could feel all of that at once, but he did.

A wry smile tugged at his lips. There was definitely talent in the drawing. Real skill. The de Vincent knack for the arts was still kicking around, it seemed.

His gaze flickered over what was written in a blockish handwriting. He'd already read it three times, but couldn't bear to read it a fourth time. Not right now. He didn't want to fold the paper and create creases in it, so he was careful as he carried it back to where he was parked.

"Gabriel de Vincent."

Frowning at the vaguely familiar voice, he turned around. A man stepped out from behind a truck. Dark, square sunglasses shielded half the man's face, but Gabe recognized him.

He sighed. "Ross Haid. To what do I owe the honor of seeing you in Baton Rouge?"

The reporter for the *Advocate* gave one of what Gabe assumed was a trademark half grin, the kind that probably got him into places and events he sure as hell didn't belong in. "Headquarters are here. You know that."

"Yeah, but you work out of the New Orleans office, Ross."

He shrugged a shoulder as he neared Gabe. "I had to come up to headquarters. Heard through the grapevine that a de Vincent was in town."

"Uh-huh." Not for one second did Gabe believe that. "And you just happened to hear that I was at this restaurant?"

The smile kicked up a notch as he ran a hand over his blond hair. "Nah. Seeing you here was just luck."

Bullshit. Ross had been sniffing after his family for about two months now, trying to get to one of them when they were out at dinner or at an event, showing up at nearly every damn function one of them was attending. But back home, in New Orleans, Ross had trouble getting near them. Well, he had trouble getting to the one he really wanted to talk to, which was Gabe's older brother.

Didn't require any leap of logic to figure out what was going on. Somehow Ross had heard that Gabe was here, and that's why Ross *conveniently* ended up here. Normally he could tolerate Ross's incessant questioning. Hell, he sort of liked the guy, appreciated his determination, but not when Ross was here and something he didn't want a reporter finding out mere feet away.

Lowering his sunglasses, Ross eyed Gabe's ride. "Nice car. Is it one of the new Porsche 911s?"

Gabe raised his brows.

"Family business must be going well. Then again, the family business is always going strong, isn't it? The de Vincents are old money. The one percent of *the* one percent."

Gabe's family was one of the oldest, linked all the way back to the days the great state of Louisiana was being created. Now they owned the most profitable oil refineries in the Gulf, coveted real estate all around the world, tech firms, and once his older brother married, they'd be in control of one of the largest shipping industries in the world. So, yeah, the de Vincents were wealthy, but the car and nearly everything Gabe owned, he bought it with the money he *worked* for. Not the money he was *born* with.

"Some say that your family has so much money that the de Vincents are above the law." Ross straightened his sunglasses. "Seems that way."

Gabe really didn't have time for this. "Whatever you want to say, can you stop beating around the damn bush and get to it? I'm planning to head home sometime in the next year."

The reporter's smile faded. "Since you're here and I'm here, and it's damn hard to talk to you all any other time. I want to chat about your father's death."

"I'm sure you do."

"I don't believe it was a suicide," Ross continued. "And I find it also convenient that Chief Cobbs, who openly and publicly wanted your father's death investigated as a homicide, ended up dead in a freak car accident."

"Is that right?"

Frustration hummed off Ross about as loud as the damn locusts. "Is that all you got to say to me about this?"

"Pretty much." Gabe grinned then. "That and you have an overactive imagination, but I'm sure you've heard that before."

"I don't think my imagination is nearly vast enough to compete with all the things the de Vincents have had their hands in."

Probably not.

"Okay, I won't ask you about your father or the chief." Ross shifted his weight as Gabe opened his driver's door. "Also heard some interesting rumors about some of the staff at the de Vincent compound."

"I'm starting to feel like you might be stalking us." Gabe placed the drawing facedown on the passenger's seat. "If you want to talk about staffing, then you need to have a chat with Dev."

"Devlin won't make time to talk to me."

"That doesn't sound like my problem."

"It seems like it is now."

Gabe laughed, but the sound was without humor as he reached inside, grabbing his sunglasses off the visor. "Trust me, Ross, this isn't my problem."

"You may not think so now, but that'll change." A muscle twitched along the man's jaw. "I plan to blow the roof off every single damn secret the de Vincents have been keeping for years. I'm going to do a story that not even your family can pay to keep quiet."

Shaking his head, Gabe slipped his sunglasses on. "I like you, Ross. You know I've never had a problem with you. So, I just want to get that out of the way. But you have got to come up with some better material, because that was cliché as shit." He rested his hand on the frame of the car door. "You've got to know you're not the first reporter to come around thinking they're somehow going to dig some skeletons out of our closets and expose us for whatever the hell you think we are. You're not going to be the last to fail."

"I don't fail," Ross said. "Not ever."

"Everyone fails." Gabe climbed in behind the wheel.

"Except the de Vincents?"

"You said it, not me." Gabe looked up at the reporter. "Some unasked-for advice? I'd find another story to investigate."

"Is this where you're going to tell me to be careful?" He sounded oddly gleeful by the prospect. "Warn me off? Because people who mess with the de Vincents end up missing or worse?"

Gabe smirked as he hit the ignition key. "Doesn't sound like I need to tell you that. Seems like you already know what happens."

NIKKI STOOD IN the center of the quiet and sterile kitchen of the de Vincent mansion, telling herself that she was not the same little idiot that almost drowned herself out in the pool six years ago.

She sure as hell wasn't the same idiot who had spent years making an utter fool out of herself, chasing after a grown man. An act, which resulted in one of the worst ideas she'd ever had in the history of bad ideas.

And Nikki had a remarkable history of making not the brightest of all decisions. Her dad said she had a bit of a wild streak in her, taking after Pappy, but Nikki liked to blame the de Vincents for the recklessness. They had this really bizarre talent of making everyone around them stick one toe into Recklessville.

Her mother claimed that most of Nikki's bad decisions came from having a *good heart*.

Nikki had the habit of picking up strays—stray cats, dogs, a lizard here and there, even a snake, and humans, too. She was a bleeding heart, hating to see anyone she cared about in pain, and she was oftentimes a bit overly affected by the troubles of strangers.

It was why she avoided the TV around the holidays, because they always played those heart-wrenching videos of freezing animals or children left to starve in war-torn countries. She hated everything about New Year's Eve because of that and spent the week between Christmas and the first of January moping around.

There was a lot of Nikki that was the same as she was the last time she walked through this house. She still got emotionally invested in animals that didn't belong to her—that was why she volunteered at the local animal shelter. She still couldn't turn away from someone who needed help, and she still found herself in weird situations, but reckless? Wild?

Not anymore.

Not since the last time she'd been in the house, right before she left for college. That had been four years ago and now she was back, and nothing and everything had changed.

"You okay, hon?" her father asked.

Turning to find her father standing just inside the large kitchen, she pulled herself out of her thoughts and smiled widely for him. Goodness, her dad was starting to look his age, and that scared her—truly terrified her. Her parents had her late in life, but she was only twenty-two, and she wanted another fifty years or so with them.

Nikki knew that wasn't going to happen.

Especially now.

She forced those thoughts from her head. "Yes. I'm just . . . it's weird being in here after being gone so long. The kitchen is different."

"It was remodeled a few years back," he replied. The mansion was constantly being remodeled, it seemed. After all, how many times had this place caught fire since it was built? Nikki had lost count. Her father drew in a deep breath, and the lines around his mouth became more pronounced. He looked so tired. "I don't know if I've said this to you or not, but thank you."

She waved him off. "You don't need to thank me, Dad."

"Yeah, I do." He walked over to where she stood. "You

went away to college to do something better than this—
better than cooking dinners and running a household. To
become *something* better."

Offended on his behalf, she crossed her arms and met his
weary gaze. "There's nothing wrong with cooking dinners
and running a household. It's good, honest work. Work that
put me through college. Right, Dad?"

"We take great pride in our job. Don't get me wrong, but
what your mother and I did all these years was so you could
do something else." He sighed. "So, it means a lot that you
would come home to help us out, Nicolette."

Only her dad and mom called her by her full name.
Everyone else called her *Nikki*. Everyone except a certain
de Vincent who shall remain nameless. He and only he
called her *Nic*.

Her parents had worked for the de Vincents, one of the
wealthiest families in the States and possibly the world,
since long before she was born. It was weird growing up
in this house, being privy to a lot of strange stuff—things
the public had no idea about and would probably pay
a large sum of money to learn. And personally? It was
like she had a foot in two different worlds, one absurdly
wealthy and the other middle working class.

Her father was basically a butler, except she always had a
small suspicion that her father had . . . taken care of things
for the de Vincents that no normal butler did. Her mother
ran the day-to-day functions of the house and prepared
the dinners. Both her parents loved working for the family
and she knew both had planned to continue to the day they
died, but her mom . . .

Nikki's chest squeezed painfully. Her mom was not well
and it had happened so fast, coming out of nowhere. The
dreaded C word.

"Honestly, this is perfect. I got my degree and this will
give me time to figure things out." In other words, figure out

what the hell she wanted to really do with her life. Get to work or go for her master's? She wasn't sure yet. "And I want to be here while Mom is going through everything."

"I know." His smile wobbled a little as he brushed a strand of blondish-brown hair out of her face.

"We could've hired someone else to step in while your mother—"

"No, you couldn't have." She laughed at the mere thought of that. "I know how weird the de Vincents are. I know how protective you two are of them. I know how to keep my mouth shut and not see what I'm not supposed to. And you two don't have to worry about someone new *not* keeping their mouth shut and *not* seeing what they're not supposed to."

Her dad arched a brow. "A lot of things have changed, honey."

She snorted as she took in the white marble countertops with gray veining. Mom had filled her in on some of those *changes* during one of her chemo treatments. After all, what else did they have to talk about while she was being pumped full of poison that would hopefully kill only the cancer cells building in her lung?

Things in the de Vincent mansion that had changed.

For starters, the patriarch of the family, one Lawrence de Vincent, had hung himself a few months back. An act that had shocked her because she figured that man would've outlived a nuclear bomb. And Lucian de Vincent apparently had a live-in girlfriend and they were about to move into their own place. That was even more insane, the idea of Lucian settling down.

The Lucian she remembered put the *play* in player. He'd been an incorrigible flirt, leaving a string of broken hearts across the state of Louisiana and beyond.

She hadn't met his girlfriend yet since they were away on some kind of trip; the rich rarely seemed to have much of a schedule. She just hoped whoever his girlfriend was, she was nice and nothing like Devlin's fiancée.

Nikki might not have been around the de Vincents in four years, but she remembered Sabrina Harrington and her brother Parker.

Sabrina had just begun seeing Devlin the year before Nikki had left for college and that had been a year's worth of snide comments and rather impressive disdainful looks. Nikki could deal with Sabrina, though. If she was the same woman as she was before, she could be as mean as a cornered rattlesnake, but Nikki normally didn't even register on her scale of people to pay attention to.

Parker, though?

Nikki suppressed a shudder, not wanting to worry her father who was watching her like a hawk.

Parker had often stared at her the way she'd wanted Gabe to look at her, especially when she had grown brave enough to move from a one-piece bathing suit to a two-piece.

And Parker . . . he had done more than look.

She drew in a deep breath. She wasn't going to think about Parker. He wasn't worth a single thought.

What happened to Lawrence and Lucian's new romance weren't the only things her mom had told her. She filled Nikki in on the whole sister-reappearing-and-then-disappearing-again thing. Something that she knew the general public had no idea had even happened. She didn't know the details around it, but Nikki knew that in typical de Vincent fashion, it had to be the most drama-llama-est thing possible.

And she also knew better than to ask questions about it.

Her father stepped back. "The boys are all out."

Thank God and baby Jesus.

"Devlin should be back this evening for dinner. He likes dinner to be ready at six. I believe Ms. Harrington will be joining him."

Well, thanking God and baby Jesus lasted all of five seconds. She resisted the urge to roll her eyes and make a gagging sound. "Okay."

"Gabriel is still in Baton Rouge, or at least, that's the last I heard," her father continued, ticking off the brothers' schedules while she wondered what Gabe was doing in Baton Rouge. Not that she cared. She totally didn't care whatsoever, but she wondered if it had anything to do with his woodworking business.

The man was talented with his hands.

Really talented.

Her cheeks flushed as an unwanted memory of how his calloused palms felt pierced her straight through the chest. *Nope. Not going there. Absolutely not.*

There were examples of Gabe's skill all around the house—the furniture, chair rails, and trim, even in the kitchen. All of the woodwork was designed and created by Gabe. As a little girl, she'd been fascinated with the idea of picking up a piece of wood and turning it into something that was truly a work of art. That fascination had turned into quite the hobby for Nikki.

It had started one long, fall afternoon when she was ten and she'd found Gabe outside, whittling away on a piece of wood. Out of boredom, she'd asked him to show her how he did it. Instead of shooing her off, Gabe had given her small scraps of wood and showed her how to use a chisel.

She'd gotten pretty good at it, but she hadn't picked up a chisel in over four years.

Nikki refocused on what her dad was telling her.

"We're a little understaffed right now," her dad continued. "So there's a lot of dusting in your near future. Devlin is very much like his father."

Great.

That was not a compliment in her book.

"Is it the ghosts?" she half joked. "Scaring off the staff?"

Her father shot her a look, but she knew damn well that her parents believed this house was haunted. Hell, they wouldn't even come here at night unless it was a dire emergency. None of the staff would and everyone in town knew the legends about the land the de Vincent mansion sat on. And who hadn't heard about the de Vincent curse more than a time or two?

Being in this house as much as she had been in the past, she had seen some weird things and heard some stuff that couldn't be explained. Plus she grew up within minutes of New Orleans. She was a believer, but unlike her friend Rosie, whom she met in college, she wasn't obsessed with all things paranormal. Nikki operated on the whole if-you-don't-acknowledge-ghosts-they-can't-bother-you theory and so far it had worked wonderfully.

Then again, Nikki had only come here at night once in her life, and that had not turned out well at all. So maybe ignoring ghosts didn't work, because she liked to think she was possessed by one of the ghosts that supposedly wandered the halls, and that was what provoked her to do what she'd done that night.

Nikki was well aware of how the house was run because she'd spent most of her summer vacations in the house watching her mom, so she got to work pretty quickly once her father left her.

First thing first was tracking down what staff they did have at the house. *Understaffed her butt!* The only staff they had left was her dad; the landscaper who was constantly mowing grass, it seemed, or re-mulching; the de Vincent driver; and Mrs. Kneely, an older woman who'd done the laundry services since Nikki was a little girl.

Beverly Kneely actually owed her own laundry business and only came to the house three times a week to take care of the linens and clothing.

According to Bev, whom she found in the large mudroom at the back of the house, packing up clothing that needed to be dry-cleaned, over the last couple of months, nearly everyone had quit.

"So, let me get this straight." Nikki smoothed back a few

strands that had escaped the knot she'd pulled her hair up in. "The waiters are gone, as are the maids?"

Bev's buxom chest heaved as she nodded. "It's just been your parents for the last three months. I think all that work was wearing poor Livie down."

Anger flashed through Nikki. Hadn't the de Vincents noticed how thin and tired her mom had been getting? How quickly she got out of breath? "Why didn't the de Vincents hire someone to help?"

"Your father tried, but no one around here wants to come close to this place, not after what happened."

She frowned. "You're talking about Lawrence? What he did?"

Bev tied up the bags. "Not like that wasn't bad enough, but that wasn't the straw that broke the camel's back around here."

Nikki had no idea what she was talking about. "I'm sorry. I don't think I've been updated on all the crazy. What else happened?"

Looking around the room, Bev arched her brows as she headed toward the side door. "Walls got ears. You know that. You want to know what's been going on here, you ask your father or one of the boys."

Her lips pursed. She was so not asking the *boys*.

Bev stopped at the door and looked back. "I don't think Devlin is going to be happy when he sees what you're wearing."

"What's wrong with what I'm wearing?" It was jeans and a black tee shirt. No way was she going to dress like her mom or her dad. Her willingness to help her parents did not extend to wearing uniforms.

She looked down at herself and saw the hole just below the knee.

Nikki sighed.

Devlin was probably going to have a problem with the hole, but what Nikki wanted to know was what the hell had happened in this house to drive almost all the staff away?

It had to be something.

Not just because the de Vincents paid extraordinarily well, but also because her father hadn't told her.

And that meant it was something really bad.

Chapter 2

*I*t was approximately one in the afternoon when Nikki was finishing up in the sitting room nearest to the first-floor office. She was dusting the chairs that seriously didn't need to be dusted when she felt a prickling sensation along the nape of her neck. Wiping a faint sheen of sweat off her forehead, she rose and turned to the doorway.

Devlin de Vincent stood there.

His presence startled her enough that she almost dropped the rag she was holding. Stepping back, she knocked into the heavy furniture that reminded her of something straight out of the Victorian age.

Goodness.

She'd seen pictures of Devlin in the gossip magazines over the years, but she hadn't seen him in person during that time.

He looked so much like his father it sent a chill down her spine. Dark hair coifed and styled short. Coldly handsome and completely remote, he was dressed as if he'd just left an important business meeting, wearing trousers and a button-down despite the fact that it was September and still hot as hell.

As a kid, she'd been slightly terrified of the eldest de Vincent brother who now had to be steadily approaching his forties.

Nikki wasn't a kid anymore, though.

His gaze drifted over Nikki, assessing her in a way that made her feel like a piece of furniture he wasn't sure he wanted to keep or store away in the attic where important, powerful people couldn't see it. "Hello, Nikki, it has been a while."

Nikki forced an easy smile as she clutched the rag. "Hi, Dev."

Something passed over his face when she used the abbreviated version of his name. Nikki wasn't sure if it was irritation or amusement. One never knew with Devlin.

"Thank you for stepping in and helping while your mother is out," he said, his voice as flat as his personality. "I do hope she is starting to feel better."

"She is . . . she's hanging in there," she replied.

"Your mother is a very strong woman. If anyone can beat this, she can."

That was possibly the nicest thing she'd ever heard come out of Devlin's mouth.

His gaze roamed over her again. "I know you have been gone for a long time, away at college and all, but I am sure you do remember that our staff wears a uniform and not ragged, hand-me-down jeans?"

Aaand there he went, ruining it by becoming Captain Dickhead de Vincent, who sounded like he was eighty instead of almost forty.

Nikki's spine stiffened. "These actually aren't hand-me-downs."

"You bought them that way?" A smirk appeared. "Perhaps you should ask for your money back."

Her lips thinned as she resisted the urge to give him the middle finger. "I'm sorry. I was told I didn't have to wear a uniform."

Not necessarily true, but whatever.

He inclined his head, a gesture she used to see from his father. "I see. Then maybe you can find something in your closet that doesn't look like we pay our help below minimum wage? Especially since you are being paid. You're not doing this for free."

She sucked in a harsh breath. *Help*. The house might've changed a little and Lucian may be a reformed man-whore, but Devlin was still the same. "I'm sure I can find something that will meet your approval."

There it was again. A flicker of emotion that was gone before Nikki could even figure out what it was.

Then Devlin was in the very room with her, only a few feet away. Her eyes widened slightly. How in the world did he move so fast and so quietly?

Was he part ghost?

More like part devil. After all, that was his nickname— what the gossip mags called him. *The Devil*.

Now he was directly in front of her, and Nikki was not a tall woman. Barely pushing five and a half feet, it was hard not to be intimidated when he towered over her. "Do I detect an attitude, *Nicolette*?"

Oh dear.

Mentally cursing herself and Devlin, she planted the brightest smile she'd ever mustered in her life. "I hope not. I was being serious. I do have nicer pants. Ones that I am *sure* you would approve of."

His eyes, the de Vincent eyes, latched onto her. "I am pleased to hear that."

Okay. He did not sound pleased. At all.

He bent his chin down and she felt the tiny hairs rise all over her body. "I would hate to have to tell your father about your attitude."

Nikki would, too.

"Do you remember what happened last time? The *only* time?" he asked. "I do."

Oh, she remembered. She'd been seventeen and gotten into the liquor cabinet when her mom wasn't looking, drinking the expensive-as-hell scotch, all to prove she wasn't a little girl anymore. Looking back, she recognized that she'd been, in fact, a little girl, but that wasn't the point. She'd mouthed off at Devlin when he'd ordered her to stop following Gabe around like a *lost, underfed puppy*.

He had such a way with words.

"I remember." Her smile was beginning to fade. "In my defense, I'd been slightly intoxicated and therefore was not wholly responsible for my actions."

One dark eyebrow rose.

Her shoulders squared. "And I also hadn't been following your brother around, so I was a little offended."

"You were attached to my brother like an underage barnacle that had no concept of why a grown man would not be remotely interested in a teenage girl."

Holy crap, he really just went there! Like totally went there.

"I . . ." Yep. Nikki had no idea what to say to that.

Because it was true. All true.

Ever since Gabe pulled her out of the pool and defended her to Devlin, she'd spent every spare moment basically stalking Gabe and trying to catch his attention. For some dumb reason, when she'd been younger, she hadn't seen the age difference as being that big of a deal.

God, she had been such an idiot.

She was completely nutso not realizing that the age difference had been a very, *very* big deal, because it was quite the age difference. He'd been *twenty-six* when he pulled her out of the pool. Ten years older than her, a full-grown man, and she had been—well, yeah, barely sixteen. Gross.

But she'd figured in her dumb hormone-riddled teenage brain that once she turned eighteen, Gabe would fall head over heels in love with her.

Honest to God, Gabe had never once given her any indication that he'd thought of her in any way that was inappropriate and illegal, but she . . . well, she had been young and dumb and in love for the very first time in her life.

"Can I be honest with you, Nikki?"

She blinked. "Of course."

"I was not at all happy about you taking your mother's place while she gets better."

Wow. What was she supposed to say to that? Thanks?

"You leaving for college was the best thing you could've done for yourself, because if you had stayed, you would've gotten yourself in a lot of trouble." He paused. "Or my brother."

Well, she hadn't exactly left before *that* happened.

Her face started to feel like it was on fire.

Devlin dipped his chin. "I do hope you don't pick up where you left off."

Nikki's mouth dried as her heart turned over heavily. "I don't know what you're talking about."

"Now, you know that's not the truth." His voice was deceptively low. "From the moment you realized you liked boys, you pranced around this house every single time Gabe was around."

Her face was seriously going to burn right off, because that was also true. She'd done just about everything to garner Gabe's undivided attention. Sometimes it had worked. Usually it hadn't.

"And those swimming lessons?" he continued, much to her horror. This was not a walk down memory lane she wanted to stroll on. She hadn't even worked up the nerve to *look* at the pool yet. "They weren't that bad when you had the body of an underdeveloped boy."

Oh my God!

"But the older you got, the skimpier your bathing suits became." His face was still completely devoid of emotion. "We all saw it whether we wanted to or not. Even though we shouldn't have."

Suddenly she was that sixteen-year-old girl again, wanting to drown herself in the pool. "I was just a teenager, Devlin."

"And you're just—what? Twenty-two now?" He'd guessed right. "Not exactly that much older. You're still just a girl, but one who is actually of legal age now."

Folding her arms across her chest to stop herself from throwing the rag in his face, she took several deep breaths before she trusted herself not to curse. "I am not a teenage girl pining after an older guy any longer. Trust me."

"I don't."

She stared at him for several moments, unsure of how to even proceed with this. "I don't know what you want me to say then." And she really didn't. "I didn't come here for Gabe. I came home to help my parents. If being here is going to be such a huge problem, then you need to hire someone else. I'm sure my father will understand."

Devlin was quiet for a moment. "You know . . . how things work here. You know what is expected."

"I do." She wished her face would stop flaming and that this conversation was already over.

The eldest de Vincent watched her intently. "The last thing my brother needs right now is another complication."

Another complication? What? Her stomach dropped. "What does that mean? Is something wrong with him?"

That was apparently the wrong thing to ask, because his eyes narrowed. She didn't regret asking the question. While she felt like an utter fool whenever she thought about Gabe and seeing him again was not something she was looking forward to, she still cared for him.

How could she not?

Gabe was completely off-limits, always was and always would be, but they'd been . . . friends once. Even with the age difference, he'd respected her. He'd been kind to her, and he used to bring her smoothies, surprising her with different flavors. Some he'd made himself. Others he picked up from her favorite shop when he was coming back from the city and knew she was there. He'd been there for her, more than once.

But she'd ruined all of that, so Devlin really had no reason to be worried that she had any plans that concerned Gabe. He was not going to welcome her with open arms, and Nikki was going to do everything in her power to avoid him as much as humanly possible.

"I hope we have an understanding," Devlin said without answering her question.

"We do."

He hadn't backed off. "Good to know."

Nikki nodded slowly, hoping beyond hope this awkward-as-hell conversation was over and she could retreat somewhere for a few moments to repeatedly punch herself in the lady bits for past crimes.

"Dev," a voice called from the hall. "Where in the hell are you?"

Her heart stopped in her chest when she heard the voice. No. Oh, sweet baby Jesus, *no.*

"Speak of the devil," Devlin muttered under his breath. His gaze lifted to the ceiling while Nikki was close to hyperventilating and maybe even passing out. "Gabe. I didn't know you were coming home today."

"Change of plans." The voice neared.

Nikki looked around wildly for a place to hide. Would dive-bombing under the raised couch that no one ever sat in look strange? Yes. Yes, it would, but she was not ready to see Gabe.

Not after this conversation.

But it was too late.

There was nowhere to hide, and Devlin was turning around. She couldn't see the doorway because of how broad Devlin was, but she squeezed her eyes shut nonetheless.

I can do this.

It's no big deal.

I'm not a teenage girl anymore.

Her pep talk wasn't helping her very much.

"What are you doing in here?" Gabe asked, and God, his voice sounded just like she remembered. Deep. Smooth. Lightly accented. "Oh, you have company." A shocked-sounding laugh came from him. "Sorry to intrude."

She almost laughed at the idea that she and Devlin could be together, but she managed to squelch it because it would probably sound a bit crazed.

"Yes, I do have company." Devlin stepped to the side. She didn't see him, because she still had her eyes closed, but she'd felt Devlin move.

Silence.

And then, "Holy shit."

Chapter 3

*N*ikki's eyes flew open, and she immediately wished they hadn't, because now she saw him.

It had been forever since she even allowed herself to look at a photo of him. Maybe she should've done that, because then she might not simultaneously feel like jumping on him like a rabid monkey and running away from this room.

She couldn't look away from him.

God, Gabe was . . . he was beautiful in this raw, masculine way. He was as she remembered, but somehow he was *more*. If anything, he seemed taller and his shoulders broader, his biceps and forearms defined in a way they hadn't been before.

Age had treated him well. Gabe was thirty-two now, and the only sign was the faint smile lines around the corners of those stunning sea-moss eyes. His cheekbones were classic de Vincent, high and angular as was the blade of the nose and that lush, lush mouth.

Oh man, he was still wearing his hair long. The deep brown, almost black hair just brushed his shoulders. A faint stubble shadowed the strong curve of his jaw as if he hadn't shaved in a day or two. He was dressed much more casually than his brother, wearing a dark pair of jeans and a pale-blue cotton shirt that was loosely tucked in the front. And he was barefoot.

Her lips twitched into a small smile.

Gabe was *always* barefoot.

"Nic?" He stepped around a chair, staring at her like . . . well, like he wasn't even sure it was really her.

While Gabe mostly looked the same, Nikki had changed in the last four years. Gone was the eighteen-year-old girl who'd fled from him in tears.

He stopped a few feet from her, still staring at her like she was a figment of his imagination. His gaze swept from the now-messy knot of hair at the top of her head, all the way down to her llama-print Vans. The way he checked her out was nothing like his brother's earlier perusal. Not when she could practically feel his gaze getting hung up on her now-much-rounder hips and fuller breasts. A sweet, unwanted, and unexpected flush swept through her.

Bad Nikki. Bad. Bad.

He could stare at her in the way she'd always wanted him and it meant nothing now. All he was to her now was a silly teenage crush. That was all.

So she had to pull it together.

She lifted an empty hand and gave an awkward finger wave once his eyes met hers again. "Hey."

"Hey?" he repeated, blinking slowly and showing off ridiculously long lashes.

Nikki swallowed hard and tried again. "Hi?"

Beside her, Devlin sighed loudly.

"Is something wrong?" Gabe's gaze bounced between his brother and her. "Did something happen to Livie?"

Nikki slowly turned to Devlin. He hadn't told Gabe? What in the hell? "I'm filling in for Mom while she's getting treatment. You didn't . . . ?"

It was obvious in the way Gabe stared at her that he had no idea, and Nikki had no clue why Devlin would've left him out on that pretty important update.

"No." Gabe's tone was short. "I wasn't told."

This was beyond awkward. She peeked at Gabe. Unease stirred in the pit of her stomach as she quickly looked away. He was still staring at her.

"I believe that Nikki has a lot of work to get done," Devlin interjected smoothly.

Grasping onto the cue to make her exit like it was the last life jacket on the *Titanic*, she got her legs moving and kept her gaze fixed on the doorway. But as she walked past him, she couldn't help herself. It was like she had no control over her eyeballs.

Nikki glanced over at him, and found that he was still watching. She wasn't even sure he'd blinked at this point. "It's good seeing you, Gabe."

There.

She said it and sounded like she meant it, even though it wasn't exactly true.

THERE WERE ONLY two times in Gabe's thirty-two years of life that a damn feather could've knocked him flat on his ass.

This was one of them.

Gabe still stared at the doorway Nic had walked out of, completely and utterly shocked. "Was that really her?"

Dev made a sound that was a cross between a laugh and a cough. "Little Nikki isn't so little anymore, is she?"

Little Nikki hadn't exactly been little the last time he'd seen her, but she hadn't looked like *that*.

Holy shit, she didn't have that ass or those tits the last time he'd seen her.

What the fuck? Did he seriously just think that?

Disgust churned in his gut. He would not—could not think of her tits or ass. Even acknowledge that she now had them aplenty based on how that shirt was stretched across her chest and how those jeans hugged her—

Damn it.

Didn't matter that she was now in her twenties—*barely* in her twenties.

But shit, Nic had always been a cute girl. A scrawny and goofy-as-hell cute girl, but she was . . . she was now fucking beautiful.

He almost laughed.

The whole late-bloomer thing whirled around in his head, but it was true. Her face had filled out during her absence, finally matching those big brown eyes and that wide, expressive mouth.

She'd gone from cute to dangerously stunning.

Gabe couldn't believe she was here. He forced himself to turn to his brother. "Were we unable to hire someone else?"

Because anyone would've been a better choice.

Dev arched a brow as he folded his arms. "As you know, we've had a problem retaining staff recently."

That they did.

"And with what has happened here, I couldn't help but accept when Richard brought up the idea of bringing Nikki in to fill her mother's spot. She was already coming home. Plus, she knows how to mind her own business and keep quiet."

Gabe's jaw tightened. Nic definitely knew how to keep quiet. Lifting a hand, he dragged it through his hair. What in the hell? He honestly had no clue how to proceed with this newest development. Like he needed another damn issue in his life right now.

He'd honestly believed he was never going to see Nic again, at least not up close. Maybe from a distance, because distances were *safe*.

Shit.

How old was she now?

He quickly did the math in his head. Twenty-two. Her birthday was coming up. November. She'd be twenty-three then. Fuck. What he remembered of twenty-three was a whole lot of partying and screwing. That was a lifetime ago.

The stupidest question surfaced. Did she still make little bracelets and necklaces out of wood? He'd hoped so. The girl had a natural talent.

"Is this going to be a problem?" Dev asked softly.

He frowned, dropping his hand. "No. Why would it be?"

"Good question."

His gaze narrowed on his older brother. There was no way Dev knew. Dev hadn't even been home that messed-up weekend, four years ago, when Gabe made the second-biggest damn mistake of his life.

But his brother missed very little.

"You had such a strange, strong reaction to seeing her," Dev pointed out.

"I was caught off guard." That was the damn truth. "Wasn't expecting to see her here. Shit. I thought something happened to Livie."

Dev watched him quietly for a moment. "I thought you weren't coming back until Thursday."

"That was the plan." Gabe sighed, looking at the doorway again. Hell. "But I decided to cut the trip short."

"Things aren't going our way in Baton Rouge?"

Gabe shook his head. As messed up as it was—and God, it was fucking messed up—he wasn't even thinking about his trip to Baton Rouge now. His mind was nowhere near that place after seeing Nic. "Can't blame them for it. They did me a favor by calling me in the first place, but they aren't just going to let me waltz in there after five years."

"We can make them."

Gabe's gaze sharpened. "Hell, no. You're not stepping in on this, Dev. This is *my* life. This is *my* shit to deal with. It has nothing to do with the family."

"It has everything to do with our family. William is—"

"Don't." Gabe met Dev's gaze as his chest turned cold. "I am handling this the best way I see fit, Devlin. It does not involve you."

A muscle flexed along Dev's jaw, a rare show of emotion and for a moment, Gabe didn't think he was going to let it drop. "Which reminds me," he said. "As I was leaving Baton Rouge, I ran into Ross Haid."

A mere glimpse of annoyance flickered across Dev's face. "Let me guess. He wanted to talk about . . . Father?"

"And the police chief. And why we're having problems hiring staff."

"Of course," Dev murmured. "He's becoming quite annoying, which means he needs—"

"To be ignored," Gabe said, holding his brother's gaze. "He needs to just be ignored. Eventually he'll move onto something else, Dev. That is all we're going to do."

"That's exactly what I was going to say." A faint smile tipped the corners of his lips, and Gabe was ready to call bullshit on that. "By the way, Sabrina is coming over for dinner tonight."

Jesus.

Could this day get any more twisted?

Well, he knew he wouldn't be having dinner here then, because being on a different planet wasn't a far enough distance between him and Dev's fiancée. Wait. Something occurred to him. "Will Nic be serving the dinner?"

"Since we don't have the staff, she will be assuming Mrs. Besson's duties fully."

And that meant she'd be serving dinner—serving Sabrina.

Fuck.

STANDING IN FRONT of the large oven with her hands planted on the window, Nikki peered inside. Her stomach rumbled. The ham and cheese sandwich she'd made for herself before the awkward-to-end-all-awkward conversations with Devlin did nothing to stave off her overeager stomach. Her tiny lunch had been hours ago.

The chicken smelled amazing, like herbs and butter and home-cooked meals. And from what she could see, the skin was crisping perfectly.

God, it made her hungry.

It also reminded her of all the afternoons sitting on one of the nearby stools, watching her mom cook for the de Vincents. Granted, the stools were newer now, a sleek gray design with thick cushions, but being in this kitchen, in this home, made her feel like a kid again.

Nikki was a damn good cook if she said so herself and she had her momma to thank for that. She actually loved cooking, something she never got to do at her dorm room in Tuscaloosa or the small apartment she'd lived in her senior year. So when she did come home for the holidays, she loved getting in the kitchen with her mom and making stuffing, pies, and more.

Except this kitchen was nothing like the kitchen at home. This kitchen was nearly the same size of the entire downstairs of her parents' house.

She rested her nose against the warm window. Who needed a kitchen this big? The de Vincents. That's who. Hell, the entire home was ginormous. Three levels and two wings veering off from the main part; there were more bedrooms than Nikki could count and more rooms than anyone would ever have use for.

The de Vincent compound had been remodeled and rebuilt over and over, but it mirrored the style of the days that parts of the South still desperately clutched on to. Each level was accessible from the porches that circled the entire property, and she knew the brothers all had their private quarters and entrances, and they were basically apartments. Those quarters had living rooms, kitchens, bedrooms, and bathrooms. Hell, their private rooms were, in fact, bigger than most apartments.

According to her father, Gabe and Dev were in the right wing and Lucian and his girlfriend were in the left wing of the house.

All the other bedrooms in between were empty, as was their mother's room and their father's. They had separate rooms, and she guessed none of the brothers wanted to take over those rooms.

Luckily, the cleaning of their rooms was something that only occurred once a week and that wouldn't be happening until Friday. She was so not looking forward to going into Gabe's apartment.

The last time she'd been in there, she been clutching this necklace she'd made for him, and . . .

Nikki flushed and cringed at once.

Her mind went back to the awkward reunion. Gabe had stared at her like . . . God, she wasn't even sure. But it wasn't good. Not at all and she couldn't—

"What are you doing?"

Squeaking, she jumped back from the oven and whipped around. Her heart lodged in her throat.

Gabe stood just inside the kitchen.

"What is it with you guys creeping up on people and making no noise?" she demanded, placing a hand to her pounding heart. "God."

His lips twitched like he was almost going to smile, but then thought better of it. "I wasn't exactly quiet."

"I didn't hear you."

"Maybe because it looked like you were trying to stick your head in the oven."

Her cheeks flushed. "The door was closed, so that wouldn't have been a very successful attempt."

"No, it wouldn't be."

Nikki drew in a stuttered breath that went nowhere when her gaze collided with his. Silence followed. He didn't speak. Neither did she. They just stood there, staring at one another. He didn't look exactly hostile, but he didn't appear warm and fuzzy either.

Her shoulders tensed as the silence continued to grow.

"Dinner smells good," Gabe said suddenly, breaking the silence. "Roasted chicken?"

She jolted. "Um, yes." She turned to the counter, where she'd just finished peeling potatoes. "And potatoes. I'm also making a salad. There'll be biscuits . . . with butter."

There'll be biscuits . . . with butter?

It took everything for Nikki not to roll her eyes at herself.

He moved forward, maybe a foot or two, but stopped like one would if they were approaching a rabid dog. A heartbeat passed. "Your hair . . ." He tilted his head to the side. "It's different."

"Yeah, it is." Her hair used to be a rather dull medium brown, but then she found this amazing hair stylist in Tuscaloosa and turned her brown hair into this array of blondes and browns, using some weird technique called *balayage*. "It's basically just highlights and stuff."

"Stuff." His gaze flickered over the bun.

Uncomfortable, she scanned the kitchen. "And my hair is longer. A lot longer."

His brows lifted.

Was she really telling him the length of her hair? This was the most strained conversation she'd ever had in her life. And that was, well, it was sad. She peeked at him. It used to not be this way. Back before . . . well, before she ruined everything, he'd be teasing her and asking about her college. He'd be talking to her like he could actually stand being in the same room with her.

She needed this conversation to be over like it was yesterday and she also needed to figure out how she could work here and not run into Gabe. The house was big enough that it should be possible. "I need to get back to—"

"Planting your face against the oven door?"

Her shoulders slumped. "Actually, I need to finish the potatoes. So, if you'll excuse me." She started to turn away, praying that he'd just leave.

"That's it? That's all you have to say to me? Because I have a lot I need to say to you," he said. "Never in a million years did I think I'd see you here again."

Nikki's spine stiffened like steel had been poured into it. Oh God. Her throat spasmed.

"We need to talk."

"No we don't," she said quickly. "We do not need to talk about anything."

"Bullshit," he snapped, and his voice was so much closer that she turned to him on instinct.

Gabe was now at the edge of the massive island, only two or three feet from her. She stepped back into the counter. Her heart thundered in her chest as her gaze flicked to the kitchen door.

"No one is coming near here," he said as if reading her mind. Her gaze flew back to his. "Dev is in his office on the second floor in a meeting and your father is out with the landscaper. No one is going to hear us."

A weird mixture of sensations assaulted her. One was a chill that skated down her spine. The other was a tight, hot shiver that danced over her skin.

Gabe kept coming at her, not stopping until he was right in front of her, separated by a few inches. She sucked in air, catching the crisp, clean scent of his cologne. It reminded her of storms, of *that* night.

That was the last thing she wanted to be reminded of.

Like his brother, he was a good head and then some taller than her, so right now, her eyes were fastened to his chest. Thank God he was wearing a shirt.

"I . . . I don't want to talk," she managed to say.

"I do."

"Gabe—"

"You owe me this."

Her body jerked as she pressed her lips together. He was right. She owed him a conversation. "Okay."

There was another beat of silence and then he asked in a voice so low she almost didn't believe she heard him right. "Did I hurt you that night?"

Chapter 4

"What?" she gasped, her gaze lifting to his.

Gabe stared—well, more like he *glared* down at her. "I saw the sheets after you left. There was blood on them."

Oh my God, the blood rushed from her face and then swept back to her cheeks so quickly she feared she might have a stroke. At that moment, it seemed entirely possible.

"Did I hurt you?" he demanded again.

"No." And that wasn't a lie. Not really. It hurt, but from what she knew, it tended to hurt the first time.

What appeared to be relief flickered across his face as he briefly closed his eyes.

She drew in a shallow breath. "It's just, you know—"

"No." That relief was gone, replaced by anger. "I *don't* know, Nic."

Really? She looked away, telling herself that she was an adult and she could have this conversation, because he was right. She did owe him this. "I was a virgin—"

"Yeah, I kind of figured that part out," he interrupted, his voice so hard it could break a board. "Seemed like more blood than there should be. Then again, I've never made it a habit of fucking virgins, so I'm a little inexperienced in that department."

Nikki flinched. Of course he wouldn't make that a habit. Gabe was a good guy. One of the *best*. "I don't know what to say, but you didn't hurt me."

A muscle thrummed along his jaw. "I don't believe that for one fucking second."

She looked up, her eyes wide as she focused on his shoulder. "You didn't, Gabe."

He leaned his head in as he placed his hands on the counter, on either side of her hips. Within a second, he'd gotten all up in her space. "I don't remember much about that night," he started.

Nikki flinched again, because she remembered everything about that night. *Everything.* And wasn't that the gut punch? It had been all she ever wanted, and he hadn't even remembered most of it.

He hadn't even known it was *her.*

"Just bits and pieces," he continued. "But what I do remember? I sure as hell didn't treat you like someone who'd never had sex."

That part was also true. Gabe had not held back and he was large. It had been . . . intense, to say the least.

"So, when I remember those parts and that blood? Yeah, I'm going to wonder if I hurt you."

She shook her head. "You didn't." Her gaze dropped to his right hand. His knuckles were bleached white from how tight he was gripping the end of the counter. "Gabe, I am so—"

"Sorry?" he queried softly. "Are you seriously going to apologize to me?"

"Well, yes. I actually apologized to you that morning. Profusely, if I remember correctly—"

"Oh, I remember that." His eyes were like sheets of ice. "But not sure how an apology is adequate for what happened."

It wasn't. It really wasn't. "But I need to." She forced herself to meet his gaze. "I am sorry. You have no idea how sorry I am."

Nothing about him softened. Not that she expected her apology to do so. "Do you even know how bad things could've gone?"

"I—"

"No," he said, and Nikki quieted. "You didn't give me a chance to say shit to you. Not in four years. Not when I tried to call you. Not when I tried to make sure you weren't fucking hurt. You disappeared when you left for college. Dropped off the face of the planet and never came back."

"Isn't that what you wanted?" she asked. "Because I am pretty sure at one point that morning that you never wanted to see 'my fucking face' again." A knot expanded at the back of her throat. It still hurt to even think about how he had looked at her, how utterly disgusted he'd been. "I remember you saying that."

He didn't respond to that.

"I also remember you telling me I dis—"

"I remember that," he bit out.

"Then why are you asking me this? It's not like you really wanted to talk to me or something," she shot back, getting angry. She knew what she'd done was wrong, beyond wrong, but the anger was still building in her. Had he really expected her to answer those calls? After what he'd said to her? After he'd seen how devastated she'd been? There'd been no way she could've talked to him. She'd been embarrassed. Humiliated. And most importantly, her heart shattered into a million, stupid little pieces.

"But now you're back," he said. "Strolling back into my life like nothing happened."

"I wasn't exactly acting like nothing happened nor was I strolling anywhere—"

"Do you realize what could've happened to me if anyone ever found out?"

She gasped as her eyes shot wide. "I was eighteen, Gabe. Not a minor—"

"That doesn't matter. You were still a fucking kid—"

"I was *not* a kid. I was eighteen."

He barked out a harsh laugh. "Yeah, eighteen ain't an adult, sweetheart."

Sweetheart.

God.

Her chest cracked. He used to call her that and it actually sounded like a nice endearment. Not so much now.

It struck her then. Coming back here was a mistake. Nikki would do anything for her parents, but this . . . this wasn't going to work.

And Gabe was on a roll. "If our roles were reversed and you were as drunk as I was, what do you think would've happened? If I had come to you when you were drunk off your ass and taken advantage of you?"

Tears of shame and regret crawled up her throat. That horrible sinking feeling threatened to drag her under.

Honest to God, she'd known he'd been drinking but she'd never seen Gabe seriously drunk. He wasn't like Lucian back then. She'd figured that he'd had a few beers. That was all. She didn't even realize until that following morning that he'd been so drunk he'd barely known what he was doing or *who* he was doing. But she'd realized that pretty damn quickly before he even woke up fully that morning.

Because he'd rolled over, curled his arm around *her* waist, and tugged her against his chest, holding her like he couldn't even bear the thought of her getting out of the bed. And those brief seconds had been wonderful. Then he called *her Emma*, blowing up every stupid dream she had.

"I didn't think you were that drunk," she whispered.

His eyes widened with disbelief. "So you honestly thought that I'd want to screw an eighteen-year-old girl? A girl who was practically a sister to me? A girl who was ten years younger than me?"

Those tears were threatening to reach her eyes. She looked away, pressing her lips together as she shook her head. She would not cry. Damn it, she would not *fucking* cry.

"Christ," he growled. "What in the hell did you think of me?"

Nikki was so not going to answer that question.

He cursed under his breath. "If your parents had found

out what happened, it would've killed me. Literally and figuratively. Besides the fact your mother would've poisoned my dinner and your father would've fed me to the alligators, I respect the hell out of them."

"I know," she whispered. "I thought . . ."

"What were you thinking, Nic? I got that you had a crush on me, but seriously? Do you know—" He drew in a breath that sounded like he was striving for patience and not doing too well at it. "Do you know how much shit I gave myself for allowing that to happen between us?"

"It wasn't your fault," she said, meeting his gaze again. "It was all mine."

Gabe was quiet for so long Nikki thought he might've lost his ability to speak. "What were you thinking?" he demanded again.

"I don't know what I was thinking. It wasn't like I planned to do that. I was eighteen and I was dumb and in—" She cut herself off.

No way in hell was she admitting that she'd been in love with him. That when she realized he'd been drunk and thought he was with someone else, it had broken her in ways she couldn't even describe.

"Look, I am sorry. Trust me. I know what I did was wrong and I am sorry that you gave yourself a hard time over it. You were not at fault and you didn't hurt me."

Gabe finally, finally looked away.

She lifted her shoulders. "I'm not the same person."

"No shit," he muttered, and she had no idea what that meant.

Nikki continued. "I'm not here to cause trouble. I'm here for my parents and that's all. I'll only be working here until my mother can come back and then you won't have to deal with me again."

His head whipped back to her. "That's good to hear, because I need you to understand one very important thing."

She was all ears.

"I don't want anything to do with you and I want you to stay the hell away from me."

GABE WAS WELL on his way to getting shit-faced.

Something he'd been doing far too often of late, but then again, his entire world had been thrown up in the air a few months ago in multiple different ways, and now a part of a past he wished he couldn't remember was currently downstairs, preparing dinner for Dev and that . . . fiancée of his.

He downed the rest of the forty-year-old Macallan scotch. The burn was barely noticeable as he placed the short glass on the bar. Lucian was a bourbon man, but Gabe loved that smart bite that scotch gave at the end.

Walking through the living area of his apartment, he opened the French doors and stepped out onto the porch. Immediately his shirt started to stick to his skin. Late September and it still felt like the weather was circling one of the rings of hell.

He'd been really hard on Nic.

The little idiot had deserved it, but damn, he'd been . . . harsh. Rubbing at his chest, he stared out over the grounds—at the pool down below. He'd seen the way her eyes turned glassy when he'd said what he said.

And he'd meant everything he'd said.

He had to.

The last thing he needed right now was Nic following him around, making him feel like he was a hero just for breathing the air around her.

But damn, he hadn't been all that honest with her or himself, now had he? His gut twisted as he closed his eyes.

Most of that night was a damn blur. Being drunk off his ass had not been an exaggeration, but he remembered. . . .

Opening his eyes, he turned and looked at the doors he'd just come through. Yeah, he remembered some of it.

He remembered being shocked to see Nic there at night,

staring at him through these very doors. He'd had no idea what that imp had been up to. With her, it could've been anyone's guess. He'd let her in, because it was Nic, and she was funny as hell most of the time. And even though he'd known she had a major crush on him, she'd been harmless.

It hadn't even been the first time she'd showed up while he'd been in his apartment. She'd knocked on these doors when fucking Danny Chrisley made fun of her the first day of her sophomore year and she'd been in tears. She'd waited out in the hallway for him when she'd been upset about not having a date to homecoming. She'd even let herself in once, waiting for him because, as she'd claimed, his father was going to yell at her for making noise.

He never in a million years could've imagined that night would've gone the way it did. If he hadn't been drinking, he would've had the damn common sense to realize that night was going to be different.

Gabe should've seen it coming.

As the time for her to leave for college grew closer and closer, she'd been attached to his hip like Velcro. Her stares had become longer, more daring, and he swore those damn bathing suits of hers had continued to shrink in size.

And he'd done everything under the damn sun not to notice the fact those fucking bathing suits barely covered anything, because even though he and his brothers treated her like a sister, Nic wasn't their kin.

Their actual sister turned out to be a lying, murderous psychopath that would make Nic's crimes seem like a walk in the damn park.

And Nic . . . she'd messed up big that night and it could've been far worse, but she had been eighteen. God knows he'd done a metric shit ton of stupid shit when he was eighteen.

Then again, even with all the stupid shit he did, he still somehow managed not to sleep with someone who was drunk off their ass.

I didn't think you were that drunk.

Shit.

Her softly spoken words echoed in his dark thoughts. It was very possible that she hadn't realized, and again, he wasn't being completely honest with himself.

Wasn't like he hadn't known who was in his room that night and ended up in his lap and then in his fucking bed.

Yeah.

He'd been sober enough to know exactly whose body was crawling all over his.

He'd just been too drunk to care.

And there was a football field's difference between being too drunk to care about consequences and too drunk to know what he was doing.

What did that say about him?

Nothing good.

Most considered him the *good* brother. The decent one. The kind one. The one who acted *right*. And here he was, practically the most fucked-up of them all.

What did those damn gossip magazines nickname him while he was in college? *Demon*. If they only knew how right they'd been.

"Fuck," he muttered, turning from the doors as he reached out, wrapping his hands around the vine-covered railing. The damn shit covered every part of the outside of the house except for the porch floors. He figured it was only a matter of time before they smothered the floorboards.

His lips twisted into a smirk as he remembered all the years his father tried to get rid of the vines. No matter how many times he'd cut it down, the ivy came back. Always.

But now his so-called father was dead and no one was going to try to cut the stuff down again. The vines won in the end.

Pushing off the railing, he headed back into his main room. His stomach rumbled as he reached for the bottle of scotch. That chicken smelled amazing.

No way in hell was he going down there, though. There was not one, but two females down there he'd die happy never seeing again.

NIKKI COULDN'T WAIT to go home.

She'd only been on the job for one day and she was five seconds from dumping what remained of the bottle of champagne on Sabrina Harrington's head.

Sabrina was everything Nikki would never be.

Extraordinarily thin, elegantly beautiful, well-mannered and manicured, extremely wealthy, and marrying a de Vincent brother.

Sabrina was also a grade-A bitch.

And Nikki didn't use that word lightly. Usually, she hated it because it was a word often used to demean women, but Sabrina? She was the epitome of everything wrong with rich people.

Standing outside the smaller dining room, because the de Vincents actually had two, she clutched the bottle instead of placing it back in the ice like she knew was expected.

She could give two shits if the champagne was the temperature of her hands. All she wanted was for them to finish their damn meal, so she could clean up, go home, and bury her head in the bed in the same damn bedroom she grew up in.

Nikki wanted to forget today.

Forget the awkward-as-hell conversation with Devlin.

And definitely, *most* definitely, forget the long-overdue confrontation with Gabe.

I don't want anything to do with you and I want you to stay the hell away from me.

She couldn't blame him for wanting that, but it still stung like she'd kicked a hornets' nest.

It had taken so long for her to move past what she'd done and to start to act like a normal girl at college. Sex had been all twisted up in her head after that night. She'd felt . . . dirty after what had happened. For a long time it hadn't mattered that she honestly hadn't known Gabe had been three sheets to the wind. It wasn't until her junior year of college that she'd even been in a place to be in a relationship and have sex without being reminded of that night.

And even then, she had little experience and even less when it came to relationships, but she'd gotten better. She'd managed to stop thinking about that night at least once a day. She'd even gotten to a point where she stopped thinking about Gabe.

So, she'd thought she could handle this.

"Excuse me? *Nikki*," Sabrina called out.

Closing her eyes, Nikki strung together an impressive list of F-bombs and then started back into the room with the round table, the one designed for more intimate gatherings.

And yet, Devlin and Sabrina sat opposite each other at the table.

"Yes?" she asked, stopping beside her.

Sabrina lifted a slender flute. "I know that you're not naturally skilled at this task or had the proper training, but you should never let a glass go empty."

Biting the inside of her cheek, she said nothing as she poured the champagne. Apparently, Sabrina's legs didn't function while eating and therefore she could not get up and refill her own damn glass.

The slender, icy blonde smiled up at her, but it was too sweet, too sugary. "That is the hallmark of a great servant."

Nikki's gaze flicked to Devlin, but he was staring down at his phone. She was sure he was completely unaware of the fact that he wasn't alone. She hadn't even heard them exchange more than five sentences. So romantic.

Stepping back, she was about to go back to her hidey-hole when Sabrina gasped. Her French-manicured hand fluttered to her throat. "The *Pérignon* is warm." She said this like that was equivalent to murdering a nun. "*Nikki*, are you not putting the bottle back in the ice? With or without experience, I am sure you would know that."

She figured the truth would be unacceptable, so she started to turn away without answering, but then she saw it—the transformation that overcame Sabrina was ah-mazing. Sabrina lost the ice princess smile and her entire face warmed like her own personal sun had just arrived.

Nikki followed Sabrina's gaze.

Her stomach dropped.

Gabe strolled into the room, and he wasn't empty-handed either. In his right hand was a glass of amber-colored liquid. Scotch. Nikki could practically smell it.

"Devlin, dear. Look who has joined us!" Her entire tone even changed, so much so that Nikki actually looked back at her. Was this woman for real?

The elder de Vincent lifted his gaze as Gabe dropped into an arrogant sprawl in the chair beside him. Devlin raised a brow. "Good evening."

Gabe gave him a chin nod as he placed his scotch on the cream linen. He didn't look at Sabrina, but he turned his head directly to where Nikki stood . . . still clutching the bottle of champagne that cost as much as a used car.

What was he doing down here?

"Nikki, get Gabe a plate of food." Sabrina's laugh sounded like wind chimes. "Goodness."

Well, obviously he was down here getting food.

Duh.

"I don't quite remember her being so dense," Sabrina said with a shake of her head, grinning at Gabe like he'd be in agreement.

And the longer she stood there, he probably was.

Snapping out of it, Nikki pivoted on her heel and hurried into the kitchen, all but dropping the champagne into its ice bucket. Her mind was blank as she started filling his plate with food. He was probably hungry, so she placed a chicken breast and a thigh on his plate and added a mound of potatoes. Then she created her own version of an endless salad bowl. With her hands full, she made her way back.

"So," Sabrina was saying. "What have you been working on recently, Gabe?"

"An order from overseas," he answered, tone bland as his gaze found Nikki the moment she appeared. He tracked her around the room, and there was no stopping the faint flush creeping up her throat as she leaned in, placing the salad and then the main dish down.

Sabrina lowered her flute. Her plate was virtually untouched. "Oh, what kind of order?"

He didn't answer Sabrina, which Nikki thought was kind of rude. As Nikki stepped back, Gabe caught her wrist, startling her. Her entire body jolted at the contact of his fingers pressing over her wildly beating pulse. "Can you get me a glass of water?" He paused. "Please?"

Swallowing hard, she nodded, but Gabe still held onto her wrist. The grip was soft but unyielding and it felt like a brand on her skin. Her gaze shot to his. What was he doing? Touching her? After he'd told her that he wanted her to stay the hell away from him?

His brows lifted, obviously waiting for something. . . .

The she realized what he was waiting for. Irritation spiked as she bit out, "Yes, I can."

"Good." A small smile appeared as he let go of her wrist. Not a real smile. It was about as fake as the one Sabrina had given her earlier.

Curling her wrist to her chest, she turned away. Her gaze connected with Sabrina's. Her expression was pinched, like the champagne had soured. Having no idea what her problem was now, Nikki went to do what Gabe had asked, retrieving a glass of water.

"Gabe, dear," Sabrina tried again. "What are you working on?"

Nikki didn't hear his response and she had no idea if he even did.

The conversation at the table was just as stilted when she returned. Good news was that Devlin's plate was cleared and most of Gabe's salad was gone. She placed the glass of water down.

"I just think you have such an amazing talent," Sabrina was prattling on. "I know you're busy, but I'd love for—"

Gabe's elbow caught the knife on the table, knocking it onto the floor. Their gazes connected, and that one-sided smile was back. He watched her. "Sorry," he murmured. "I'll need a new knife."

You've got to be kidding me, she thought, bending down and snatching up the knife. She returned with a new one, and by then, Gabe had finished off the water, wanted another, and then he wanted fresh salad, and even Devlin was staring at him with a flicker of inquisitiveness. At that point, Nikki knew he was doing this on purpose.

Fine.

Whatever.

He wanted to be a jerk. Have at it.

Truth be told, she deserved worse, but if this was the best punishment he could dish out, she could easily take it. So she brought him another glass and more salad.

"My glass is empty *yet* again," Sabrina said just as Nikki was placing another full glass of water in front of Gabe.

How much liquid did these people drink? Lord.

Swallowing a sigh, she straightened and muttered under her breath, "Fuck my life."

Gabe made this noise that sounded an awful lot like a laugh.

Sabrina's eyes widened. "Excuse me?"

Oh crap. Nikki smiled brightly. "I said, 'I'm so bad at this.'"

The woman studied her. "I'm sure that's what you said."

Glancing back at Gabe, she was surprised to see an actual real grin on his lips as he lifted the glass of scotch to his mouth. Nikki grabbed the champagne.

"When do you think the other one is coming back?" Sabrina was asking this of Devlin, who just shrugged in response. "I do hope it's soon. This one seems ill equipped for the job. Actually—" she glanced up at Nikki "—that's pretty sad. This isn't hard."

Nikki's hand tightened on the bottle.

Sabrina tilted her head to the side, and Nikki would swear the blond bob barely moved. What kind of hair spray did this woman use? "Devlin was telling me you just graduated college? I'm finding that difficult to believe. I think whatever your employment or educational history is, it should've been vetted."

"She went to college," Gabe answered, shocking the hell out of several people in the room. Namely Nikki. "Majored in social work. Right? Graduated with honors."

Nikki stood beside an equally frozen Sabrina. How in the world did he know that? Well, the answer was obvious. Her parents most likely kept him and all the brothers up to date, whether they wanted to be or not.

But was he actually trying to defend her? After everything?

"Well—" Sabrina lifted her flute higher "—then I have no idea why she can't figure out how to fill a glass correctly."

Nikki had no idea why she did what she did. It was probably that wild streak her Pappy had left her, but she acted without thought, something she of all people should've known better than to do.

Planting the biggest and brightest smile on her face, she poured the champagne into the glass and just kept on pouring.

Sabrina shrieked as the god-awful-expensive champagne coursed down her slim fingers and splattered off her white pants. She launched from the seat like a rocket, knocking the heavy chair over. "Oh my God!" Sabrina stared down at her legs. "I cannot believe you did that!"

"I'm so sorry," Nikki said, blinking slowly. "Let me get

you a napkin." She reached for the pale-blue napkin that had been barely touched. "I'm just so unskilled at this. I wish there was training, but . . ."

There was a strange huffing or choking sound coming from one of the brothers, but Nikki didn't dare look at them, because they'd know if she did. They'd take one look at her face and know.

"Don't!" Sabrina's voice was shrill. "Don't you touch it. You'll just make it worse."

"Sabrina," Devlin sighed. "Sit down."

Her head jerked up in disbelief. "I can't sit down. I need to get these to the dry cleaners immediately before they're ruined."

Devlin placed an arm on the table as he stared back at his fiancée. "They are just pants. I will buy you three new pairs to replace this one. Sit down."

Sabrina sat down, but she glared up at Nikki. "The cost to clean these pants should be taken out your paycheck."

"Dev already said he'd buy you a new pair," Gabe interjected. "They're just pants."

Sabrina gasped. "They're not just pants. They're *Armani*. They don't even make these pants any longer."

Across the table, Devlin sighed once more. "I will buy you an entire closet's worth of Armani pants if you will stop talking about *those* pants."

Sabrina's lips thinned, but she was quiet as she picked up her napkin and blotted at the wet spot.

Because Nikki couldn't help herself, she asked, "Would you like me to get you another glass?"

"No," snapped Sabrina, her pale cheeks flushing pink.

"As you wish." A quick glance across the table told Nikki that the brothers did, in fact, know what had happened was no accident.

Apologizing once more, Nikki crept back from the table, fighting the laugh bubbling up in her throat. As she left the room, she couldn't help but notice that Gabe wasn't grinning as he watched her from under his thick lashes.

Oh, no, the man was smiling that smile that had gotten her in trouble all those years ago, and her stupid, *stupid* reckless heart jumped in her chest.

AFTER THE WORST first day on a job, Nikki couldn't get out of the de Vincent compound fast enough. Slipping out the back entrance, she hurried to where her nearly decade-old Ford Focus was parked next to the garage that housed who knew how many cars.

Turning on the car, she immediately cranked up the music and an old eighties song blared out of the speakers. Immediately, she recognized the song. It was "Jesse's Girl."

Man, she loved that song.

For some reason, she loved songs from the eighties. Maybe it had to do with her parents listening to it as she grew up, but she hated most of the music of today, preferring to sing along to David Bowie or Talking Heads than whoever was currently popular.

Though, she did go through a One Direction phase at one point in her younger years.

Like she always did when she was restless, she started to sing along, bobbing her head. "Where can I find a woman— blah, blah—Jesse's girl!"

God. She sucked, but she kept on, following the curve of the road as she drove past ancient oaks. That way, as she focused on not butchering the lyrics, she didn't think about her craptastic day as she drove down the winding, tree-lined road that led to the main highway. She didn't think about how she was going to have to face Gabe again and again.

Reaching the end of the private road, she slowed and leaned forward. No cars coming. She pulled out, hanging a right—heading back out into the real world, where people didn't have someone waiting in the wings to refill their champagne glasses or—

Bright light suddenly poured through the back window of her Focus, startling her. Glancing in the rearview mirror, her brows pinched as headlights appeared. Strange. Her hands tightened on the steering wheel. No one had been on the road when she pulled out. There was no way someone would get behind her that quickly unless they'd . . . they'd pulled out of the de Vincent road.

Her stomach dipped.

That would be impossible, because who would've been on that road? No one else was there, and wouldn't she have seen a car sitting along that road? Her gaze flipped back to the rearview mirror. The car was still there, not on her ass, but it was close. There was a good chance that a car could've been parked between any number of the trees or on one of the dirt access roads used by the landscapers.

But who'd be sitting there?

No one would dare loiter on the de Vincent property.

Unease blossomed as she continued down the highway, slowing down as traffic picked up around her. She kept looking in the mirror and each time she did, she saw the car right behind her. All she could make out in the fading sunlight was that it was a dark-colored sedan. When she turned off to take one of the streets to her parents' house, the car—holy crap—the car made the same turn.

Nikki's heart lurched into her throat as she hit the button on the steering wheel to turn the radio down. She needed to concentrate.

Was she being followed?

That . . . that would be ridiculous.

She glanced up. The car was still there. Her throat felt funny as she thought of her phone. It was in her purse. She started to reach for it, but then stopped. Who was she going to call? The police? And tell them what? Possibly some car was following her? Again, that sounded ridiculous.

Pressing her lips together, she focused on the busy street and houses practically stacked on top of one another. The street to her parents' house was coming up, in two blocks. If the car turned . . .

Nikki would call the police. No matter how stupid it sounded, she would call them.

Nearly holding her breath, she turned and sped up, hastily looking in the rearview mirror. The car slowed at the intersection, causing her to suck in a sharp breath. She was wrong. The car was a two-door—a coupe of some sort, but she couldn't make out the model.

The car sped up, clearing the intersection.

It did not turn.

Nikki let out a rough breath as she neared her parents' house, waiting for the relief to kick in—the laughter to spill out of her, but it didn't come and the unease didn't go away.

Chapter 5

"How was it, being back there?" Livie Besson asked as she shuffled over to the kitchen table. Despite the warm temps outside that the old central air could barely beat back, she was bundled up in her robe. It swallowed her thin body as she sat down.

Sipping her coffee, Nikki watched her mom try to get comfortable. The treatments were pretty aggressive, taking her hair and then her strength. Even the days when her mother wasn't spending eight hours getting chemo and fluids through an IV, she was still exhausted. She'd be more at ease in her recliner, but her mom wanted to keep to old habits. Although she'd switched out her coffee for some kind of tea that was supposed to be better for her.

"It's weird," Nikki answered, pushing past the concern and the seed of fear steadily growing in her stomach, the one that whispered, *Would Mom get better?* "Some things are the same. Like Devlin. And parts of the house, but it . . . feels different. I don't know how to explain it."

"How is Devlin doing?"

"Okay, I guess? He didn't like that my jeans had a hole in them."

A fond smile graced her lips. "Devlin likes things to be a certain way."

She rolled her eyes. Only her mother could feel fondness for Devlin. "I haven't seen Lucian yet, but . . . Gabe came home yesterday."

Her mom took another drink of her tea. "Was he in Baton Rouge?"

"Yeah." Curiosity filled her. "What's he been doing there?"

"I believe tending to some personal business," her mom answered in a way Nikki couldn't be sure if she knew more than what she was saying or not.

A weird, uncomfortable burn lit up her chest nonetheless. Was the personal business a girlfriend? He had to have one. Probably several. He'd gone a little wild after he and his college girlfriend broke up. *Emma*. God, just thinking her name was like a throat punch. Nikki barely knew the woman and she'd been crazy jealous of her.

Not anymore.

Because *Nic* didn't exist anymore.

Nikki dragged her fingers along one of the deep scratches on the kitchen table. "What happened to all the staff?"

Her mom glanced at the clock and then straightened the colorful floral scarf she was wearing over her head. "There have been some incidents at the house that have made the staff very uncomfortable."

"Bev made it sound like it was more than what happened with their father." Which was a big deal. Knowing that they'd found the man hanging in his office was horrible. She couldn't imagine what the brothers felt. "That it was something else. Was it their sister reappearing?"

Nikki had never spent any amount of time with Madeline de Vincent when she was younger, considering Madeline disappeared when Nikki was twelve, vanishing into thin air the same night the de Vincents' mother threw herself off the roof.

Things had been rough for many years after that for the brothers, and before that, Nikki was simply never around Madeline. But she was dying to know where Madeline had been for ten years, where she was now, and why everyone had kept it quiet.

A moment passed. "There are things that have happened in the last couple of months that are not my story to tell."

"Mom—"

"You know I would, if I could." She reached across the table, placing her cool hand over Nikki's. She squeezed gently. "You know how their family is. Things just happen to them. Bad things."

Bad things happening to the de Vincents was, like, the understatement of the year. After all, it was believed that the de Vincents were cursed. Like seriously. That was how bad the bad things that happened to them were.

"What I can tell you is that there was another death there recently," her mom said. "It was in the papers, so I'm not breaking any confidence by telling you."

She hadn't seen anything, but then again, she'd purposely ignored all things de Vincent related. "What death?"

"Do you remember their cousin Daniel?" When Nikki nodded, her mom continued. "Well, he broke into the house one night, threatened Lucian and his dear girlfriend. Was going to kill them. Devlin . . . Devlin defended them."

"What?" Nikki gasped. "Devlin killed Daniel?"

"In self-defense," her mom stressed. "And there was some speculation about Mr. de Vincent's suicide—that it wasn't one. That someone had hung that man up there and framed it as a suicide."

Nikki's jaw was practically on the table.

"One of the detectives thinks it might've been Daniel's doing."

"Why?"

"He was out of money. Needed some, and you know what money does to people."

Nikki was stunned. She hadn't known Daniel that well either. He was always with Madeline. "What does Daniel have to do with Madeline's reappearance?"

Her mother sat back. "Well, that goes to a place I'm not

comfortable talking about, but I'm sure you remember how close he and Madeline were?"

She started to open her mouth, but an understanding flared, and she snapped her jaw shut. Was her mom insinuating that Madeline had been with Daniel this whole time? And if she had been, were they like *together* together?

What in the hell?

They were cousins! Nikki almost spit up her coffee. She'd been right with her earlier assumption. Whatever happened with Madeline had to be utterly dramalicious.

"How was seeing Gabriel again?" her mom asked suddenly.

This time Nikki almost choked on her coffee. "Um, it was okay."

A knowing look settled into her mom's face. "Hmm . . ."

Uncomfortable with the change in subject, Nikki shifted in the chair. She had no idea if her parents had known how bad her crush on Gabe had been, but they weren't blind, and according to Devlin, everyone had seen it. She did know that they had no idea what happened that night before she left for college—Gabe was right about that.

The de Vincents weren't the only ones in that house capable of murder.

Her parents would've straight up killed Gabe and locked her ass away for an eternity if they knew.

IT WAS TOO damn early for Gabe to be awake, but there he was, eyes open and staring at the damn ceiling.

His temples throbbed.

And his dick was so hard he could hammer a damn nail with it.

Hell.

He'd drunk too much last night, not stopping after he knew Nic left. And he knew exactly when she had left in her older Ford, because he'd been out on the porch when she drove down the winding driveway.

Watching her like some kind of creep.

He didn't even know why he'd gone out there and watched. No clue. He was going to blame the damn alcohol for that one.

An unwanted grin tugged at his lips as he recalled last night's dinner. He'd sworn to himself that he wasn't going down there, but that's where he found himself.

Fucking scotch.

As expected, Sabrina had acted like a bitch toward Nic, and Gabe knew in his core that Nic was only going to take so much from Sabrina before she did something.

Nic had a recklessness in her that was the size of Lake Pontchartrain. Didn't he know that? Probably didn't help that he'd also been messing with her throughout dinner.

He wasn't even sure why he'd been such an asshole. Actually, that was kind of a lie. He was angry with her and he was—hell, he wasn't finishing that train wreck of a thought process.

But Nikki had definitely spilled that champagne on purpose.

A hoarse chuckle rumbled out of him as he closed his eyes. Aw Christ, he could still hear Sabrina's horrified shriek. One would think Nic had punched her or something.

Fucking Nic. What a . . .

There were way too many adjectives to describe her and why was he lying in bed thinking about her? Shit. Lifting his hands, he dragged his palms over his face. She was the last person he needed to be worrying about.

Things between them were clear. He'd told her to stay away from him, and as long as he kept his ass away from her, then it was done. He'd said his piece to her. She'd heard him.

It was time to close that chapter of his fucking life.

Besides, he had a bigger chapter that had barely started. When he left Baton Rouge, he promised he'd give the Rothchilds three months without him coming by. He promised that, and he'd be damned if he'd go back on that even if it felt like a part of him was there.

A part of him actually was there.

He had three months. That would give him time to find a place up there so he could go back and forth, so that he wouldn't be coming into their lives like a damn wrecking ball.

Three months.

Lowering his arms to the bed, he figured he might as well get the hell up and do something productive. Head to his warehouse in the city. He had work to do.

But he was going to have to take care of his throbbing dick first.

Shoving at the sheets twisted at his hips, he reached down, fisting himself. Closing his eyes, he dragged his hand up and down the thick length. In his mind, the woman was faceless, but she was riding him, and what was between her legs replaced his hand.

He kept that fantasy going. A fine sheen of sweat broke out across his forehead as he stroked himself, faster and harder. Wasn't long before he felt the familiar coiling at the base of his spine, the tightening in his sac.

"Christ," he grunted.

His hips punched up as he gripped his cock, squeezing tight. In an instant, the nameless, faceless woman in his mind disappeared, replaced by blondish-brown hair and big, brown doe-eyes. The body was a mystery to him, but before he could stop it, the face pieced together out of the wisps of his consciousness. Tiny nose. Wide, expressive mouth. High cheekbones.

Nic.

A deep moan rumbled out of Gabe. Release powered down his spine, so intense it felt like it was frying the shit out of his nerve endings as it made its way to the head of his cock. He couldn't even push the image aside. It was too late. Within seconds, it was Nic riding his cock, it was her clenching and dragging him under. He came, his back bowing as he spilled into his hand, onto the sheets in a powerful rush of sensations.

Gabe fell back to the bed, his chest rising and falling heavily. When was the last time he'd jerked off and it felt like *that*?

Not since he was a goddamn teenager.

At least it was the twenty-two-year-old Nic he was jerking off to and not the eighteen-year-old version. There was that, right?

No.

That wasn't any better. Not at all.

"Shit," he growled, heart racing as he let go of his dick and dropped his hand to the sheets. He stared at the ceiling.

This . . . shit; this was going to be a problem.

FRESH FLOWERS ARRIVED Tuesday afternoon, like they had for years. It was something the de Vincents' mother started and after she'd passed, Nikki's mother continued the tradition, personally picking out the arrangements.

Ten large bouquets were delivered, all identical. The crisp white lilies were seated among white cushion and bronzed, disbudded chrysanthemums. They were arranged in mercury glass julep vases that belonged to the de Vincents.

Nikki snapped a quick picture and sent it to her mom, knowing she took great pride in the bouquets. Then she went about placing them throughout the designated areas. The flowers were heavy, but the ones downstairs were easy. She carried one to each of the dining rooms and seven more went to various sitting rooms on the main floor.

Only one had to go upstairs, thank God. Her arms were already starting to ache from having to carry the heavy bouquets. Dev liked one in his office, so she took the back staircase and headed upstairs.

She was feeling a little out of shape when her legs started to burn as she reached the second level. Maybe she should run for something other than beignets, because goodness, she felt like she needed to sit down.

Shifting the vase into the nook of her arm, she turned the knob. It didn't budge. "What the hell?"

Nikki tried it again, but it was locked. She stood there for a moment, as if it would magically unlock or an explanation would come out of the thin air as to why the door was locked.

She even tried it again.

Nothing.

Groaning, she turned and looked up the third flight of stairs. She could try that door and then access the second floor from the outside stairwell. Her gaze dropped to the pretty flowers.

"Ugh."

Nikki climbed to the third level, and hallelujah, that door was unlocked. She entered the third floor, keeping her gaze on the beams of sunlight streaming through the door at the end of the hall. When she passed the open archway to the right, she didn't look. That was the hall that led to Gabe's apartment.

She hurried down the corridor and then out onto the porch. Cradling the vase in both hands again, she kept her gaze glued to the white boards of the floor as she hung a left.

The last time she'd been on this very porch was that night—she cut those thoughts off. Gabe had said his piece. She had said hers. Sort of. Either way, she wasn't going to think about that anymore.

Nikki reached the top of the stairs and started to step down. A floorboard creaked behind her. Someone was up here? She turned.

Weight slammed into her back, between her shoulder

blades. Shoved hard, her foot slipped on the edge of the step. A startled scream punched out of her as she tipped over. There wasn't enough time to drop the flowers so she could grab the railing. She pitched forward, into the air and then down, over the steep, hard stairs.

Chapter 6

Gabe had just opened the porch doors when he heard a scream break the silence. Birds scattered from the nearby trees as he shot out onto the porch. Where had the sound come from? His left?

He took off, rounding the corner of the porch. He didn't see anything. Maybe he was hearing stuff? With this house, it was anyone's guess. Passing the entry to the third-floor hallway, he hung a left, his steps slowing as he neared the top of the stairs.

One thick, long vine had broken free of the railing and had found its way across the floor, curling along the side of the house. He frowned as he stared down at it.

Now that was some shit.

Hadn't he just thought about the vines making their way over the floors? Just yesterday? His gaze flickered down the steps.

That's when he saw her.

"Holy shit." His heart about stopped in his chest and then sped up. He shot down the steps, taking them two at a time. "Nic."

She was lying on her side in the landing, a bouquet larger than her head cradled in her arms.

"Nic!" Was she moving? Didn't look like it. Pressure clamped down on his chest as he dropped onto his knees beside her. He reached for her. "God damn it, Nic, say something."

"Ow," she muttered, pulling one leg up.

Oh, thank Jesus. His hands were frozen just above her hip. "Are you okay?"

"I think so?" She rose onto her elbow.

If she fell down those stairs, he didn't see how she could be okay. It was at least ten damn steps. Shit. Her hair shielded her face, and that was why he reached out and touched her.

Her entire body jolted as his fingers brushed her cheek and she sucked in a sharp gasp. "Did that hurt?" he asked, scooping her hair back from her face.

"N-No."

His gaze flickered over her face. She was pale, but he didn't see any obvious wounds. At least to her face. "Does anything hurt?"

She stared at the flowers. She shook her head. "Not really." Her shoulders rose with a deep breath, the kind of breath that had to mean she hadn't hurt her ribs. "I t-think the flowers are okay."

What the hell? "I don't give a damn about the flowers. Are you okay?"

Nic looked at him, those big eyes somehow even bigger. She stared at him like she wasn't sure she heard him right. Now Gabe was starting to get worried. He thought about that time Julia—Lucian's girl—had fallen in the shower and knocked her head real good. She'd been disorientated as hell, too, and there'd been a lot of blood. Nic wasn't bleeding, but she didn't seem all there.

She didn't seem right at all.

"You can let go of the flowers now," he suggested.

She glanced down at them. "I didn't . . . want to ruin them."

"You didn't." Gabe reached for them, and her grip tightened. He lifted a brow. "You can let go of them, Nic."

Nic held on for a moment longer and then she finally let go. Taking the vase, he set it aside. His heart was finally starting to settle down. "Do you think you can sit up?"

When she nodded, he gently took ahold of her arm. She jerked again, and his gaze flew to her face. "You still feeling okay?"

"Yeah." She straightened, exhaling heavily as she lifted her left arm, turning it to the side. A streak of bright red coursed down her arm. "Ew."

Ew? That was all she had to say? "Let me see that."

"It's not bad."

He ignored her as he took her wrist in his hands and gently turned her arm. Some pretty gnarly scratches ran from her elbow up under the sleeve. Her shirt was torn. "I don't think this needs stitches." He peeled back the little sleeve on her shirt and leaned in. As he checked her out, he tried to ignore how damn . . . good she smelled. Like jasmine. "But we should probably call Doc. Have him—"

"I'm fine. Really," she said, leaning away. "You don't need to call a doctor."

"These stairs are no joke. You could've hurt yourself and not realized it yet, Nic. You need to let a doc look at you."

"I didn't hit my head." Nic pushed the hair back out of her face. "I'm okay."

He wasn't so sure about that. "Nic—"

"Seriously. I'm okay. It's just a cut. I don't know how, but I didn't really hurt myself."

Frustration rose. "You fell down a flight of stairs and you're bleeding. Why are you being so difficult about this?"

"I'm not," she snapped, as she pulled her arm free. "Why do you care anyway?"

He drew back. "Why do I care?"

"Figured you'd throw a party if I broke my neck."

Gabe stared at her a moment, shocked at first. Then he thought about what he'd said to her the day before and he kind of couldn't blame her for thinking that. "I wouldn't be happy if you were hurt. Jesus." He lowered his hands to his knees and started to rise. "At least let me get your father—"

"No." She grabbed his arm, and his gaze shot back to her. She stared up at him. "Please don't say a thing to my father. I don't want him to worry and get upset over nothing."

"Over nothing? Nic, you could've—"

"He has enough to worry about right now. He doesn't need to freak out about this for no reason," she said, her gaze pleading. "Please, Gabe. Don't say anything."

Her concern for her father touched a part of him he'd rather not have her dig her fingers into. Reaching down, he placed his hand over where she gripped him. Despite what had happened between them that night four years ago, he always, *always* had a hard time telling her no.

"I won't say anything," he said, voice gruff as he pulled her hand away. "As long as you're not hurt. I'm going to get something for your arm and then I'm going to sit here with you for a few minutes and make sure that's the case."

She looked like she wanted to argue, but after a moment, she nodded.

Wary of leaving her, he hesitated for a moment and then went up the stairs, stopping at the top to grab the damn vine she obviously tripped over. He ripped it free and tossed it over the railing. Then he went to his apartment. He quickly grabbed an array of items before making his way back to her. He found her sitting next to the vase, her feet resting on the step below. He had a sudden memory of her, when she was younger, sitting in that very spot, waiting for him to come home, her hair pulled into a high ponytail, her knobby knees knocking together.

Shaking the image from his thoughts, he stepped around her and sat on the step her feet rested on. "Let me see your arm."

"I can take care of it." She reached for the damp cloth he held.

Gabe lifted his brows. "Give me your arm, Nic."

She stared at him a moment and then rolled her eyes. "Whatever."

Biting back a grin as she shoved her arm out, he carefully began wiping up the blood. He glanced down at her shoes. They were flats with some kind of thin, useless sole. "You need to start wearing shoes with better tread on them. Then you won't be tripping over vines and falling down steps."

"I didn't trip over a vine or slip down the steps," she protested as he tossed the towel up on the landing and reached for the peroxide and cotton balls he'd grabbed.

He coated the cotton in peroxide. "Sure looks like you did to me. Probably didn't even see the vine, but it was lying on the floor, right at the top of the steps." The skin above her elbow was angry and raw. "You're so damn lucky," he muttered, shaking his head. "Could've been so much worse. This might sting."

"I know I'm lucky." She sucked in a sharp breath as he pressed the cotton to the scratches. "But I didn't trip or slip. Someone pushed me."

His hand stilled as his gaze found hers. "What?"

"Someone pushed me. I mean, that's what it felt like." The corners of her mouth pursed as the peroxide fizzled over her skin. "I heard what sounded like a step behind me and then I felt something hit my back."

Gabe frowned as he reached for the small tube of antibacterial cream. He'd brought the whole pharmacy with him. "I came as soon as I heard you scream. There was no one up here."

"I didn't see anyone, but I know what I felt." A shudder rolled through Nic. "I didn't just slip. I'm not clumsy."

"You were pretty clumsy back in the day." He gently rubbed the cream over her arm, his eyes shooting to her face when he heard the harsh inhale. "Sorry."

Her cheeks flushed in the prettiest way as she shook her head. "There was no vine at the top of the steps."

"There was. I just snapped it off and tossed it."

"I didn't . . . I didn't see it."

Gabe was silent as he finished with the cream and then picked up the gauze. Could she have been pushed and not have tripped over the vine? The mere thought of that pissed him off, but he had no idea who could've done it. Or why.

Taping the ends of the gauze together, he lowered her arm to her thigh. "How are you feeling? Dizzy? Nauseous?"

"I feel fine," she insisted. "Thank you for cleaning up my arm."

"It's no big deal—" He looked up as he heard footsteps. A second later, Dev appeared at the top of the steps. Right behind him was Sabrina.

Gabe felt Nic stiffen.

Dev stared down the steps, his expression unreadable. "Do I even want to know what is going on?"

"Nothing." Gabe looked over at Nic. "Everything is fine."

"It does not look like everything is fine," Dev replied. "Are you injured, Nikki?"

"No," she answered, craning her neck to look up the steps. "I'm okay."

"Did you fall down the steps?" Sabrina asked the question in a way that sounded like she was trying not to laugh.

"Yeah." Nic looked away, focusing on the steps before her. "I fell."

"Oh no." Sabrina placed a hand on Dev's arm. "I do hope she doesn't try to get workmen's comp." She gasped. "Or sue you."

Gabe opened his mouth, but Nic was faster. "Contrary to what you might think, I'm not desperate enough for money to throw myself down the stairs."

Sabrina's eyes narrowed.

"That's good to hear." Dev's response was dry. "So, you did fall down the steps?"

Gabe waited for her to say she was pushed, but he heard Nic sigh as she picked up the bouquet and said, "I did, but I saved the flowers."

THE NEXT DAY Nikki felt like she'd fallen down a flight of steps because, well, she'd fallen down a flight of steps.

God, she'd been so lucky she hadn't cracked her head open or worse. She wasn't even sure how she ended up only with a few scratches. Kind of felt like she had a guardian angel perched on her shoulder yesterday.

She still couldn't believe that Gabe had been the one to find her. Not only that, but he'd actually taken care of her as if he didn't hate her.

But he hated her.

He just wasn't going to let her lie on the stairs, bleeding and banged up.

Nikki winced as she reached up, grabbing two cans of cream of chicken soup. She cradled them to her chest as she picked up a pack of noodles.

Was I pushed?

That question had been haunting her since yesterday afternoon. She knew she'd felt something hit her back. She hadn't just lost her balance. Someone pushed her, but who? Gabe had said no one was up there and he said there was a vine covering the floor, and she doubted that he'd lie about that. She hadn't seen anyone nor heard anyone run away. Granted, she'd been falling down the stairs screaming, so she probably wouldn't have heard anyone, but she knew she'd been pushed. If it wasn't a person then the only other option was a . . . ghost had pushed her.

She didn't laugh at the absurdity of the idea. She'd basically grown up in this house. She'd never seen anything, but she'd heard stuff—footsteps in the hallway when no one was there, a woman's laughter when there was no other female around, and things moving.

A shiver danced down her spine. She wasn't sure what was worse. An actual living, breathing human being who wanted to see her injured or a ghost who decided she needed to take a quick trip down the steps.

Either way, she was grateful that Gabe hadn't said anything to her father. She'd been able to hide the bandage yesterday by wearing a cardigan and today she wore a shirt where the sleeves went to her elbows.

She thought about the car that had seemed like it had been following her almost to the front door of her parents' house. Another shiver shook her. The car hadn't been following her and maybe . . . maybe she did trip over the vine. That sounded more likely than someone pushing her.

Nikki left the pantry and made her way back in the kitchen. As she reached the island, she heard the sharp rap of heels clicking off the wood floors. She knew who it was before she walked into the kitchen.

Irritation pricked at her skin as Sabrina entered. The woman looked flawless, as usual. Her chic bob defied the laws of physics by not having one single strand of hair out of place. She wore dark slacks that seemed to repel lint of all forms and a pressed, wrinkle-free blouse that was tucked into her pants so perfectly Nikki wondered how that was even possible.

Nikki also wondered what in the world she was doing in the kitchen. She doubted that woman knew the difference between a spatula and a fork.

"Hello, *Nikki*," she said, saying her name like it was a newly discovered STD. "I wanted to make sure you were aware that I'll be joining Devlin for dinner tonight."

Unfortunately she was aware. "Yes. I was informed of that this morning."

Her gaze flicked to the island. "I do hope you're not making whatever that is for dinner."

"A casserole was—"

"I don't care what was on the menu," she interrupted. "I will not eat a *casserole* for dinner."

"Then you might want to order out," Nikki replied, keeping her voice level.

Sabrina's gaze sharpened. "Is that a serious response or are you just being a smartass?"

Honestly, she wasn't being a smartass. Sort of. "Only the chicken has thawed out. For me to make something else, the meat wouldn't be ready—"

"Then I would like a broiled herb butter chicken breast," she cut in, and Nikki suddenly wondered if she was working at a restaurant. "Would that be too difficult of a request to make? Too hard for your obviously limited skillset?"

Limited skillset? Aw, Jesus be testing her. "I can make that for you. Would you also like a salad?"

Sabrina's lips twisted into a smirk. "You should've offered that before telling me I needed to order out."

Counting to ten and only making it to five, Nikki bit back a curse. "Would you like a salad with your chicken breast?"

"Yes, I would love a salad with my chicken breast."

Nikki nodded and then turned away, hoping Sabrina would take the hint.

She didn't. "How are you feeling after your fall?"

A chill skated down her spine as she turned back to Sabrina. There wasn't a single second where Nikki believed genuine concern had prompted that question. "I'm feeling fine. Thanks for asking."

Sabrina nodded. "I'm glad to hear that."

Nikki was going to call BS on that.

"I would hate to see something tragic like a serious fall happen to you, when you're so young." Sabrina smiled then. "I'll see you at dinner."

Another icy chill danced over her skin as Nikki watched Sabrina leave. A horrible thought occurred to her as she stood there. Had . . . had it been Sabrina who'd pushed her? She'd been at the house yesterday. Obviously. Could she have snuck away from Devlin and done it? Nikki had spilled the champagne on her, but that seemed like a drastic retaliation even for someone as petty as Sabrina.

But what if it had been her?

Chapter 7

$\mathcal{T}$hank God that after Wednesday, Nikki had to only worry about getting dinner prepared and served to Devlin, which was like serving food to a wall, and Gabe, which was like serving a water buffalo.

Over the next two days, she only saw Gabe during dinner and other than retrieving endless glasses of water for him, he hadn't said much of anything to her other than asking how her arm was on Wednesday.

Which was perfect.

She hadn't seen him during the day. For all she knew, he wasn't even home, and Devlin was like one of the ghosts in the house. She'd see him out of the corner of her eyes and when she'd turn to acknowledge him, he was gone.

Creepy.

Devlin was probably checking to make sure her jeans didn't have holes in them and that she wasn't falling down any more sets of steps.

And so far, she hadn't, but every time Nikki went up and down any stairs in the house, she looked over her shoulder.

She hadn't been able to shake the possibility that Sabrina had pushed her, but whenever she really sat and thought about it, it seemed crazy to her, that Sabrina would do something so insane.

It just couldn't have been her.

Mainly because Sabrina would've been petrified of breaking a nail.

Which left the question of who or what had done it, and Nikki had no idea. All these years she had spent in this house, she only felt uncomfortable a few times, but now she walked through the silent rooms and halls feeling like someone was always with her, right behind her.

Nikki was making her rounds Friday afternoon, cleaning the game room that had a fully stocked bar, when her phone vibrated in the back pocket of her jeans. Well, they really weren't *jeans* jeans. They were jeggings—the lovechild of denim and leggings, and the best pairs actually had pockets, so no one could tell the difference.

She practically lived in leggings.

Setting the bottle of scotch on the bar, she pulled her phone out and saw that it was a text from Rosie. A smile tugged at her lips as she tucked a stray hair behind her ear.

Drinks & bad life decisions commence at 8pm tomorrow night!

Rosie was a riot. Nikki had met her during her freshman year at UA. The tiny redhead was several years older than Nikki and was taking the *scenic route* through college, meaning it was taking her, on average, two years for every year it took a normal student to complete. It didn't help that Rosie had changed her major three times since Nikki had known her.

She'd finally graduated the same semester as Nikki, obtaining a degree in philosophy.

Nikki would never forget the first time she learned how old Rosie really was. The woman looked ten years younger than thirty-three and acted roughly Nikki's age. Not that Nikki acted immature. Well, if she was being honest, she had her moments, but Rosie still had this thirst for life that Nikki wondered if it came from the freedom of not really being bogged down by a career, a significant other, children, or a mortgage.

Nikki sent a message back.

Can't do this weekend, but can do next Saturday.

A frownie face emoticon came back and then Rosie texted the first message over again, changing the date to next Saturday. Nikki slipped her phone back in her pocket, actually looking forward to seeing Rosie. She'd been home a couple of weeks before she started working here and she hadn't done anything other than have dinner a few times with one of her childhood friends and visit the local animal shelter. She needed to get out of her house and hooking up with Rosie in the evening would be perfect since it would give Nikki most of Saturday to spend with her mom.

She'd been getting home from the de Vincent compound after her mom was already asleep, worn out by the toll treatment was taking on her. So Nikki had now taken to dragging her butt out of bed an hour early to eat breakfast with her mom before she left for work.

Breaking a sweat lifting the damn bottles and climbing up and down the stepladder, she was on the tips of her toes so she could place the last bottle when she heard footsteps outside the hall.

Her stomach dropped a little as she twisted at the waist. She knew it wasn't her father. He was out running errands. Stretching as she gripped the top of the stepladder, she tried to see in the hall, but from what she could see, there was no one.

She bit down on her lip.

A wave of sharp tingles danced along the nape of her neck as she turned back to the shelves. Probably Devlin out there, creeping—

The sound of glass scratching across wood was like a blast of cold air to her stomach. Turning at the waist so fast she was shocked she didn't fall off, her gaze dropped to the cherry oak bar top.

Five recently cleaned tumbler glasses sat side by side, like she'd left them.

All except one.

One of them was several inches to the right of the group.

Nikki's lips parted on a sharp inhale as the fine hairs on the nape of her neck rose. "This damn house," she whispered.

Those glasses were super heavy. If she threw one and hit someone in the head, it would knock them right out. No way would it just move.

"Nope." She crept down the ladder and reached out, hesitating for a second. "Not today, Satan. Knock it off."

Picking up the glass, she quickly put it away and did the same with the rest. Then she moved out from behind the bar, almost done. Thank God. The dark, windowless room was starting to creep her out.

On her way to the door, she saw a balled-up napkin under the pool table and veered over to it, shivering. Was it her or did this room feel substantially cooler than the rest of the house? Probably the fact there was no windows for the sun to beat heat through. Or there was definitely a ghost.

There were no in-betweens.

She was just glad there weren't any staircases nearby.

Bending over, she snatched the napkin off the floor.

"Well, hello."

The male voice startled Nikki. She jerked up, smacking the side of her head on the bottom of the pool table. She fell back, landing on her butt as she pressed her palm to the side of her head. "Ouch!"

A deep chuckle raised her hackles. What the hell was funny with her nearly giving herself a concussion? Or the fact that this house was trying to kill her?

"I'm used to women throwing themselves at me, but not knocking themselves out. That's a new one for me," the oddly familiar voice said. "Are you okay?"

Squinting against the dull ache, she saw a hand appear

in front of her face. Her gaze tracked up the arm, over the white dress shirt that was rolled up to the elbows.

"Hello?" he said, wiggling his fingers.

Her gaze shot to the man's face as she lowered her hand from her slightly throbbing head. *Oh crap.* No wonder she recognized the voice.

It belonged to Parker Harrington.

No way was she taking his hand.

She'd rather reach into a burning inferno than take his hand.

What in the hell was he doing roaming here? Usually her father was on the ball, making sure no visitors had free, random access to the house and Parker knew that. He'd been to this house thousands of times when Nikki was younger, being that he was close to the brothers, and she guessed even more so now that Devlin was marrying his sister. Still, no one but the family moved about these halls without being escorted by someone. But since her dad wasn't here, obviously Parker was taking advantage of that.

Refusing to take his hand, she pushed to her feet and stood, ignoring the ache along the side of her head. "You startled me."

"I can tell." His pale-blue gaze, the same as his sister's, dropped to his empty hand. He slowly lowered it with a slight frown. "I'll admit I was being quiet. Saw you in here, and well, I was admiring the view."

Ew.

Not only did Parker behave the way she remembered, which was like a creep, he looked the same, just older. His light blond hair was styled back from a face that was attractive but also hawkish. He had this intense way about the set of his thin lips that always reminded her of a bird of prey. He was younger than Sabrina, around Lucian's age.

"Hell, I haven't seen you in forever," he continued. "Look at you." He checked her out so blatantly that it crossed that line on what was respectful and belly-flopped straight into disrespectful territory. "All grown up now. You've really filled out nicely, Nikki."

Double ew.

Nikki stepped back, clutching the damn napkin in her hand. "Nice seeing you," she said, getting her tone short. "Hope all is well, but I need to get to work."

Parker stepped to the side as she did, staying between her and the door. Exasperation spiked, but so did a little burst of panic. They'd been in this situation before.

This was just what she needed to end her first week here. Obnoxious, and unfortunately, the friendlier Harrington sibling.

"When Sabrina mentioned you were now working for the de Vincents, I almost didn't believe it." He smiled, flashing ultra-bright and ultra-straight white teeth. "But here you are."

She sighed heavily. "Yes. Here I am. And I'm pretty busy—"

"Come on, Nikki. It's been forever since we've seen each other." He dropped a heavy hand on her shoulder. "Let's reconnect."

Her lips turned down at the corners as she stepped back, out of his reach. "We never connected to reconnect."

Parker let out a low laugh. "That's not exactly true."

She sucked in a shrill breath, somewhat shocked that he would even think about bringing up what he surely was. "That was not a connection. That was you being—"

"Being what? Trying to be nice and friendly when you were always a bit of a stuck-up bitch?"

Nikki's eyebrows practically landed in her hairline. "I was the stuck-up bitch?" Had he met his sister? Looked in the mirror recently?

"Yeah." He was still smiling, but his eyes weren't warm. They were just like his sister's. "I remember trying to get to know you better when you were here, waiting for that housekeeper to get off."

"*That* housekeeper is my mom," she retorted. "And I don't think we have the same idea of getting to know one another."

They definitely didn't. He'd cornered her once, when she was seventeen. It had been one particularly hot July afternoon. The boys, namely Devlin, were home and they'd had friends with them. She'd headed inside the pool house to change since she'd been wading around the shallow end and Parker had walked in on her while she had nothing on but a towel. Instead of immediately running from the pool house like any decent guy would, he'd gotten close to her, *too* close.

And he . . .

Nikki's mouth dried.

Parker had scared her, and if it hadn't been for Lucian coming in to grab a towel, Nikki knew she would've been more than scared. Of course, Parker had played the whole thing off. That he hadn't known Nikki was in there, and why wouldn't Lucian believe him? Nikki hadn't said anything, even though she wanted to badly.

And Parker knew why she hadn't.

"Oh, I'm sure we have the same idea of getting to know each other better." He blocked her again, but this time he stepped forward. "Same way you wanted to get to know Gabe."

Nikki's back hit the pool table. "I don't know what you're talking about."

"Really?" Parker laughed as he leaned in, placing one hand on the pool table next to her. Every muscle in her body locked up. Gabe had done a similar thing in the kitchen on Monday, but it was nothing like this. "You were like a cat in heat whenever Gabe came around. I doubt that's changed."

Her mouth dropped open. Her tongue burned to let loose on him, but she held back. Ha. A total adult move that she thought she deserved a beignet for later. It didn't matter if what he said was true or not. Denying it or arguing with him would only prolong this conversation. "I have work to do, Parker."

"I know." He shifted his hips, placing his other hand on the pool table. "What are you doing later?"

Now her jaw hit the floor. "Are you serious?"

"What do you think?"

"You're asking me out?"

Parker dipped his chin, forcing her to lean back as far as her spine would allow her. His hair didn't even move. Just like his sister's. "You can come check out my place. Got a new penthouse over at Woodward. I think you'll like it."

For several seconds, Nikki couldn't even think, but then she let out a loud laugh. "You're not asking me out to dinner, but to go 'check out' your penthouse?"

"Yeah." The smile started to fade from his face. "Why would I ask you out to dinner?"

"Oh my God." She laughed again, out of shock. He couldn't be real. Wow. His offer was so dumb and trashy, she couldn't even be offended.

A throat cleared. "Am I interrupting?"

Oh God.

Nikki snapped her mouth shut as Parker briefly closed his eyes. A weird tremor coursed through him. Pushing away from the pool table, away from her, he turned around. "Hey, Gabe." His tone was light. "I didn't know you were home. Would've swung upstairs and said hi."

Her gaze collided with Gabe's. He was looking at them like he was ten seconds away from throwing one or both of them out of the house.

"What are you doing in here, Parker?" Gabe's jaw was so hard it could crack granite.

Parker grinned. "I was going to see Devlin, but then I saw Nikki and had to say hi. Hell, I haven't seen this girl in four years. Crazy."

Drawing in a deep breath through her nose, she crossed her arms. "He was just leaving," she said.

"Good to hear," Gabe replied, widening his stance. Her gaze dropped, and yep, his bare feet poked out from the hem of his jeans.

Parker looked over his shoulder at her. "Don't forget about my offer. It's always open."

Nikki didn't get the chance to tell him that she was about as interested in seeing his penthouse as she would be in swimming in one of the swamps nearby. He was already walking past Gabe.

He nodded at the de Vincent brother. "I'll see myself out."

Detecting a bit of tension there, Nikki remained quiet and then Gabe and she were alone for the first time since he bandaged up her arm.

Was going to ask her to get water?

A giggle tickled its way up her throat, but the look on Gabe's face as he eyed her from where he stood by the bar told her that would not be wise.

Oh boy.

Stepping away from the pool table, she said, "I need to get started on dinner."

"What you need to do is stay away from Parker Harrington."

Disbelief thundered through Nikki. She stopped and turned to Gabe. "I wasn't planning to be near him."

His eyes were sharp. "That's not what it looked like to me."

"I don't know what it looked like to you, but he came in here while I was cleaning up. I didn't search him out."

"Looked like to me, you two were getting reacquainted with one another."

Nikki's head was about to explode. "Then you were seeing wrong."

He didn't appear to believe her. "Parker's only going to want one thing from you, Nic. And it isn't going to be a relationship."

"No shit," she said, and then laughed again, because this conversation was ridiculous for several reasons. If he knew what Parker really was like, he wouldn't be even suggesting that.

Then again, maybe he wouldn't care, all things considered.

He stared at her as he stepped forward. She held her ground. "And that's good enough for you? To be a quick fuck to be thrown away, because people like Parker only get with people like the Harrington family. Everyone else is disposal to them."

Several seconds passed before she could even work out what he was saying and when she did, she all but exploded. She didn't care that Gabe hated her, but she wasn't going to stand here and be lectured over Parker Harrington. "First off, let me make this clear. I have absolutely no interest in Parker and let me explain this *again* to you, Gabe. I was in here doing my job and he came in here. I cannot stand him. Trust me."

Nothing about Gabe's face softened.

"Secondly, I don't know if you don't realize this or not, but when I think of 'people like the Harringtons,' I think of the de Vincents."

"We are nothing like them," he growled. "And you damn well know that."

"Devlin is marrying one of them," she pointed out.

"That's Dev."

She threw her hands up. "He's a de Vincent!"

Gabe moved into her space, his voice dropping low. "And you know I'm nothing like Dev."

"This has nothing to do with you or Devlin." Frustration pricked at her skin. What in the hell? "Let me get back on topic here. I'm not interested in anything to do with Parker, but if I was, that's none of your business, Gabe."

"Is that so?" A ghost of a smile curled at his mouth.

"Yes." She glared at him. "But contrary to what you think, I don't go around throwing myself at guys, so—"

"Really?" he replied dryly. "That hasn't been my experience."

Nikki jerked back as if she'd been slapped. The anger twisted into something ugly deep inside her, causing her chest to squeeze. What Gabe was saying cut into her.

"You think that because—" She sucked in a breath, stepping away from Gabe. "You think that because of what I did when I was *eighteen*? You honestly think I throw myself at guys?"

He didn't respond, but a shadow crossed his face. Looked like regret for a moment, but then his striking features smoothed out. She'd have to be crazy if she really thought he felt bad for saying that.

Nikki shook her head, her throat thickening. "I've spent the last four years regretting that night, thinking I'd scraped the bottom of that big old barrel of regret, but I was wrong. Because I haven't regretted it more than I do right now."

That shadow was back. "Nic—"

"I get it. You think the worst of me. I understand that, but I was eighteen and I made a mistake that I've been paying for in ways you have no fucking idea. I am not that same girl." Her voice shook. "But you don't know that. You don't know me at all."

Chapter 8

As embarrassing as it was to acknowledge, Nikki went home that night and cried like she was that very same girl she'd told Gabe she wasn't, and that pissed her off. Why did his super-wrong assumption hurt that badly?

The answer, the only answer, terrified her.

Because it had to mean that a stupid, asinine part of her still cared about what he thought and how he felt—cared beyond the superficial level, and that was unacceptable.

Nikki was over him—over her silly infatuation. That's what she kept telling herself over the weekend and when she arrived at the de Vincent compound the following Monday. And when thoughts of Gabe crept unwanted into her head, she got her shit straight, right then and there, focusing on more important things.

Like what the hell was she going to do after this?

As highly as she thought of her parents' jobs here, this was not what she wanted from life. While she walked all the poor doggies at the shelter on Sunday, she went over her options in nauseating detail. Having not made up her mind yet about continuing on in her education to get a master's or doctorate in social work or going straight to work, she only knew one thing. That no matter what, she wanted to stay close to home.

The health scare with her mother showed her that time with her parents was running out. As much as she hated to admit it, even when her mom got better—and she *would* get better—the years weren't stretched out in front of her like they used to be.

So Nikki was staying local no matter what.

Either way, she needed to find a cheap and safe place to live. What little money she had saved up from the part-time job working in the campus bookstore wasn't going to get her very far, but she was getting a paycheck from the de Vincents, which made her feel weird. Her parents refused to allow her to hand over the whole paycheck. She knew they needed the money with everything going on, so after a whole lot of arguing, she was pocketing half and giving the rest to them.

And that felt right, because she was nowhere near as good at running the de Vincent household as her mom was.

Something she was sure Devlin was thinking every time he saw her.

First thing she needed to do was to find a place. Then she would decide what to do in terms of her career, and maybe she'd find someone to . . . distract her. Hadn't exactly worked well in college, but she'd decided that she hadn't fully committed herself to being with someone.

She'd dated Calvin most of her junior and senior year. Even taken him home one Mardi Gras to meet her parents. He'd been a really good guy, but she hadn't . . . yeah, she hadn't really been *there*, and he'd sensed that. Calvin had eventually given up on her.

No more of that nonsense.

She was going to go on a date—no, *dates*, and she wouldn't compare how she *used* to feel toward Gabe to how she felt about every man she met since then.

There would be no more of that.

Focusing on her actual life and what to do with it helped her not fall down that rabbit hole known as Gabe. Operation Avoid Him at All Costs, OAHAC for short, was working.

Mainly because he hadn't showed up for dinner since last Thursday and whenever she saw him in the halls or heard his voice, she engaged ninja stealth mode and darted into whatever room was nearby.

A few times she wasn't successful.

Now was about to become one of them, because she could hear him talking on the phone as she just finished stacking fresh towels outside the sauna.

Yes.

They had a sauna.

Whipping toward the open door, she wished she'd thought about locking it behind her. She looked over her shoulder. Could she hide in the sauna? Okay, that was excessive. She felt like she did when she was younger, stuck in the pool in her ugly one-piece bathing suit, too embarrassed and awkward to even move.

What was it about this house that made her feel like she'd taken one giant leap backward when it came to personal growth?

"Yeah, I'll have the frame finished up by the beginning of next weekend," he was saying, and there was a pause while Nikki seriously considered throwing open the nearby window and crawling out of it.

Gabe laughed.

The air hitched in Nikki's throat. *His laugh.* It had been so long since she had heard that sound. It was deep and infectious, and tugged at the corners of her lips. It made her think of lazy summer afternoons when she'd do something stupid just to hear his laugh.

Nikki hadn't heard that laugh in years.

"The freight charge is going to be the least of his worries." He was getting closer.

"Damn," she muttered as she realized she was completely trapped if he came in here.

A second later, Gabe was in the doorway, and her heart stopped in her chest and then restarted, pounding way too fast.

Gabe was shirtless.

Code red! Code red!

Her brain screamed as her greedy, gluttonous eyes took in every bare inch of his skin. Not like she hadn't seen him shirtless before. She'd seen him hundreds of times without a shirt and she had seen him naked. This wasn't anything new, but it had been a long time and her memories hadn't done him justice.

Nikki shouldn't look, but she couldn't even help herself. The nylon pants he wore hung indecently low, showing off those drool-worthy indents on either side of his hips. His stomach was ripped. She knew he had that wickedly defined six pack because the man worked out religiously. There was a faint line of hair that trailed from his navel, down his lower stomach, disappearing under the nylon pants. Her heart skipped a beat as she forced her gaze up over the smooth skin of his pecs and the broad width of his shoulders. Earbuds hung from a cord around his neck. He had his hair pulled back into a small bun that was oddly and ridiculously attractive to her.

Only a handful of seconds had passed from the moment Gabe walked into the gym, and she knew the exact moment he realized she was there, standing petrified by the rack of towels.

His gaze connected with hers, and the grin slipped off his face. "Hey, I've got to go."

Didn't seem like he waited for a response, because a heartbeat later he was lowering the phone. Her heart was currently lodged somewhere in her throat.

Almost a week had passed since they'd last spoken.

"What are you doing in here?" he asked.

"I was putting fresh towels away."

"Sort of looks like you're just standing there, frozen like a statue."

She couldn't tell if he was teasing her or not, but it didn't matter. Her muscles finally unlocked and she got her feet moving. She went the shortest route that put as much space between them as possible. That required her to walk over one of the four treadmills. She didn't care how stupid it looked. Not when she could feel his intense gaze following her process.

"You know, there's an actual floor you can walk on," he commented.

"I know." She nodded and then tucked a strand of hair back behind her ear, feeling about five different levels of awkward. "I like walking on treadmills."

"Uh-huh."

Her cheeks started to warm as she stepped off the treadmill. There were only a few feet between her and freedom. *Just keep walking. Just keep—*

"Nic."

She stopped. It was like she had no control.

Silence.

Biting down on her lip and telling herself she was probably going to regret this, she slowly faced him.

Somehow, and she didn't know how, he'd gotten closer to her. His gaze was sheltered as he stared at her. She wondered if he was going to ask about her arm. A terse moment passed and then he said, "You didn't clean my apartment last week."

Oh.

That was not what she was expecting him to say. "Yeah, I figured you didn't want me to do that."

His head tilted just the slightest. "That's your job, isn't it?" His cold tone would've impressed Devlin. "Why would I not want you to do it?"

It's your job.

A sharp stab pierced her chest. She had no idea why that statement bothered her so much. Maybe it was because she knew damn well he would never speak to her mom or father with that tone. And maybe it was because it was a painful reminder of just who she was to him now.

A staff member that worked for his family.

That ugly feeling from before turned to a messy knot in her throat, but she lifted her chin. She was done crying over Gabe.

"I figured you wouldn't like if I was in your room," she said, keeping her voice level. "But I can clean it this afternoon if you like."

Something flashed in those eyes and the muscle throbbed along his jaw. "I don't want you cleaning it today."

"Then I can do it tomorrow."

"Tomorrow won't work either."

Her brows pinched. "Since tomorrow is Friday, I'm not sure when else I can do it. Next week—"

"You could've done it last week like you're paid to do."

She folded her arms over her chest like that could somehow help ease the sting of his words. "I'm sorry." It took every ounce of her self-control to say what she did next. "You're right. I should've done it last week, but I can either do it today or tomorrow. If not, then I will do it next week."

His features tightened with what appeared to be frustration, but she wasn't sure what he had to be frustrated about at this moment. He was the one being difficult. "Your suggestions aren't acceptable."

Irritation swelled inside her, washing away the hurt. It loosened her tongue. "Then how about you clean your apartment then?"

Surprise parted his lips.

"I mean, you *are* a grown man who is more than capable of changing his own bedsheets and picking up after himself," she snapped, uncrossing her arms. "I'm not your *mother*."

"No shit," he shot back. "But thanks for clearing that last part up."

"So, I don't know what you want me to say or do. Either I clean your rooms when I said I could or you do it yourself."

The corner of his lips twitched. "I can't believe you're talking to me like this."

Nikki was beyond telling herself to shut her mouth and

she snapped like a twig breaking under strong winds. "I can't believe you're being such a dick."

A surprised laugh burst out of him, and Nikki couldn't tell if that was a good thing or a bad thing. She didn't care at the moment, because she was pissed. "I may be working here for right now, but you need to remember I'm not your servant, here for your beck and call."

"Actually, you are here for our beck and call." Gabe smirked. "That's what you're being paid real money to do."

He had a point, but he wasn't getting it. Not even remotely. "What happened to you?" The question burst out of her. "You were never like this. Devlin? Yes. But you? No. What in the hell happened?"

"*You* happened to me."

His words were like a psychical push. She stumbled back a step as her gaze latched onto his. She snapped her mouth shut, because that knot had expanded three sizes bigger and she had no idea if she was going to start cursing him or crying.

Nikki did the only smart thing.

Pivoting on her heel, she hurried out of the gym and she thought she heard him curse. And then she flinched, because she thought she heard him throw something—something that shattered against the wall.

And a spiteful part of her really, really hoped it was his phone.

Chapter 9

A shadow fell over Gabe's workbench, stilling his hands. Gabe looked up from the frame he was chiseling. Despite the shit day he was having, he smiled when he saw Lucian standing there.

And he wasn't alone.

Troy LeMere was with him and they hadn't come empty-handed either.

Lucian placed an opened bottle of beer on the bench as Gabe tugged his earbuds out and turned off the music app on his phone. "Figured we'd find you here."

Grinning, Gabe rose, giving his younger brother a one-arm hug and a clap on the back. The bastard had been gone for about three weeks. "Glad you're back home." He turned to Troy, giving him the same treatment. They all went way back, having forged a friendship on basketball courts. "And what did I do to deserve a face-to-face with you?"

Troy grinned as he dragged a hand over his shaved head. "It's guys' night?"

Gabe lifted a brow as he picked up the beer. "Guys' night and you're spending it at my workshop in the Warehouse District?"

The dark-skinned detective tipped his head back and laughed. "When you get married, that's how guys' nights go down."

"True," Lucian murmured, taking a swig of his beer.

"What?" Gabe laughed, leaning against the bench. "You aren't married."

"Yet," Troy chimed in, sitting down on one of the stools. "I'm betting they're married before the year's out."

Lucian said nothing, and Gabe shook his head. The last person Gabe ever expected to settle down was his younger brother, but look at him now—wrapped around Julia's pinky finger and he didn't even care. "Where is your pretty girl?" Gabe's smile was daring as he took a drink. "I miss her."

Lucian's eyes narrowed. "You have no business missing her."

He chuckled, loving nothing more than needling his brother when it came to Julia. "Seriously, though, where is she? You're here and she's usually wherever you are."

"She was tired after traveling all day. She's currently all curled up in my bed, waiting for me." He eyed the dresser frame Gabe had been working on. "Why in the hell are you here on a Saturday night?"

Gabe shrugged, thinking it must be nice to have someone like Lucian and Troy did. Someone you wanted to get home to and looked forward to ending and beginning the day with. He'd had that with Emma. He'd fucked that up along with the help of his family.

He pushed thoughts of Emma out of his head. "Need to get the order done."

"Uh-huh." Troy kicked his long legs up on the bench. "Heard you weren't in Baton Rouge for more than a few days. What changed?"

His grip tightened on the bottle. Both knew why he'd been going to Baton Rouge. "I needed to give them a little space. That's the best thing to do."

Lucian was quiet for a moment. "That's got to be hard."

"It is." He drank half the bottle after admitting that. "You have no idea."

"I don't," his brother agreed. "You know Dev's going to want to step in."

"Your brother has no sense of boundaries." Troy scratched at the label on his bottle.

Gabe snorted. "Don't we know." He crossed his ankles. "I don't care what Dev's opinion is on the matter. I told him to stay out of it, and if he knows what's smart for him, he will. This isn't his life."

"Dev will back off," Lucian said. "But not for long. You know what he'll do."

Setting the bottle aside, Gabe folded his arms. He knew exactly what Dev was capable of. So did Lucian, and Gabe knew Troy had his suspicions, especially about what really went down with their fucking cousin Daniel—ones Troy wouldn't vocalize, because once he did, he'd have to act on them. Troy was like a brother to them, but he was a cop, one who took his job seriously.

Gabe just hoped Troy's duty to the badge never came between them.

"So." Lucian drew the word out as he ran a hand through his blond hair. If it weren't for the de Vincent eyes, people wouldn't even think they were brothers. The fact that Lucian and his twin looked so different from Gabe and Dev had always been a red flag to them. Except, as it turned out, he and Dev had it backward. The whole damn family had. Only Lucian and Madeline were the children of Lawrence. Gabe and Dev had no idea who their father was.

"I learned something else when I got caught up with Dev," Lucian said. "Heard your long-lost love was back."

Everything about Gabe stiffened.

Everything.

"Fuck, Dev." Gabe uncrossed his ankles, widening his stance. "Don't say that."

Confusion crept in Troy's features. "Long-lost love?"

Lucian grinned. "Yep."

"Do I even want to know who this is about?" Troy asked, lowering his beer.

Lucian chuckled at Gabe's dark look and then he turned to Troy. "Remember Nikki? Livie and Richard's daughter?"

Their friend's eyes widened. "Yeah. She's at college. Alabama, right?"

"Not anymore." Lucian pushed away from the bench. "She's filling in for her mom at the house."

"I'm going to ask again," Troy said. "Do I want to know why you're calling her Gabe's long-lost love? Because seriously."

Completely unrepentant, Lucian laughed again. "When she was younger, she had it bad for Gabe. Used to follow him around the house and somehow connived him into swimming lessons."

Nic hadn't connived Gabe into those lessons. Like a dumbass, he offered after she almost killed herself in the pool. "Shut up, Lucian."

Lucian wasn't shutting up, because of course not. "Gabe just can't help it. Women just get obsessed with him. I think it's the hair." He reached toward Gabe's head.

Gabe leaned out of the way.

"Women? As in plural?" Troy asked.

Lucian nodded. "Yeah, you don't know about Sabrina?"

"Dev's fiancée?"

Gabe was about five seconds away from punching Lucian.

"Yep. One and the same. Did you know that Sabrina actually met Gabe in college? Met him first." Lucian's eyes glimmered with amusement. "Ever since then, she's been chasing after Gabe's dick like it's the last one left in the world."

Troy's mouth dropped open. "But it ain't the last dick. It ain't even the last de Vincent dick."

"Can you all stop talking about my dick?" Gabe grumbled.

They ignored him.

"Well, this dick didn't want anything to do with her, rightfully so, because that woman is a bitch. Hate using that word, but it's true. Anyways, she went for the next best dick. Dev."

"No shit," muttered Troy, shaking his head. "Does Dev know this?"

Lucian shrugged. "Not sure how he can't. Don't think he cares, though."

"Dev doesn't know she was on my ass all through college. She's annoying, but she's harmless," Gabe said, lip curling in disgust. "And I'd honestly rather forget about all that. Sabrina's marrying Dev. God help him, but she's not my problem."

"Except for when she hunts you down every time you're home," Lucian pointed out slyly.

Yeah, and that was another reason getting a place in Baton Rouge was at the top of his priority list. He was not going to live in the same house as Sabrina. *Hell no.*

"Okay." Troy arched a brow. "So, let's backtrack. What's this shit about Nikki?"

Lucian was about as happy as a damn pig rolling in shit at this point. "The thing is, when Nikki was younger, no big deal. Right? Then Nikki started growing up, and well, I made it my life's mission to remind Gabe that she may not have looked it at the time, but she was just a teenager."

His gaze connected with his brother's. Lucian quirked a brow, and irritation flared deep inside Gabe. People who didn't know Lucian didn't give him enough credit. The younger de Vincent missed *nothing.*

Troy's gaze narrowed on Gabe. "Did you need reminding?"

"Fuck no," he shot back. Despite what happened before Nic left for college, he hadn't needed a reminder of her age. No matter how beautiful she was becoming back then, it was hands off and eyes off. "And stop calling her a teenager. Jesus. She's fucking twenty-two now."

Thank fuck.

"Well, I am reassured to hear that. Age of consent might be seventeen here to avoid a statutory charge, but that little piece of law ain't going to stop a bullet in the back of the head." Troy took a drink of his beer.

"Damn, bro. You're a cop," Lucian said with a laugh.

He raised a shoulder. "Hell. Richard may be all calm and shit, but I've looked into that man's eyes. He'd straight up kill a motherfucker who messed with his daughter."

Yeah, he would.

It wouldn't have mattered to Richard that Nic had been eighteen. Shit, still wouldn't matter now. Gabe twisted at the waist, picking up his beer. Why in the hell was he even thinking about a *now*?

Probably because the three times he jerked off this week *alone*, her fucking face appeared in the middle of it.

But there was a *now*.

Lucian grinned as he watched Gabe. "Well, she might be twenty-two now, but she'll always be Little Nikki to me."

"Christ," Gabe muttered, rubbing at his chest. A moment passed. "Found Parker sniffing around her last week."

"Fuck Parker," muttered Troy.

Gabe nodded as guilt stirred in his gut. He was man enough to admit that he'd handled Nic wrong when it came to Parker. He'd been caught off guard when he'd seen her with him—that bastard all in her space and her laughing. He'd also been knocked off his game by his reaction to seeing them together.

He'd wanted to rip Parker's throat out.

And he had no right to that feeling or to say anything to Nic about it. She'd been correct when she threw that in his face, and he was also man enough to know he owed her a damn apology for that . . . and for how he talked to her Thursday, in the gym.

What happened to you? She'd asked that and what had he said? *You.*

Jesus, he'd been a dick and that wasn't him. He wasn't that guy. Or at least he hadn't been, but that was the guy he was turning into. That shit didn't sit well with him. But he knew one damn thing. What had happened between them four years ago was no excuse. Neither was how his head was still twisted up over the shit with Emma a good enough excuse for how he talked to her.

For how he knew he made her feel.

"What was Parker doing at the house?" Lucian asked, the easy grin gone from his face.

"Supposedly visiting Dev." Gabe finished off his beer and tossed it into a nearby trashcan. "Richard was out of the house, so Parker was just roaming around."

A muscle ticked in Lucian's jaw. "What was he doing with Nikki?"

Gabe lifted a shoulder. "Talking."

"Parker wouldn't be visiting Nikki with just talking in mind," Troy commented, and hell if Gabe didn't already know that.

Lucian was quiet as he focused on one of the ornate chairs Gabe had finished, but still needed to paint. "Yeah," he murmured.

Gabe frowned, sensing there was more. "What?"

A long moment passed. "I don't know." Lucian tossed his empty bottle. "Probably nothing, but there was this thing that happened. Forgot about it until just now. Shit."

"Details?" Gabe turned to his brother.

"I think Nikki was around seventeen? She was in the pool house. I didn't know she was out there. Not at first." He paused. "Anyway, I'd gone in to grab a towel."

Gabe stilled.

"I walked in and Parker was in there with Nikki. She was just in a towel—"

"What the fuck?" Gabe exploded. How in the hell was this the first time he was hearing this?

"Yeah." Lucian dragged a hand through his hair and let it fall. "He said he'd just walked in, like a few seconds before me, and that was possible. I'd gone into the house to get changed and just came back out to go to the pool house. Nikki didn't say anything to me. She looked embarrassed, but . . ."

"But what?" Troy leaned forward, dropping both feet onto the floor.

"But it didn't sit right with me." Lucian's jaw worked. "When I asked him afterward about him being in there, he'd sworn he was only there for seconds. I told him to stay away from her at that point. I don't think anything happened. I mean, I feel like Nikki would've said something, but I . . . yeah, I wish I'd done more."

"Like knocking him the fuck out?" Troy asked. "Because I have a hard time believing it was just seconds he was in there. Shit. You walk in on a girl who's in a towel and you're not supposed to be in there? You turn into the Flash and get the hell out of there."

Gabe was barely hearing what they were saying. He didn't know about this. Had something happened in the pool house? And he remembered how Nikki had reacted earlier to his accusing her of throwing herself at Parker. There was no mistaking the shock and disgust and . . . and something else he'd seen in her eyes.

Shit.

TROY DIDN'T STAY long, wanting to get back to his wife, and Gabe figured Lucian would be right behind him since it seemed like he didn't spend more than a few hours apart from Julia.

Lucian didn't leave, though. He took Troy's seat, kicking his legs up on the workbench Gabe was leaning against. "How've you been?" he asked. "We haven't really gotten a chance to talk after . . . everything happened."

Gabe smirked. "Probably best, all things considered."

"Except more shit kept happening," Lucian replied, rocking his feet. "Everything with Emma—"

"Don't want to talk about Emma," he cut Lucian off.

"Maybe you should," his brother said softly.

Jaw hardening, he picked up the chisel he'd been working with and walked it over to the table. Talking about Emma—damn, thinking about Emma always ended the same way.

Drinking about his weight in scotch.

He didn't want to spend the night like that.

"I know it's a no-fly zone for you, but you got to get that shit out of you." He paused. "Or you'll end up like Dev."

Gabe snorted as he tossed the chisel on the table. Some days he wished he was more like Dev, who was about as caring as a rattlesnake with its head chopped off.

"I know something's up. You wouldn't be here on a Saturday night if there weren't," Lucian continued. "You'd be at the Red Stallion, finding yourself a woman to spend the night with. Maybe two."

He faced his brother. "Are you playing therapist tonight?"

Lucian grinned. "What's going on? You don't keep me in the dark. Maybe Dev. But not me."

That was true. There were few secrets between him and Lucian. He walked over to the stool he'd been using and dropped onto it, running his hands over his face. He needed to keep his mouth shut. That was the best thing to do, but he knew his brother. He'd end up annoying the living fuck out of him until he told him what was up.

He exhaled heavily, letting his hands hang between his knees. "It has to do with Nic."

Surprise flickered across Lucian's face. "It does?"

"Something happened between us."

Lucian's stare sharpened. A heartbeat passed. "What happened between you two?" A terse pause. "And when?"

Letting his head fall back, Gabe stretched his back. "Fuck. I can't believe I'm even going to talk about this."

"Whatever it is, you better get talking, because my head is going in a lot of different places."

He lowered his chin. "It's probably going in the right direction."

Lucian's eyes widened slightly and then he murmured, "Shit."

Threading his fingers together, he did something he never thought he would ever do—told someone else the story of that night. "Right before Nic left for college, she came to the house. Her parents had already left for the evening, and I have no idea where you and Dev were, but you guys weren't there. I'd been drinking. A lot that night. I was drunk but honest? I would've let her in anyway. It wasn't the first time she came to my apartment. It was different, though. It was at night."

Lucian became very, very still.

"I let her in, and I don't know how it happened," he said, closing his eyes. That was a mistake, because what he did remember from that night came back in flashes. Teasing her like he normally would. Then her telling him that she was going to miss him when she left for college. At some point she started to cry when she talked about not seeing him, and he'd hugged her. Somehow, and he couldn't even figure out how, she ended up in his lap . . . and then under him. "But it happened."

"I'm assuming that by *it*, you mean you two hugged it out?"

Gabe barked out a short laugh, but it was without humor. "We had sex."

The only other time Gabe had seen his brother shocked was when they'd learned the truth about their mother and father. This was the second time he'd seen Lucian shocked into silence.

Lucian pulled his feet off the bench, dropping them heavily to the floor. His mouth opened, but he didn't speak.

He needed to keep going. "When I woke up hours later and she was in my bed, at first, I had no clue—" He cut himself off, swallowing. "I flipped the fuck out on her. Nic bailed out of there so fast, and the first time I'd seen her since that night was when she showed up to work."

"Fuck," Lucian said.

"Yeah. That about sums it up."

Lucian stared at him. "I'm actually at a loss for words. That never happens."

"That's not making me feel better about this."

"Not trying to make you feel better." Lucian shook his head. "She was eighteen when she left for college, right?"

"Yes. But that doesn't make a—"

"Bullshit. That makes a difference. Not a huge one, but it makes a difference." His jaw worked. "You were drunk?"

"I was shit-faced. Nic swears she didn't realize how drunk I was and I . . . I believe her."

His brother blinked slowly. "Exactly how drunk were you that you ended up having sex with Livie and Richard's eighteen-year-old daughter?"

"Drunk enough to not care," he replied honestly, and fuck, saying it out loud was like some kind of weight lifted from his shoulders. He hadn't been an unwilling participant. Honest? He'd been willing. "That's how drunk."

"Shit, man." Lucian leaned back. "And you and Nic talked about this?"

"Last week when I saw her. I was pissed. She never gave me a chance to talk to her about it before. And I tried. Called her. Texted her after she left, to make sure she was okay—"

"Shit. Was she?"

"*Yeah*," he replied with heavy meaning. "For four years, I couldn't fathom what the hell she was thinking. Damn. Even when I think about it now, I get pissed, because she just left and ignored me and I had no idea if I . . ." He drew in a deep breath. "I know she spent these years not realizing I wasn't that drunk and I spent these years trying to forget it even happened, grateful that her father hasn't found out yet and shot me."

Lucian snickered at that, because he knew it was the truth. "I wouldn't be worried about that, though. He loves you. It's her mom who would do it."

A small smile pulled at Gabe's mouth. "Yeah, you're right about that."

"They'd never think you'd do something like that, though. Me? Hell. They'd probably be surprised I didn't try something. But you? Nah. They'd never think it. You're the good one out of us."

Gabe lifted a brow.

"It's true."

A moment passed before Lucian blinked and rubbed his face. "Wow. Well, shit, man. I don't know what to say. I mean, that is fucked-up. For both of you. Got to be awkward now."

"Yeah, doesn't help that I've been nothing but a dick to her since she's returned. Fucking yelled at her last week when I saw her with Parker. Accused her of throwing herself at him. Then I just . . . yeah, I haven't been nice to her."

Lucian's gaze zeroed in on him. "Do you think you should be nice to her?"

Gabe thought about it, really thought about it. "For the last four years, I wanted to simultaneously strangle her and ask her if she was okay. I've hated her for what could've come from that night, but I got to take responsibility for it, too. Not like she slipped and fell on my dick. I was drunk, Lucian. But I knew it was her. I knew what I was doing." He let out a ragged breath. "That makes me a shit person, doesn't it?"

"No. I don't think so. It just makes the situation complicated."

"Complicated" didn't feel like a strong enough word to describe everything in his head, but he knew one thing. He didn't hate Nic now. He didn't know what the hell that meant, but he didn't hate her.

"Well, you know what I think?" Lucian said.

"I'm afraid to ask."

"I think you know what you need to do." And then Lucian surprised the shit out of him, because he grinned in a way that set off about five hundred warning bells in Gabe. "Yeah, I think you do."

Chapter 10

$\mathcal{I}$ would sell my soul to gain access to that house." Rosie's chocolate-brown eyes were glassy, but there was no mistaking the seriousness in her voice. "Come on, Nikki. Help a chick out."

Nikki giggled as she twirled the straw in whatever drink Rosie had convinced her she just needed to have. She had no idea what it was, which wasn't at all surprising since they were at Cure, a bar on Freret Street known for their unique cocktails. "Not going to happen."

"Seriously," Bree chimed in from across the table. She would know exactly how impossible it would be to open the door to Rosie's unique blend of craziness. She was Bev's daughter, and while Nikki knew Bev didn't gossip about things she saw or heard while retrieving the laundry, Bree knew enough to know how the de Vincents were. "No one gets into the de Vincent compound without permission."

Nikki should never have told Rosie about what happened the last week, the whole glass moving by itself, because now she was more determined than ever to get inside the de Vincent compound.

"You can sneak me in!" Rosie lifted her hands. "I thought you said the cameras inside are for show, because they *mysteriously* don't work."

"They don't work." Which was just one of the mysteries at the de Vincent house. No cameras ever recorded in the house beyond a camera on a phone. She knew they had electricians and technicians out there many times over the years, and no one could explain why. "Because of ghosts."

"Exactly!" Rosie slammed her hands down on the table, jarring it. The people at the table behind them looked over. "That is why I need to get in there with NOPE."

NOPE stood for New Orleans Paranormal Explorations, the team Rosie worked with. Nikki snort-laughed and it didn't sound attractive, but she couldn't help it. "Devlin would have a stroke if I let a paranormal investigative team into his house."

"Uh-huh." Bree nodded, sending tight braids over her shoulders. "That he would. I only met that guy once and I know that. Hell, they don't even let me in the house, and my mom has worked for them for *decades*."

"Ugh." Rosie plopped her chin on her fist. "I would shave my head to get inside the house."

"You could pull that off," Nikki said dryly. And it was true. Rosie was Louisiana Creole and she had the most beautiful honey-colored skin Nikki had ever seen. "So that wouldn't exactly be a sacrifice."

"Agreed." Bree finished off her drink.

Nikki rolled her eyes at Bree. "As if you couldn't do the same. I, on the other hand, would look like a hot mess."

"You always look one step away from being a hot mess." Bree grinned when Nikki threw her napkin at her. "Crap." Bree checked the time on her phone. "I've got to go. Gotta work in the morning." Ignoring their boos, she slid off her stool and gave them a quick kiss on the cheek. "Don't be hos tonight without me."

Rosie laughed as she nodded her head at Nikki. "As if this one over here even knows what being a ho is."

Bree laughed. "Too true. Be safe."

"I know what being a ho is," Nikki said after wiggling her fingers goodbye to Bree. "I've got my ho on more than once."

Rosie arched a brow as she knocked an auburn curl out

of her face. "Honey, when is the last time you even went out on a date?"

Huh. Scrunching up her nose, she had to really think about that. "Um, I had one . . . in March, I think?"

"That was seven months ago."

"So? I was busy with finals and then moving back home." She sipped more of whatever the citrusy stuff was. "What about you?"

"Last night." Rosie grinned. "It wasn't a sleepover." There was a shrug. "But it was nice."

"Nice." Nikki laughed, but it came out sounding like a snort once more, which meant it was time to stop the drinking. Sighing, she pushed the drink away.

Rosie was studying her closely. "How are things with Gabe?"

"Ugh," she groaned. Rosie knew about Gabe—knew *everything*. Her confession occurred one night a few years ago where nearly an entire bottle of tequila had been consumed between them. Rosie was the only person who knew what happened. "Not good."

Rosie reached over. Orange and red bangles clanked together as she patted Nikki on the arm. "Talk to me."

Leaning forward so Rosie could hear her, Nikki told her about the confrontation in the kitchen and then what happened yesterday. When she finished, Rosie let out a low whistle. "Damn, girl, I don't know what to say."

"Exactly," Nikki muttered. "I'm trying to stay away from him. I have been! Except when I don't have a choice, but . . ."

"But what?"

She raised her shoulders. "I know I messed up, but I . . . I just wish it wasn't like this. I mean, I'm pissed at him. What he said to me yesterday was not cool."

"Damn straight it wasn't."

She toyed with the edge of the drinks menu as laughter exploded from the bar. "But I wish things could be the way they used to be with us. He's a good guy. I mean, he could've easily ignored me like his brothers did for the most part, but he didn't. He was kind to me, always made time when I know I was being annoying."

"You've got to understand that the past is the past. There is no going back to that," she said. "You've got to accept that and let it go."

Nikki knew that.

She also knew it was easier said than done.

"Seriously, Nikki. I've known you for how many years now? You're a good woman, and it's time for you to get some good in return."

Nikki opened her mouth.

Rosie wasn't done. "You don't let any guy get close to you. And poor Calvin? He was a good guy, Nikki. He wasn't a stray."

She winced at the mention of her ex-boyfriend.

"He was patient and understanding, but you didn't love him. You could've fallen in love with him, but you didn't *let* yourself love him."

Her gaze lifted to her friend and her dumb throat started to thicken. Rosie was dropping truth bombs like it was D-Day.

"You're not going to be able to move on, have fun, and maybe find someone until you let all that bullshit go." Rosie sounded surprisingly sober in that moment. "You were eighteen and blinded by your first love. You made dumb choices because of it. You didn't murder someone. You didn't set out to trick him. It happened. It's over. Stop punishing yourself."

Her lips lifted in a weak smile. "You're gonna make me cry."

"Don't do that. You'll ruin your mascara, and then you won't have any hopes of being a ho tonight."

Nikki broke out into a loud laugh. "I'm not ho-ing to-night."

A guy walking past their table glanced over with interest. He stopped.

"You couldn't afford her," Rosie said, dismissing him. "Move along."

"Oh, geez." Nikki swallowed a giggle. "Thank you. I think I . . . I think I needed to hear all of that."

"You did." Leaning over, Rosie kissed her cheek. "You're too young to live like you're my age, because I don't even live like that. Now let's order a shot."

Thankfully their night stopped at one shot and didn't turn into the kind of night where you ended up in the French Quarter, stumbling through what was most definitely *not* puddles of just water.

The night had been good, though. Nikki truly realized it as she said goodbye to Rosie, who was heading to a friend's place instead of her apartment on Chartres. She *had* punished herself long enough for being young, dumb, and in love once upon a time. Not anymore. Starting right now, she was letting it go. All of it.

Hopefully her new motto in life wasn't fueled by liquid courage.

She'd called for an Uber as she'd walked out of the bar, but as she scanned the street, she didn't see the green Prius that was supposed to be coming for her. Checking her app, she sighed when she saw the car was still over on Canal, stuck in traffic.

That was going to take fifteen minutes or more for the driver to get to Uptown. Sighing, she curled her arm around her waist as she eyed the benches along the building. Most of them were full of people chatting and smoking.

At least it was a nice night, not raining or too ridiculously hot. She moved to stand by the curb and looked down Freret, spying a huge crowd near where the comedy theater used to be. What were they doing? Probably a street performer or an overdose. One never knew in New Orleans. Tucking her hair back behind her ear, she looked away and tipped her head up. Stars were out, battling against the twinkling lights of the city. When she'd been at Tuscaloosa, she'd missed the sights and sounds of New Orleans.

She started to glance down at her phone, but stopped when a weird sensation skated along the nape of her neck. Turning to the side, she almost expected to find someone walking up behind her, but there was no one there. No one really paying attention to her, but she couldn't shake the feeling of eyes drilling holes through her back. Not until the green Prius finally showed up. Not until she was back home, safe in bed.

IT FELT LIKE Nikki had only slept for a few hours when there was a knock on her bedroom door, followed by her father calling her name.

Pushing the covers off her head, she sat up, wincing as the harsh morning sun did a number on her poor eyes and head. "Yeah?" she croaked out, and then groaned. She sounded terrible. "What, Dad?"

"You awake?" he called out.

Uh, now she was. Sitting up, she pushed the rat's nest of hair out of her face. "Yeah. You can come in."

The door cracked open and her father stuck his head in. "You have a visitor."

"What?" She squinted at him and then looked at the clock on her nightstand. It was nine in the morning. No one she knew would be at her house at nine in the morning on a Sunday.

Her dad's face was strangely blank. "It's a very odd visitor . . ." He looked over his shoulder. "Come downstairs."

She watched her dad close the door. "What the hell?"

The air around her didn't answer, so after a moment of sitting there trying to clear the cobwebs of sleep from her mind, she threw the covers off and swung her legs over the edge of the bed. She started toward her bathroom, but decided against it. Whoever was downstairs wouldn't require brushed hair or a fresh face. And since she was wearing loose flannel bottoms and a cami with a built-in bra, all she grabbed was a lightweight cardigan.

Smothering a yawn, she headed down the narrow hall and staircase. She shuffled into the kitchen, relieved when she smelled coffee.

She was going to need a gallon of that stuff and a handful of aspirins.

Trailing a hand over the worn wallpaper in the cozy dining room, she hung a right and then the kitchen came into view.

Nikki came to a sudden stop.

Was she still drunk from last night? Had she drunk more than she realized? Because that had to be the case.

That was the only option, because there was no way Gabriel de Vincent was sitting in her parents' kitchen with a smoothie in front of him.

Chapter 11

Gabe could barely keep the smile off his face. It was a struggle, and he ended up pressing his fingers over his mouth, because Nic looked thoroughly confused. He couldn't blame her for that. And she also looked . . . adorably rumpled. Like she'd just rolled out of a bed and come down here.

Her wide eyes lost the unfocused quality to them. "What's going on?" Her gaze bounced around the kitchen, landing on where her father stood, pouring himself a cup of coffee. "Is Mom okay?"

"Your mom is in bed," her father answered, turning from the counter. "She's feeling a little run down, but she's okay."

"Okay." She glanced at Gabe, worry creeping into her face. "Is everything all right on your end?"

That surprised him. After the way he'd been treating her, he couldn't believe that she would even care if things weren't okay. "Yeah, they are."

Her mouth opened, but she didn't speak, and Gabe found himself staring at her mouth. He didn't notice how full her lips were. Plump, actually. Or maybe he did notice and just never acknowledged it before.

Probably the latter.

"He says he was in the neighborhood and thought he'd swing by and say hi," her father answered, tone deadpanned. "Though I can't imagine why he'd be in our neighborhood at nine on a Sunday morning."

It wasn't the greatest reasoning he'd ever come up with. "I was out driving around. Couldn't sleep and found myself near here." That part wasn't exactly a lie, but him being here wasn't by accident. "I picked up a smoothie. Strawberry."

Nic stared at him.

Her father cleared his throat as he shuffled over the tile floors in his slippers. "I'll be upstairs," he announced, patting Nic on the shoulder. "If you guys need anything."

Gabe smiled at her father and waited until he disappeared around the corner before he spoke. "You still like smoothies, right?"

She was still gaping at him. "Are you . . . high?"

"What?" he laughed. "No."

Nic glanced over her shoulder and a moment passed. "Are you sure about that?"

Fighting a grin, he nodded.

"So, you were out driving around and decided to pick up a smoothie and bring it to me?"

"Yes." He couldn't stop the grin now. Not with that completely blown-away look on her face. "Is it that hard to believe?"

"Yes." Then she nodded for extra emphasis. "Yes, it is."

His gut clenched at her honest response and his grin faded. "I wanted to talk to you."

Nic stood extremely still and after a long moment he half expected her to ask him to leave. If she did, it was about to get awkward, because he wasn't leaving until they talked.

But then she gathered the edges of the thin gray sweater and tugged it around her waist. "We can go out back. It's probably still cool outside."

"It is." Rising from the chair, he picked up the smoothie and walked around the table. "Not much has changed here."

She looked at him warily. "No, it hasn't." She stepped out into a hall lined with photos of her, all through the ages.

"I like it."

"Really?" she said dryly.

"Yeah, it's cozy. It's . . . real." He checked out the photos as she made her way toward the back door. One caught his attention. It was a senior portrait by the looks of it. The wide, proud smile on her pixieish face wasn't one he'd seen in a while. "You can tell a family actually lives here."

Nic looked over her shoulder at him, but didn't respond. He was speaking the truth, though. He'd only been once before, and that had been a brief trip, but it smelled the same to him. Like apple pie. His family home, on the other hand, smelled like disinfectant and fresh linen. Always. And there were no pictures. No smiling faces. Not out where anyone could see them.

When Gabe was younger and with Emma, he always thought this was what he'd have eventually with her. A house smaller than the de Vincent compound, one that was warmer and full of photos of them on vacations and eventually framed pictures of their children, chronicling every important moment.

He didn't get that.

He wasn't ever going to get that.

Nic opened the door and stepped out onto a small patio that fed into a narrow courtyard. Overhead, an ivy-covered awning cast a thick shadow over the old iron chairs and the wooden swing, blocking out the morning sun.

The smoothie was starting to make his fingers wet. "Do you want this?"

She glanced down at it and then snatched it out of his hands like he was going to take it back from her. "Thank you," she muttered, clutching the plastic container and backing up to the swing. She sat down. "Pretty sure my father doesn't believe you were out there, just driving around aimlessly."

He watched her for a moment and then sat in one of the old chairs across from her. "Do you remember the last time I was here?"

Not answering him, she took a sip of the smoothie from the straw.

"You were sixteen and you got drunk at your friend's house."

"I wasn't drunk," she grumbled after a moment. "I was buzzing."

He struggled to keep his lips from kicking up into a smile. "You were drunk, Nic. If I remember correctly, it was the first time you ever really drank. You called me because you and your friend got into a fight and you wanted to go home, but you didn't want to wake up your parents." He paused. "You called me, and I came."

Several strands of hair had fallen forward, shielding her face as she continued to drink the smoothie. Damn. Her hair had gotten a lot longer.

"You puked in my car," he added.

Nic stopped slurping.

"And then you cried, because you were afraid I'd be mad at you." And he had been mad. Not that she'd vomited in his Porsche, but because she'd been drinking that much in the first place.

She lifted her head. "Is there any reason why you're talking about this?"

He wasn't sure himself, so he lifted a shoulder. "I brought you home. Your dad was up. Thought he was going to lock you up for life after that."

Nic went back to attacking her smoothie.

"There were a lot of times like that. You called. I came. I didn't even think about how that would look to outsiders. Fully grown man answering the beck and call of a teenage girl who wasn't related to him. Looking back, that should've raised some red flags."

"You thought of me as a sister," she muttered around the straw. "You weren't being a pervert."

"True." He watched the slight breeze play with her hair.

"Why are you here? It can't be for this—this walk down memory lane. You came to talk about something else."

There was a lot they needed to talk about.

This conversation could've waited, but Gabe didn't wait on things he knew he needed to do. He'd wanted to search her down last night, but it had been late, and by the looks of it, Nikki wouldn't have been in any condition to have a serious conversation.

Which made him very, very curious about what the hell she'd been doing last night. "You look a little hungover."

She peeked up through lashes he didn't remember being quite as thick before. "A little."

His eyes narrowed and he found himself liking the idea of her drinking now just as much as he did when she was younger. "What were you doing?"

She lowered the smoothie, which seemed like a great feat considering half of it was already gone. "I met up with some friends at Cure."

"Nice place." A lot of the younger locals went there. "Get in late?"

"Not really." Her brows were furrowed together, like she was trying to figure out the purpose behind what he was saying. "Why are you here, Gabe?"

Her attitude didn't bother him. Just like it hadn't bothered him when she told him to clean his own rooms. It had done something else entirely. It was doing something else now.

He leaned forward in the chair. "You had a crush on me."

"Gabe—"

"Just hear me out, okay? I'm not here to make you feel like shit, and I get that you probably think I am. I've given you no reason to believe otherwise, but I'm not. I just want to . . . talk."

The look of suspicion eased only slightly from her face. "Then talk."

He bit back a grin. "You had a crush on me, and I knew you did. I thought it was harmless."

Nic visibly stiffened.

"And that night, when you came to me?" His voice dropped low. "When I let you inside, it wasn't like I forgot that you had those feelings. I shouldn't have let you in. I'm going to take responsibility for that. I wasn't so drunk that I forgot who you were."

She lowered the smoothie to her lap.

"I know we've both said things about that night, but I haven't said what really needed to be said," he continued, trying not to notice how a pink flush was creeping across her cheeks. "I was drunk, but I wasn't so drunk that I didn't know what I was doing."

Her lips parted in a sharp inhale that was lost in the breeze.

He drew in a deep breath. "I was drunk enough to not care."

Nic blinked slowly. "Then why . . . why did you . . . ?"

"Not tell you that before? I don't know. I was a dick about it. No excuse."

Her brow snapped again and she looked like she was about to say something, but changed her mind.

"We both made mistakes that night. It wasn't just you. I want you to know that," he said, meaning it. "I need you to know that. It's important . . . to me."

Nic's throat worked on a swallow as she looked away. Her voice was barely above a whisper. "I . . . I hated myself for that night."

There was a twisting motion in his chest and he was moving before he even knew what he was doing. He crossed the distance between them and sat down on the swing beside her, relieved that the old thing didn't come crashing down when her wide-eyed gaze collided with his again.

"Stop," he said as quietly as she spoke. "Stop hating yourself. We both did wrong. It's over. It's in the past."

"But . . . you hate me—"

"No, I don't." As fucked-up as it was, part of him wished he did, because then all of this mess would be easier to deal with. "I don't hate you, Nic. And I hope you don't hate me. Not that I'd blame you if you did. I've been a fucking dick to you and I'm sorry for that."

"I couldn't hate you," she replied quickly, and the pink in her cheeks increased. "I mean, I don't hate you."

"Good." Relief settled into his muscles, easing the tension around his neck. Maybe he'd be able to sleep past four A.M. now.

"But yeah, you've been a dick," she added.

Gabe arched a brow as he looked away. His gaze was snagged by the nail polish on her toes. It was a teal-blue color. "I know. But I'm not going to be a dick anymore. Not when I want us to be friends."

"Friends?" she squeaked like a little toy. Cute.

"*Friends*," he repeated.

THERE WAS A good chance all of this was some kind of hallucination and maybe, just maybe, she and Rosie hadn't stopped at one shot last night and now she was having imaginary conversations with Gabe.

That made more sense than him actually being at her house, with a smoothie, asking to be friends with her.

Gabe glanced over at her, sucking his lower lip between his teeth. "Do you want to be friends? If not, this convo is probably going to get really awkward."

Her stupid-ass heart took over and she opened her mouth to scream yes, they could be friends, but she stopped herself.

Could they be friends?

Better yet, could she be friends with him, after everything? Did she want to be? After deciding last night that she had this new motto in life? Wait. What was that motto? She couldn't remember, but she was sure it didn't include being friends with Gabe.

"Nic?" His gaze searched her face.

"How?" she blurted out. "And I'm not talking about what happened between us. How can we be friends? You're a de Vincent. My parents are your house staff."

The corners of his lips turned down. "So? That has never been a problem before."

"Well, I was also an annoying little girl that you felt bad for."

His frown increased. "I didn't feel bad for you."

She snorted. "Whatever. What I'm trying to say is that we have nothing in common anymore." She lifted the smoothie. "I know how to swim now, Gabe."

"I don't care if you don't need me for swimming lessons." He reached over, taking the smoothie from her. Her mouth dropped open.

He took her smoothie!

There was still at least two good slurps left. Ugh.

"And I think we have a lot in common," he continued.

"Like what?"

"We both know how to take a plain block of wood and turn it into something amazing."

Not anymore, but Nikki didn't say that.

"And well, we both can legally drink now," he quipped.

Her brows lifted. "That's literally the best you can come up with?"

He grinned as he lifted the smoothie. "I was kidding."

She was struck speechless as he folded those wonderful lips over the straw and finished off her drink—using the straw she'd just been drinking out of.

Okay.

Friends did that. They shared drinks and stuff.

But why were her lady bits suddenly very much awake?

She ignored those idiotic parts of her. "I work for your family now, Gabe. Your brother is my employer."

He snorted. "If that was truly the case, you wouldn't have mouthed off at me and told me to clean my own rooms."

"Well, you should be cleaning your own apartment. I mean, come on. You aren't that busy that you can't clean up after yourself or actually serve your own ass food."

A deep laugh rumbled out of him, and her chest seized at the sound. That laugh. Damn it. "See," he said, leaning over and placing the empty smoothie on the nearby iron bistro-style table. "If you truly thought of yourself as an employee, those words would never come out of your mouth. You'd think them, but you wouldn't say them."

"Whatever," she muttered, keeping her arms tight to her sides, so she wasn't accidentally touching him.

"And by the way, I normally don't have my dinners served."

"What?" Her head swung toward him.

He was close, so close that she could see those faint lines around his eyes that hadn't been there four years ago. "I usually get my own food unless it's some kind of special occasion. I've never allowed your parents to serve me."

"You had me serving you!" she exclaimed. "You had me getting you so much water I worried you had a kidney infection."

Gabe let out another loud laugh. "I was being a dick."

"Yes, you were!" Without thinking, she slapped his arm hard enough that her palm actually stung.

"Hey." He was still chuckling. "Now you're hitting me, so you're just proving my point."

Her eyes narrowed and then she asked probably the most important question. "Why do you want to be friends with me? I mean, I appreciate you apologizing and clearing the air. Trust me. You will never understand how much that—" Her voice cracked, and she cleared her throat. She wasn't going to let him see how much that did mean. "I needed that, but we could just be . . . cool with one another. You know, not be mean to each other. We don't have to be friends."

His gaze found its way back to hers. "But what if that's what I want?"

A tremor danced between her shoulder blades. Their gazes collided again and held. "Why?" she whispered. "Why would you want that?"

His gaze dropped and for a stuttered heartbeat, she thought he was looking at her mouth, but that made no sense whatsoever. Then his gaze was fastened to hers again. "Honest?"

"Honest."

"I . . . I don't know," he said, and his lashes lowered. "I just know what I want."

Nikki really had no response to that.

That half grin returned. "And you might as well agree to it."

"Why?"

"Because I'm a de Vincent," he said. "And we always get what we want."

She stared at him, unsure of what to make of any of what he was saying. "Is that so?"

"So."

Her lips twitched as she looked away. She honestly didn't know what to say to him. Wasn't it just last night when she was saying to Rosie that she wanted things to go back to the way they were before that night? Gabe was offering that to her, but how he'd treated her since she'd been back had hurt and Gabe wasn't the same guy she remembered. Neither was—crap! She shot out of the swing. "What time is it?"

"Don't know." He leaned back, pulling his cellphone out of his pocket. "It's almost ten—"

"Damn it. I'm going to be late."

"Late for what? It's Sunday."

"I know what day it is." She hurried toward the back door. "I have to go."

"Nic." Gabe rose.

She yanked open the storm door. "We'll have to pick up this conversation later."

Or maybe never.

Never sounded good.

"WHAT ARE YOU doing?" Nikki demanded as she drew up short, her car keys in one hand and purse in the other.

Gabe blocked her access to the driver's door of her car.

He was leaning against it actually, his arms folded across his chest, ankles crossed. He had donned a pair of silver aviator-style sunglasses, and as much as she hated to admit it, he looked good in them.

Real good.

A little under an hour had passed since she'd left Gabe on the back porch, having just enough time to shower, halfway blow-dry her hair, and pull it up in a bun. She'd figured he'd left, and honestly, she didn't even have time to think about their conversation.

"Waiting," he answered. "For you."

Stepping around a little garden gnome her mom had by the sidewalk, she walked over to him. "I really don't have time. I'm going to—"

"The shelter to walk the dogs," he cut in. "I know. Your mother told me while I visited her."

Nikki hadn't even seen her mom this morning and Gabe had? Something was wrong with that. "Then you know I have to go."

"Yep." He pushed away from her car. "And I'm driving."

"What?" She lowered her keys.

"I'm going to go with you." He stepped in front of her, blocking out the early morning sun. "Quality friend time."

Nikki's brows furrowed together. "I know I've already asked you this, but I'm going to ask you again. Are you high?"

His laugh startled her again, because it was another real laugh. He moved and before she could figure out what he was doing, he snatched the keys out from between her fingers and took her hand. Stunned, she let him lead her over to his much newer and much nicer car.

A Porsche.

Which kind, she had no idea, but she knew she could probably lease an apartment for several years for the cost of one. A really nice apartment. He only let go of her hand to open the passenger door for her. She didn't get in. "What are you doing, Gabe?"

"Pretty sure we just had that conversation. You're going to the shelter, the one out on Jefferson Highway?"

"Yes, but—"

"I'm going to go with you."

"Why would—"

"They always need volunteers, right?"

"Yes, but you haven't filled out any of their applications."

"They would turn me away?" A half grin appeared as he gestured at the front seat. "A de Vincent?"

They most definitely wouldn't turn away a de Vincent, but that wasn't the point. "Look, I get you want to prove we're going to be friends forever, but this isn't necessary."

"With the way the sarcasm dripped from your voice, this is necessary," Gabe replied, and she rolled her eyes. "And I honestly don't have anything else to do. I'm up. Want to feel helpful and shit, and the longer you stand here and argue with me, the later you're going to be."

A thousand retorts rose onto the tip of her tongue, but he was right. The longer she took here, the longer those dogs would have to wait before they got out of their kennels.

She couldn't help but think he was up to something, but she figured the moment he realized he had to clean up after the dogs, he was probably going to regret this choice.

So, Nikki smiled brightly and then slipped past him, sliding into the front seat of the car. "Fine. Let's go."

HONEST TO GOD, Gabe had no idea why he was going with her to the shelter. He figured there were easier, less involved ways for him to prove he was serious about wanting to make amends, but he guessed when he really thought about it, it had been the doubt and wariness in her voice and eyes.

Nikki hadn't believed him, and he really couldn't blame her for that. So, he was a little surprised that she relented. He half expected her to gut punch him, take her keys, and run off to her car. Something she would've done when she was younger.

Her accepting his presence rather easily and her silence left him a little unnerved, but there was something he still wanted to talk to her about.

As he pulled away from the curb, he glanced over at her. She was pulling a pair of sunglasses out of her purse. "Lucian's home," he said. "You haven't had a chance to meet Julia yet."

"No." She slipped her sunglasses on.

"You'll like her."

Nic glanced over at him. A moment passed. "Have to admit, I was shocked when I heard he was in a serious relationship. I was not expecting that."

Gabe chuckled as he slowed at the stoplight. "Pretty sure no one was expecting that, but he really lucked out with Julia. She's a good woman."

"Nothing like Sabrina?" she asked.

He snorted. "Leagues above her."

Nic smiled at that. "That's a relief."

The light turned green. "So Lucian and I were talking last night and he told me something that happened when you were younger. He said he walked in on you and Parker in the pool house?"

"What?" She drew back, pressing against the leather seat. "He did, but I—"

"I know." Gabe thought he probably could've broached this subject better. "Lucian didn't insinuate that you were welcoming of anything." He paused, asking what he knew he needed to even if he wasn't sure how he'd handle the answer. "Did Parker . . . try something with you?"

Nic was quiet for so long, he glanced over at her. She was staring down at her hands. They were balled into tight fists.

His stomach clenched. "Nic?"

She lifted her chin. "He walked in on me when I was getting changed and he got . . . *friendly*."

Muscles locked up along his spine as he focused on the road. Another red light. "Friendly?"

"He grabbed me and tried—" She cut herself off.

"Tried what?" he prodded softly, the steering wheel creaking under his grip.

Nic twisted in the seat toward him. "Is that why you came over this morning? Because Lucian told you about Parker?"

"No." He didn't hesitate. "I came over to apologize for being a dick."

"And?"

His jaw locked as he stared at the light. They'd only made it about two blocks from her house. "And yeah, I wanted to ask you about Parker. Just so you know, those two things are not mutually exclusive."

She didn't respond as she straightened in her seat.

Gabe sighed. "Are you going to tell me what happened, Nic?"

"He was being a creep like usual," she said finally, her voice tight. "Telling me I was really becoming pretty and hitting on me. It was weird and gross, and . . ."

"And what?"

"Nothing else. Lucian walked in."

Gabe wasn't sure if he believed her or not. "I'm sorry that happened. Wish you would've said something. I would've taken care of it. Made sure he never looked in your direction once. Nic, I—"

It sounded like a gunshot, cutting Gabe off. Nic shrieked as Gabe's gaze snapped to the passenger window. A crack splintered and then glass exploded.

Chapter 12

*N*ikki threw her hands up, shielding her face, but she was too late. Tiny shards of glass smacked off her cheeks and sunglasses, raining down on her.

"Christ!" Gabe jerked the steering wheel to the right, and Nikki threw out her hands, pulling them back a half a second before slamming them on the glass-covered dashboard. "What the hell?" he thundered as the car jerked to a halt. "Nic!"

Heart pounding, she slowly opened her eyes. "Holy shit," she whispered.

The passenger window was gone, like the Hulk got all Hulk-smash and punched his fist through it. Hands shaking, she started to lower her arms, but locked up when she saw her lap was covered in glass. How . . . how was this possible?

"Are you okay?" he demanded again.

"Yeah," she whispered, pretty sure she was okay even though she had no idea how.

"Don't move," Gabe ordered, and he didn't need to tell her that twice. She was frozen. Having managed to stop the car in the one open spot along the narrow street, he threw open the door and was out.

She had no idea what had happened. They were just driving along and then bam! Glass shooting everywhere! Obviously someone had to have thrown something but she didn't see anyone running.

Kids throwing rocks at cars happened. Hell, sometimes

they stood on overpasses and dropped them, but her parents' neighborhood was quiet. Things like this didn't happen.

The passenger door yanked open, and suddenly, there Gabe was, kneeling beside her. The sunglasses were shoved up. Concern was etched into his striking face. "You sure you're okay?" he repeated himself. "Nic?"

Was she? She swallowed. "Yeah. I think so? I mean, I don't feel any pain."

"That's good—that's real good." Relief colored his tone as he gently took ahold of her sunglasses, pulling them off. His gaze crawled over her face as he placed her sunglasses on the ground. "Jesus, Nic." His voice rough. "I have no idea how you're not even scratched."

She didn't either.

"You're covered in glass, so I just want you to sit still while I unbuckle you, all right?"

"All right," she repeated, too shocked to argue. She swallowed hard as she willed her heart to slow down. "What happened?"

"Something hit the fucking window," he bit out as he carefully reached around her. His hand brushed her hip. Glass tinkled as he found the seatbelt. "I have no idea what it was," he said, craning his neck. With the side of his hand, he brushed off the glass on her thighs. "Shit. Okay. Move your leg out, but careful you don't slide it along the seat. There's glass everywhere. Are you sure you're fine?"

"Yes."

"I don't see how. Fucking miracle," he growled. "Get that leg up."

Nikki lifted her leg, biting down on her lip when he curled his hand under her knee to help her. Then his other hand went under her arm. Gabe all but lifted her out of the vehicle, then planted her on her feet.

Glass fell, clinking off the asphalt. Looking down, she could see pieces stuck to the front of her shirt. She started to brush the pieces off, but Gabe caught her wrists, drawing her gaze to his. "Let me."

There was no chance to protest, because he dropped her wrists and then his hands were moving over her stomach, the swell of her chest. Air hitched in her throat. His movements were clinical and methodical, not at all romantic, but an acute heaviness filled her chest with each quick brush.

She was totally blaming the exploding window.

"Damn it," he gritted. "You've got glass everywhere—in your hair." He looked over his shoulder. "I don't see a damn person."

That much was true. No one had even come out of the houses here to check on them. "The window didn't just explode, right? Unless that's a new feature with Porsches?"

He stopped with his hands hovering over her shoulders and looked down at her. A harsh laugh burst out of him. "No, Nic. Not that I know of."

She turned slightly, wincing as glass crunched under her sneakers. "I need to get my purse and call the shelter."

"Let me get it. Probably covered in glass."

"The last time I checked, you also have skin that can be pierced by glass," she pointed out.

"Yeah, but my skin is thicker, and before you say anything, that's actually true. Science." He started to touch her but stopped. "What the fuck?"

"What?" Her eyes widened, half expecting something to come winging at them.

"There's something on the floor." He bent over, reaching inside the car. He picked something up off the floor. It looked like a white rock. A rather small rock, one Nikki couldn't fathom being responsible for breaking the glass. "The hell? It's a piece of ceramic."

LUCIAN LET OUT a low whistle as he stared at the passenger side window of Gabe's car. "Damn. Took out the entire window?"

"Yep. One tiny thing did that."

Gabe was doing his best to keep his anger under wraps at the moment. Between the broken window and the fact Nic could've been hurt because of some dumbass person out there.

"Is that normal for this type of car?" Julia asked, frowning from where she stood next to Lucian. "I mean, I would think with a Porsche, they'd have better windows."

"They have tempered glass, but it's not infallible." Irritated, Gabe tossed the keys onto the bench at the back of the garage. "It'll be fixed by tomorrow. I'm just glad Nic wasn't hurt."

"Me too," commented Lucian. "Shocked that she wasn't."

It really was a damn miracle. If she hadn't been wearing her sunglasses, there was a good chance that those tiny pieces of glass would've gotten in her eyes. Shit. That wouldn't be good.

"Kids really need better hobbies," Julia remarked, shaking her head.

The police thought it was a kid or a group of them being little punks and while the neighborhood Nic's parents lived in was quiet, there were kids on their street. Wasn't out of the realm of logic that they saw a nice car and decided to be little shits about it, but Gabe just wasn't sure.

"You're thinking something." Lucian was looking at him.

"Yeah." He reached behind his head and tugged out the small leather band and then gathered his hair, securing it once more. He really needed to get this shit cut. "I don't know. Just seems off that a kid would do that, aiming it right at the passenger window."

"Maybe they were aiming at the windshield and missed," Julia suggested.

That was possible, too, but it didn't ease the agitation.

"You think someone threw the rock at that window on purpose, aiming for Nikki?" Lucian asked.

That also sounded ridiculous, because who the hell would

want to possibly hurt Nic? Gabe didn't say anything as he folded his arms.

"What were you doing at Nikki's house anyway?" Lucian asked.

He arched a brow as he looked at his brother.

"What?" Lucian grinned. "Did you really think I wasn't going to ask about that?"

"Lucian." Julia elbowed him. "Don't be nosy."

"I cannot help but be nosy. It's my second middle name."

Julia pinned a look on him, but Lucian's grin grew about five sizes bigger in response. "You haven't met Nikki yet, but let me tell you—" He stopped, turning.

The sound of an approaching car silenced Lucian, thank fuck. Gabe spied Troy's tinted-out, police department SUV rolling to a stop by the other end of the garage. Unfolding his arms, he walked over to where Troy was climbing out.

"Hey," he called out as Troy came around the back of the SUV. "Get to see you twice in twenty-four hours. Feeling lucky."

Troy snorted as he gave Lucian a chin nod and a smile for Julia. "Yeah, well, you should feel loved, because I'm off today."

"You didn't have to come out over a broken window," Gabe pointed out, knowing damn well detectives didn't handle that kind of nonsense.

"True, but I was in the area, and Officer Newman—the one who took your call—let me know what went down since he knew we were friends. He showed me what went through your window, and I figured I needed to have a one-on-one with you."

"Over a busted window?" Lucian curled an arm around Julia's waist as he spoke. "And some kids?"

"Well, it's not like someone threw just a rock." Walking to the passenger door of his SUV, he opened it and pulled out a small clear bag. Inside was what Gabe had found on the driver's floor. "Do you know what this is?"

Gabe frowned. "Yeah, a piece of ceramic."

"Not just any piece of ceramic. It's part of a spark plug," he explained, turning the bag over, and Gabe now recognized the coiled part of the plug. "They call these things *ninja rocks*."

"Seriously?" Julia's brows lifted.

Troy nodded. "Yep. You throw one of these things at a moderate speed and it's going to shatter just about any window."

"Damn," Lucian muttered.

"That's why it took out your entire window like that." Troy lowered the bag. "And here's the thing. Most kids don't know about ninja rocks. That's a good thing."

"But then that means it might not have been a kid?" The agitation grew in Gabe.

"Just means that it was someone who knew what to use, and that's why I figured you'd need to know that." Troy met his gaze. "So, you could possibly start thinking about anyone who'd like to damage your property before it escalates. You feel me?"

"Yeah." A muscle ticked along Gabe's jaw. "I feel you."

"Is EVERYTHING OKAY with you and Gabriel?" her mother had asked that night at supper. "I cannot believe it happened," she said, shaking her head. "You two could've been seriously injured. What if that piece of whatever it was hit you?"

"It didn't," Nikki reassured her. "I'm fine. Gabe is fine. It was just some bizarre incident."

"Nothing like that has happened on our street before," her mom returned, and then she let out a heavy sigh. "But I guess there's a first time for everything. Some kids need a stronger hand when it comes to discipline."

Nikki couldn't agree more. How bored and utterly reckless could you be that you spent your spare time throwing rocks and objects at cars? But that was what the police believed even though they didn't see anyone outside.

Granted, both she and Gabe had been so shocked that it would've been easy for someone to run away without being seen. And what had the young officer said? The type of car Gabe had been driving would've drawn a lot of attention.

Gabe hadn't exactly responded well to that.

Needless to say, Nikki never made it to the shelter. Not with the whole waiting-for-the-police thing and then having to go home to make sure she didn't have glass on her. And she had. Everywhere. Even down her shirt.

She still had no idea how she didn't get scratched. Just like when she'd fallen down the steps at the de Vincent compound, she should've been seriously injured but wasn't.

Maybe she really did have a guardian angel looking out for her.

Nikki swiftly changed the subject with her mom to some of the apartments she'd been scouring on the internet earlier. She hadn't wanted her parents to keep questioning what was up with Gabe's unexpected visit, because her parents weren't stupid.

Any de Vincent being in their Creole-style cottage was not normal.

LUCKILY SHE WAS able to get them somewhat distracted. Now that it was Monday and she was currently walking into the kitchen, she still wondered if she'd hallucinated Gabe's visit.

It still didn't make any sense to her.

Or Rosie.

Because Nikki had called her friend after the police and Gabe had left and told her all about the conversation. Even Rosie had no idea what the hell was up with Gabe, but she'd thought it was a good sign.

A good sign for what, Nikki wasn't sure, but the fact that he admitted to knowing what was happening that night had lifted some of the unseen weight off her shoulders. He'd known it was her, at least that night he had, but what did that really mean? That he *had* wanted her or . . . or that he'd just been drunk enough to want her?

None of that mattered now. It couldn't.

It *didn't*.

Pushing those thoughts aside, she walked over to where her father was placing a ceramic canister on a tray. He turned to her. "Can you do me a favor?"

"Sure."

Picking up a tray with two cups and saucers, along with a steaming pot, he turned to her. "Can you take this to Devlin's office? He's with the senator, but we're expecting the arrival of an electrician any second, and I need to be down here for this."

"No problem." She just finished dusting rooms that were never used. Taking the tray, she started to turn, but her father stopped her.

"I'm going to be leaving early today to spend some time with your momma while she receives her treatments," he reminded her. "Are you sure you're okay here without me?"

Holding onto the tray, she nodded. "I know the landscaper needs to be paid today. The check for that is in the staff office. Bev already picked up dry cleaning, and there's no dinner tonight since Devlin is going to some charity thing." *Thank God.* "So, don't worry. Spend time with Mom. I got this."

Her father smiled as he stepped around her and kissed her temple. "Yes, you do."

Taking the tray, Nikki pivoted and made her way up the back staircase toward Devlin's office. It was at the end of the hall, beyond the paneled, double doors. One was ajar. Using her elbow, she knocked.

"Come in," came Devlin's voice.

Nudging the door open with her hip, she stepped into the office. All the blinds were up, letting the sunlight pour in. Half of the rounded walls were lined with built-in bookcases filled with digests that looked about as interesting as reading the dictionary. The other half were covered with certificates, licenses, and degrees.

Nikki thought about what Gabe had said about the pictures in her parents' house. There was nothing personal at all about this room.

Devlin sat behind the large cherry oak desk, but it was the older man who sat in the chair with his elbow propped on the arm and his chin in his hand that unnerved her.

Senator Stefan de Vincent was the identical twin of the brothers' father. Seeing him now, knowing that Lawrence was dead, was like seeing a ghost.

With dark brown hair turning silver at the temples, the senator was handsome like all the de Vincents were. He was proof that each of those brothers was going to age very well.

He was also proof that money could almost certainly ensure you could get away with just about anything.

She made herself walk at a normal, sedate pace as she crossed the rather large room.

"Nicolette Besson," the senator said, one finger resting just below his lip. "It has been a very long time since I've last seen you." His gaze flicked to Devlin. "Women from the past are having a habit of reappearing lately, are they not?"

"Appears so," commented Devlin.

Nikki had no idea on how to respond to that, so she just smiled and nodded as she placed the tray on the credenza. She started to turn to leave, but realized that she needed to pour the tea.

Ugh.

Eye roll.

"I'm still not sure why you're so worried about the Harrington financials," Devlin was saying as Nikki turned the cups over. "With my marriage to Sabrina, I gain control of the shipping businesses. Besides, it's not like they're in dire straits. You can tell Parker he can keep his new penthouse."

Nikki kept her face blank as she poured the steaming tea.

"This has nothing to do with Parker," the senator replied.

"Oh, really?" mused Devlin. "He was here last week, worried that I would end my engagement to Sabrina. I doubt it was out of brotherly concern."

"You haven't set a date," the senator said. "You can't blame Sabrina for having concerns."

"If she has concerns, then *she* should come to me. Not her brother. Not you."

Wholly aware of the senator watching her as she placed the cup in front of Devlin, she tried to ignore his stare and not eavesdrop, but it was hard.

Rich people always talked in front of their staff like they weren't even in the room. It was insane and Nikki knew better, but this was juicy. Was Devlin thinking about ending the engagement?

He should.

He really should.

"You know how Parker is," the senator replied. "But I'm more concerned about their ability to donate to my upcoming campaign than whether or not Parker gets a sizable allowance once their father passes."

"Which I hear won't be too far from now." Devlin sat back as Nikki placed the little canister on his desk. She started to put the spoon down, but realized the little dish was for that. "Perhaps you should be worried more about that missing intern than the campaign donations."

Oh, *dear.*

Nikki turned back to the tray, blinking rapidly as she picked up the teapot again.

"I'm sure Ms. Joan will turn up, sooner or later." There was a pause. "Funny how people go missing or die under mysterious causes around these parts."

"Hmm?" Devlin murmured.

This conversation was turning dark.

Nikki poured the senator's tea.

"Like that police chief who was investigating Lawrence's

death. Died in a car accident—a single-vehicle car accident," Stefan continued. "That journalist from the *Advocate* contacted my office *again*, wanting to talk."

"I do believe they said the chief suffered a medical emergency before the crash," Devlin replied. "And Ross Haid can call all he wants. No one is talking to him."

"I guess Mr. Haid is curious about the chief's death. Odd considering the chief was a healthy man who didn't believe for one second my brother hung himself." Stefan didn't lean back as she placed the tea in front of him, so she had to stretch over his leg, and of course, the cup clattered off the saucer.

"I see some things never change." The senator's tone was dry. "You're still incapable of not making noise."

Sharp tingles spread across her neck as her head whipped around toward him. That was something Lawrence always said to her. Not the senator. She'd only ever been able to tell them apart when they'd been together. The senator never paid any mind to her while Lawrence was pretty much always scowling at her.

Senator de Vincent arched a brow. "Can I help you?"

"No." She blinked. "Sorry." She straightened and backed off. "And I'm sorry to hear about your brother."

A faint, tight smile crossed the senator's face. "Thank you."

She glanced back at Devlin who was staring at her curiously. "Is there anything else you need?"

"No," Devlin said quickly. "Thank you, Nikki."

Nodding, she got out of there as fast as possible, her thoughts racing. The Harrington family was having financial issues? Parker had an allowance? That made her want to laugh. And what the hell was up with the whole chief of police thing? She had no idea, but she'd heard about the missing intern, because there'd been no escaping that news. It had been plastered everywhere about a year or so ago.

Her disappearance had been super suspicious and mysterious. From what Nikki could remember, it was like the intern vanished into thin air. Her purse, along with her car keys and ID, had been found in her apartment. Her car was in the driveway. No prints. No leads. Nothing except the rumored relationship between her and Stefan de Vincent.

The curse strikes yet again.

Lord help her, but the de Vincents were bananas. All of them. Back out in the hallway, she started for the outdoor stairway. Nikki had just made it to the porch, about to round a corner, when a woman suddenly appeared in front of her.

Startled, Nikki gasped and stepped back, nearly dropping the tray. It was then when she realized that she was supposed to leave the tray behind to clean once Devlin was done with his meeting. She really sucked at this, but none of that mattered at the moment.

A tall and curvy brunette stood there, wearing a pretty dress that flowed to the straps on her flats and had super-cute fluttery sleeves. Her dark brown hair was loose, falling around a gorgeous face.

"Oh!" the woman exclaimed. "I'm sorry. I scared you!" She laughed, her warm brown eyes dancing. "And in this house, you don't need any additional reasons to be startled."

It clicked who she was. "Julia?"

"That's me." A wide, welcoming smile graced her lips. "And you must be Nikki? Well, I know you're Nikki. I just saw your father and he said you were upstairs, so I planned on waiting in the hall, but here you are."

Nikki lowered the tray, finding herself grinning. So this was Lucian's girlfriend? She looked nothing like Sabrina nor did she act like her, so she already got a ton of bonus points just for that reason.

"It's nice to finally meet you." Nikki stuck out her hand.

Julia shook it. "You heading back to the kitchen? I'll walk with you."

They fell into step. "So, did you guys just get back? I haven't seen Lucian yet."

"We got back Saturday evening, but Lucian is around here somewhere. This house is crazy," Julia said. "An entire family of five could live here and you'd never cross paths with them."

Nikki laughed. "It is. When I was little, I used to get lost in here." As soon as she said it, she realized that Julia might not know exactly who she was. "My parents are—"

"Livie and Richard." She tucked her hair back from her face. "I know. Lucian told me who you were. You kind of grew up in this house."

Relieved that she wasn't going to have to give a complete rundown, she nodded. "I was here mostly during the summers and sometimes after school in the afternoons. Childcare was just too expensive."

"Isn't it, though? I don't have kids. Never have, but when I used to work back home, some of the parents would spend at least half of their paycheck on childcare. It's insane." There was a pause. "It's nice that you were allowed to come here."

They reached the main-floor entrance. Julia opened the door, waiting for her.

"Yeah, I think even my parents were surprised that Mr. de Vincent was okay with it, but he was." Nikki pursed her lips as a rush of cool air greeted them. "As long as I was quiet."

Julia giggled. "I never met him, but . . ."

"He was not . . . the nicest man," Nikki said quietly, thinking of the senator upstairs.

"That's what I figured. Lucian doesn't . . ." Her expression darkened, and Nikki recalled what her mom had told her about Daniel, the de Vincents' cousin. "Well, these boys didn't seem to have much of a mother or a father."

They'd stopped in the back hallway. "They didn't."

"Which reminds me." Her expression smoothed out. "How is your mother doing?"

"Good. She's a little worn down, but she's doing great."

They started walking again, toward the kitchen. "I'm glad to hear that. Your mother is great."

"She really is."

"I heard about what happened yesterday with you and Gabe," Julia said. "Thank God neither of you were hurt. It's just all so bizarre when you think about it."

"Bizarre things happen whenever you're around them . . ." Nikki trailed off when they entered the kitchen through the back entrance. It wasn't empty.

The remaining de Vincent brothers were at the island. Lucian had his back to her, but Gabe was facing the entrance. His hair was loose, hanging forward and brushing the chiseled line of his jaw as he grinned at whatever Lucian was saying or doing.

Her stomach clenched when Gabe looked up. It was like he sensed her or something, because his gaze immediately found her. She hadn't seen him since yesterday, and she had no idea what to expect from him.

One side of his lips kicked up as he straightened from where he was leaning on the island. He smiled—wasn't a big one, but it was a real one, and her heart threw itself against her ribs in elation.

Nikki let out a breath she hadn't realized she'd been holding and smiled back.

"Hey . . ." Lucian turned at the waist. He only had eyes for Julia as he rose from the barstool and crossed the room. He picked up Julia, causing her to squeak as he spun her around. "I missed you, woman."

Nikki felt her mouth drop as she watched them. There was a part of her that thrilled that they were so obviously in love, but the other half was shocked that it was Lucian.

The man had a reputation. . . .

Julia laughed as he buried his head in her hair. "You literally saw me about thirty minutes ago."

"Still missed you." Setting her down, he kissed her cheek and then smacked her rear before turning to Nikki. "Well, isn't it Little Nikki, back from college, and all grown up."

She rolled her eyes as she placed the tray on the counter. "Hi, Lucian."

He chuckled as he walked over to her, giving her a less enthused greeting, but a nice one nonetheless. "How have you been?"

"Good. You?" She peeked around Lucian at Gabe, who was watching them.

"You know, nothing's really changed. Just living a life of leisure with my woman." Lucian turned, winking when Julia made a noise. "Do I detect a sarcastic snort from you?"

Julia sat on the stool, tucking her feet on the bottom rail. "Possibly."

"My heart." He placed a hand on his chest. "You wound me."

"Whatever." Julia grinned across the island at Gabe. "I don't know how you've managed to deal with him all these years. He's so needy."

Gabe smirked. "I've learned to block him out. It's a skill you're going to need to work on if you want to make this long term."

His brother flipped him off. "That's rude."

Lifting a shrug, Gabe walked away from the island. Those sea-green eyes focused on her. "How's your Monday been?"

"Um, good. Busy." Feeling incredibly awkward and unsure of how to proceed with Gabe, she clasped her hands together. "Yours?"

"Headed into the city to get a little work done and just got back, which reminds me." Gabe opened the fridge door, and it was then that Nikki saw the thin layer of wood dust on his jeans. "Swung by D'Juice and picked you up a smoothie."

Surprise scuttled through her as he pulled out a tall, reddish-orange smoothie. The smoothie yesterday had been shocking and the one today was equally surprising. He'd used to do this all the time back in the day, but it seemed . . . different now.

"Thank you." She took it, tugging the paper off the top of the straw as she glanced over at Lucian and Julia. Both of them were staring at her and Gabe, but it was the de Vincent's small, oddly knowing grin that caused her cheeks to flush. "That's nice of you."

Gabe lifted a shoulder. "Picked one up for myself. Sucked that down like water, though."

She smiled as she took a sip, swallowing a moan of pleasure. It was like a mango-strawberry orgasm in her mouth. "Oh, this is so good."

"Thought you'd like it." He grinned as he leaned against the counter, crossing his arms. "Then again, pretty sure you'd like anything with strawberries in it."

The fact he remembered that stunned her. "Just not blueberries. Not a blueberry fan."

He shook his head. "You don't know what you're missing out on with your illogical distaste for blueberries."

Unable to help herself, she giggled. "They're gross."

"Uh-huh. Yet you like raspberries."

"They are not the same thing though," she argued. "Blueberries are too tart."

"But in real life, outside of your taste buds, raspberries are actually more tart than blueberries."

"Liar," she said, taking another yummy-filled gulp of the smoothie as she turned to Lucian and Julia. They were still staring at them.

Lucian had plopped his chin on his palm, watching them. "Sooo." He drew the word out. "Julia is making dinner tonight."

"Oh." Nikki stepped away from Gabe, knowing she needed to get back to work. The reminder was stark. She wasn't one of them. "Yes, I saw that there wasn't a meal planned for tonight."

"I love to cook. I don't get to do it often here, but—" Julia dipped her chin "—when the grumpy cat's away, the mice will play."

Nikki laughed, knowing she was referencing Devlin.

"That is one of the big reasons why I can't wait to move into our place." Julia elbowed Lucian. "And it's why it's taking so long to move in. Kitchen renovations."

Nikki imagined that Julia would probably end up with an amazing, gorgeous kitchen just based on the way Lucian looked at her. "Where did you guys find a place?"

"Over in the Garden District. The realtor swears it's not haunted," Julia added with a grin. "But I've resigned myself to the fact that every place around here probably has a ghost or two."

Shaking his head, Gabe sighed. "You could always have the house blessed first."

"Can we do that?" Julia looked at Lucian. "Can we—"

"Whatever you want, babe. House blessing. Cleansing. Full exorcism. As long as you're happy."

Julia beamed, and there was a twinge in Nikki's chest, because there wasn't an ounce of condescension or sarcasm in his tone. He'd meant what he said, no matter how crazy it might sound.

That was love, like, true love, and Nikki had no idea what that felt like to be on the receiving end of. Worst part, if she was being honest with herself, Calvin could've been that man for her, if she had let it happen.

"You should join us for dinner," Lucian announced suddenly, and it took her a second to realize he was talking to her.

What the what?

"I'm making spaghetti—home-cooked spaghetti with meatballs and garlic bread, full of carbs and fat and calories." Julia patted her stomach. "The best kind."

That sounded amazing actually, but . . .

Nikki glanced at Gabe. He wanted to be friends and had

attempted to go to the shelter with her, but she hesitated. Friends or not, she was still staff and staff *never* ate dinner with the de Vincents at their table. "I don't know. I should—"

"You should stay and have dinner with us." Lucian leaned over, dropping an arm around Julia's shoulder. "Right, Gabe?"

Gabe nodded from where he stood. "Julia makes amazing spaghetti."

"Thank you. It sounds delish, but I don't know." Nikki fidgeted with the straw. "I don't think Devlin would be thrilled about me doing the dinner thing—"

"Do any of us look like we give a fuck what Dev thinks?" Gabe asked. "Because we don't. At all."

"Not even remotely," Lucian added.

Julia grinned as she nodded. "I'm not going to say what they're saying, because Devlin still kind of scares me."

"Devlin scares everyone," Nikki murmured.

"Come on." Gabe faced her. "Join us for dinner. It will be fun."

"Lots of fun," Lucian chimed in.

Nikki glanced between the brothers, knowing she should say no, because she wasn't one of them. She was never really one of them.

"Have dinner with us, Nic." Gabe reached out, tapping her arm. "Please?"

And it was suddenly like being that little girl again with a huge, undying crush, because she couldn't say no to Gabe.

Chapter 13

Gabe found he was having a hard time not staring at Nic during dinner. He wasn't sure why. Maybe it was because when she showed up at the beginning, she'd taken her hair down and now looked less like someone who'd spent the day dusting furniture and compiling the week's grocery shopping list.

Maybe it was because she was holding a wine glass and smiling at Lucian and Julia in a way she hadn't smiled at him in a long time.

Or maybe it was because when her cheeks got flushed and those big brown eyes started to dance, she was fucking beautiful.

It didn't matter.

Sitting back with his cheek resting on his palm, he knew he needed to stop staring at her, because he wasn't exactly being inconspicuous about it.

He didn't stop.

Gabe couldn't even blame it on liquor. All he'd been drinking tonight was water and sweetened tea.

"So what made you decide to go into social work?" Julia asked, picking up her glass of red wine. "That has to be a hard job."

"Can't be any harder than nursing," Nic said as she reached for a piece of garlic bread. She hadn't been watching him. Hell, it was like she barely knew he was there, which he found fucking irritating, because they were *friends* now.

Gabe noted she hadn't answered Julia's question so he opened his big mouth. "Nic has always been a *helper*."

Her gaze shot to his from across the round table. Finally.

"A *helper*?" Lucian slid a long look in his direction.

Gabe ignored it. "Yeah, she's always wanted to help people."

Nic blinked slowly and then focused on Julia. "My friend Rosie says I have a savior complex. I don't think it's that extreme, but I do want to help people. I know that sounds cheesy—"

"It doesn't," Gabe interjected. "The world needs more people like you and Julia and fewer people like us."

"Agreed," snickered Lucian around the rim of his wine glass.

Julia put her glass down. "You guys donate a lot of money to charities."

"Giving money is easy," Gabe replied. "Giving time isn't."

Nic bit down on her lower lip as her lashes swept down.

"So are you done with school or not?" Julia asked.

"I have my bachelor's and I'm currently deciding if I want to get a master's or PhD. Kind of going back and forth on it," Nic answered, breaking a part the piece of garlic bread into little sections, getting crumbs all over her plate. "I could get started and take evening classes."

"That would be really hard."

"It would be," Nic agreed, popping a piece of the buttery bread into her mouth. "But getting out there and doing the job sounds more enticing than grad school."

"No doubt." Lucian rocked back on his chair as he toyed with a strand of Julia's hair. "Did you know that Gabe isn't the only one good with his hands when it comes to wood-work?"

Julia looked over at Nic. "You?"

"Um." She took a rather long sip of her wine. "I used to be able to create like these stupid little charm bracelets and figurines—"

"They weren't stupid." Gabe straightened in his chair, frowning. "Nic has a talent."

"I wouldn't call it a talent," Nic began.

"I'm not going to sit here while you're being all modest and shit. The little pieces of jewelry she used to make were amazing." Gabe was speaking the truth. "So were the figurines. You're still doing that, right?"

She avoided his gaze. "With school and everything, I didn't have a lot of time to mess around with that stuff." She lifted a shoulder. "It's not something I really do anymore."

"Really?" Surprise flickered through him. "I thought you wanted to open up a little shop and sell your work. It was all you talked about—"

"People change. I'm just not into the same things I was when I was a kid."

A kid? She'd been into it right up until that night, and she sure as fuck hadn't been a kid that night.

Nic turned to Julia. "How did you and Lucian meet? You're from Pennsylvania, right?"

His eyes narrowed as Nic changed the subject. She obviously didn't like the focus being on her, which was new. The younger Nic loved to be the center of attention—the center of *his* attention.

Julia glanced at Lucian. "Well, I was . . ."

"She was hired to care for Madeline," Lucian finished for her since it was obvious Julia didn't know how much she could share. "Did you know she returned?"

Since she was chewing on a piece of bread, Nic only nodded at first. "I was told that she had returned, but nothing beyond that. How . . . is she doing?"

Gabe raised a brow, letting Lucian take the lead on this since anything he had to say about Madeline would most likely upset his younger brother. Lucian now knew just how messed up Madeline had been, but she was still his twin. That biological connection was hard to get over.

"Not well," Lucian said after a moment. "She's dead."

"What?" Nic gasped, and he'd swear a tiny piece of garlic bread fell out her mouth. Her wide gaze swung to his before darting back to Lucian. "Oh my God, I'm sorry."

"Thank you, but don't feel sorry. Not for Maddie." Lucian sat back with a sigh. "How much do you know about what's been happening here?"

Nic had lost the pretty flush in her cheeks. "I knew that Madeline had come back and something happened with Daniel? He threatened you and Julia?"

"That's the watered-down version, but Madeline did show up. Found her one night floating in the pool outside," Lucian explained. "She was virtually comatose and we had to hire someone."

"Which was me." Julia's arm moved under the table, and Gabe knew she was comforting Lucian. Most likely placing a hand on the tapping leg of his. "We believed she was in some sort of locked-in state of consciousness, but that wasn't the case."

"Remember the night our mother died?" Lucian asked.

Nic nodded. "How could I forget? I was young, but that kind of stuff sticks with you."

Gabe remembered Nic crying when she heard the news, not because she really knew their mother, but because she was so upset for them—the brothers.

"Turned out Mom didn't kill herself. She and Maddie had been up on the rooftop arguing." His brother's voice sounded detached, but Gabe knew better. That whole mess still cut him deep. "Fighting over our cousin Daniel. Maddie had been with him, and yeah, as in having relations with him."

"Oh my," whispered Nic.

"The argument escalated and—" Lucian drew in a deep breath—"Maddie pushed her off the roof."

Nic jolted. "Oh my God."

"It gets worse." Gabe reached for the water, wishing it

was liquor. "She'd spent the last ten years hiding out with Daniel. They ran out of money, concocted some wild-ass plan for getting ahold of the de Vincent fortune."

"Almost worked," Lucian said quietly. "She had me fooled, right up until the night Daniel threatened Julia."

Surprised that Lucian was opening up, he sat back and said nothing, glad that his brother *was* talking about it.

"I . . . I don't know what to say." Nic reached for her wine again, then stopped herself. "How did she even think that she could get the money?"

Julia sipped her wine while Lucian seemed to choose his words wisely. "Her plan was ridiculous, but well, you know it's never been a secret that Maddie and I weren't the offspring of dear old dad."

If Nic hadn't heard that rumor, she didn't show it.

"Come to find out, Maddie knew the truth about who father's true heirs were." Lucian smiled but there was no humor to it. "Maddie and I were Lawrence's children. Dev and Gabe were not."

Nic's lips parted as her gaze darted to Gabe. Her face had paled considerably, so much so that he was a bit concerned. "I . . . I really have no idea what to say."

"It is what it is." Lucian picked up his fork, lazily dragging it through what was left of his spaghetti. "Not much has changed. Dev is still the heir. Gabe is still the spare."

Gabe raised his hand.

"And I'm still Lucian and I don't have to worry about business meetings or deal with Senator Dickhead. And honest? Maddie was a true sociopath, but in a way, I'm thankful." Lucian looked at Julia. "If she hadn't come back, I would've never met Julia."

"That's . . . sweet," Nic murmured, blinking rapidly.

Gabe grinned as her gaze connected with his. "It's a lot to process. Besides your parents and our doctor, no one outside of the family knew that Madeline was back."

"It has to stay that way." Nic picked up her wine glass and finished it off. "I understand."

"Well, that was a bit of a conversation killer, wasn't it?" Julia laughed nervously. "I think we need to stop telling the truth."

"We did meet at a bar first." Lucian grinned at her. "We should just go with that version."

"Yeah, I think you should most definitely go with that version," Nic said, eyes widening. "It's a lot less intense."

Julia kissed Lucian's cheek and then turned to Gabe. "Are you heading up to Baton Rouge this week?"

He shook his head. "No."

"What do you have going on in Baton Rouge?" Nic asked.

The question was innocent enough. Gabe knew damn well neither Livie nor Richard would've said a single thing about his now-frequent trips.

"A few personal things," he said.

"Oh." Disappointment flashed across her face, and he felt like an ass. He could've come up with a better answer, but *that* was just something he wasn't ready to talk to her about.

Or talk to her at all about it.

Lucian came to the rescue. Sort of. "So, are you seeing anyone, Nikki?"

Gabe's hand stilled along the arm of the chair. This was an interesting question.

Nic's brows flew up. "Um, no. No. Single." Her nose scrunched. "Well, I was seeing this guy in college."

"And that didn't last?" Gabe asked before he could stop himself.

Her gaze darted to him. "We broke up a bit ago."

"Interesting," he murmured.

She started to frown.

Lucian stared at him.

And then he realized that his response was a bit odd. "It's interesting because . . . most college relationships don't work out."

Okay.

That sounded stupid.

But then something flickered over Nic's face before she quickly looked away, but he knew what she was thinking about. Hell, he knew what he was thinking about now.

Or whom, to be more exact.

Emma.

DINNER HAD BEEN . . . ENLIGHTENING.

That was all Nikki could think as she grabbed her purse from the staff office. She couldn't even process what Lucian had told her about their sister and father. The de Vincents had some crazy drama in their background, but that was beyond anything she could've imagined.

And she had no idea how Gabe was dealing with it. She'd always had the impression that Lucian had never been close to Lawrence, but Gabe and Dev had been. Well, they had been as close to him as anyone could be to that man.

To learn that the man you thought was always your father wasn't? And who was their dad? God.

Digging her keys out of her purse, she started to head out the back door but stopped.

Nikki remembered how bad it had been after their mother had died. They'd grown up thinking she'd killed herself, and this whole time, she'd been taken away from them by their sister.

How did one even begin to get over that?

As she stood in the small ten-by-ten room, she suddenly thought about the de Vincent curse.

What was it? Women never lasted long here. Yeah, that was it. They either lost their minds . . . or died.

Nikki never really believed in the curse and the brothers had always been so blasé about it, but now she was beginning to think it was onto something and that the brothers weren't so dismissive of it, because sweet Jesus. Wow.

She looked over her shoulder, toward the back hallway. How would she feel if she found her dad wasn't her father? It would kill her in a way. He'd always be her father, because he was who raised her and that was all that mattered, but still. And then to find out their own sister killed their mother because their sister was screwing her cousin and their mother objected?

Sorrow wrapped its way around her heart, and she was moving without telling her legs where to go.

In the back of her mind she could hear Rosie saying, *Don't listen to your bleeding heart. . . .*

Unfortunately, she was listening, and it wasn't that big of a deal. Not like she was in search of Gabe to throw herself at him. She just wanted—God help her—to make sure he was okay, really okay.

Because that's what friends did.

She cut down the back hallway, making her way to the rec room. Some kind of bizarre sixth sense guided her down the long hallway and to the door that was cracked open. Placing her fingers on the engraved wood panel—the panel that Gabe himself had carved the vines into—she pushed.

He was alone.

Gabe was behind one of the pool tables, lining up a shot. The cue stick jutted out, smacking into the ball. It shot across the table, knocking into a red solid, sending it to spin into a corner pocket.

Her gaze dropped.

Gabe was barefoot.

Straightening, he looked up. "Nic?"

"Hey." She stepped into the room, wondering what the hell she was doing. It was already dark outside, and Lord knows she didn't have a track record of being smart once the night fell here, so she should be well on her way out of here, but here she was. "You're playing pool by yourself?"

"Lucian wanted some alone time with Julia." He placed the stick against the pool table. "So here I am, playing pool by myself."

"That's kind of . . . sad."

One side of his lips kicked up. "Is it?"

"Yeah." Dropping her keys back into her purse, she draped the strap over her shoulder. "I mean, pool is a game for more than one person."

"Some consider it a sport," he corrected, leaning a hip against the table.

She rolled her eyes. "I truly feel like for something to be considered a sport, you have to break a sweat."

"You aren't playing pool right if you're not breaking a sweat."

A smile pulled at her lips. "I'll have to take your word on that."

Gabe cocked his head, and a strand of hair fell forward, brushing his cheek. "I thought you had left."

"I was going, but . . ."

Everything about Gabe appeared to go on alert. "But?"

What was she doing? She wasn't so sure. Okay, she wasn't being honest with herself. She was now wasting time and being stupid. "I wanted to check on your car."

"Check on my car?"

"Yeah. The window?"

"It's been fixed. My car is whole and happy."

"That's . . . good," she said lamely.

A knowing look settled on his features. "That's not why you're still here."

Hating that he could read her so well, Nikki took a deep breath. "I just wanted to say that I'm sorry about everything that happened with your sister, your mom . . . and your dad."

He stared at her for a moment and then looked away. "It's no big deal."

"No big deal?" she repeated, stunned. "Dude, that's a huge deal. All of it. Every last piece of it."

He let out a soft laugh. "And you only know half of it."

"Half of what?"

A muscle flexed in his jaw as he turned back to her and a long moment passed. Long enough that Nikki began to really worry. "Thank you, though. For saying that."

She didn't miss that he hadn't answered her question.

"But you don't have to apologize."

"I know." She inched closer. "But I can't imagine what you guys must've gone through—are going through."

Lifting a hand, he brushed the hair out of his face. "What can we do, though? We can't change what our sister did or the stuff with our mother and father. No point in dwelling on any of it."

Fidgeting with the strap on her purse, she inched a little closer. "Do you and Devlin have any idea of who your father could be?"

He shook his head, but Nikki didn't miss the way his jaw tightened. He may be standing there acting like everything was a nothing burger, but Nikki knew better. Maybe someone like Devlin would be wholly unaffected by the events but not the Gabe she knew.

Before she gave herself time to think about what she was doing, she sprang forward and all but tackle-hugged Gabe. Wrapping her arms around his waist, she squeezed him and said, "I really am sorry for everything that has happened."

Gabe was utterly frozen. His entire body was so stiff she wasn't even sure if he breathed or not, and for a really tense moment, she feared that she'd let her heart guide her into making another bad decision.

But then she felt Gabe's chest rise under her cheek and his arms swept around her, folding across her back. He held her, and she couldn't even remember the last time they'd hugged or been this close.

Actually, she did.

That night she'd gone to him they'd hugged and obviously that hug had turned into a hell of a lot more. Four years was a long time between hugs, and being this close to him again did crazy strange things to her senses. The entire front of her body tingled sharply and when she inhaled, she was surrounded by the crisp scent of his cologne.

It was just a hug.

That's what she kept telling herself even as she knew she needed to pull away. It was just a hug—one that probably had little to no impact on Gabe while it was absolutely destroying her best of intentions.

Gabe's arms tightened around her and she bit down on her lip when she felt his chin brush the top of her head. One of his hands moved, dragging down the line of her spine. His palm flatted at the small of her back.

Just a hug. Just a hug.

Her body wasn't on the same wavelength as her brain. Heat flashed through her, intense and wanting. The feel of his chest against her and—

Oh my God.

Nikki's eyes flew open. She felt *him*, hard and thick, pressing against her stomach.

Gabe suddenly let go and stepped back, putting distance between them as her wide-eyed gaze swung to his. "You should leave." His voice was rough, deep. Abrasive. Nikki shivered. "Now."

Resisting the idiotic voice that always got her into a world of trouble and wanted her to ignore what he was saying, she turned and got the hell out of there.

Chapter 14

$\mathcal{N}$ikki didn't see Gabe for two whole days after the hug apocalypse in the rec room, but then he'd brought her a banana-strawberry smoothie on Thursday, and from there, a routine began. For the next week, Gabe brought her a smoothie from D'Juice just after lunch, and he chatted with her while she prepped for dinner.

He'd asked her again about why she hadn't found time to create the jewelry she used to be so obsessed with doing. She'd given him the same answer, mainly because she'd been too embarrassed to tell the truth.

What she used to enjoy had been tainted after that night.

Not that she'd ever tell him that, not when they were becoming friends.

He'd asked her about college. She'd asked him about how much his woodworking business had grown. She told him about her plans to find an apartment, and he offered to help her move when that day came.

A de Vincent moving her stuff?

She'd laughed then when he suggested it and could laugh now even thinking about it.

They didn't talk about what happened with his sister or about his father and there was definitely no mention of what had happened during the impromptu hug.

Nikki was even beginning to think that she possibly imagined what she'd felt pressed against her. She hadn't even told Rosie about that, and if she hadn't imagined it, then she chalked it up to him just having a physical reaction to being close to a woman's body.

Because Nikki seriously believed that some guys could get hard if the wind blew across their pelvic area.

After all, that was all it had to be, because Gabe showed no outward interest in her beyond what he'd said he wanted, which was to be friends.

It was Wednesday evening, right before dinnertime, when Gabe appeared in the kitchen. "Heads up," he said, strolling past her. He picked up her braid and flipped it over her shoulder. "Ms. Harrington is in the house."

"Ugh," she muttered, already knowing that Devlin was planning to have dinner with her tonight. "Is her brother with her?"

"Unfortunately. Make it four for dinner," he said, drawing her gaze to him. "No way am I leaving you to fend for yourself with them."

Oh, that was . . . sweet, and sounded like the Gabe she knew. "Thanks."

"And I have another purpose for being here other than watching you check the roast beef, which, by the way, smells amazing."

She smiled at that and ignored the way her belly jumped around. "I think it's going to turn out pretty good." Closing the oven door, she faced him and got a little tongue-tied. Why, oh why, did he have to be so . . . freaking hot. "Why else are you here? I don't see a smoothie."

"No smoothie. Yet."

"Oh." She didn't know what to say to that.

A half smile appeared. "What are you doing after you get off?"

Oh.

Oh my.

That was not a question she was expecting. "Uh, nothing. I was heading home."

"So, no plans?" When she nodded, he said, "That works out perfect, because now you do."

"I do?" she squeaked. Like a mouse. Ugh.

His grin kicked up a notch. "Yep."

Now her heart was jumping along with her stomach. "What am I doing?"

"It's a surprise."

She stilled, barely breathing. "I don't like surprises."

"Whatever," he laughed. "Yes, you do."

"Not anymore."

Pushing away from the counter, he slid her a knowing look. "You'll like this one. Trust me."

"But—"

Gabe was already strolling out of the kitchen, leaving her standing there with her mouth hanging open.

That was how Parker found her.

Because she had the worst luck known to man.

He walked through the main doorway. "Nikki."

Her spine stiffened. "What are you doing in here?"

"Getting a drink." He swaggered into the kitchen like he belonged in there.

Nikki knew damn well he knew to ask her father if he wanted a drink, which meant he snuck around her dad somehow.

"But now that I see you in here, I'll let you do your job." He flashed those bright teeth. "I would like a scotch on the rocks."

Resisting the urge to tell him to help himself, she pivoted around and headed for the pantry where the liquor was stored off the kitchen.

"Make sure you get the good stuff."

Nikki jumped at the closeness of his voice. She should've known he'd follow her. "You didn't need to come in here."

"Thought I'd keep you company," he replied. "Just like Gabe was keeping you company."

Climbing up the small ladder, she looked down at where he stood, blocking the damn door like the jerk-face he was. How long had he been waiting out in the hall to come in? She grabbed a top-shelf bottle.

"Gabe doesn't like me," he said, sounding indifferent.

Well, guess that answered her question.

What a creeper.

"I really wouldn't know." She came down the ladder. "Excuse me."

He didn't move. "He's going to have to get used to me. His brother is marrying my sister."

"Has Devlin picked a date yet?" The question came out of her mouth before she could stop herself.

His lips thinned slightly. "He will. Soon."

"Hmm." She stepped to the side. "If you want me to make you this drink, you're going to have to move."

"What if I don't want to move?"

Irritated, she squared her shoulders. "Look, I'm just trying to do my job. Can you please move?"

He bent at the waist, lowering his head so they were eye level. "Say it nicely and maybe I will."

She drew back, seconds from slamming her foot on his. "Can you *please* move aside, Parker?"

"That wasn't really that nice, but I do want that drink." He stepped back. "And I want you to make it for me."

Swallowing a load of curses that would make a truck driver pleased, she went back into the kitchen and grabbed a tumbler.

"You don't like me either." He'd followed her back into the kitchen. "Don't even deny it. I know you don't."

Well, he said not to deny it, so she kept her mouth shut as she filled his glass with ice.

"I don't get it," he continued. "You should be thrilled that I even notice you."

Okay. Now she was unable to keep her mouth closed. "Perhaps *that* is why I don't like you." She poured the scotch and then picked up the glass, offering it to him. "Besides the fact you have no sense of personal boundaries? You're arrogant because you're rich and you're used to getting whatever you want. That's why I don't like you."

Parker laughed.

She wasn't sure how she expected him to respond, but laughing wasn't one of them.

Taking his glass, he stared down at her with what her mom would say were *airs*. Like he was a million leagues better than her. "I have some advice for you, Nikki."

"Can't wait to hear it."

His nostrils flared. "You better improve that attitude of yours before my sister does marry Dev." He reached out, placing a cool finger on her cheek as he said, "Actually, you should start right now."

Nikki jerked back. "Don't touch me."

"You're not listening to me." He smirked, lowering his hand. "You should be nicer to me, because even if you're gone by the time Sabrina marries Dev, she can make damn sure that your parents no longer have a job here."

Sucking in a shocked gasp, she stared up at Parker. A wicked sense of déjà vu swept over her. "You're threatening my parents' employment? Again?"

"You know it's not a threat. It's a piece of advice. Drop the bitch act and maybe when your mom is feeling better, she'll still have a job." He paused. "And considering her health, her and her husband losing their jobs because their daughter is a little bitch is the last thing they need."

Her lips parted. Shocked, she couldn't believe what she was hearing. Why she was surprised in the first place was beyond her. That's what he'd done the last time, when he tried to pull her towel off her and managed to shove his hand under it. He'd threatened her and it had worked. But now? Maybe it had to do with the fact he knew how sick her mother was and he was still threatening her employment.

Nikki was disgusted and horrified.

Switching his glass to his other hand, he reached out before she could move, dragging his damp finger along the curve of her cheek.

"Just something to think about the next time we cross paths." One side of his mouth curled up. "Okay?"

Parker didn't wait for an answer. Nikki bit back a curse as she watched him leave the kitchen just as her father appeared, looking harried and beyond annoyed.

Parker nodded at him as he passed.

"Is everything okay?" Her father hurried over.

Clearing her throat, she nodded, not wanting her father to worry. He had enough to stress over. "Yeah, everything is great."

FOR WHAT FELT like the hundredth time since Nic got in his car, he glanced over at her.

She'd been strangely quiet for the drive into the city, sitting still and staring at the window. She'd been the same way during the dinner, barely making eye contact with anyone, including him. He'd thought she'd be in a jovial mood considering Parker ended up not joining his sister for dinner. Hell, he hadn't even seen the punk ass.

Hands tightening on the steering wheel, he glanced over at her again when the traffic slowed on the highway. "You okay, Nic?"

She nodded. "Yeah."

"Hey." He reached over, touching her arm lightly. She jumped, and he frowned. "You sure about that?"

"Yeah. Yes. Sorry." She looked over at him. The overhead street lamp glanced off her shadowed face. "Just lost in my head. So, you going to tell me about this surprise?"

"If I did, then it wouldn't be a surprise." He took the exit to the Business District.

Gabe wasn't even sure why he was doing this. It was just something that had stuck in his head ever since spaghetti night.

She shot him a look as she fiddled with the edge of her braid. A moment passed and then she asked, "Do you really think Devlin is going to marry Sabrina?"

"That's a random question," he said with a laugh.

"I know." She dropped her hands to her lap. "It's just that they barely talk to one another. Sabrina paid more attention to you at dinner than she did Devlin."

His lip curled with disgust. "Yeah, well, Sabrina wants what she can't have."

"You?"

"I met her in college, after Dev graduated. She was interested." He turned down Iberville. "I wasn't. Still not."

"Did something happen between you guys?"

"No," he said, speaking the truth. "She tried a time or two back in college, but nothing ever happened."

Lucian always believed otherwise, but his brother was wrong. Other than being somewhat kind to Sabrina in the beginning, Gabe did nothing to encourage her.

"I don't like her," Nic said with a sigh.

"Yeah." He remembered how Sabrina had talked to her during the first dinner. He hadn't helped matters. "Sorry about how I acted that one dinner. I shouldn't have acted like that."

Nic waved it off, but he knew what he'd done had bothered her. "We're going to your workshop, aren't we?"

"Yep."

"Why?" Interest filled her voice.

"You'll see."

She sighed heavily. "Sabrina brought up Baton Rouge during dinner. Seems like you go there a lot."

He nodded as he cut down a narrow alley. "I have been."

Gabe could feel her gaze on him. "So what are you doing up there?"

"I've been looking for a place," he answered, which was true.

"You're moving there?" She sounded surprised.

"Part-time. That's the plan."

"Why?"

He didn't answer, because he wasn't sure how he could without feeling like shit and having her think the worst of him. Because once she learned the truth, she would wonder what everyone would, which was how in the fuck was he here and not there.

It was a question he kept asking himself.

"Are you . . . seeing someone there?" she asked, her voice quiet.

His head shot in her direction as he parked the Porsche. She wasn't looking at him, but she was messing with her braid again. "No, I'm not seeing someone there."

"Oh."

He reached over, gently wrapping his fingers around her wrist. Her gaze flew to his as he pulled her hand away from her hair. "I just have some stuff going on there, okay?"

Her brows knitted together. "Okay."

Exhaling heavily, he let go of her wrist, refusing to acknowledge just how soft her damn skin was. "You ready?"

"For the surprise?" She smiled. "I think so."

Laughing under his breath, he unhooked his seatbelt. "Hold on."

Gabe climbed out and jogged around the front of the car, going to her side. He opened the door for her. Closing it behind her, he led her in through the back entrance of his workshop.

A blast of cold air and the scent of raw wood greeted them as he opened the door. He flipped the overhead light on. The lights whirled to life, casting the shop out of darkness.

Nic brushed past him, and the slight touch of her hip against his was like a punch to the gut. There was no ignoring the visceral reaction to her. His dick immediately roared to life, a sure sign he needed to get laid, because handling it himself wasn't working.

She was a beautiful woman. That was all it was. And she was forbidden, a big no-no, which made her even more . . . *there*, right in front of him.

That's what he kept telling himself as she stepped out of the hall and into the open space. "Wow." She scanned the various projects he had going. "This place is bigger than I imagined."

Nic moved further into the shop and knelt down, tracing the scrollwork on the leg of a chair. "This is beautiful, Gabe." She looked up at him through thick lashes. "Really."

He was oddly jealous of that chair leg.

"I always thought it was strange." She stroked her hand across the carved wood.

"What?" He watched her tilt her head to the side.

"Lucian paints. Madeline was also a painter. You can turn a couple of sheets of plywood and lumber into something stunning." She rose fluidly, with the grace of a lithe dancer. "But Devlin, he doesn't have a talent."

"Does pissing people off count as a talent? Because if so, he fucking excels at it."

Her laugh was soft, but hell, it rolled and licked over his skin. "True."

"Dev does have a hidden talent," he said, unable to drag his gaze off her as she moved over to a workbench. She touched each tool left out with just one finger and then two, and he swore to God, his dick got harder.

How fucked-up was that?

He really needed to go out, find someone to screw his brains out, because the raw lust pounding through his veins needed an outlet.

And that outlet wasn't Nic.

No matter how tempting she was.

"What's his talent?" she asked, picking up a small chisel.

"He can sing." He eased past her, running a hand over a table he'd been working on earlier in the day.

"What?" She laughed. "Are you for real?"

He nodded as he stopped on the other side of her. One would think talking about his brother would do something about the hard-on he was rocking at the moment, but apparently not. "Would I lie about something like that?"

"I don't know. Maybe?"

"Well, I'm not. The man can sing. But you'd have to get him drunk before that happens." He was done talking about his brother. "Come on. Your surprise is through that door over there."

Her gaze drifted over his shoulder. "I really have no idea what this surprise is."

Because he was into self-torture, he took her hand, somewhat awed by how small it felt in his.

He was being a dumbass.

Folding his fingers around hers, he avoided her gaze as he pulled her across the main floor. "So, I thought that since you haven't decided what to do about school or work, you had some extra time on your hands."

He stopped in front of the door and turned the handle with his free hand. "And I know you said you weren't into the same things you were back then, but I think you just might be."

Pushing open the door, he reached inside and flipped on the light. He tugged on her hand, letting her squeeze past him.

The contact of her smaller body brushing against his fried his senses, but he ignored that as he focused on her face.

And saw the exact moment she understood what she was looking at.

Those pink lips parted on a soft inhale as those big eyes got even bigger. "Gabe . . ."

She twisted toward him, and he smiled at her. "I've been keeping the spare pieces of wood over the years, just tossing them in here. Not even sure why." He frowned, not really wanting to look too closely at the reason for doing so. "Anyway, I asked Richard if you still had a woodcarving kit. He said he didn't think so."

He'd cleaned up the room over the weekend and put a little desk in there, one that he'd made himself but never sold. It had the same vine work as the trim at home. On the desk was a black, smooth box sitting next to a lamp he'd dug out of storage.

"I ordered a new kit," he continued. "And all that wood in the corner is yours if you want it. Actually, this room is yours if you want to use it since I doubt your parents want dust and shavings all over their house again."

"Are you . . . are you serious?" she whispered.

"Yeah." He took a breath. "You're free to use it whenever. Got an extra key and everything."

"I don't know what to say." Blinking rapidly, she turned back to the room. Nic squeezed his hand, and that's when he realized he was still holding her damn hand.

He let go and folded his arms across his chest. "Well, I'm hoping you'll say you love it and you'll make use of it."

Nic tucked her hands under her chin as her shoulders rose with a deep breath. She stepped into the room and then reached out, touching the kit. A second later she opened it, and then did what she'd done out in the main area. She ran her fingers along the tools.

His damn dick jumped.

"This had to cost a fortune," she said, her voice filled with wonder. "This isn't a cheap set."

He grumbled a nonresponse.

"I love it," she said, and then she spun on him. "And I'll make use of it."

Then the strangest damn thing occurred in that moment. He'd wondered if he made a mistake.

Gabe's gaze dropped to her mouth.

A second later, she threw herself at him, like she'd done the night she'd learned about his father, like she'd done a hundred times before things went to shit.

He caught her, taking her weight as she threw her arms around him. He hugged her back, praying that she didn't feel his cock, because shit, that would complicate things.

"Thank you," she said, her voice muffled and oddly hoarse. "You have no idea what this means to me."

Gabe kind of thought he did as he dropped his chin and caught the scent of her shampoo. Strawberries. Her and her damn strawberries.

Briefly, he closed his eyes and then he pulled back, letting his hands slip to her arms. Then he held her back. "I'm glad you like it."

"I love it," she corrected.

Yeah, he liked hearing that. Liked it too much. And yeah, he was thinking that he made a mistake and he had no idea how badly he was going to regret it later on, but he knew he wouldn't have changed a damn thing.

Chapter 15

*H*e did what?" Rosie whisper-yelled.

Nikki nodded as she picked at her beignet. It was late Saturday morning and she was with Rosie at the Café du Monde, scarfing down the powdery pieces of perfection. The fact they'd been able to grab a table surprised both of them since the temps had cooled a little.

She'd just filled her friend in on Gabe's surprise. "Yep. And he even had brand-new saws—a hacksaw and coping saw. I mean, he set me up in my own little shop basically."

"That's insane." Rosie took a bite of a beignet, managing to not get any of the sugar on her, which meant she had to have sold her soul to the devil. "I mean, I didn't even know you could do that stuff with wood. Why did you never tell me?"

Nikki lifted a shoulder. "I just . . . I think if I talked about it, it would make me want to get back to it, and honestly I didn't have time in school and it . . ."

"It reminded you of Gabe?"

"Yeah," she sighed. "Anyway, I don't know what I was expecting, but it wasn't *that*."

Rosie picked up her bottle of water. "Are you going to make use of it—of the tools and the shop?"

There was a flutter deep in her chest. Like a nest of butterflies were waking up. "I think so. I mean, he went to all that trouble."

Oversized sunglasses shielded her eyes, so it was hard to

tell what Rosie was thinking. "Are you going to make use of his wood?"

"Of course. He saved—wait." Nikki picked up her napkin and threw it at her smirking friend. "It isn't like that."

"It's not?"

Now those butterflies were trying to eat their way out, because she thought of the hug and the way she was sure he'd been staring at her mouth. She shifted in her chair, crossing her legs. "Shut up."

"Seriously, though? He had a room full of spare wood?" She leaned forward, tipping her nose down. "And he didn't know why he was saving the wood?"

"That's what he said." The butterflies had moved to her stomach.

"You know what I think?" She straightened. "I'm going to tell you. I think he was keeping the spare wood for you."

The mere idea of Gabe doing that over the years shook her. If it was the case, she didn't know what to think about that.

She couldn't think about that.

Because her heart was already swelling to the point it might burst, and that was not a good sign.

Rosie must've sensed it, because she said, "You just need to be careful, Nikki."

"I'm not reading into it."

"No, I think you do need to read into it."

She frowned. "I'm not really following you."

"Look, what he did for you is not something someone who spent the last four years possibly hating you would do."

"Wow." She picked up her coffee. "When you put it that way."

"What he did was a big deal. He had to know that, even if he doesn't know why you stopped the whole woodworking thing." Plucking up a napkin, she wiped at her fingers. "So, I think you need to read between the lines."

Nikki took a breath that went nowhere. "I can't let myself do that."

"I'm saying you need to be careful. He is a grown-ass man who is very experienced and you, on the other hand, are not very experienced."

"Thanks," she muttered.

"And you guys have this messy past between you. It's going to be tricky."

She shook her head. "I don't know. I mean, what you're suggesting—that he could have some kind of motive beyond being friends with me—just seems insane when you said it yourself; he spent four years hating me."

"Did you ever think that maybe he spent four years hating himself more?" A hot-pink bangle slipped down her arm as she plopped her elbow on the table. "That maybe he wanted you back then and he hated himself for it?"

Nikki opened her mouth.

"You know I have a degree in psychology, right?" Rosie tapped a purple-painted fingernail on her temple. "I know these things."

Could Gabe have hated himself more? That was more than likely, but not for the reasons Rosie was suggesting. "I think he wanted me when it was happening, because he was drunk at the time."

Rosie shook her head, sending curls bouncing in every direction. "All I'm saying is that I think you need to proceed with caution."

"I'm not proceeding with anything." She picked up what was left of her beignet. "We're friends and I think what he did was like a . . . token of our friendship. A true white flag."

"Well, I'm happy to hear that, because I have something for you."

With Rosie, her surprise could be anything from a Ouija board to a voodoo doll. A *used* voodoo doll.

"I have someone I want you to meet."

"Rosie—"

"He's single. He's got a job. Doesn't live in a haunted house, which is a negative for me, but whatever. Not everyone can be perfect. But you don't work for his family. He's good looking aaand you didn't sleep with him when you were eighteen."

"There are a lot of people I didn't sleep with when I was eighteen," Nikki replied with a wry sigh.

"Yep." She smiled widely. "And here's the best part. He actually asked me about you."

She started to frown. "What?"

"He saw us together at Cure, actually, and thought you were just the hottest thing since Hot Pockets."

"Um . . ."

"I don't know why he didn't come over and say hi. I think he got nervous or something. And you know what else I think? I think you should go out on a date with him."

She opened her mouth to say no, absolutely not.

Rosie beat her to it. "If you really are ready to move on with your life, the first thing to do is to get out there and meet someone who isn't Gabe."

Nikki thought there were a whole lot of things that she could do other than going out with some random guy. "I did have dates in college—"

"Barely."

"And I had a boyfriend—"

"We know how that turned out," Rosie quipped.

Nikki's eyes narrowed, but seriously? Why was she being so resistant to a date? She'd even decided that it was time for her to get out there and go on dates. *Nothing* was holding her back. "You know what? Yes. I will go out on a date."

Excitement filled her brown eyes that were more hazel in the light. "Really?"

Nikki nodded. "Set it up."

ABOVE THEIR HEADS, something crashed into a wall—something fragile by the sound of it. Probably something expensive, too.

Gabe's gaze lifted to the ceiling. "That sounded like a glass."

"Or a vase," Lucian commented.

"I hope it wasn't a window." Julia lowered her pool stick.

Gabe smirked. "Sabrina knows better than that."

For the last thirty minutes or so, Sabrina had been up in Dev's office and every so often, they heard Sabrina's shrill voice. They couldn't tell what they were arguing about, but they had their guesses.

This wasn't anything new.

Most likely she was pressuring Dev about setting a date and each time she did, it ended with her throwing something when Dev refused to cave.

Walking around the pool table, Lucian came to Julia's side. "Why don't you head upstairs and pick out a movie for us to watch?" He hooked his arm around Julia's shoulders, tugging her into his side. "I'll be up in a little bit."

Julia arched a brow, but stretched up and kissed his cheek. "I'll be waiting."

"Damn straight." He smacked her ass as she pulled away, earning him a narrowed glare. "That's me warming up."

"Whatever," she muttered, her face flushing as she waved goodnight to Gabe and then left the room.

Gabe leaned back, resting his arms on the bar behind him. "Smart move."

"Hmm." Lucian walked behind the bar and picked up several glasses. "You think Dev is going to pick a date?"

"If he did, she wouldn't be up there throwing shit." Gabe turned on the stool, facing his brother as he poured bourbon into the three glasses.

"Dev isn't who she wants."

Gabe snorted as he took his drink. "Yeah, well, not my problem."

"Until she moves in here." Lucian leaned against the bar. "You think she's going to magically stop trying to jump on your dick?"

The image those words provoked curled Gabe's lip. "She's out of her mind if she thinks going down that road with me is going to be successful."

Lucian tipped his glass to Gabe.

Pulling his phone out of his pocket, Gabe checked the app for the alarm system at his workshop. It hadn't been turned off, which meant Nic hadn't been there yet.

She hadn't come to the shop since he took her there on Wednesday, but she did take the kit and a piece of wood with her when they left.

As he sat there, swirling the amber liquid around in his glass, he wondered what Nic was up to. Was she out in the Quarter? It was a Saturday night, and he doubted she was sitting at home.

Hell, what was he doing sitting at home?

He'd gotten a text earlier in the evening from one of the women he usually crossed paths with at the Red Stallion. Alyssa was always down for a good time, no strings attached. Normally, he would've responded—he would've dragged his ass down there. That would be the smart thing to do.

Except he had no interest in going to the bar.

He had no interest in seeing Alyssa.

"Have you paid any more mind to what Troy said to you about the car?" Lucian asked.

He'd paid a lot of mind to it. "We've all pissed off people, but for someone to know where I was and to do that? I don't know who that could be."

"So you think it was a kid then?"

He lifted a shoulder. "Don't know. I just don't think it has anything to do with Nic. She hasn't been home in four years and who'd be pissed enough at her to do that?"

"Not you," his brother replied smoothly.

Gabe ignored that comment.

Lucian was quiet for a moment. "You don't think it has anything to do with the Rothchilds?"

The question jolted him. "You think they threw something through my car window?"

"Not them, but maybe someone they hired." Lucian shrugged. "You have the potential to change their life and not in a way they're going to like. I know it sounds crazy that they'd be involved, but we've seen crazier."

It was crazy, but Lucian was also right. They'd seen crazier. "I don't think it's them. It would be stupid if so. I'm not being the bad guy with them. I've been more than reasonable."

"That you have been, but . . ." Lucian trailed off.

He didn't need to finish his thought. Gabe knew what he was thinking. People were truly capable of anything.

Gabe was finishing off the glass of bourbon when Dev made his grand appearance, raising both of Gabe's brows. Dev's normally pressed, wrinkle-free shirt was half untucked. There was a red mark along the left side of his face.

"Whoa." Lucian slid the third untouched glass toward Dev. "Looks like you've had an interesting visit with Sabrina."

Dev snorted as he picked up the glass, downing the drink in one gulp.

"Did she hit you?" Gabe asked. Sure, Sabrina had a habit of throwing stuff—usually whatever was the most expensive within grabbing distance, but hitting?

Dev lowered the glass to the bar. "Let's just say her tantrum reached an all-new high."

"Or low, depending on how you look at it," Lucian suggested. "I have got to ask this. Why are you marrying her, Dev?"

Sitting on the stool next to Gabe, Dev folded his arms on the bar. "Why not?"

Gabe looked at his older brother. "That's not exactly the best answer to give to that question."

His brother shrugged. "Their company could be a valuable asset down the road."

"Wow," Gabe murmured. "And some say romance is dead."

Lucian snickered. "We don't need their company. We have more money than any future generations could ever hope for."

Dev didn't say anything as he focused on the shelves behind the bar. "The labels aren't facing the same direction."

Gabe followed his gaze. He was right. Some were cock-eyed.

"That would be Nikki." Dev sighed. "I'm going to have to talk to her."

"About the bottles of whiskey not being straight?" Gabe's shoulders tensed. "Are you fucking serious?"

Dev's gaze slid to his. "No. But that's a bit of a strong reaction."

Gabe ignored that comment. "What do you want to talk to her about?"

"How she talks to Sabrina."

Sitting back on the stool, Gabe held Dev's stare. "And how does she talk to Sabrina that Sabrina wouldn't be deserving of?"

"It doesn't matter what Sabrina deserves. She's to become my wife, and Nikki needs to respect that—respect her."

"Kind of hard to respect someone who treats you like a servant," Gabe fired back.

"Last I checked, that *is* Nikki's job. At least for right now." Dev motioned for Lucian to refill his drink. "Nikki might not be a permanent staff here, but when she's here, she needs to act as such."

"Exactly what is Sabrina bitching about?" Lucian asked, pouring the bourbon. "I've seen Nikki around her. She usually keeps quiet and ignores Sabrina's incessant insults."

"Except when she poured champagne on her," Dev commented.

Gabe's lips twitched. "That was an accident."

"You and I both know that wasn't an accident."

"That happened weeks ago."

Dev picked up his glass again. "Apparently Nikki made a snide comment to Sabrina's brother about there not being a date for the wedding. This upset Sabrina, which led to her little meltdown tonight."

Gabe's eyes narrowed. When would Nic have seen Parker? He'd thought back to Wednesday. Parker had been here, and Nic had been awfully quiet in the car ride to the workshop.

"I'll talk to Nic," Gabe said.

"Is that so?" murmured Dev.

"I think that's a good idea," Lucian chimed in. "Better than you talking to her."

"And why is that?" Dev asked.

"Because you're an asshole," Lucian replied, grinning. "And Nikki stepped in to help her mom—who has cancer. The last thing that girl needs is you lecturing her on how to speak to her 'betters.'"

"The last thing she needs is you speaking to her at all." Gabe folded his arms. "I'll make sure she stays away from both Sabrina and Parker. I'll handle her."

Dev's lips curled in a semblance of a smile around the rim of his glass. "You know what I think, Gabe?"

"Can't wait to hear this."

He took a sip and then looked at him. "I think the last thing you need is to be *handling* Nikki in any sense of the word."

Chapter 16

Sunday afternoon, Nikki stood in the center of the small room Gabe had put together for her. In her arms, she cradled the woodcarving kit and the block of wood she had taken home with her on Wednesday.

It had been ages since she'd done anything of the sort, so she'd used the block of wood as a practice run, like she'd done when Gabe had first taught her how to use the carving tools.

She'd carved a crescent moon into the block of raw wood, surprised by how much easier it had been once she got going. It didn't matter how much time had passed. Her fingers knew what to do the moment she sat down with the chisel.

Nikki placed the moon on the desk. Maybe she'd cut it out later, but what she really wanted to do was make her mom a bracelet. She saw it in her head already, six long beads to represent each cycle of treatment she'd receive . . . and survive.

And when her mom finished her last cycle, Nikki planned on giving her the bracelet.

Walking around to the neatly stacked pile of wood, she picked up a section of wood and then grabbed the Dremel tool. Tapping on the music app on her phone, she sat down behind the desk and got to work.

Nikki had no idea how much time passed. The special thing about working with her hands, concentrating on evening out the centers, was that she didn't think—she didn't stress. She didn't obsess over Gabe, worry about her mom, or stress over Parker's not-so-veiled threat. Her mind went blissfully blank while she worked, and God, she had no idea how much she'd missed that until she was sitting behind the desk Gabe had obviously made with his own hands.

So caught up in what she was doing, she didn't realize she had company until there was a soft knock on the open door.

Looking up, she wasn't all that surprised to see Gabe standing there. "Hey," he said, grinning. "Good afternoon."

"Hi." She lowered the Dremel. "I hope you don't mind that I'm here."

"Of course not. I told you that you could use this place whenever you wanted." He leaned against the doorjamb. "I'm happy to see you in here."

Her stomach dipped, and she thought about what Rosie said yesterday. *I think you need to read into it.* Her breath caught. "Thank you again for this."

He shrugged. "It's no big deal."

Gabe had said that before, but it was a big deal to her. Even if he hadn't been keeping the spare wood for her over the past years, this still meant a lot.

"What are you working on?" he asked.

"A bracelet for my mom." She bit down on her lip and she glanced at the two beads she'd finished. "Not sure what color I'm going to paint them, but I think I'm going to try to carve roses in them. It's her favorite flower."

"That's going to be tricky."

"It will be, but thanks to you, I have the perfect tools." She brushed the fine layer of dust off her hands. "What are you up to?"

"Thought I'd swing by and do some work." He pushed away from the door. "Have you eaten yet?"

Nikki shook her head. "No."

"Want to grab something to eat?" he offered. "There's this diner right down the street. They have amazing wings."

Now her heart was joining in with her stomach. *It's just lunch*, she told herself as she nodded. "Yeah, um, let me grab my stuff."

Gabe waited for her as she snatched her phone off the desk and grabbed her purse. She headed out of the office, brushing past Gabe in the process. The slight touch of her arm against his was a shock to the system, sending sharp tingles all through her body.

Arousal, swift and sharp, swept over her, leaving her a little breathless and, oh Lord, turned on. Her stomach felt weird. Her breasts were heavy, and acute throbbing picked up between her thighs.

Okay, she needed to get out more, and like, meet people, because seriously, her body was ridiculous if brushing against his *arm* could turn her on.

"You okay?" Gabe stopped in front of the front door.

Not really. She felt flushed . . . and stupid. "Yeah, I just need to eat."

"Then let's do that before you pass out."

As he turned around, she closed her eyes and pictured herself punching herself in the face. Repeatedly.

The diner was just down the block, like he said, and after getting seated near a window, Nikki felt an ungodly amount of nervous energy as Gabe ordered a water and she went for a sweet tea.

Her gaze kept darting from his face to the street outside. Part of her couldn't believe she was sitting here with Gabe. If anyone had asked her if that was possible a year ago she would've laughed straight in their face.

"By the way, there is something I want to talk to you about," he said, drawing her attention. "I think it would be really smart of you to stay as far away from Sabrina and her brother as humanly possible."

"What?" She frowned. "That's a really random statement, and you know I would rather be on the moon during a solar eclipse than be in the same room with them."

"On the moon during a solar eclipse?" he repeated quietly and then shook his head. "Sabrina complained to Dev about you."

Her stomach dropped. "About what?"

"About you making some kind of comment to her brother about their lack of a wedding date."

Fucking Parker. Her hands balled into fists. "I *hate* him."

Gabe watched closely. "Hate's a pretty strong feeling."

"Yeah, well, I hate him. He's arrogant and when I said that to him, I wasn't saying it to be an ass." She stopped herself. "Okay. I was being an ass, but whatever."

His lips twitched at the last part. "When did you see Parker?"

"On Wednesday, when he was there for dinner. He came into the kitchen for a drink."

Understanding crept in his face. "What happened on Wednesday?"

The urge to tell him what Parker had said to her was strong, but she knew if she did, Gabe would say something to him and then Parker would complain to Sabrina. Based on what Gabe was now telling her about Devlin, Sabrina would go to Devlin, and she couldn't jeopardize her parents' employment.

"Nothing happened."

"Doesn't sound like nothing."

"He was just being his normal jerk self." She drew in a shallow breath. "I'll be on my best behavior."

"Not sure you have a best behavior." He grinned.

It took her a moment to realize he was teasing her. "I do. Sometimes. But promise me you won't say anything to Parker. You know if you do, it will just make the situation worse."

"Is there a situation that can be made worse?" His voice turned so cold that she shivered.

"No. There's not, but if you say something to him, then

there will be a situation. Promise me you won't say anything."

"I promise I won't, but I also want you to promise me that if there *is* a situation, you'll be honest with me."

"I promise—wait." Disappointment sparked to life in her. She remembered the conversation in the car the day he tried to go to the shelter with her. "Is that why you asked me to lunch? To talk about me being nicer or whatever to Sabrina?"

"No." He frowned. "I asked you to lunch because I wanted to have lunch with you. I could've waited to talk to you about Sabrina tomorrow."

"Oh." He had a point.

"So, did you do anything exciting with your weekend?" he asked, changing the subject.

"Not really." She toyed with the edge of the menu. "I met with Rosie yesterday at du Monde and ate my weight in beignets. How about you?"

He grinned. "Just spent time at home." He paused. "I'm surprised you didn't go out or something."

"Why?" She smiled when the waitress appeared with their drinks. They placed an order for wings, her earning a look of disapproval when she asked for hers to be naked while Gabe went with some flavor guaranteed to burn the roof of his mouth off.

"I just remember what it was like when I was in my twenties," he said after the waitress left. "This city was like one giant playground."

She laughed. "You make it sound like that was ages ago."

"It was."

"Did you also walk to school in one foot of snow, barefoot?" she teased, and he chuckled. "I haven't really been going out since I've been home."

Interest sparked in his eyes. "Did you go out a lot when you were up at UA?"

Nikki shook her head, unsure of how to explain that

she didn't have the stereotypical college experience. "You know, I actually didn't go out a lot there either."

"You were a dedicated student?" he teased.

She laughed. "Not quite. I just . . ."

"What?"

Looking out the window, she watched a woman walk by pushing a stroller. Instead of answering, she shrugged.

A moment passed, and she could feel his intense gaze on her. "Can I ask you a question and you be real with me?"

Her heart turned over heavily as she looked at him. "Sure."

Gabe had leaned forward, resting his arms on the table. "You weren't holding back on doing things because of what happened between us, were you?"

Damn. He'd connected those dots way too quickly for her comfort. Granted, they talked about her life at college before and she'd always skated around the whole dating and partying scene.

"Fuck," he muttered, sitting back. He looked out the fingerprint-smudged window. A muscle ticked along his jaw. "I hate knowing that's the case. I always figured you'd go buck wild at college, probably burn a building down or two."

She didn't know what to say at first. "It wasn't just that. I'm serious. You know I was a weird, awkward kid. I was still weird and awkward in college. So what? I didn't date a lot—"

"But you had a boyfriend?"

"Yeah. And he was a good guy."

"Then what happened?" His gaze had swung back to her, and his eyes were more blue than green today. "If he was a good guy, why aren't you still with him?"

This wasn't exactly the conversation she planned on having with him, like, ever. "I wasn't . . . the easiest girlfriend to have."

"Do tell?"

She rolled her eyes. "I just wasn't really . . . open. Like he really tried and he was patient, but I wasn't there for it."

"I'm not following."

Of course he wasn't. "Okay, so like we'd make plans, and I'd always forget about them. It wasn't on purpose. I was just not thinking about it. He'd want to go out—like to the movies and do dinner, and I wasn't really interested. I used to think it was because I was a homebody, but I just didn't want to go out with him—with anyone really. Because when he would come chill with me at my dorm, I was just annoyed with him being there. No matter what he did."

"Damn." He tapped a finger on the table. "That's kind of harsh."

She shifted in the booth, uncomfortable. "Yeah. Pretty much. He ended up calling me out on it, after I kind of forgot our anniversary. One year. And I forgot."

"Shit, that's got to be awkward."

"It was. Especially when he asked me if I loved him, and I couldn't answer him. I mean, I could, but it wasn't what he wanted to hear. That's when he broke up with me."

He seemed to mull that over. "Sounds like you didn't really want to be with him."

"I don't think I did."

"Then why were you?"

"Honest? God. This is embarrassing to admit, but I didn't want to be alone and I wanted to be . . . normal. Like everyone else was hooking up or in a relationship and there I was, sitting around like a dork."

"And you didn't go out with other people?" he asked and when she shook her head, disbelief crept into his face. "Hooked up?"

This conversation just kept getting worse and worse. How could she explain that she had been scared to go out and experiment? To let loose and have fun? Or that it was more than that and even hard for her to understand?

Nikki couldn't just hook up. God, she wished she could. It sounded fun and freeing and *normal* by societal standards, but she had to be into someone on a deeper level to want to have sex with them. Hookups usually didn't allow for that. "This is such an awkward conversation. Seriously."

"If you can't talk about it, you shouldn't be doing it."

"Shut up."

He was leaning forward again. "You guys—"

"Are you seriously asking if Calvin and I had sex?" she asked, voice low.

He tilted his head. "Yes. I was going to say fuck, but having sex sounds more . . . tame."

Nikki flushed to the roots of her hair. "Not like that's any of your business, but yeah, we did."

His eyes latched onto hers. "Was he the only person besides me?"

"Oh my God." She pressed back against the booth. "I can't believe you're asking me this question. I honestly cannot believe it."

"Well, believe it, because I am. Have you slept with anyone else?"

Nikki gaped at him. "I am not answering that question."

One side of his lips kicked up. "And why not?"

"You seriously don't know why?" Popping forward in her seat, she gripped the edge of the table. "Okay. I'm done talking about me. Let's talk about you."

His eyes narrowed.

"Whatever happened between you and that chick you dated when you were in college? The one you were in love with?" She watched him pull back, satisfied and annoyed. "What was her name? Emma?"

His expression hardened. "We're not talking about that."

The annoyance was now outweighing the satisfaction of putting him in his place. "Well, now you know how it feels to be on the receiving end of those kinds of questions."

"It's different."

"Really?" She cocked her head to the side. "How so?"

"Because I loved her and you didn't love this guy."

Nikki sucked in a sharp breath. There. He said what she always suspected about the girl he dated in college. He had loved her. And because she was a grade-A idiot, she asked, "Do you still love her?"

Gabe looked away, his shoulders tense. A heartbeat passed, and something . . . something inside of Nikki, near the vicinity of her useless heart, cracked a little, and that was insane, because it proved that he still held a place there.

"I will always love her."

THE LUNCH HAD fallen apart after that.

Neither of them really said much of anything and the walk back was about as fucking awkward as a damn monkey trying to fuck a football.

Gabe couldn't believe she brought up Emma.

Hell, his brothers knew better than to go there. Well, except Lucian, but he knew when to shut the hell up about her.

But Nic?

She'd flat out asked him the one question that not even Lucian had the balls to ask. She may not know his whole history with Emma, but Nic was observant. She saw enough to know that was a no-go with him.

And fuck him if he hadn't answered it honestly.

What he said was true. A part of him would always love Emma and that fact ate at him—had been eating at him for years.

Unable to sit and work like he planned, he left Nic at the workshop, got in his car, and drove. Without realizing it, he found himself pulling into Metairie Cemetery. Parking alongside the manicured green lawns, he climbed out and started walking, making his way past the famous pyramid as a light breeze stirred the trees above, sending leaves floating to the ground.

He wasn't alone.

People strolled past him. Some were tourists. Others were there visiting tombs of their loved ones. Cemeteries were a big deal in New Orleans. They were old, but even the newer ones were busy. There were always people dying, always people grieving. A lot of money was spent on the dead.

Gabe cut between a row of tombs. Up ahead, he saw the tall mausoleum, guarded by not one but two weeping angels.

Back in the day, the de Vincents used the crypt that was on the back of the property, nearer the swamp. He wasn't sure why the family started burying people at Metairie. Probably because the family crypt on their property couldn't keep up with all the deaths.

This was where his grandmother was buried, along with several aunts and uncles. The man that raised him, the man he always believed was his father, was here, along with his mother.

And after Madeline, his sister, had died, for real this time, she had been interred privately. An endeavor that had cost Dev a lot of money to keep quiet.

Madeline would've killed him—killed all of them—but she was still family. Fucked-up family, but family nonetheless. She hadn't been placed next to their mother.

Hell no.

Gabe stepped to the side and sat down on the bench. Squinting in the sunlight, he reached inside his pocket and pulled out his phone. Scrolling through his contacts, he hit Call and lifted the phone to his ear.

Samuel Rothchild answered on the third ring, and like always, the man was as blunt as a fingernail. "You said you'd give us three months. You're just now coming up on a month."

Felt longer than that. "I'm not going back on the promise I made you."

There was a beat of silence. "Then why are you calling, Gabriel?"

His jaw hardened as he closed his eyes. "I wanted to check and see how everyone is doing."

"Everyone is fine," was the clipped response.

Gabe sighed. "I know you don't like me and I know you're worried about what I'm going to do. I get that. But I have a right to make this phone call. I have the right to a lot more, Samuel."

"Five years, Gabriel."

"Yeah, five years of me not having a single clue." Irritation filled his tone as he opened his eyes. "You can't forget that. You can't put that on me. If I'd known, I'd have been there five years ago."

There was another pause of silence. "I know. That's what scares us."

Jaw working, he shook his head as he lifted his gaze to the clouds slowly drifting across the sky. "How is he?"

There was a heavy sigh. "He's doing good. Has a bit of a cold, but nothing serious."

Gabe's hand tightened on his phone. "Shit. You're sure it's just a cold?"

"Just a cold." Samuel's voice softened a bit. "He was asking about you. Wanted to know when you were coming back."

That was a damn sucker punch to his chest. "And what did you tell him?"

"I told him you had business to attend to, but you would be back," he replied. "Didn't lie to him."

"Thank you." There was so much he wanted to say, but pressure clamped down on his chest, shutting off those words, leaving the only thing he could say. "Take care of my son, Samuel."

Chapter 17

*G*abe knew she was probably expecting things to be awkward between them after their lunch, and he couldn't blame her, especially how it ended, but when he saw her on Monday, he made it a point to not act like a jackass.

Seemed to work, because even though she was a little stiff around him at first, she loosened up and relaxed.

The smoothie and chocolate chip cookie he brought her probably helped smooth things over.

And when she mentioned that she was thinking about going to the workshop in the evening, after work, he'd been . . . interested in hearing that. With a busy afternoon, he wasn't able to get to the shop himself until after dinner. It *conveniently* worked out.

So there they sat Tuesday evening, working almost side by side as the traffic from outside hummed in the background.

Gabe had new orders to work on. One being a wine rack to match a cabinet he'd done for the governor a few years back. While that was a smaller piece, it required more time due to the design. He'd cut the frame yesterday and pieced it together.

"How's your mother doing?" he asked, realizing he hadn't asked about her in a bit.

Nic looked up from where she sat cross-legged on the floor instead of at the desk. He kind of liked that about her. "She's doing okay, but . . ." She drew in a deep breath as she stared down at the bead she was working on. "She's really worn out. The treatment is taking a lot out of her."

Concern for the woman who was basically a second mom to him rose. "She's a really strong woman, though."

"I know, but I don't think it matters how strong anyone is." She bit down on her lower lip. "Her white cell count dropped and they had to give her a booster shot before they could continue with the chemo."

"Did the shot work?"

She nodded. "Yeah, it did."

He could see the worry etched into her face, and he wanted to ease some of her concern, but he knew that all he had for her were words. "She'll be okay."

Nic peeked up again. "You think so?"

"I do." Well, he hoped so. He really fucking did.

A smile appeared, and damn, she went from gorgeous to mind-numbingly beautiful in a nanosecond. Nothing about her in that moment reminded him of the Nic who grew up following him around.

Nothing about her reminded him of Emma.

Hell.

He really had no idea where that thought came from, but that's what made its way through his head.

Nic went back to work on her bead, and companionable silence fell between them as they worked. It had never been like that with anyone. Not even Lucian who often joined him. His brother wasn't quiet for more than a few minutes at a time, but Nic . . . well, she knew what it was like to get lost in the hum of a saw or the nick of a blade. That was rare.

Could he see himself sitting here with—

He cut himself off and then . . . and then he forced himself to finish that question. Could he see himself sitting here with Emma like this?

No.

Not at all.

Emma was quiet, but it came from an inherent nervousness more than anything else. She liked to mull over everything she'd do or say, so she'd been prone to long stretches of silence. Not the companionable kind like this. Gabe knew that when Emma was quiet, it meant she was thinking hard about something and working up the nerve to discuss it. He used to think that was cute about her. Except toward the end—toward the end it just pissed him off, because he knew she was thinking a lot of shit that had to do with him instead of talking to him.

But with Nic? He knew she was lost in what she was doing at the moment. Whatever was going on in her head was going in and out. She wasn't over there plotting out an entire conversation that she might get around to bringing up a week from now.

So, yeah, he couldn't see himself sitting here with Emma, even when things had been good between them.

Gabe had no idea what the hell that meant, but he felt like an ass for how he shut down the conversation about Emma with Nic.

Normally he wouldn't care. He didn't talk about Emma, but with Nic, it felt different, wrong not to somehow. Maybe it was because he and Nic shared something as messed up as he'd once shared with Emma.

For the first time in his life, he felt the urge to talk about Emma—to talk to someone about her.

He lowered the rack he was working on. "When we went to lunch, you brought up Emma."

Nic looked up and the centers of her cheeks flushed. "Yeah, I'm sorry about that. It was—"

"Don't apologize. You didn't do anything wrong. That was all me being an ass. Not you."

She lowered her hands, but didn't say anything as she stared at him from where she sat.

He drew in a deep breath, his gaze falling to his now-empty hands. "Do you remember Emma? She came home with me one Christmas. You were there one of those days."

"I remember," she said after a long moment. "She was really nice."

"Yeah." Gabe nodded slowly. "She was. Sometimes too nice. Like you."

"I don't think you'd believe I'm 'too nice' if you knew what I was thinking about people half the time."

A wry grin tugged at his mouth. "You're still nice. Just like Emma. She was . . . she was a good person. To the heart. Anyone who met her couldn't have a bad thing to say about her. Lucian thought the world of her. Even Dev liked her."

"Why did you guys break up?" Nic asked. "I mean, it was obvious when you guys were dating, you were in love with her."

That was a loaded question, one with an answer that he didn't want resting on Nic's shoulders. "During our senior year, there was a party. I wasn't there. Can't even remember why I didn't go, but . . . Emma got hurt."

"What do you mean . . . she got hurt?"

He looked over at her as his hands closed into fists. "A guy she was friends with didn't understand the word no."

"Oh, God," she whispered, blanching.

Helpless anger rose in him as he looked away. "She didn't want to go to the police. I wasn't exactly thrilled with that decision but I respected her choice. That was her right and I supported it while trying to get her to go to the police, but—" he shook his head "—I confronted him. Things happened, and our relationship fell apart after that."

He hadn't heard Nic move, but he sensed that she was closer, and when he looked up, she was now sitting down on the dusty floor beside him. Those doe-eyes were heavy and somber. "I cannot even imagine what she was going through," she said. "I'm so sorry."

Gabe's gaze flickered over her face. "I couldn't either. I tried, and I think—no, I *know* I made things worse when I did try."

Her head tilted to the side as she placed a hand on his

arm. "There's not a manual for how to handle these kinds of things, Gabe. You can't be too hard on yourself."

He laughed, but it was harsh and brittle. If she only knew what he and his brothers had done, she would be singing another tune. Hell, she wouldn't want to be in the same room with him let alone touching him.

"So, that's why you guys broke up?" She squeezed his arm, and the touch, well, it was supposed to be comforting but it sent mixed sensations through him.

Clearing this throat, he nodded. "We did. Fucking killed me. I loved her, but she needed space and I think I did, too. In the back of my head, I always figured we'd come back together. I mean, when you love someone and they love you, things just find a way to work, right?"

"Right," she whispered, pulling her hand away as she settled on her knees.

He dragged a hand over his head, loosening the strands he had pulled back. "About five years ago, I was at this charity event. Didn't even want to go, but Lucian connived me into it." A faint smile crossed his lips. "And there she was. Years later, there she was."

"What happened?"

The best and the worst thing, he supposed. "We got caught up, you know? Talked and ended up spending the whole weekend together, but she had her own life in Baton Rouge and I had mine."

Something flickered across her face. "Baton Rouge?"

"Yeah, anyway. That was it." He rose, picking up one of his tools and walking it over to the table. "We had a weekend, and I never heard from her again. Tried calling her, but she didn't answer. Obviously, she didn't want me back in her life. That was a bitter fucking pill to swallow, because that weekend proved that I still loved her." He tossed the tool on the table. "And then my phone rang three months ago."

Nic was quiet, so quiet that he turned to her. She wasn't

watching him, but staring into the space he'd been sitting in. She was so incredibly still.

"It wasn't her," he said. Her head turned and her eyes met his. "It was her father. Emma had been in a car accident and it was bad. She was in a coma and they . . . they thought I should know."

Nic placed her hand to her mouth.

"I went up there. She was in the hospital, in that bed, and it didn't even look like her." His stomach filled with acid. "As I sat beside her, while she was in the damn bed, all I could think about was everything I never told her. I thought about how I'd made things worse when she was at her most vulnerable. I sat there hating myself and . . . fuck, hating her for never returning my call, because there weren't going to be any more chances."

Truth was, he'd already known that before he'd gotten that call. Could they have gotten back together? Who knew, but it was unlikely. Not when he learned about the secret she'd been keeping from him.

Some things could be forgiven.

Some things couldn't.

"She was in a coma when I got there, and . . ." He exhaled roughly, rubbing at the center of his chest with the palm of his hand. "There was no brain activity. So many tests were done. None of them gave a glimmer of good news or hope. She was gone, and her parents were left with the decision to pull her off life support. They did it about a week after I went up there."

Then he said the two words he hadn't spoken in these months. The words that haunted him, because of everything that had been left unsaid between them—because of those five years between now and the last time he saw her, because of what he did that drove them apart. "Emma's dead."

Nikki sat in her parents' living room, watching the steady rise and fall of her mother's chest. Her mother had been asleep on the couch when she got home, and her father hadn't had the heart to wake her up. He was now shuffling around in the kitchen, doing Lord knows what. The house was comfortable, but her mother was bundled up under several soft blankets.

Nikki had read that one of the many side effects of chemo was feeling cold. Not everyone felt that. Some only experienced it when they were receiving chemo, but her mom seemed to get this side effect, among others.

She looked away as she sat back in the old recliner, pulling her legs up so her knees pressed into her chest.

Emma was dead.

That had been a shock to Nikki. She'd always assumed that Emma was still alive. And when he said Baton Rouge, she automatically and understandably assumed that was why he was looking for a place there.

Because Emma was there.

But Emma was . . . she was dead.

Wrapping her arms around her legs, she rested her chin on her knees and closed her eyes. Gabe and Emma reconnected five years ago. A year before she left for college, and if she really thought hard about it, Gabe had definitely been moodier during that time, staying home and drinking more. The only time he'd seemed to be like his old self was when he was working.

And the morning after she'd come to him, before he'd been fully awake, he'd called her Emma. He'd been in love with Emma then and there was still a part of him that was in love with her now.

Nikki was . . . she was happy that he'd confided in her. It was obvious that Gabe needed to talk to someone, and she almost couldn't believe it was her. That was a huge deal. A big one, and God help her, she couldn't stop the sorrow rising and she couldn't stop the feeling of disappointment.

And she knew that the latter signaled something in her that was just like Gabe. He'd spent how many years thinking he and Emma would find their way back to one another? She really was no different than Gabe. Even as foolish and pointless and utterly hopeless as it was, there was still a part of her that . . . that cared for him more than she should.

That wasn't breaking news, though.

But if the conversation today proved anything to her, she needed to do exactly what Rosie had said, which was to proceed with caution.

Gabe wasn't still in love with a woman who didn't want him. He was in love with a ghost, and no one could compete with that.

Chapter 18

*G*abe was watching Nic.

Again.

He was doing that a lot lately. So much so, he was beginning to wonder if he had a problem. It was Thursday night and it was getting late. She should be on her way home soon since it wasn't like she lived around the corner.

Maybe he'd start bringing her here after work and then dropping her off on the way home. It would be safer that way. Smarter. He should definitely offer that to her.

He thought about what her father would think of that, and instead of cringing, he grinned at the thought.

Something . . . something had changed in Gabe after talking to Nic about Emma. As fucking cliché as it sounded, he felt lighter.

Lucian was right when he said that maybe Gabe needed to talk about Emma. The last couple of nights he actually slept the whole way through. Freaking miracle right there.

Nic was looking around, the corners of her lips turned down. Then her gaze swept up to the shelving against the back wall. Setting the bead and chisel aside, she rose, dusting her hands off.

"Is that the saw up there?" She pointed at the top shelf.

"Yeah. You need it?"

She crossed the room. "I can get it."

Swallowing a laugh, he rose from where he sat. There was no way she was going to reach that shelf. Not when she was compact size basically.

But there she was, stretching up on the tips of her toes, straining for the handle of the saw as she gripped one of the lower shelves.

"You're going to end up pulling that whole shelf down on you." He walked over to her. "Here." He reached around her at the same time she settled back on her feet.

Gabe didn't know what happened.

One second he was reaching for the saw and then the next, his front was against her back as she stumbled into him.

"Whoa," he said, his hand landing on her hip.

In an instant, the air around them seemed to spit fire. For what felt like an eternity, neither of them moved, and then Nic shifted, pressing her rear against him.

Sweet Jesus.

His jaw clenched as pure primal lust pounded through his veins. Did she do that on purpose? Hell if it mattered. He looked down at her, seeing her chest rise and fall heavily, straining against the front of her shirt. His head dipped and he inhaled deeply, catching the strawberry scent of hers.

Christ.

His body practically surrounded hers, but her mere closeness overpowered him. He should back off. He should definitely get his hand off her damn hip.

He didn't do either of those things.

His thoughts clouded as the smallest shudder coursed through her. Gabe's brain clicked off. His hand tightened on her hip as his arm flexed, tugged her back with just the slightest amount of pressure. Fuck. His blood caught fire. She fit perfectly against him. Better yet, she *felt* perfect against him.

Took no effort to picture himself spinning her around and bending her over the bench. Except nothing would be between them as he slipped his hand between her thighs and pounded into—

Holy fuck, that line of thought was not helping. At all.

But could she feel him? How fucking hard he was against the cleft of her ass?

Then he felt her shiver. Full-bodied shiver. Her head turned to the side, and he waited for her to pull away or push him away. To do something. She didn't. Nic stood there while her ass practically cradled his dick, letting him . . .

Letting him do what exactly?

Dry-hump her ass? Gabe swallowed a groan, because right about now that sounded amazing. And when was the last time he dry-humped a woman? Shit. When he was a teen? Hell, he knew there was a good chance he could come doing just that.

He felt her take her next breath. "Have you . . . got the saw yet?"

His eyes drifted shut. So, they were going to pretend like his dick wasn't pressing against her ass? All right. He could do that. He could pretend. "Not yet."

She placed her hands on the lower shelf, and yeah, he realized right then, he wouldn't need to turn her around. He could make this work just as well. "Do you need help?"

Yeah, he needed help.

Primal instinct told him that she would let him do just about anything right then, and that instinct had nothing to do with their past. Not a damn thing.

Nic's hips moved again, this time in the smallest damn circle, and he had to wonder if she was even aware she was doing it or what it was doing to him.

He needed to stop this before he fucking came in his jeans.

His hand tightened on her hip as he reached up, grabbing the saw off the top shelf. He let himself have one more moment, one more breath of the air she breathed, and then he started to act like he had at least an ounce of common decency left in him.

"Sorry," he bit out, voice gruff as he backed off. "Lost my balance there."

"It's okay." Her face was ten different shades of pink as she faced him. She lifted her hand. It trembled. "Thank you."

He nodded as he turned and made his way back to the workbench. Sitting wasn't exactly what he wanted to be doing, but that's what he did.

Fuck.

He couldn't even pretend anymore—couldn't lie to himself.

It wasn't his dry spell that had him rocking a hard-on every time he was near Nic. It was her.

His gaze found its way to her.

Brushing a strand of hair out of her face, she glanced over and sent him a small, tentative smile as her fingers around the saw remained steady.

The little smile went straight to his cock.

He didn't smile back. He was beyond that. His entire body was taut and strained. He wanted *her.* Under him. On him. In front of him. On her knees. And with his head between her thighs. He wanted her every which way he could think and damn, he had an active imagination.

Lust, pure and simple, was a powerful drug.

He watched her go back to carving the tiny piece of wood. Would he go down that road with her?

Gabe didn't need to really ask himself that.

He already knew the answer.

LATER THAT NIGHT, Nikki lay in bed and stared at the ceiling, unable to sleep. Her body and mind were traitorous bitches, replaying the evening over and over again in her head.

My God, what had happened between them?

Something had. There was no denying what she felt pressed against her rear.

Her stomach twisted and lower, much lower, she *clenched* as she drew her legs up, bending at the knees.

Hours later and Nikki could still feel his hand on her hip. It was like he'd branded her with his touch. And the way his hand tightened and pulled her back?

"God," she whispered, pressing her thighs together. That did nothing to alleviate the ache building between her thighs. It actually made it worse. So much worse.

Gabe had to have known what he was doing. There was no way. Just like she'd known what she had been allowing by standing there, letting him press into her.

They both pretended like nothing was happening, but he'd wanted her. She could feel that. And oh Lordy Lord, as reckless and dumb as it made her, she wanted him *still*.

Badly.

Except now she at least had a working knowledge of what wanting him entailed. She might've only had sex with him and Calvin, but she knew what it could feel like.

The tips of her breasts hardened as she closed her eyes. Her thoughts got away from her, and she was back in that workshop with Gabe, all big and strong, standing behind her, pressing into her.

What if he'd pushed on her back, bending her over? Nikki sucked in a shallow breath. Would she have stopped him? She knew the answer as her hand slipped between the covers tangled at her waist. She wouldn't have stopped him. She would've spread her legs, just as she was doing now, giving him more access to do . . . to do whatever he wanted.

Her fingers inched under the band of her bottoms. She was wet. She already knew that as she touched herself. She'd been so wet just standing in front of him tonight, letting him . . .

Nikki's jaw clenched as she slipped a finger inside and pressed her palm against her most sensitive part.

Just a fantasy.

What she was doing meant nothing and she knew that there wasn't anything real between them, not when he was in love with a woman who was no longer here.

Just a fantasy.

In her mind, it was Gabe's hand replacing hers. It was his hand she was thrusting against, his fingers she was clenching around as he stood behind her, pressing his hardness into her as he worked her with his hand.

It didn't take long.

Muscles tightened and tension coiled deep in her core. Her legs locked as her fingers pumped faster and faster. She twisted, pressing her face into her pillow as she came.

Panting, she fell back against the mattress and opened her eyes. Moments passed as she pulled her hand away. Her legs were limp, but she still felt . . . empty.

She exhaled slowly. A part of her couldn't believe she just did that. Not like it was her first time, but she never let herself picture Gabe. Not after that night.

But it was just a fantasy and fantasies were okay. They were safe. Healthy even. Fantasies weren't real.

Chapter 19

It was Friday afternoon when Gabe entered the kitchen, his arrival like clockwork. In his hand, he carried what appeared to be a straight strawberry smoothie.

"Hey." Tossing the thick braid over her shoulder, she closed the fridge door and placed the pack of meat on the counter. "That for me?"

"Of course." He met her at the island, handing it over. "It's your favorite. Boring. But whatever."

"Boring is good." She grinned as she took the smoothie from him. Their fingers brushed. His were rough and sent a jolt up her arm. Nikki stepped back. She'd been careful not to touch him since the . . . *incident* at his workshop. "Thank you."

"No problem." He lowered his hand and backed off, hopping up on one of the stools. "So, what's for dinner?"

"You're actually joining Devlin?"

He lifted a shoulder. "Maybe."

She tugged the paper off the straw, tossing it into the trash. Gabe hadn't been attending dinner since the first week she'd been here. Lucian and Julia sporadically joined, but when they did, they got their own food. There hadn't been any more dinners that Nikki had been invited to.

"Lamb is on the menu." Glancing over her shoulder at the meat, she curled her lip. "Ew."

"Lamb is tasty." He spread his thighs, hooking his bare feet on the bottom of the stool.

She shook her head. "Lambs are too cute to eat."

A grin appeared as he pulled his phone out of his pocket, placing it on the island. "And I'm guessing you don't find cows cute, because you have no problem eating them. Or chickens."

"Cows and chickens are cute, but I choose to not think about them while I'm eating them." When he arched a brow, she grinned. "Don't question my logic."

"Would never dare to do so." He trailed a finger along the edge of the island. "So, you got any big plans this weekend?"

Actually she did.

And it wasn't finishing the beads for her mother's bracelet, either. Shocker. Her belly flipped and then flopped. "I'm going to look at an apartment later."

"You found one?" Genuine interest filled his tone.

She nodded, having kept him up to date on her apartment search. "It's nice and in a good area, just outside of the city. I hope it's the one. Don't get me wrong. I love being back with my parents, but living with them is not exactly what I thought I'd be doing when I'm about to turn twenty-three."

He grinned. "Well, I'm not going to judge. All of us are still living here, at the family home."

"That's different. This place is so big, a whole family could move in and you guys would never know," she reasoned, taking a sip of her smoothie. "Besides, you all have your own apartments. You don't have to see anyone unless you want to, where if I stay out past eleven I feel like I'm sixteen sneaking back into my parents' house."

Gabe laughed. "I'm crossing my fingers for you."

"Thanks."

"Got anything else planned?"

She did. Turning from Gabe, she took her smoothie back to the counter. "I . . . I have a date tomorrow night."

Silence.

Telling herself not to, she didn't listen and looked over

her shoulder at Gabe. His expression—yikes. His face was harsh. It kind of scared her. "Um, my friend Rosie set me up on a date."

His hand stilled along the kitchen island. "So, it's a blind date?"

"Yeah." She turned away and moved down a foot. Bending, she opened the cabinet and pulled out a large roasting pan.

"Is that safe?"

She kind of thought that was a weird question. "Rosie knows him, and I trust her. She wouldn't fix me up on a date with a creep."

"What's his name?" His tone was flat, like he didn't believe what she said, which was ridiculous, because he'd never met Rosie.

Though the idea of Rosie meeting any of the de Vincents made her grin. Especially Devlin.

"His name is Gerald." She placed the pan on the counter. "I doubt you know him."

"Gerald?" He laughed loudly. "What kind of name is that?"

She twisted at the waist, her brows lifting. "It's a name."

He smirked. "Sounds like an old man's name."

"You're an old man," she retorted.

"Not old enough to be named *Gerald*."

"Whatever." She rolled her eyes. "We're going to Crescent City."

"*Crescent City*?"

"There is nothing wrong with Crescent City. They have amazing steaks and I love their French fries."

"I'd at least take you to Morton's. You'd love their fries."

Her eyes narrowed. "Sorry. Morton's is not on most people's budget. Anyway, we're just grabbing dinner. So, whatever."

He was silent for the moment. "You don't sound very excited about your date with Gerald."

"I'm excited." That was the truth. Kind of. She was excited to go out and have a nice dinner and she was excited because she was meeting someone new. And after what happened between them at the shop, she *really* needed to meet someone.

Anyone other than him.

"Uh-huh."

Shaking her head, she walked over to the spice cabinet. It was time to change the subject. "What are you doing this weekend?"

"Working. Don't change the subject. I want to know more about Granddad Gerald."

"Oh my God," she laughed, turning around completely. "I'm pretty sure Gerald is my age, so knock it off, *Pappy*."

Those stunning eyes were sharp as they focused on her, and she realized in that very second, something had changed. She couldn't put her finger on it, but her senses were firing off left and right. "Didn't realize you were looking to be in a relationship."

"I didn't say I was."

He straightened. "Then why are you going out on a date?"

She stared at him, sort of struck speechless for a good half a minute. "Why do people go out on dates, Gabe?"

"To fuck?" he answered.

Whoa. That was not exactly where she was going with that train of thought, but hearing that come out of his mouth made her feel warm in areas that did not need to feel warm. At all. "I was going to say to meet new people, but I mean, I guess if that's what happens, it happens."

She had no idea if that would happen, but she knew she'd need to be into Gerald for that to go down, and she hoped she was.

His head tilted to the side. "So, you're looking for a hookup?"

"I'm not saying that I am actively seeking a hookup—"

"But you'd be down for it if Gerald is?"

"I thought we agreed on not having this conversation," she reminded him.

"I don't know what you think we agreed on. I want to talk about you and Gerald." He rose from the stool and crossed the kitchen, coming straight for her. "Do you even know what he looks like?"

"Um, yeah, Rosie showed me a picture." Her hand tightened on the bottle of cumin. "He's cute."

"Cute?" He stopped in front of her.

Nikki tilted her head back. "Yeah."

"Interesting." He stepped forward and his bare feet brushed her flats.

She pressed against the counter, still holding on to the stupid bottle of spice "I am not sure why you find any of this interesting."

Placing his hands on either side of her hips, he dipped his chin and suddenly their mouths were lined up. She sucked in a soft breath as her heart threatened to slam its way out of her chest.

"What are you doing?" she whispered.

"About to have an awkward conversation with you again."

"And that requires you to be all up in my personal space?"

"Yes." A small grin tipped his lips.

"I do not think that's the case."

He tilted his head slightly, and when he spoke, his breath danced over her lips, sending shivers down her spine. Did he realize how close their mouths were?

Better yet, was he out of his mind?

"You know what I can't picture?" he asked.

"I guess you're going to tell me."

Thick lashes lowered, shielding his eyes. "I am. Ready for it? I can't picture you hooking up with some guy named Gerald."

How mad would he get if she threw the cumin on him? "Is it because you think I'm still little Nikki?"

"Pretty sure I stopped seeing you as little Nikki about four years ago."

Her eyes widened. What did he just say?

"Back to my point. Do you know why I can't picture you hooking up with some guy named Gerald?"

"Why?" she whispered.

Gabe leaned in, brushing his nose against hers. Her chest rose sharply as she sucked in air. "That right there," he said. "That little inhale you just made. That's why."

A sweet and heady flush coursed down the front of her body. All she could think about was those brief moments at his workshop. Him pressed against her, his hand clenching her hip.

That had not been her imagination.

"I don't . . . I don't know what you're talking about," she said, swallowing hard.

"Yeah, you do." His nose brushed hers again, sending another tight wave of shivers throughout her body, and then he pulled back. "You sure you want to go out on that date?"

What date?

Breathing heavy, she watched him step away and then turn. He picked up her smoothie and took a long drink. She was about to ask him exactly what the hell he was up to, but the sound of heels drew her attention.

Freaking Sabrina entered the kitchen.

There were few stronger wake-up calls than seeing Sabrina Harrington. Her slim figure looked absolutely elegant in a pale-blue dress that complemented her skin tone. The icy-blonde hair was coifed back behind her ears, showing off glittering diamond earrings.

Parker's threat surfaced, and Nikki turned back to the lamb. Looking down at the spice in her hand, she wondered what the hell she planned on doing with it.

"I was looking for Devlin," Sabrina said.

"I don't know why you'd think Dev would be in the kitchen." Gabe placed the smoothie on the counter.

Out of the corners of her eyes, she could see him crossing his arms as he leaned against the counter.

"Well, you're in the kitchen, aren't you?" Sabrina's tone was thick and sweet like molasses.

"I live here."

Sabrina laughed, but Nikki wasn't sure what was so funny. "Devlin lives here, too. He could be in the kitchen."

"You obviously don't know the man if you think he's in here." Gabe's tone was flat, like it had been when he was pestering her about the date. "Did you need help with something?"

Nikki stepped around Gabe and opened the fridge, grabbing the fresh thyme she needed to cut up.

"That's sweet of you to offer." Sabrina's voice sounded closer.

Rolling her eyes as she picked up the cutting board, Nikki glanced over at Gabe. He arched a brow. Biting down on her lip to keep from smiling, she pulled the packaging off the herb. It was like she didn't even exist in the room and that was fine by her.

"I was hoping you could help me, actually," Sabrina said. "I brought this painting over that I wanted Devlin to hang in his office. Since I can't find him, could you help me?"

"Did you try looking for him in his office?"

"Of course." She laughed again, the sound grating. "I even looked for Mr. Besson, but I believe he must be on break."

Nikki picked up the knife.

"Richard has the afternoon off." He pushed away from the counter. "I'll help you."

"That's so kind of you."

Gabe's arm brushed hers. "We'll finish our conversation later."

Nikki said nothing as she nodded, because as far as she was concerned their conversation was already over.

Because her date was something she wasn't discussing with Gabe.

GABE WAS BARELY listening to Sabrina prattle on about whatever painting she had in her car as they walked out the front door, to where her red BMW was parked.

"It's in the backseat," she was saying. "It's a surprise for Devlin. Do you think you can hang it up for me?"

"I'll let Dev do the hanging. It's his office." He was careful to keep a good foot's worth of distance between them.

Sabrina opened the back door, and Gabe peered in. Was she for real? The painting was maybe a foot long and a foot wide. "You couldn't carry this?"

"It's heavier than it looks."

He bent in, easily picking up the wrapped painting with one hand. Without saying a word, he turned and started back to the house.

Sabrina hurried to catch up to him. "Please be careful."

"It's fine. I'll carry it to his office. You can wait for him in one of the sitting rooms."

"Wait for him like I'm a guest?" She placed a hand on Gabe's upper arm. "Darling, I'm going to be your sister-in-law soon. I don't need to wait in the sitting room like I'm a guest."

Shaking off her touch, he opened the front door. "Until you're married to him, you're a guest in this house."

He started for the stairs, but Sabrina darted in front of him. "While I have your attention, I thought there was something we needed to talk about."

"I don't think there is anything we need to talk about." It was a struggle to keep his tone even. "You want me to carry this upstairs? You're going to have to move."

Sabrina looked around before she stepped forward, lowering her chin in what Gabe could only guess was an attempt at looking demure. "Do you remember college? We used to be friends once."

"We were never friends, Sabrina."

"That's not true." She started to place her hand on his chest, but he stepped back, and her fingers closed around air. "Well, I suppose I was closer to Emma than you. Such a tragedy what happened to her then."

His jaw locked down. "How in the hell do you know about that?"

Sabrina's calculating gaze lifted to his. "Oh, you didn't realize that I knew what had happened to her?"

All he could do was stare at Sabrina.

She tsked softly. "What was his name again? Oh. I remember. Christopher Fitzpatrick. I do wonder what happened to him." She tilted her head to the side. "Didn't he . . . go missing? How convenient what happens to those who have gone against the de Vincent family or those they care about."

Chapter 20

Gabe slammed Dev's door shut behind him. His brother was there, behind the desk looking through some paperwork just before dinner on Friday night. "What in the hell does Sabrina know about Emma and Christopher Fitzpatrick?"

Arching a brow, Dev looked up. "That is a very random question."

"And you know what else is random?" Gabe stalked forward. "Your fiancée bringing up Emma and that bastard earlier."

A slight frown crossed Dev's face. "Sabrina shouldn't know anything about Christopher."

"Then why would she bring him up?"

"I really don't have an answer for that." Dev closed whatever file he was looking over. "Sabrina did know Emma. It's a good chance she said something to Sabrina."

"She barely knew Emma. I have no idea if she would've told Sabrina what happened to her, but I know damn well she never would've told her what happened to Christopher."

Dev was quiet for a moment. "Sabrina likes to sound like she knows things. I wouldn't pay any attention to it."

Gabe wasn't so sure about that. The way Sabrina had said what she said told Gabe that somehow Sabrina knew that Christopher Fitzpatrick wasn't simply a missing person.

"Since you're here—" Dev tossed the closed file across the desk "—you'll be happy to know that the investigation into our . . . into Lawrence's death has officially been closed."

Gabe picked up the file and opened it, flipping through what appeared to be copies of the police report Troy had filed and the autopsy report.

"They now believe that the scratches along his neck came from him possibly changing his mind," Dev said, sitting back and crossing one leg over the other. "Since there were no wounds or trauma, it has been officially ruled as a suicide."

Gabe closed the file and dropped it on the desk.

"And the new police chief sends his apologies over the inconvenience of them investigating the death," Dev continued, smiling slightly. "He's assured me that the case is truly closed."

"Even if Stefan continues to push it?"

"If Stefan has any hopes of retaining the Harringtons as donors, then he'll leave it alone." Dev glanced at his watch. "It's nearly time for dinner. Are you joining me?"

He nodded absently, his mind elsewhere. Neither he nor Lucian truly believed that Lawrence de Vincent killed himself and there was a reason they didn't speak of that suspicion to Dev.

Because there was only one person Gabe believed would've killed Lawrence, and it wasn't their sister Madeline.

Wondering if there was a cold draft in the office, Gabe turned. As he did, he noticed the painting he'd carried upstairs earlier. Dev hadn't hung it up, but it was propped against the credenza, unwrapped.

It was a painting of Sabrina.

A nude painting.

Jesus.

NIKKI COULDN'T REMEMBER the last time she laughed so much, but her stomach practically ached from doing so and their meal had just arrived.

Her date with Gerald wasn't going bad at all.

First off, Gerald was definitely as cute as he looked in the pic Rosie had showed her. Come to find out, contrary to Gabe's smartass mouth, Gerald wasn't very much older than her. Only six years. Definitely not in *Granddad Gerald* territory.

He was also funny as hell, and had a knack for telling stories.

And bonus points for the fact he looked nothing like Gabe. Not that she was thinking of Gabe while on her date with Gerald—not at all. Gerald was a blond and his hair was cropped short. He wasn't as tall or broad as Gabe, but he was taller than her. Well, most people were taller than her, but he would probably only come up to Gabe's shoulders—

Okay, so she was thinking about Gabe just a little bit.

"So," he said, picking up his glass. "Rosie was telling me you work for the de Vincents? Like *the* de Vincents?"

Her eyes widened slightly. Could he read minds? You never knew when it came to the people Rosie hung out with. "Temporarily. My parents have worked for them for years."

"Man, I bet you guys have seen and heard some stuff."

She stiffened. "Why do you think that?"

"Because of what they're called. Their nicknames the magazines use? What are they? Devil? Lucifer. There was one more—damn, I can't remember."

"Demon," she said, sighing. They called Gabe *Demon*. A weird need to protect them rose. "They really don't live up to those nicknames the papers give them."

"They don't?" He sounded surprised. "That's kind of disappointing. Sounds sort of badass to be called *Lucifer.*"

She wasn't so sure she agreed with that. "It's funny how the newspapers always focus on rumors and stupid stuff, but never on how much work they do for charities and the millions of dollars they donate."

"Well, people would rather read about scandals than good deeds."

Sad but true.

"And the de Vincents have had their fair share of scandal." He took a drink. "The thing with their father recently? Such a damn shame."

"It was," she murmured, wanting to change the subject. "So, you were telling me about Rosie wanting to investigate where you work or something?"

"Ah, yes." He laughed. "Rosie once convinced me to let her investigate the office building I work in."

"Oh, no." She grinned as she cut into her steak. Crescent City Steaks was packed on a Saturday night, with the waiters rushing back and forth between the tables. "I'm sure that didn't end well."

"It didn't. She brought this medium with her. Someone named Princess Silvermoon—"

"No way," gasped Nikki. "That was not her name."

He placed his hand to his chest. "Scouts' honor. That was her name. Princess Silvermoon."

Laughing, she took a drink of her wine. Scouts' honor. She liked that. It was cute. Everything about him was cute. He was actually perfect, but . . .

Nikki's smile faded.

But from the point they met outside, while they waited for their table, ordered the appetizers, and the main course, she waited for that *spark*. That undeniable attraction that wasn't just physical, but went beyond that.

The spark hadn't happened.

Yet.

"So, Princess Silvermoon walked through the first floor and did a reading of the place. She immediately said that there was a young girl there who died of one of the flu outbreaks. The girl ghost was looking for her—"

Her phone rang from inside her purse. Since everyone who would need to get ahold of her knew she was on a date, a kernel of concern blossomed.

"I'm sorry." She reached for her purse. "Do you mind if

I see who this is? My mother has been sick and I just want to make sure it's not an emergency."

"It's okay," he replied. "Totally fine."

Smiling, she reached inside her bag and tugged her phone out of its little pocket. Turning it over, she saw that it was a local number, but she didn't recognize it.

"Is it your family?"

She shook her head as she placed her phone back in her bag, draping the strap over the back of the chair. "No. I actually don't recognize the number. Must be a wrong number. So back to the ghost girl. What did she want?"

He smiled as he picked up his glass of water. "She was apparently looking for someone to play with."

"That's kind of sad." Nikki heard her phone beep like it received a text or voicemail, but she ignored it.

"It is, but then things got really weird when Silvermoon went upstairs. She claimed that the back office, the one where my boss works, was haunted by a 'woman of the night.'"

Her lips twitched. "A prostitute?"

"Yep. And apparently, she was a vengeful spirit, having been murdered by one of her customers."

As Gerald talked, Nikki finished off her steak and found herself looking for the waiter. She could really use another glass of wine. Maybe that would help find the missing spark.

At least temporarily.

Nikki sat back, folding an arm in her lap as she toyed with the stem of her glass. He was really cute. Had a nice smile.

". . . Then Rosie decided that we just had to do a séance. I don't even know why I agreed to it. I really shouldn't have, because my boss walked in about fifteen minutes—"

A shadow fell over their table, and Gerald trailed off. Thinking it was their waiter, she twisted in her seat. The first thing she caught was the fresh, crisp scent of cologne. Warning bells went off as she lifted her chin.

"What in the hell?"

Her jaw hit the floor as she looked up, seeing Gabe standing there. She had to be hallucinating, so she blinked once and then twice. Nope, he was still there.

He was staring—no, *glaring* at Gerald like he was five seconds from yanking him out of his chair.

"Gabe?"

"Are you fucking kidding me?" Gabe demanded.

Nikki jolted as her gaze swung toward Gerald. She didn't understand his reaction. "What are you doing here, Gabe?"

"Is this the guy you said you were going out on a date with?" he asked instead of answering her question. "*Gerald?*"

"Gabe, what are—?"

Gerald leaned back in his chair. "Wasn't expecting to see you tonight, Gabriel."

Nikki turned to Gerald, her stomach twisting with unease. "You know Gabe?" There was no way. When he talked about the de Vincents, he didn't speak of them as if he was on a first-name basis.

"His name isn't Gerald," snapped Gabe, his eyes burning. People at nearby tables were starting to pay attention.

"What?" she whispered, beyond confused. "That's not your name?"

"It's my middle name," Gerald replied, plucking his napkin out of his lap and tossing it on the table. "I'm not lying about my name."

"Oh, so it's convenient that you forgot to mention your name is Ross Haid?"

That name meant nothing to Nikki, but she had a really bad feeling about this. "Ross?"

"Ross Gerald Haid." Gerald slash Ross smiled faintly.

"And you forgot to mention you're a journalist for the *Advocate*?"

Everything in Nikki stilled. "A journalist? You told me you were a writer. That's what Rosie said."

"A journalist is a writer," Ross said.

Gabe placed a hand on the back of her chair. "Yeah, a writer for the *Advocate*, who's been working on a story about my family."

Shock splashed through her. "You're doing a story on them?"

"I am." His gaze flicked to Gabe. "But that's not why I wanted to go out with you, Nikki."

"Bullshit," Gabe said, voice low. "You've been slithering around like a snake these last couple of months. You found out that Nikki was working for us and then you went after her."

Oh my God.

Nikki sat back in her seat, dumbfounded. There was no way Rosie would've known this. No way. She hadn't been set up on a date. She'd been *set up*. That was why he started talking about the de Vincents. It wasn't the normal curiosity one would expect. He'd gone through Rosie to get to her to get to the de Vincents. . . .

Embarrassment washed over her as everything clicked into place. This date—her first get-out-there-and-be-a-normal-woman date—was a freaking disaster in the most unbelievable way.

"You son of a bitch." Gabe leaned forward, placing his other hand on the table. "You go near Nikki again . . ."

"And what?" There was no mistaking the eagerness in Ross's tone. "You're afraid that Nikki might tell me something I can use?"

Something I can use?

Oh hell no.

"You don't even want to know what will happen," Gabe warned.

"Are you threatening me?" Ross asked.

"Use that imagination of yours to figure out what it is."

In the back of her mind, she realized she'd never heard

Gabe speak like that, but she was too far beyond pissed for that to truly register.

"Hold up." Her shoulders squared as she stared across the table. "You asked me out so that you could hopefully glean information out of me on the de Vincents?"

"I wouldn't say that was the *only* reason." His gaze shifted to her.

Gabe made a sound that reminded her an awful lot of an actual growl. She gripped his arm as she rose from her chair. She snatched up her purse and then she extended her middle finger right in Ross's face. "Fuck you, dude."

"Hey." The smile slipped from Ross's face. "I was being serious. I wasn't asking you out just because—"

"Shut up," Gabe growled.

He wasn't budging, so Nikki tugged on his arm. "Let it go," she said. "It's not worth it. He's not worth it."

"Oh, I think it would be worth it." Gabe stared down at Ross. "Way worth it."

While Nikki sort of wanted to see Ross knocked the hell out, if he really was a reporter, this wouldn't end well for Gabe. She needed to get him out of here before he did something stupid. "Let's go," she whispered. "Please."

Gabe's gaze swung to hers and then he pushed off the table, rattling the glasses. "I mean it, Ross. You can have a hard-on for my family, but you stay the fuck away from Nikki. Do you understand me?"

Her heart skipped over itself as Ross bit out, "Oh, I understand perfectly."

She really had no idea if he did, but Gabe turned and took her hand. Wholly aware of the stares, she kept her gaze glued to Gabe's back and her mouth shut as he led her around the packed tables and out into the cooler night air.

Once they were outside, Nikki pulled her hand free. She didn't even know what to say as she turned to look up at Gabe. "That was so embarrassing."

"Nic—"

"He was using me to get gossip on your family!" She turned, staring back at the entrance, half tempted to storm back in there and smack Ross or whatever his name was across the face. Then she gasped and she whirled back to Gabe. "I didn't tell him anything. Nothing about—"

"I know." His jaw softened. "I know you wouldn't. I didn't think that for one second, and don't feel embarrassed. You didn't know who he was. You did nothing wrong."

Some of the tension crept out of her shoulders, but she still felt like a flaming idiot. "And there's no way Rosie knew what he really intended. She would've never fixed me up with him if she knew."

"I believe you."

Nikki exhaled roughly. That was . . . that was a relief.

"You look absolutely beautiful, by the way." Gabe faced her, and even in the low light from the restaurant, she could see his gaze sweeping over her. "That dress . . . the hair. Those shoes. Jesus. *He* really didn't fucking deserve all of that."

She flushed as she glanced down at herself. She'd taken time getting ready for tonight. The dress was a sexy one—a simple LBD. A little black dress that hugged her breasts and stomach before flaring out slightly at the hips. The skirt of the dress was loose around her thighs. She'd done her hair, using a wand until the strands fell in loose waves around her face. And she knew her makeup was on point, because she took the time to perfect the smoky eye look and the red pout.

She cleared her throat. "Um, thanks. What happened—?"

"I want you to know that," he interrupted her. "You look beautiful, Nikki. Too beautiful for Ross, even if he weren't who he was."

She didn't know what to say to that, so she decided it was time to change the subject. "How did you know it was him?"

"I didn't. Not until I saw him."

"But why did you come to the restaurant?" she asked.

"I'd tried to call you."

That was his number? How did he get her phone—wait. He would have her number from her employment papers for tax purposes and all that jazz.

Gabe started walking. "So, you're probably going to be mad at first but then you'll thank me later."

"What?" She caught up to him, which was a feat in the heels she was wearing.

"I had no idea that Gerald was Ross. I was going to interrupt your date and tell you there was an emergency," he said, glancing down at her. A half grin appeared. "Thought I'd do you a solid and swoop in and save you."

For the umpteenth time, her mouth dropped open. "You're joking, right?"

"Nope."

"You're telling me you would've interrupted my date for no good reason?"

"Well, it turned out to be a damn good reason."

"But you didn't know who he was. What if he wasn't a reporter—"

"What-ifs are stupid, Nic."

"No they're not, you asshole." Someone passing them by shot them a look, but Nikki was beyond caring. "You have got to be kidding me."

He was grinning—actually grinning at her. "I'm not kidding. Let's pretend that wasn't Ross, the dirtbag reporter who just wanted to use you. What if he was just Gerald? He's lame as fuck and you look way too hot to be sitting in there with him."

Nikki stopped in the middle of the sidewalk, spun, and smacked his arm—smacked it hard.

"Ouch." He laughed, and he really laughed. Tipping his head back and letting loose. "Told you. Said you were going to be angry at first."

"I'm pissed," she seethed. "What is wrong with you?"

"Did you drive yourself?" he asked, not even fazed.

"No. I took an Uber. I hate driving anywhere in the city on a Saturday night."

"Awesome." He started walking again, leading her toward Toulouse Street. "I'll take you home."

"You're not taking me anywhere." She reached for her purse. "I can't believe you. I honestly—"

"What are you doing?"

"Ordering a car." She stopped.

"No, you're not."

"Oh, yes I am," she snapped, digging around in her purse. It didn't matter that her date was a front for a damn reporter. Gabe had come there to ruin her date, not save her.

"If you don't start walking, I will throw you over my shoulder and carry you to where I'm parked in a garage."

"You wouldn't dare."

He stared down at her. "Do I look like I'm joking?"

As much as it annoyed her, he didn't. "No."

"That's what I thought." He sounded so, so smug. "If you behave and don't try to hit me, I'll stop and get you a smoothie."

"If I behave?" She glared daggers at him. "I'm not a child, Gabe."

"I know you're not a child." He slowed his steps to match hers. "And telling you to behave does not mean what you think it does."

She didn't even know what he meant by that. "I'm going to ninja kick you in the back of the head."

He laughed as they came to an intersection. "You couldn't even reach the back of my head."

Ugh.

That was true.

But that didn't mean she didn't want to try.

Nikki was torn between being beyond confused by his appearance and furious as they crossed the road. "Why did you do this?" she asked, glancing up at him. "If you didn't know who Gerald really was, then why did you do this?"

The street lamps cast a soft glow along his cheekbones. He was quiet for a moment. "I was at the workshop and I was sitting there, thinking about what you said on Friday about why you wanted to go out on a date. About how you weren't looking for a relationship, but you'd be interested in a hookup if that was what happened."

Nikki's brows pulled together as she frowned. "I'm pretty sure that's not exactly what I said."

"But that's what you meant."

Her hand tightened on the strap of her purse. "And?"

"And I didn't like it."

She was absolutely dumbfounded. So much so that she didn't speak as they walked into the silent, shadowy parking garage. Because Gabe must've made a deal with the devil, somehow he'd gotten a parking space on the first level.

Her heels clicked on the cement, echoing around them. "I don't understand this—understand you at all."

His steps slowed. "I think you do. You just don't want to acknowledge it."

"No," she said. "I honestly do not understand this."

He didn't speak until they reached his car at the very back of the parking garage. "Are we going to pretend that nothing happened between us at the workshop? Is that what we're going to do?"

She stopped as he opened up the passenger door for her. "I . . . I don't know what you're talking about."

"You're lying." He took her purse from her and placed it on the seat.

Nikki was, because she was comfortable with pretending like that didn't happen. It was safe.

He turned to her. "I know you felt how into you I was standing behind you."

Her cheeks flushed, and she thanked God that it was too dark in there for him to see her blush. "You're a guy. You all get turned on if the wind hits you the right way."

Gabe laughed. "I wish that was true, but it isn't. And you know that—you knew exactly what I was feeling, because you were feeling the same."

Her heart stuttered in her chest. There was no way she could admit that. It didn't matter what they mutually had been feeling. "I'm not interested in you anymore."

"Bullshit."

Nikki gasped. "Your arrogance really has no limit."

"It's not arrogance." He stepped into her, forcing her to step back until she bumped into the side of his car. "And it has nothing to do with what happened between us before you left for college."

"Everything has to do with that," she snapped. "Everything."

He stared down at her. "Okay. Let's say it does. Even so, it doesn't change one fact."

"And what is that?"

"You went out with that guy when you'd rather have been with me."

Her eyes just about popped out of her head. A thousand denials rose to the tip of her tongue, but Gabe moved so fast that it wasn't until he had her turned around, her back pressed to his front, that she realized what he was up to.

"What are you doing?" she asked as he curled an arm around her waist.

"Proving what I just said."

Her wild gaze darted around the parking garage. "You do not need to prove anything."

"Oh, I think I do." His hips brushed her rear, and yep, she felt him. No denying that. "You still want me. You probably never stopped wanting me."

"Are you drunk?" she gasped.

"I haven't had a single drink all day. It's not like that night."

The implications of what he said made her shudder. So did the hand that coursed over her hip. "Gabe."

"You tell me to stop and I will."

Her lips parted. She needed to tell him to stop, because she knew that whatever was happening right now was going to change everything between them, and she knew this time there wouldn't be any repairing the damage it would wreak on their friendship . . . and possibly her life.

This blurred too many lines for her, and especially after learning what had happened to Emma, this wasn't smart at all. Because no matter what, his heart belonged to someone else, and what did that leave her with?

Just *this*, whatever *this* was.

She still didn't tell him to stop.

His breath danced over her temple. "You have no idea what I wanted to do when you said you had a date. Well, maybe you're getting a good idea of what that was now." His fingers reached the hem of her skirt. "And maybe this is crazy. I don't care."

"You should care," she whispered, her heart thundering.

"Then tell me to stop." His lips brushed her temple, causing her to gasp. "You still haven't."

Nikki hadn't.

She had no idea how she started off her evening with one guy and was now getting pleasantly fondled by Gabe de Vincent in a parking garage.

Other than once this past week, she hadn't even dared to let herself fantasize something like this.

His chuckle was deep and rumbled through her. "That's because you don't want me to, but Ross? Even if he wasn't a fucking dick?"

She couldn't breathe as his hand slipped under the skirt of her dress and ran up her thigh. The calluses on his hand drove her crazy.

"He wouldn't even have gotten this far with you." Those fingers trailed up to the thin slip of material curving over her hip. "Would he?"

No, he wouldn't have.

"Answer me, Nic." He hooked a finger around the side of her thong.

She drew in a stuttered breath. "No. He wouldn't have."

His lips brushed the lobe of her ear, sending a shiver down her spine. "And why is that?"

Her throat was dry. "There was no spark."

"Why?" He tugged hard on her thong and her hips jerked as he snapped each side.

Holy *shit*.

Gabe pulled the material away, and she had no idea what he did with her ruined undies at that point. "Why was there no spark, Nic?"

She could barely think as his hand slid across her lower belly and then dipped, coming so, so close to where she throbbed. "It just wasn't there."

"Now, that's not the reason." His fingers stilled. "Tell me why there wasn't a spark and I'll show you what a spark is."

Her chest was heaving as she swallowed hard. "He wasn't . . . he wasn't you."

"That's my girl." His fingers slipped between her thighs, wringing a gasp out of her.

Oh God, this was really happening. Gabe was touching her and they were in the middle of a parking garage. Anyone could walk up on them, but she didn't even care. The only thing she could focus on was Gabe, on the heated sensations he was building in her and the swelling in her chest.

She had wanted him for so long.

Always wanted him.

"Fuck, you're so wet," he growled.

Her knees felt weak as she started to press her legs together.

"Don't. Don't do that." He nipped at her ear, causing her to gasp. "I love it."

She kept her legs open.

"Do you know what I wanted to do the night in the shop? It's all I've been thinking about." He dragged his finger through the wetness, teasing her. "I wanted to bend you over and fuck you so hard you wouldn't even think about going out on a date with another man."

Oh God.

"Can't do that, though." His finger circled her clit. "But you know what we can do?"

"What?" she whispered, her eyes darting around the garage.

He leaned away from her and she felt his hand at his waist. She heard his zipper coming down, and then he pressed into her.

Nikki's body quivered—actually *quivered*. She felt him against her rear, hard and thick and bare. A seed of panic took root. "Condom—"

"We're not having sex, Nic." His hips moved against her ass. "Trust me."

And with that, he sunk his finger into her.

Nikki's entire body arched as he went as deep as he could. It was nothing like when she did it. Oh hell no, this was something else entirely.

His curse was a heated breath against her as he twisted the rough skin of his palm against the most sensitive part of her. He moved his hips behind her, dragging his cock up and down her ass as he added another finger, stretching her. She jerked in response, eyes widening.

Gabe's fingers stilled. "Am I hurting you?"

"No," she gasped. "It's just . . . it's been a while."

"I can tell."

Could he really? But that thought disappeared as his fingers started moving again. She was completely at his will as she curled one hand over his arm, digging her nails into his skin as she planted her other hand against the side of his Porsche.

Her thoughts were spinning. Her body was coiling tight. There was no holding herself back. She was moving against him, riding his hand just like she'd fantasized.

"That's it." His voice was almost guttural, a tone she'd never heard from him before. "Fuck my fingers."

His words scorched her skin, and maybe tomorrow she'd be embarrassed by them, but tonight, those words turned her on. Her blood turned to lava and every point of her body seemed to be tightening all at once. His fingers pumped inside her as he thrust against her ass. He must've felt her start to come and known she wasn't going to be able to be quiet. His hand folded over her mouth, muffling her cries as she came.

Ripples of pleasure were still coursing throughout her as Gabe made this deep sound that came from the back of his throat. He ground against her, stilling as his entire body shuddered. She felt him then, pulsing against the cheek of her ass as she rested her head on his chest.

All Nikki knew was that they both were out of their minds.

Chapter 21

*L*uckily Gabe had an extra shirt in the back of the car and was able to use it to clean Nic up as best as he could. And for some fucked-up reason, he was way too into the fact that it was his come he was cleaning off of her.

Once in the car, he glanced over at her. She was holding on to the edges of her skirt and staring straight ahead. If it wasn't for the sated little half smile on her face, he'd be really worried.

Still, he was concerned.

Things had progressed further than he anticipated. Wasn't like when he left the shop to put an end to her stupid date, he'd planned on ripping off her panties and fucking her with his fingers.

Gabe hit the ignition button and the engine purred to life.

Honest to God, he didn't even know how it all escalated so quickly, but fuck, wasn't like he could turn back time.

"Hey." He reached between them, placing his hand over one of hers. "You okay?"

"Yeah." She cleared her throat. "Yes."

His gaze searched every square inch of her face, searching for who knows what, but then that tiny smile spread. She looked away, but not before he saw the deepening in her cheeks, the pink turning rose-colored.

This night was . . . different.

He almost killed a man in the middle of a restaurant and then he had one of the best orgasms of his life in a parking garage without actually having sex.

Not exactly a normal Saturday night.

"You know what I could go for right now?" he said, backing out of the parking garage.

She glanced over at him. "A nap?"

He chuckled as he drove through the garage. "That would be nice, but not what I had in mind. I think I could go for a smoothie."

When he glanced over at her, she was grinning. "Yeah, I could go for one myself."

"Then let's do it."

And that's what they did.

He drove to the closest one, which turned out to be Smoothie King. He went in and grabbed her a strawberry one while he ordered a blueberry one that she would most definitely turn her nose up at.

"Thank you," she said, taking it from him when he slid into the driver's seat.

"No problem." He reached to turn the car on, but stopped. Depending on the traffic, it wouldn't take more than twenty minutes to get her home. "Mind if I finish this before we get back on the road?"

"Of course not." She took a sip of her smoothie.

He suddenly remembered her plans last night. "What happened with that apartment you were looking at?"

"Oh! It's perfect. I filled out the paperwork and I'm just waiting to hear back from the property management. If I'm approved, it's mine."

"That's awesome."

"Thanks. I should know something this week."

"Then you need to get a dog or something."

She laughed softly. "Maybe a cat."

"Or an armadillo."

"An armadillo? What?"

Grinning, he lifted a shoulder. "I remember you trying to save an armadillo when you were like thirteen."

She was quiet for a moment. "Oh my God, I can't believe

I forgot that. Mom flipped out because I was trying to pick it up—"

"An understandable reaction to seeing your child trying to pick up an armadillo."

"It wouldn't have hurt me. It liked me."

Gabe shook his head.

"I still think armadillos are the cutest things ever." A moment passed and then she peeked over at him. "You're staring at me."

"No, I'm not." He totally was.

She turned her head to him. "You're not? You're doing it right now."

"Okay." Grinning around the straw, he looked up at the front of the smoothie joint. "I'm not staring at you now."

"But you *were*."

"Maybe."

She laughed, but it faded all too quickly. "Gabe?"

"Yeah?" Tipping his head back against the seat, he looked over at her. God, she was . . . There really weren't words.

"What . . . what are we doing?" she asked quietly.

He didn't know how to answer that. While he'd been at his shop, sitting there staring at the damn rack, all he could think about was her on that date. Before he knew what he was doing, he was in his car, calling her and driving to Crescent City Steaks. Irritation of a primitive nature had overcome him, and if he was being honest with himself, so did another emotion. One that fueled his decision to basically bust up her date, which he was glad about for multiple reasons, because God knows Ross would've tried to get between her legs, investigating his family or not. Look at her. She was fucking gorgeous.

"I don't know," he answered, meeting her gaze. "Honest to God, I really don't. I just . . . I didn't like the idea of you being on that date."

Her brows rose as she took a nice, long drink of her

smoothie. "So, you didn't like the idea of me being on a date and you decided giving me an orgasm in a parking garage was the way to go?"

Unable to help himself, Gabe laughed. "You weren't the only one who got off."

"Oh. I know," she replied dryly.

"I didn't plan that." And that was the truth. "It . . . just happened."

She lowered her smoothie as she stared at him. "It's kind of hard for something like that to *just* happen."

"You have a point." He scratched his fingers through his hair. "I guess I felt the need to prove that you're into me as much as I'm into you."

"You're into me?"

"You sound surprised." Gabe laughed. "What just happened—me coming like that? Pretty sure that hasn't happened since high school."

"Oh." She shoved the straw in her mouth.

He watched her for a moment, amused by her, and there was something else going on inside him, an odd feeling he hadn't experienced in a while. Tenderness? Of course, he'd feel tenderness for Nic. "Anyway, when you said you weren't into me anymore, I guess I rose to the challenge."

Nic seemed to consider that for a moment. "Was that what it was? To prove something or a challenge?"

"Shit. No. That's not what I meant." He took a drink of his smoothie, trying to make sense of what he was thinking, but that was no fucking use, because he had no idea. "Not at all."

She exhaled raggedly, drawing his gaze. Hers flitted away. "Do you regret it?"

Her question was barely above a whisper and at first he couldn't believe she'd ask that since he hadn't given any indication that he did. But then he got it. Their history was like a damn viper between them.

"No." Reaching over, he cupped his fingers around her

chin and turned her gaze to his. What he felt about what just happened and how he felt for her was one hell of a confusing ball of emotion settling in his chest. "I don't know what that was. Or what it means tomorrow, but know one thing, Nic, not one fucking piece of me regrets it."

THE JARRING RING of Nikki's phone was what woke her finally. She had the distinct impression that it had been ringing for a while.

Groaning, she rolled over and slapped around on the nightstand until she found the stupid phone. One eye opened.

Rosie.

Hitting the Answer button, she brought the phone to her ear and croaked, "What time is it?"

"Time for you to tell what the hell happened last night!"

Last night felt like a dream, not at all real to her in the early morning hours. "I'm guessing you talked to Gerald. Oh wait, what's his real name? Ross Haid, a reporter—"

"I knew he wrote for the *Advocate* every once in a while, but I didn't think that was going to be an issue. He texted me last night, but I didn't see his messages until this morning. The first text was, and I quote, 'Gabriel de Vincent just kidnapped my date.' At first I thought he had to be joking," Rosie said. "But then there was another text where he explains that he's doing a story on the de Vincents. He swears that's not why he wanted to go out with you, but I'm going to murder him for real. What the hell happened, Nikki?"

How in the world could she explain this when she wasn't even quite sure she knew what happened herself? "Well, you got the brief version of what happened."

"So Gabe figured out it was Ross?" Rosie's voice rose, causing Nikki to wince.

Groaning, Nikki rolled onto her back. "No. He had no idea until he got there. He said he was coming to save me from what was probably an awful date."

"Really?" Her tone was dry.

"Yeah." Nikki tossed an arm over her eyes. "I was caught off guard by him showing up and finding out who Gerald was. It was crazy."

"And then what happened?" Rosie demanded. "Did he take you home and tuck you in?"

Nikki's lips pursed. "No."

"So, he just came out and whisked you away and that was it?"

"Not really," Nikki muttered as she dropped her arm to the bed.

"I feel like this conversation needs to happen in person," Rosie decided. "You need to get up—"

"I'm not getting up."

"Then you need to tell me what happened last night."

There was a part of her that didn't want to tell Rosie, because it felt like it would tarnish what happened. But she also knew Rosie. She wouldn't put it past the woman to show up at the house, demanding to know answers.

"Something did happen between us," she said, glancing at the closed bedroom door. Having this conversation in her parents' house was weird. "I don't even know how it happened."

"How *what* happened?" Rosie's voice was calmer, which meant instead of being at a level ten, she was now at a level seven. That was progress.

"We were . . . kind of arguing. I guess? About him wanting to ruin my date without knowing who Gerald really was, which, looking back, is a ridiculous argument, but whatever. He said something about me still being into him, and I said I wasn't." She rubbed at her eyes. "Then he sort of proved that I was lying."

"Okay. I'm going to need more detail," Rosie said. "How did he prove you were lying?"

Feeling her cheeks heat, she shook her head. "We sort of, kind of made out."

There was a stretch of silence. "How does one sort of, kind of make out?"

She sighed heavily. "Imagine making out, but not kissing and fingers were involved."

"Holy shit," Rosie breathed.

"Yeah."

"Fingers? As in plural?"

Nikki laughed as she rolled onto her side. "Yeah."

"Holy shit," she repeated.

"I know. Things kind of escalated pretty quickly and . . ." And he'd given her the best damn orgasm of her life. "And I don't know. It happened. Afterward, we grabbed a smoothie."

"Wait. What?"

"You heard me correctly. We grabbed a smoothie."

"I don't even know how to respond to that, Nikki." There was a pause. "Did you guys talk about what happened?"

"Yeah. We did. I asked him what was going on, and he said he didn't know. He also said he didn't regret it." Nikki pressed her lips together as she flopped onto her back again. "I believe him. I don't think he planned on that happening and I don't think he regretted it."

"Nikki," sighed Rosie.

"Look, I know it was crazy. Given our history that was the last thing we should've done, but—"

"But you still care for him."

"I wasn't going to say that, but yeah, I care about him. Obviously."

"You know what type of caring I'm talking about," she replied. "What were you going to say?"

Nikki frowned. "I was going to say that I'm not reading into what happened. I don't have expectations."

"Girl." Rosie's tone was heading upward again. "Like I told you last time, you need to start reading into his actions. I'm also going to tell you something new. You also need to stop lying to yourself."

"I'm not lying to myself."

"Yes. You are. Look, I'm not judging you. Obviously. I don't know Gabe or what type of guy he is, but there's something between you two. There *has* been, and I don't know if that's a good thing or a bad thing, but what I do know is bad is you pretending like this is no big deal. It is."

She opened her mouth to deny it, but Rosie was right. Nikki was totally lying to herself. Well, she hadn't really given herself a chance to even fully process everything, but what happened between them was a big deal. It was either a step toward a future or a step toward a disaster, but it was a step she damn well knew she'd be taking.

"I hate you," Nikki muttered.

Rosie laughed. "Can I ask you something and you be real honest?"

Oh God. "Go for it."

"Did you ever stop loving him?" she asked.

Nikki's breath caught, not mistaking what Rosie asked. She didn't ask if Nikki was in love with Gabe. She'd asked if Nikki had ever stopped, and that question tore through her. A cyclone of emotions whirled. Fear. Anticipation. Dread. Excitement. Just for a tiny second, she let herself feel it all, everything, and it was wonderful and terrifying.

Could it be possible that she'd actually been in love with Gabe when she was younger? That it hadn't been a silly infatuation, and that what she was feeling again, what she'd felt last night in his arms, wasn't an infatuation? That it wasn't just lust?

She couldn't answer Rosie's question.

Rosie sighed. "That's what I thought."

Chapter 22

It took one phone call for Gabe to find what he needed Sunday morning and that was why he was standing in front of the chocolate-brown door of one of the newer shotgun-style homes over on Pritchard Place.

He banged the side of his fist on the door and then waited and he didn't have to wait that long. Footsteps neared the other side and then the door cracked open, revealing half of Ross Haid's face.

"What the hell?" Ross blinked rapidly as he opened the door to reveal he was wearing nothing more than a white undershirt and flannel bottoms.

Without saying a word, Gabe pushed forward, forcing Ross to take a step back as he walked into his house. Gabe caught the door and closed it shut behind him.

A healthy dose of fear filled Ross's wide eyes. "What are you doing, man? You know who I am and who I work for—"

Cocking back his arm, he slammed his fist into Ross's jaw, knocking his head back. Ross dropped like a sack of potatoes, landing on his ass as he palmed his jaw.

"I wanted to do that last night." Gabe opened his fist as he bent over Ross. "Took every bit of my self-control to not lay you flat on your back right then and there."

"Fuck." Ross spit out a mouthful of blood. "I think you cracked one of my teeth. Are you out of your mind?"

"You should be asking yourself that question," Gabe replied, straightening. "You can sniff around my brothers and me all you want, but you stay the fuck away from Nic."

"Shit." Ross rolled onto his back. "Pretty sure you made that clear last night."

"I'm making damn sure it's clear right now." Punching Ross had given him a moment of satisfaction, but he wanted to rip the man apart for embarrassing Nic and trying to use her. "Because next time will be your last time."

"You're seriously going to walk into my house, punch me, and then threaten me?"

"I know you're going to keep your mouth shut about this. Want to know why? Because you're not that fucking stupid. You report this, and then I make sure the whole damn world knows exactly why I about knocked your ass out. Sure your bosses over at the *Advocate* want that kind of press? Using a woman?" Gabe asked. "I'll give them a story and it won't be the one you were hoping to report."

"Damn." Ross coughed out a wet-sounding laugh. "And here I've heard you're the calm and levelheaded de Vincent. Got to think people have that wrong."

"They do when it comes to people I care about."

"And you care about Nikki? A twenty-some-year-old daughter of your house staff?" Ross laughed again, and Gabe thought there might be a good chance that he'd punch the son of a bitch again. Ross lowered his hand as he rose onto his elbow. "What is she to you?"

Gabe knew where he was going with this. "If I see one thing written about her anywhere, I'm going to hold you personally responsible."

"I'm not going to write about her. I actually like her."

"That last part was the wrong thing to say," Gabe warned him.

"Was it?" He curled one leg up. "I'm beginning to think my theory about your family is correct."

"I don't give a fuck about what you think."

"You should." Ross sat up, wiping away a trail of blood leaking from the corner of his mouth. "I don't think your father committed suicide. I think he did something and one of you—one of you killed him for it."

NIKKI WAS SO nervous come Monday morning that she walked by the deep freezer twice before realizing she'd gone into the pantry to take out the steaks for dinner.

She hadn't heard from Gabe since he dropped her off at home Saturday night and she'd hadn't seen him yet. Having no idea if that meant anything or not, she tried to gather her scattered thoughts and get to work.

It was Monday, so that meant endless dusting of things that were never used and she doubted that the de Vincents even knew they had.

Pulling her hair up, she threw herself into work. The downside of doing something so monotonous was that her brain was given free rein to obsess over every little thing that had happened between her and Gabe on Saturday night.

Which wasn't exactly what she needed.

Or wanted.

No matter how hard she focused on how she was going to decorate the cute apartment she hoped she got approved for or stressed over the decision to apply for a caseworker job with the county or enroll in grad school, her mind wandered back to Gabe.

She sort of wanted to punch herself. Hard.

The best thing she could do was proceed as if nothing had happened. That wouldn't be the easiest thing to do, but the smartest. Obviously he was physically attracted to her. She obviously had the hots for him, but the difference was that she knew it wouldn't just be something physical for her.

It would become more.

And she couldn't risk that.

It was close to noon when she was vacuuming one of the

unused bedrooms on the second floor of the wing Lucian and Julia occupied. Because the plush carpet was virtually spotless, she'd toed off her flats and left them in the hallway. She was humming along to the whirl of the vacuum when it suddenly turned off.

Frowning, she fiddled with the on/off switch and then turned at the waist, scanning the room. The cord was unplugged.

"Odd," she murmured, walking over to the thing. The cord was long, so it wasn't like she'd pulled it out of the wall.

Freaking weird, demon-possessed house.

She plugged it back in and the vacuum roared to life. Sighing, she turned and let out a startled squeak.

Gabe stood in the doorway, arms crossed as he leaned against the doorframe. "Having difficulties with the vacuum?"

"Did you unplug it?" she asked as she hurried over to the vacuum, turning it off.

"No. Why would I do that?"

She narrowed her eyes at him. "I don't know, but it unplugged itself."

"Ghosts."

"I didn't think you believed in ghosts."

He lifted a shoulder. "I've never seen anything, but I've heard enough weird shit in this house that I do have to wonder."

She wasn't sure if he was messing with her or not, but she was fully aware of the fact that they were the only ones on the second floor, in a room with a bed.

Nikki cleared her throat as she folded her hand over the handle of the vacuum. "Well, I need to get back to work, so . . ."

Gabe frowned. "Is that how this is going to be?"

"I don't understand." And she really didn't. "I have to vacuum this room. You know, one of the five on this floor that hasn't ever been used. It's very important that I finish this."

He grinned. "And why is that?"

"I'm guessing if I don't, the dust bunnies under the bed will multiply and take over the house, causing Devlin to go into shock. We can't have that happening."

Gabe laughed. "The dust bunnies can wait."

"They really can't. You know how dust bunnies are. Always getting together, multiplying, and making little dust bunny babies. Plus, it's my job."

"I've been looking for you," he said, ignoring what she said.

"Well, you found me, but as you can see, I'm pretty busy—" She took a little step back as he pushed away from the frame and entered the room, stopping to close the door behind him. "What are you doing?"

He locked the door, and her heart launched itself into her throat like a rocket. Gabe was silent as he stalked toward her, and that's what he did. He *stalked*, like a big cat that had caught sight of its prey.

"Gabe—"

"Have you been hiding from me all day?"

"What? No. I've been working—"

"Uh-huh." He crossed the space between them. "I remember when you were younger, you used to hide in these rooms whenever Lawrence was here."

"Well, he didn't like all the noise I made—"

"You never made that much noise." Stopping directly in front of her, he grasped her by the hips. "Anyway, I'm glad I found you in here."

Her pulse was pounding out of control as she lifted her head. "Why?"

"Because there's something I spent all last night thinking about."

She was half afraid to ask. "What would that be?"

His hands on her waist tightened and then he lifted her

up. She didn't get a chance to protest. One second she was standing and the next, her back was hitting the center of the bed, and he was above her, his arms and knees caging her in.

Oh. My. God.

"You were thinking about throwing me on the bed?" she asked.

He chuckled again, the sound curling her toes. "No, that's not what I've been thinking about, but it was fun."

"For you, maybe."

"You liked it."

Okay, she kind of did, but she wasn't admitting that. Ever. "What are you doing?"

"Following through on what I've been thinking about all night. I told you that." Grinning, he shifted his weight onto his knees and straightened. "Keep up with me."

"Keep up with you? You come in here, throw me on a bed, and I'm supposed to know what you're up to?" She started to sit up. "Gabe—"

"Do you want to know what I've been thinking about?" he asked.

"Not really," she replied.

"Oh, yeah, you're going to want to know." His hands found their way to her waist, causing her to suck in a sharp breath. "But I think I'm just going to show you."

"I don't think—*Gabe!*" she gasped as he curled his fingers around the band of her black leggings. "What are you doing?"

"You'll see." He tugged, and she gripped his wrists. "And I have this suspicion that you're really, really going to enjoy it."

Her chest rose and fell with fast breaths. She had no idea how she'd gone from vacuuming to this. It was spiraling so fast that she wondered if she even had an ounce of control from the moment he'd walked into the room.

Or if she wanted to control it.

Her grip loosened.

Gabe's grin spread as those thick lashes lowered. "How has your day been?"

His question caught her off guard. "Um, good? A normal Monday."

He tugged again, managing to get the leggings an inch down her hips. "Have you heard back on the apartment?"

"Not yet," she said, finding this to be the most bizarre positioning to have a conversation in.

"I have a few pieces in storage that would be perfect for your apartment," he said, dragging his thumb over her hip bone. "I got a coffee table, a dresser, and an end table. You can have them."

So surprised by the offer, she could only stare at him at first. "That's not right. Your stuff costs as much as one semester at UA—"

"I don't care. I want you to have them." His thumb moved on her other hip, slipping over her lower belly. "They were pieces I never sold and I made them ages ago."

"Gabe—"

His gaze pierced hers. "They're mine to give away, and I choose you."

I choose you.

Oh Lord, those words sent a bolt straight to her heart. He didn't mean them the way her heart took them, but still.

"Just think of them as a housewarming gift," he said, as if he wasn't talking about a gift that cost tens of thousands of dollars. "And now you're supposed to ask me about my day."

Her nose wrinkled. "How was your day?"

Gabe laughed. "You could at least sound like you care."

"I do." She rolled her eyes.

"I woke up early and couldn't fall back to sleep. I was thinking about Saturday night, about how amazing my dick felt against your ass."

Oh my.

Her stomach dipped as a sharp tingle zipped through her veins in response.

"And I was thinking about how good you felt around my fingers when you started to come," he continued, his words scorching her skin. "Made me hard as a fucking rock, you know that?"

"No," she whispered as her blood caught fire.

He bit down on his lip as his gaze drifted down, over her breasts and lower. "I had to do something about that. Wasn't as good as Saturday night, but it worked. For a time."

Her eyes widened at what he was implying.

Gabe tugged again, getting her leggings down far enough that a strip of her undies was visible. He cocked his head to the side. "Are they *butterflies*?"

"Shut up." She flushed.

"Cute. I want to see the rest of them."

Her gaze darted to the closed door. "Are you out of your mind?" She held on to his hands. "What if someone walks in—"

"No one is going to find us. I locked the door." He tugged again, gaining another inch. "And this is a hell of a lot more private than a parking garage."

Her skin flamed with a whole different kind of heat.

Then he pulled again, and Nikki couldn't even lie to herself. She didn't really try to stop him, because she was grade-A certifiable at this point. All earlier thoughts of doing anything with Gabe being too risky dive-bombed out of the nearest window as he moved down the bed, pulling her pants off.

Nikki could barely breathe as he dragged his hands up her calves and over the outside of her thighs. He hooked his fingers around her panties.

This wasn't like Saturday night.

Not at all.

If she let him do this, she was bare to him in ways she hadn't been bare to another living soul in a very long time.

Nikki didn't stop him.

Gabe made this deep sound as she lifted her rear, helping him pull them off. He tugged them off, letting them fall to God knew where. Then he was sliding his hands up the insides of her legs, skimming over her thighs.

Air lodged in her throat as she fell back to her elbows. Her skin was burning, but she couldn't look away from him staring at the most intimate part of her.

"You're beautiful." He drew a finger up the crease at her thigh and then did it on her other leg. "Fucking perfect."

"We . . . we probably shouldn't be doing this."

His gaze lifted to hers. "Why not?"

She had a hard time remembering all the very valid reasons this was dumb as hell as he spread her legs, opening her up. Instinct to close her legs got her nowhere. Not when he draped her one leg over his shoulder and came down between her thighs.

"Why shouldn't I do this?" he asked.

A strangled gasp parted her lips as his breath danced over her heated flesh.

"I said Saturday night I don't know what we're doing, where it's going to lead." He turned his head, kissing her inner thigh. The rough skin of his jaw drove her crazy. "That didn't mean I wasn't going to travel that road and find out."

He hadn't even touched her and she was already throbbing. Her senses were scattered, and that's what she was going to blame for the next stupid thing that came out of her mouth. "You didn't call or text yesterday. I thought . . ." She stopped herself. "I mean, I figured you'd decided to forget it happened."

His gaze found hers again. He didn't say anything as he dragged his jaw along her inner thigh. A heartbeat passed while she cursed herself. He kissed her thigh again. "I won't forget it happened. And I won't give that impression again."

"Oh," she said, because she had no idea what else to say to that.

And then she wasn't thinking about any of that, because Gabe's mouth was on the move. He kissed just below her navel, and then lower. His lips ghosted over her, sending a tight shiver throughout her body.

Nikki shuddered as he got his hands in there, slipping them between her legs, opening her even further, and then his mouth was on her.

"This . . ." He dragged his tongue up her center. "This is what I've been thinking about. What you taste like. I just had to find out."

Nikki cried out as he did just that. He tasted her. Tongue. Lips. Licking. Sucking. Going deep and then pulling away. Any reservations she might've had were lost in a tidal wave of pure sensation. Her body took over as a certain mindless abandon swept over her. She gripped the comforter as her hips moved of their own accord, rolling against his mouth as her gasp gave way to moans.

He so knew what he was doing.

Gabe got his hands under her rear and lifted her up. He . . . he *feasted* on her. Devoured her. That was how it felt. There was no escaping the raw sensations he was dragging out of her with every dip of his tongue, not that she wanted to. Then his mouth closed over the tight bundle of nerves, and Nikki exploded.

Her head kicked back as her back arched, shoulders digging into the bed as her hands tore at the comforter. She lost a little bit of herself as waves and waves of pleasure washed over her. Her leg slipped over his shoulder as he eased off, lifting his head to press a kiss to the space below her navel.

"You taste better than I imagined." His voice was rough as he nipped at her skin, causing her to jerk.

Forcing her eyes open, she stared down at him. His lips glistened. She shivered. Their gazes connected as her breathing slowed. Dropping his hands to the mattress, he pushed up, sitting back on his knees. Her gaze dropped. She could see him, straining against his jeans. Her stomach bottomed out as her lips parted. She wanted to do the same.

He must've been reading her mind, because his hands dropped to the buckle on his belt. His nimble fingers made quick work of the belt and then the zipper. He peeled the sides of his pants away and shoved them down, along with his tight, black boxer briefs. He sprung free, thick and hard.

She wet her lips. "I want to taste you."

"My new favorites words in the English language."

"You look incredibly smug today."

Gabe shrugged as he crossed his ankles, resting his feet on the ottoman in one of the smaller rooms on the main floor. Outfitted with a TV, it was the closest thing the house had to a living room. He'd always liked the room. Probably had to do with his mother. She favored this room in the evening, gathering up the boys and Madeline. This was where they watched movies.

Sucked that the senator was now in the room.

But not even his random appearance on Tuesday could ruin Gabe's mood. A beautiful woman eagerly and joyfully sucking your dick was nature's best defense against annoying sons of bitches. Twenty-four hours later, and Gabe was still smiling.

And man, he could still taste her on the tip of his tongue. She was like ambrosia.

He hadn't made the same mistake he had on Sunday. Truth be told, it had been so long since he actually worried about what a woman he'd been with in any sense of the word worried about after they parted ways that when it had crossed his mind to reach out to her, he'd shrugged it off out of habit.

Dumbass move.

Gabe cared about what Nic worried about afterward. So he texted her last night since she was having dinner with her parents instead of going to the shop. And he texted her good morning this morning.

Right now he was going to let Nic seek him out. She was here, somewhere in the house. He was giving her time.

"I came to see Dev." Stefan sat in the recliner across from Gabe. "But he's with Sabrina."

Gabe couldn't keep the look of disgust off his face, and it didn't go unnoticed by his uncle. "You don't like Ms. Harrington, do you?" he noted.

Gabe smirked. "Who does?"

"Your brother."

He laughed at that. "I don't even think he likes her that much."

"Well, I guess you don't have to like a person to marry them," Stefan commented, crossing one leg over the other. His finger tapped along the arm of the recliner. "The same could be said about your mother and Lawrence."

His gaze narrowed on Stefan. It was no secret that his parents didn't get along. The fact that Lawrence turned out not to be Dev's and his father was evidence enough of that.

"I guess Lucian will be the first to break that tradition," Stefan continued, talking to hear himself talk, Gabe guessed. "Since he's marrying a nurse."

"There isn't a damn thing wrong with Julia or the fact she actually has a necessary skillset," Gabe fired back. "And I really don't think someone who has been married three times and divorced that many times should be commenting on anyone else's relationships."

"Touché," Stefan murmured.

Shaking his head, Gabe looked away just as Nic entered the room, carrying a small tray with one glass on it. Irritation flared. He didn't like seeing her serve his fucking uncle.

She picked up the glass and placed it on the coaster next to the recliner. Nic shot him a quick grin as she turned and glanced at him, and when he winked, her entire face flushed a pretty pink. She hurried out of the room, and it took everything in him not to chase after her.

He didn't know what Nic was to him, but she was like a goddamn addiction.

"I see some things never change."

He looked over at Stefan sharply. "What does that mean?"

Stefan shrugged, and he didn't respond. Probably was a good thing, because no more than a minute later, Sabrina entered the room.

Right behind her was Parker.

Sabrina caught sight of him and her red-painted lips spread so widely he thought her face would crack. "Gabe, what a pleasant surprise."

Fuck.

He was not going to let this woman ruin his mood. He started to rise.

"Now look at what you've done, Sabrina." Stefan grinned around his glass. "You're chasing my nephew off."

"I did no such thing." The tips of her cheeks flushed.

Gabe rose, coming to his full height. He looked at the siblings closely and then focused on Parker. "I find it odd that you've been here so much lately," Gabe said. "Wonder why that is."

Parker shrugged. "Just getting to know my future in-laws better."

From the recliner came a derisive snort. "I'm sure it has nothing to do with the hot little housekeeper running around."

Gabe's jaw locked down. "It better not be."

"Of course not." Sabrina sounded legitimately bewildered by the suggestion. "That's the most foolish thing I've heard all day."

Gabe held Parker's gaze. The fucker stared back at him boldly.

"You seem oddly concerned about that if it were the case," Parker replied.

"She's like family to us." Gabe stepped forward, smiling when Parker inched back a step. "Unlike those in this room."

Sabrina sucked in a sharp breath.

The senator laughed. "Come spend time with me, Sabrina. Tell me about the charity you're working on. What is it? Is it for the Daughters of something or another?"

Gabe scanned the room, wondering what the hell these three were up to, because this wasn't the first time the three of them had spent time together.

Whatever it was, he wanted to be as far away from it as possible.

Leaving the three together, he went in search of Nic. Screw waiting around on her. He found her in the kitchen, staring at a slip of paper. Her back was to him, but she heard him.

Looking over her shoulder, she smiled. It was shy, and for some damn reason, he felt a surge of protectiveness he couldn't quite explain. "Hey," she said, turning back to her paper. "Guess what?"

He knew he shouldn't do what he was about to do. Not with his house full of Harringtons and her father roaming around, but that didn't stop him.

Gabe came up behind her, placing his hands on her hips. "What?"

He felt Nic's reaction to his touch. The tiniest shiver that coursed through her as he tugged her back against his chest. "I just got a call about an hour ago from the property manager of the apartment I was looking at."

"What's the deal?" He slid his hands around, over her stomach.

The pink from earlier returned to her cheeks. "I got the apartment."

"That's awesome." He turned her around, so she was facing him. "Seriously."

"I know." She held the slip of paper between them. "I'm super stoked about it."

"When you going to move?"

"I don't know." A big smile crossed her face, a beautiful one. "You know me. I'm impatient, so probably as soon as the space is empty."

He laughed. "Yeah, I give you two weeks tops to move in."

"So, that stuff you said I could have . . . ?"

"Yours."

She laughed. "I really should pay you for that."

"You can." His gaze dropped to her mouth. Her lips weren't the only place he hadn't tasted yet. So were her breasts. Now was neither the time nor the place for either of those things. "Let me take you out to dinner to celebrate."

"For real?" Surprise colored her voice.

"Yeah." He grinned at her. "This Friday. Have dinner with me."

She stared at him a moment and then glanced over his shoulder. "Aren't you worried about what people will think?"

"We're going out to dinner. Not robbing a store."

Nic cocked her head to the side as she raised her brows. "If people see us, they're going to talk."

"People always talk when they see a de Vincent," he replied. "I don't care. Do you?"

She took a moment to answer that, long enough to really start to worry him, but then a teasing gleam filled her eyes. "People will think I'm out having dinner with an older brother or something."

He let out a low chuckle. "Nice, Nic."

She laughed. "I'm kidding. I don't care what people think. I'll have dinner with you."

"That's my girl," he said, sliding his hands off her before he did something stupid.

She stepped back, staring up at him through those long eyelashes. "It better be that super expensive steakhouse you talked about before."

Chapter 23

"Cheers to new apartments!" Bree raised her margarita. Grinning, Nikki raised hers in toast, as did Rosie. "Cheers!"

It was Tuesday evening and she'd joined the girls for Taco Tuesdays and drinks to celebrate her apartment. She'd left the de Vincent house and drove straight to the complex to sign the lease.

"I cannot believe you're moving in next weekend." Bree shook her head. "I'd need at least a month to pack and label everything accordingly."

"That's because you're a bit obsessive," Rosie pointed out.

"True." Bree shrugged. "I like things to be orderly. There's nothing wrong with that."

"I don't have enough stuff to do that much packing." Nikki picked at what was left of her taco. "Most of my stuff from college is in storage."

"And did you hear?" Rosie turned to Bree. "Gabe is furnishing her entire apartment with his handcrafted goods."

Bree's mouth dropped open, and Nikki swore a piece of lettuce had fallen out. "What?"

"He is not." She shot Rosie a dark look. "He offered just a couple of pieces."

Slowly, Bree lowered her glass to the table. "His stuff costs—"

"I know how much it costs." Nikki picked up her drink. "It's just old stuff he's had for a while."

Bree stared at her.

"Oh, and he's also taking her out on a date to celebrate," Rosie added. "Let's not forget that."

"It's not a date," she argued even though her heart did a happy little cartwheel. "We're just doing a celebratory dinner."

"Nikki, don't pee on my leg and tell me it's raining," Rosie replied, and Nikki wrinkled her nose. "I know you two aren't just friends. Don't forget that I know things."

"Know what things?" Bree demanded.

Nikki sat back, nursing her drink while Rosie gave Bree the lowdown on what had happened between her and Gabe the night of her failed date with Gerald. Thank God she hadn't told Rosie about the most recent event.

When Rosie was done, Nikki narrowed her eyes. "I'm never telling you anything again."

Rosie laughed.

"I can't believe you didn't tell me." Bree leaned forward, her eyes wide. "You have to tell me. Does he have a big—"

"Can we please change the subject?" Nikki asked. "We're celebrating my apartment. Not my celebratory dinner date."

"So it *is* a date," Rosie jumped in.

Bree burst into laughter while Nikki flicked salt at Rosie. Luckily the conversation did change.

"Oh, before I forget." Rosie reached into her purse, pulling out a red velvet bag. "This is for the bracelet you're working on. One of my friends who runs a healing shop that focuses on chromotherapy—"

"Chromotherapy?" Bree frowned. "You know what? I don't even need to know what that is."

Rosie flipped her off. "Anyway, she was telling me that the color red helps stimulate energy and vitality."

"And here I thought the color red would have something to do with sex," Bree muttered.

"Of course you would." Rosie shook her head.

Nikki leaned over and took the bag. "Thank you. This

will be perfect to put the bracelet in." She didn't know if chromotherapy worked, but it couldn't hurt. "I just need to paint it. Now I know what color."

Walking out into the cool evening air, Nikki said goodbye to her friends and headed down the block to where she parked. She folded her arms over her waist and picked up the pace. It was that weird time of the year when there'd be pockets of heat and humidity throughout the day and then surprisingly cooler temps at night. Then again, she knew that people up north would think nothing of what they considered cold, but Nikki was wishing she'd remembered to bring a cardigan with her.

She rounded the corner and stepped off the curb, mindful of the traffic as she edged along the side of her car. As she hit the key fob, unlocking the door, she felt a sharp swirl of tingles along the base of her neck, an acute sense of awareness that raised the tiny hairs all over her body.

It felt like . . . like someone was watching her. It was the same feeling she'd gotten the night she'd left Cure.

Looking over her shoulder, her gaze darted along the block. There were people, but like before, no one was paying attention to her. Not that she could see, but as she opened up the car door, the feeling didn't go away.

BITING DOWN ON her lip to stop from crying out, Nikki wasn't exactly successful at staying completely quiet. How could she? Not when he thrust another finger inside her as he sucked deep and hard. She came hard and fast, and would've fallen over if it weren't for him holding onto her hips.

Goodness, he was really, really good at this.

"You totally wore a skirt today on purpose, didn't you?" He dragged his mouth along the inside of her thigh.

Holding onto the counter behind her, she lifted a shoulder. "Maybe."

"Easy access?" he asked, leaning back and straightening her skirt so it slipped back down her legs. "If so, I fully support this plan."

She laughed as he rose. He'd found her in one of the bathrooms on the third floor Thursday afternoon, and while fooling around like this came with the risk of being caught, it hadn't stopped them.

It wasn't going to stop her.

Placing her hands on his chest, she slipped out from between him and the counter. She pushed him back against where she'd stood.

A single eyebrow rose. "What are you up to?"

"You'll see." She reached between them, finding the button on his jeans. His eyes flared as she unhooked the button and pulled the zipper down. "I think you're starting to figure it out."

"I am." His voice was dark, rough.

Grinning, she gripped his pants and pulled them down. Gabe had gone commando today and the hard, thick length of him jutted out. She knew from that one night, long ago, that he would fill and stretch her, but if they hadn't had sex, she would've realized that the moment she saw him.

She lowered herself to her knees as she wrapped one hand around the base of his cock. His hips jerked in response and he exhaled raggedly. She was in awe of how her touch could affect him.

Nikki knew he was watching her as she leaned in, running her tongue over the glistening head. She knew he didn't take his eyes off her as he reached down and gathered up her hair, holding it back as she licked her way from tip to base and then made her way back, flicking the little indent. And she knew that he was wholly focused on her, only her, when she closed her mouth around him.

"Hell," he groaned.

The hand in her hair tightened, tangling it, and with the

slightest pressure, he urged her to take him as deep as she could, which wasn't all that far. She used her hand, timing the movements with her mouth.

"You're going to kill me," he said.

She hadn't given a lot of blow jobs in her life, but she was quick to realize that if a guy was into you, you pretty much couldn't do it wrong. And besides, she loved doing this for him. She figured that made up for the lack of experience.

"Fuck. Nic," he growled. He held her in place as his hips moved, taking over. "Look at you. Jesus."

There was something hot about that—about having him take over, take control. He wasn't afraid to hold back. He moved against her hand, in her mouth, and the way he fucked her mouth had her squeezing her thighs together to alleviate the ache that was springing back to life there.

His movements picked up, and she felt the deep pulse along his vein. He groaned, and her eyes flew open, wanting to see the moment he let go.

It was beautiful to her.

That striking face of his tensed as he kicked his head back, exposing his throat. Who knew a throat could be so damn sexy, but the straining muscle and veins were incredibly hot.

Gabe came, and Nikki didn't get a chance to pull away, not with his hand where it was, keeping her in place. She didn't want to, though. She wanted to finish him off and so she did, taking everything she could, sucking until he finally started to soften and he was pulling away.

He didn't let go of her right away. His hand was still balled in her hair as he dropped his chin and stared down at her. A long moment passed where there were no words between them. He cupped her cheek with his other hand, dragging his thumb under what felt like a swollen lower lip.

"Does it make me sound like a chauvinistic pig if I admit to wanting to keep you like this? On your knees, ready for me?"

"Yeah. It does," she said, cracking a grin as she turned her cheek into his hand. "But I wouldn't mind keeping you on your knees, so what room do I have to talk?"

Gabe made this sound, half groan, half laugh, as he pulled her onto her feet and then against his chest. He folded his other arm around her waist as he dropped his face to her neck. "You're going to kill me." He kissed her there, eliciting a shiver. "You know that, right?"

"Because you're old and going to have a heart attack?" she teased.

"Sweetheart, I could be your age and it would still feel like I'm seconds away from having a heart attack when you're sucking my dick."

"Not sure if I should feel flattered by that."

"You should." He kissed the side of her neck again. "You'll be the death of me, yet."

Nikki closed her eyes as her heart flipped over in her chest at the gesture. She wasn't so sure about that. She had a feeling it would be the other way around when this was all over.

Because it would end, wouldn't it?

The thought killed the mood about as effectively as getting doused with ice water. She wasn't sure where the thought even came from, but maybe it was because she was trying to hold a piece of her back from him, and was slowly and surely failing at doing so.

Because she knew she was falling for him.

Falling for him *again*, and this time it would be harder and further before she hit bottom. She could tell Rosie that she was in control of this all she wanted, but she knew the truth.

She wasn't in control.

And they . . . they hadn't kissed. Not even that night four years ago and not once since they started . . . *whatever* this was. She felt stupid to put so much weight behind something like kissing, but didn't that mean something? She wasn't sure if that was just a silly notion or if it was a red flag.

"Hey." His lips moved briefly against her neck before he straightened. She opened her eyes, finding him watching her intently. "What's going on in your head?"

"Nothing."

His eyes searched hers. "Are you sure?"

"Yes." She forced a smile. "But I do need to get back to work."

His arm tightened around her as he untangled his hand from her hair. She was so going to need to find a brush stat. "What if I want to keep you?"

She liked the sound of that too much. "I don't think that will go unnoticed come dinnertime."

"True." He sighed. Dipping his head, he pressed a kiss to her cheek, and her chest squeezed. "Can't have Dev going unfed."

"It would be an epic tragedy." She slipped out of his grasp and made her way out of the bathroom.

He caught up with her as she tried to smooth her hair with her hands. "You still look like you got fucked."

Nikki's cheeks caught fire. "Wow. Thanks."

Gabe chuckled as he faced her. "But I like the look."

"I'm sure you do," she replied dryly as she worked her fingers through a knot. "You need to go."

"Don't forget we're having dinner tomorrow night."

She shoved him with one hand. "I haven't forgotten."

He barely budged. "I think maybe we should do dinner tonight, except skip dinner and go straight for the—"

"Get," she said, shooing him out.

He turned, grinning at her as he walked backward, laughing as he bumped into the wall. She giggled as she whirled around, shaking her head.

Gabe was . . . God, she didn't even know what to say.

Walking back to the bathroom, she worked at her hair until she didn't look like she'd just had sex.

Especially since she didn't have *sex* sex.

Once satisfied, she shut the bathroom door and walked out into the bedroom, closing that door behind her. She was halfway down the hall, when she heard the slow creak of a door opening behind her.

Nikki's heart jumped as she turned around. No one was in the hall, but the door next to the one she and Gabe had been in was open halfway.

"Shit," she whispered.

Part of her didn't want to check it out, but she forced herself to do so. Tiny goosebumps rose all over her arms as she peered inside the bedroom. No one was there.

The room was like an icebox, though.

The goosebumps spread as the prickly sensation exploded all along the back of her neck. The same feeling she had before. The feeling that screamed that someone or *something* was watching her—was right behind her.

Holding her breath, she slowly turned around.

No one was in the hall.

But the door leading out to the porch was open, the gauzy curtains billowing as the breeze caught them.

And that door had been closed seconds ago.

Chapter 24

$\mathscr{I}$t was getting late when Nikki decided to call it quits and head home. Gabe was still at work, his hands covered with a fine layer of dust while he dragged the sander over the plank of wood.

She was lingering by the little room he'd made for her, still unsure of how to say goodbye. Should she just wave? Walk over and hug him? She couldn't believe she was even stressing that much about it, but things were very up in the air between them. Yes, he'd given her amazing orgasms and had his hands and mouth in just about every intimate place she could think of, but he wasn't her boyfriend.

Nikki wasn't at all sure what he was to her, so she stood there, worrying her lip and wondering what was the appropriate way to say goodbye. Like an idiot.

Straightening, Gabe looked over his shoulder at her. The corners of his lips curved up. "You leaving?"

"Yeah."

"You going to come over and say goodbye?"

"Yeah." She figured she couldn't stand by the door anymore, so she shuffled over to him, feeling her cheeks flush. She opened her mouth to say something, but he'd put the sander down and turned to her.

Before she could say anything, he swept an arm around her and lifted her up onto the tips of her toes. He'd brought her to him, pressing the length of her body against his. He dipped his head, and her heart did a back handspring in her chest. Was he going to kiss her?

His mouth skated over her cheek and then she felt his lips against the space below her ear. She shivered, and then a faint smile tugged at her lips when he lifted his mouth and kissed her forehead. "See you tomorrow."

Trying to not be disappointed that he hadn't kissed her, she smiled up at him as he let go. "See you tomorrow, Gabe." She backed up and gave him a little wave before she turned and headed for the door. She'd reached it when he called out for her. She faced him.

He had that damn grin on his face, the one that twisted her insides up in all kinds of delicious ways. "Do me a favor?"

"Sure."

"Wear a pretty dress for me tomorrow night?"

That got a laugh from her. "I can do that."

"You better, because I'll make it worth the effort." He picked up the sander. "'Night, Nic."

"Goodnight," she murmured, feeling a little flushed as she stepped out into the night. It wasn't a kiss, his goodbye, but it was . . . it was Gabe.

Pulling her keys out, she headed toward the diner, where she was parked. She spotted her car under the street lamp and was about to step off the curb when she heard her name.

"Nikki?"

Frowning at the vaguely familiar voice, she turned and her mouth about hit the sidewalk. "Are you fucking serious?"

Ross Gerald Haid was walking across the sidewalk toward her. His steps slowed as he lifted his hands. "I'm not here to cause you any trouble."

"Really? You're not? I don't believe that for a second."

"You have every reason to be suspicious, but I swear I just wanted to talk to you real quick." He shoved his hands into the pockets of his jeans. "I tried to get your number from Rosie so I could apologize, but she's pissed—"

"Damn straight she is. You used her to get to me so you could do your stupid story on the de Vincents. Yeah, she's pissed and so am I." Nikki's grip tightened on the keys to stop herself from throwing them in his face. "And how did you even know I was here—wait, you're a reporter." Suddenly she thought about the feeling outside of the bar and Cure—the first night she'd worked at the de Vincents and swore a car had been following her. Holy shit, was it him? "Have you been watching me?"

"I'm a reporter. Not a stalker."

She didn't believe him for one second. "Sounds about the same to me."

His jaw hardened. "I just wanted to apologize, Nikki. I did enjoy the dinner. Would've loved to have another one with you—"

"You are insane." Anger burned through her. "Gabe is right in there, and if he comes out here—"

"He won't be happy. I know." Ross kept his hands in his pockets. "But I'm risking that to apologize. I owe that to you."

"There is only one thing you owe me," she snapped. "It's for me never to see your face again."

"I can do that," he said, keeping his voice low as a couple walked past them. "But I feel like I owe you more than that."

"An apology? You can take it and shove it up—"

"A warning," he cut her off. "You seem like a nice woman and Rosie loves you. So, I feel like I need to say this to you. You've known the de Vincents a long time, so you think you know them, but you don't, Nikki. You don't know them at all."

A fierce need to protect them swept through her. "And you do?"

"I know enough to know that good people get hurt around them, and you seem like a good person," he said, his gaze finding hers in the dim street light. "And I'd hate to see you get hurt."

GABE WATCHED THE candlelight flicker across Nic's face as she lifted the glass of wine to those lush lips. God, when he walked into the restaurant and saw her standing there, he almost picked her up and carried her out of Firestones like a fucking caveman.

He'd never in his life had such a visceral reaction like that. Nic looked beautiful. Hair pulled up in a simple twist showed off those high, wide cheekbones of hers and her amazing, expressive eyes. He hadn't realized until that moment how elegant the curve of her neck was. And that dress? Fuck. It was like a second layer of skin in royal blue. Off the shoulder and dipping low enough to reveal just the hint of what swelled underneath that dress.

And the fact that several men dressed for what appeared to be a business dinner were blatantly leering at her didn't help quell the primitive urge to secret her away.

He'd wanted to pick her up tonight, but she'd insisted on meeting him at the restaurant. He'd only relented because it would be hard to explain to Richard and Livie why he was taking Nic out to dinner.

And what would he say to them?

That was a good question. One that had been plaguing him all day. Hell, one he'd been asking himself over and over during the last week or so. If they found out what he was doing with their daughter? He didn't like that he was hiding this from them.

That Nic was also doing the same.

And here he was, also lying to his family. Lucian had asked him what he was doing tonight, if he wanted to join Julia and him for dinner. Gabe refused and then brushed off an explanation of why. Truth was, he knew that any number of people here could recognize him, but they wouldn't know who Nic was.

Felt like he was hiding her because, well, he was. He was hiding her from all that mattered. None of it sat well on his chest.

None of that changed what he was doing.

Or what he wanted.

Now they were sitting in a booth that was the closest thing to private. Their dinner was drawing to a close. The check had already been paid, and he was thinking about all the hotels nearby. Would she accept an offer to spend the night at one of them?

God, he hoped so.

"You're staring at me again," she said, putting the glass aside.

"I am."

She grinned as she ducked her chin. "It's a little unnerving."

"Is it?"

Nic nodded.

"Why is that?"

She lifted one shoulder. Her skin seemed to gleam. "I'm pretty sure anyone is unnerved when they're being stared at."

"But I like it when you stare at me."

Her gaze flew to his. "Well, you're not just anyone."

Gabe chuckled. "That is true."

She looked away, biting down on her lip. This was the first lull in conversation since dinner began. They'd talked about everything from the upcoming holidays to what their favorite classes in college had been. For him, that felt like a lifetime ago, but it had been easy to recall, talking to her.

Which reminded him of something they hadn't discussed. "Have you given any more thought to going back to grad school?"

"I have." She toyed with the stem of her glass. "If everything works out with Mom's treatment, she thinks she'll be able to return to work at the beginning of next year. It will be part-time at first, until she gets back into the swing of things, but I won't be needed."

Gabe was happy to hear that Livie was planning on returning to work, but he wasn't exactly thrilled that it meant he wouldn't have the virtually unlimited access to Nic.

Wait.

He was thinking that far in advance? That was months from now. *Months.*

"So, with getting the apartment, I'm thinking it will be smart for me to get started working in my field. That way I'm making money and getting experience. Then once I'm settled in, I'll look at getting my master's. I can do both."

"I think that's a wise choice."

"You do?" she asked, her question genuine.

He nodded. "Getting out there and getting to work is probably going to do a hell of a lot more for you right now than taking more classes. Not that furthering your education is bad, but I think . . . I think you'll be happier working."

A brief grin appeared. "That is true."

"It'll be a lot of hard work, doing both, though."

"I know." She sighed. "Not exactly looking forward to that, but you do what you have to do."

"Right." He sat back. "At the risk of sounding like the old man you think I am, I'm incredibly proud of you."

Nic smiled. "You are an old man."

He huffed. "Seriously, though. You were the first in your family to go to college and graduate. You did this while working a part-time job. That's not easy, and you did that while making the dean's list."

"How did you—?" She cut herself off. "Mom or Dad tell you about that?"

"Both. They were proud. You should be proud."

"Flattery will get you everywhere," she teased.

Gabe grinned. "And when your family needed you, you were here, without a moment of hesitation."

"Well, that's not something to be proud of," she said, placing the napkin that had been in her lap onto her plate. "That's what you do for family."

"Not everyone." He glanced at his watch. "There's something I want to show you. That is unless you have other plans?"

"I don't have another dinner planned immediately after this."

"I would hope not." Rising, he walked around the table and offered his hand. "Come with me?"

Nic didn't hesitate.

Picking up her clutch, she placed her hand into his. He guided her out of the booth, toward the door marked EMPLOYEES ONLY. "Have you ever been to the rooftop of Firestones?"

"No." She laughed when he pushed open the door, leading her into the busy kitchen.

He winked at her when her eyes widened. The moment reminded him of when he and Lucian had brought Julia back here.

"I'm assuming no one has a problem with us being back here?" she whispered, folding her other hand over his arm.

"No." He pulled Nic out of the way of a waiter carrying a tray of steaming food above his head. "The entrance to the rooftops is private. Only a handful of people have keys to the elevator."

Nic eyed the ancient-looking elevator they were approaching. "So is this one of those hidden New Orleans gems? How in the world have I not heard about this?"

"It's *very* hidden." Letting go of her hand, he reached for his wallet and pulled out the card used to activate the elevator.

"Aren't you just special," she said as the doors creaked open.

Taking her hand once more, he pulled her into the elevator. "It's a little shaky, just a heads-up."

An eyebrow rose as the doors rattled shut and the elevator jerked into motion. "I really do not want to die in this elevator," she said, looking around.

Chuckling, he pulled her into his side as he finally, finally allowed himself to touch her. He did so by dropping her hand and letting his fall to her hip, running it up the flare of her hip and the curve of her waist. He felt the fine tremble course through her as his hand stopped just below the swell of her breast.

"I really like this dress, by the way."

One side of her lips curved up. "I thought you might."

The elevator stopped. Cold air flowed in as the doors opened. Folding his hand around hers once more, he led her out on the dimly lit rooftop.

Walking past several rippling curtained enclosures, he guided her over to the ledge. She slipped her hand free and walked ahead. "Wow," she breathed, placing her hands on the ledge as she stared out over the twinkling lights of buildings and cars down below.

"You like it?" He joined her, propping his hip against the ledge.

"I do." Her smile about stopped his damn heart. "As long as I've lived here, I've never seen the city from up here."

"Really?" That surprised him. The view up here was unique, giving the viewer a look at the Quarter from one side and Mid City from the other, but he figured at some point she'd gotten to see the city at night.

She nodded. "As many times as I've been down here at night, I've never been high enough to see something like this. It's really beautiful."

"Yeah." He watched a wisp of hair graze her cheek. "It is."

Nic glanced over at him. "I imagine you've brought a lot of women up here."

"Only one other," he admitted. "And that was Julia."

She angled her body toward his. "I feel like I need a further explanation of this."

He chuckled. "Lucian was with us."

"You may want to start with that statement."

"Good point," he agreed, inclining his head. "Is it too cold up here?"

"No. It's perfect." Looking over her shoulder, her gaze trickled over the softly moving white canopies. "What's behind there?"

"You want to see?"

"Yes." She looked up at him, and her upturned face was beautiful in the silvery moonlight. He knew right then and there, he'd have a hell of a time refusing her anything. "Yes, I do."

IF NIKKI THOUGHT the view was something to marvel at, the otherworldliness behind the white curtains gave it a run for its money.

Gabe had brushed one of the curtains aside for her to enter, and that was when she got her first glimpse of the plush white couches and chaise longues circling a white marble gas fire pit that threw off just enough heat to keep the chilliness beyond the canopies at bay. And once Gabe lowered the canopy back into place, sealing them in, it was almost like they weren't even on the rooftop.

Nikki's gaze fell back to the couch and her mind belly-flopped into naughty land when she wondered what people did behind these curtains. They weren't exactly thick, but they provided just enough privacy that only the very outline of a person would be visible.

"What do you think?" Gabe brushed past her as he walked around the fire pit and sat on the center of the couch.

"I like it." She looked around. "I imagine it's not too comfortable during the summer."

"They lift the canopies then and bring out these huge industrial fans. Still hot as hell, but there's a pool on the other side."

"Ah, I thought I smelled chlorine."

He leaned back, tossing an arm over the back of the couch. Nikki found the arrogant sprawl to be incredibly sexy. The white dress shirt he wore was unbuttoned at the top, and skin the color of sunbaked clay peeked out. His hair was down, the edges brushing the strong cut of his jaw.

"Now you're staring at me," he said, the look to his eyes soft.

"I am."

"And I like it."

Maybe it was the wine she had with dinner. It was an expensive kind she couldn't even begin to pronounce and would probably never drink again. Maybe it was the amazing dinner. Maybe it was the stunning view of New Orleans. Maybe it was just her and Gabe. Whatever it was, she was feeling a little wild and a little bold.

Walking around the fire pit, she dropped her clutch on the couch beside him and then she climbed onto his lap, placing her knees on either side of his legs.

His hands immediately went to her hips. "What are you up to, Nic?"

"I was getting tired of standing."

"Well, babe, anytime you get tired of standing, you are more than welcome to use my lap." He tugged her further down, seating her so she could feel him pressing up against her. "Anytime."

She flushed as she rested her hands on his shoulders. "Thank you for dinner."

"No thanks are necessary."

"It *was* an amazing steak," she said, her breath catching as he slid his hands up her waist.

He chuckled as his thumb brushed along the swell of her breast. "I'm beginning to think the only reason why you agreed to go out with me was to get another steak dinner."

"Maybe."

"I don't mind being used." That thumb had traveled further north, smoothing over the center of her breast. Her nipples immediately beaded.

The dress had one of those built-in bras that offered enough support for her to get away without wearing a bra, so when she reached up, crossing her arms as she gripped the tiny sleeves, she didn't let herself think about what she was doing.

Later, when she was all alone and asking herself if she really did this, she'd blame the wine.

Aware that Gabe's gaze was fastened on her, she shimmied the sleeves down. She felt the material give and then slip down her chest, pooling just below her breasts.

Gabe sucked in a ragged breath.

Cool air combatted the heated flush crawling down her throat and over her chest as she resisted the desire to cover herself. Instead, she placed her hands on his chest and let him look his fill.

And he did.

She wasn't exactly well endowed. Probably average when it came to breast size, but he looked at her like she unearthed some sort of treasure.

"Beautiful," he said, dragging his gaze to hers.

She bit down on her lip, and she thought that his hands trembled when he lifted them, cupping her breasts. Her entire body jerked at the contact.

"I don't remember this. From that night," he said, and Nikki jolted. They hadn't talked about that night since the first day he brought her the smoothie. "There are glimpses of memories, but I don't remember these."

Nikki's tongue was tied as he drew his thumbs over the tips of her breasts.

"I don't remember what they looked like. My imagination has been vast. Don't get me wrong." He plucked at one nipple, wringing a sharp gasp out of her. "But I don't remember how they felt, and my imagination only gets me so far."

"Well, I hope they lived up to whatever your imagination has conjured."

Thick lashes lifted, and his intense gaze pierced her. "They surpass my imagination."

Gabe slid his hands to her ribs and then he lifted her slightly, bringing her forward as he leaned in. His mouth closed over her nipple and he sucked deep. Sensation exploded as her back arched.

"Did I do this? That night?" he asked, voice ragged.

"No," she whispered.

He nipped at the sensitive flesh. "I didn't take my time with you. I remember that."

He hadn't.

"I'm going to fix that." His tongue swirled over her nipple as he caught the other one between his fingers. Her head fell back as she rocked her hips against his.

Aching emptiness roared to life. She wanted him to carry through on his promise to fix that night right now. She didn't care that they were here, on the rooftop. She needed him, wanting him so bad it—

"Gabe? You up here?" Devlin's voice suddenly rang out, rippling over the rooftop.

Nikki gasped as Gabe stiffened under her. For a moment, she couldn't react, couldn't even think, and then her brain screamed *Devlin is here!* And here she was, straddling Gabe with the top of her dress tugged down, exposing her breasts.

She was absolutely frozen, knowing that the curtains around the couches would only offer so much cover. Not with the soft glow of the gas fire pit.

Well, Devlin was about to find out firsthand exactly what Gabe was doing up here and that involved her.

This was not how she wanted what they were doing to get out. It meant she was going to have to tell her parents, because there was no way she expected Devlin to keep his mouth shut. And even if he did, knowing that someone so close to them knew, she'd have to tell them.

That thought didn't horrify her as much as she used to think it would. This was going to be measurably embarrassing, but a stupid grin tugged at her lips as a giggle rose in her throat. They were about to be caught like two horny teenagers. Ridiculous.

Gabe pulled back and . . . and *everything* about him changed in an instant.

"Shit," he muttered, gripping the bodice of her dress and tugging it up, over her chest. The giggle died in her throat as he gripped her hips and lifted her off him, onto her feet. He rose swiftly, his gaze focused on the slight gap in the curtains, and then he turned to her. "If you head out that way, you'll be able to come back around and go to the elevator without running into him. I'll keep him distracted."

The grin faded as she turned, her brain slow to process what he was saying. He wanted her to get out of here before Devlin saw them—saw them together.

I thought you didn't care who saw us?

The question rose, but it never made it to her lips. The back of her throat burned as stupid, *stupid* tears caused her to blink. She shouldn't be surprised. Why was she?

"Go." Gabe kissed her cheek and patted her hip. "I'll text you later."

Numbly, Nikki did just that.

She turned and left, heading in the direction Gabe had told her, wondering what the hell they were doing.

What was *she* thinking?

Chapter 25

Cursing his brother and himself, he watched Nic slip out between the curtains and disappear. What in the hell was Dev doing here?

He adjusted himself, because the last thing he needed to do was to meet his brother with a raging, evident hard-on, and then parted the curtains. Stepping out under the night sky, he scanned the rooftop, finding his brother by one of the tall plants. He had a drink in his hand.

"What are you doing up here?" he asked, striding across the rooftop.

"There you are." Dev turned to him. "I was told you headed up here with a very pretty lady." He frowned, looking around. "I was curious."

"You heard wrong."

Dev's gaze slid back to his. "What a strange thing to have heard wrong."

He didn't respond to that, because there was a good chance he was going to coldcock his brother for interrupting what had been turning out to be one of the best moments of his life.

"If you weren't with someone, what were you doing?"

Gabe exhaled through his nose. "Just enjoying the solitude. Obviously that didn't work out for me."

"Really?" His brother's response was dry. "Seems counterproductive to come to a restaurant to seek solitude."

"I did have dinner," Gabe replied, "and then I thought I'd come up here."

His brother smirked as he took a drink. "Interesting."

Nothing about the way he said that made Gabe think for one second he believed a single thing coming out of his mouth.

Dev confirmed his suspicions a moment later. "The waiter who mentioned you said you were with a *young* lady."

Gabe stiffened, and not in a good way.

"Said she was very beautiful with big brown eyes," Dev continued. "Reminded me of someone we both know."

"You know a lot of pretty ladies."

"I do." He glanced over at Gabe. "But not many you'd bring up here. I can only think of one."

Gabe said nothing.

Silence fell between them and then Dev asked, "What are you doing, Gabe? I'd expect something like this from Lucian—well, before he met Julia. I never worried that you would be spending your evenings with a—"

"Careful how you finish that sentence," Gabe warned.

"So, it's true?" Dev faced him. "Don't even bother lying. You've had this ridiculous habit of defending Nikki since she was a girl, getting herself in trouble."

Gabe said nothing.

"What are you thinking?" Dev demanded once more. "Wait. I get it. She's twenty-two and she's beautiful. What man wouldn't be interested? But you of all people should know better. Getting off can't mean—"

"Enough," snarled Gabe, stepping toward his brother. "Nic is not up for discussion with you. Not now. Not ever."

His brother tilted his head. A moment passed. "I'm here with a few of the board members. Since it appears I'm no longer interrupting anything, why don't you join us. At least for a drink or two?"

Gabe's jaw locked down. Joining his brother was the last thing he wanted to do. He'd rather find Nic. He felt like shit for running her off like that, but she did not need Dev finding them like that.

Dev waited.

"I'll be down in a moment," he said.

"We'll be waiting."

Gabe watched his brother disappear as he pulled his phone out of his pocket, opening up his messages. After debating on what the hell to say, he sent a quick text to Nic.

Sorry about that. Text me when you can.

Gabe stared at the message for a moment and then cursed. He got his feet moving and then he was heading down to join his damn brother.

She hadn't responded by the time he found his brother at his table, practically holding fucking court, and as minutes ticked into hours, she didn't respond.

NIKKI FELT . . . GROSS.

Not sick gross, but like she'd-done-something-bad-and-needed-to-shower kind of gross. She'd felt that way before, four years ago, and after Friday night, she was feeling that way again.

And if that wasn't a wake-up call, she didn't know what was.

When that stupid reporter had talked about good people like her getting hurt, she was sure he hadn't meant in this way, but he'd been right.

Her *heart* hurt.

That angered her, because she'd brought this on herself. She really had, because what in the hell had she been thinking messing around with Gabe?

Why in the world did she think her heart wasn't going to get involved?

She didn't even know why she was surprised or disappointed by the fact he hadn't wanted Dev to see him with her. Even though he'd claimed not to care, he did.

And she cared about people finding out, because she . . .

she didn't want to feel like she had to hide this thing with Gabe. But the truth was, she was being hidden.

So Nikki ignored Gabe's text on Saturday, holing up in her room and focusing on packing what few belongings she had that weren't in storage. Then she finished the bracelet, painting it red to match the bag Rosie had given her. She placed it on a piece of ripped cardboard and left it out to dry.

After taking a quick shower, she picked up her purse and headed downstairs. Her mom was in the living room, thumbing through a magazine. The color was already starting to return to her cheeks.

"I'm heading out to grab some extra boxes. Do you need anything?"

Her mom looked up, shaking her head. "No, but thank you."

She walked over to her, kissing her cheek. "You look good today."

"I feel good." Her mom smiled as Nikki straightened. "Thinking about getting out in the backyard and doing some weeding."

"And what will Dad say about that?"

Her mother snorted. "If he knows what's good for him, he won't say anything other than *Get them weeds, honey*."

Nikki laughed, knowing that was not what her father was going to say. "I'll see you guys later."

The skies were overcast as Nikki walked out front to her old Ford. She hoped that her mom wasn't outside if it started to rain. Colds could turn into pneumonia when your immune system had been all but obliterated from chemo.

Backing out of the driveway, Nikki knew of one place that had a lot of empty boxes and that was Gabe's workshop. She seriously doubted he'd be there at this time, so close to dinner. Not that she was avoiding him, because seriously, she was going to have to see him on Monday. She just didn't know what to say to him at this point.

Traffic made the drive to his shop take longer than necessary, but she was relieved to find a parking spot on the same block.

Unlocking the front door, she took a deep breath and peeked in. The main floor was dark. Relief coursed through her. Quickly closing the door behind her, she locked it and hurried toward the back hall, to a small room where she knew Gabe had broken-down boxes stored.

She crossed the main floor, not hesitating. All she wanted to do was get the boxes and get out. Reaching the hall, she glanced at the closed door a few feet down the hall, the one she knew led to Gabe's office.

Shaking her head, she reached for the other door and opened it. Nikki took one step when her heart lurched into her throat as the office door swung open.

Gabe stepped out into the narrow hall.

Shit.

That was all she could think. *Shit.*

Several seconds passed as they stared at each other. "Why have you been ignoring my texts?" he asked—no, he *demanded*.

Her spine straightened. "Why are you here?"

One eyebrow lifted. "It's my workshop."

"Yeah, but all the lights were turned off, and you're in your office, door closed, and . . . and stuff." That last part sounded lame to her own ears.

"I'm in my office, because I needed to find an order someone called about. The lights aren't on, because I hadn't planned on working," he replied. "And you haven't answered my question. Why have you been ignoring my texts?"

"I haven't been ignoring your texts," she lied. "I've been busy. I'm actually still pretty busy. Packing. I came here to grab some extra boxes I saw."

"Bullshit." He stepped forward, and since the hall wasn't that big, he was right there, looming over her. "I've texted five times."

"No," she said. "You texted—"

"Three times today and twice last night, and the last time I checked, three plus two equals five."

Her eyes narrowed. "I thought you meant today, smart-ass."

"No one is too busy to return a damn text."

That was true. "Whatever. I just need to grab some boxes—" She started to turn, but he caught her hand. Her eyes flew to his. "Seriously. I just want to grab boxes and get out of here."

His shoulders tensed. "You're pissed."

Nikki was about to deny that, but then, she just let it out. All those ugly feelings she had been stewing in since last night erupted from her. "Last night made me feel like shit," she said, yanking her hand free from his. "Like I was something to be hidden, to be ashamed of—"

"I'm not ashamed of you, Nic." His eyes widened. "How could you think that?"

"Really?" She laughed. "You literally lifted me off you and told me to run away before Devlin found us. How was that supposed to make me feel?"

"You really wanted Dev to find us like that?" he asked. "Dev?"

"Obviously I didn't want to be found with my breasts all out there for the world to see—"

"Glad we're on the same page when it comes to that."

She ignored that. "But I also don't like being made to feel like I have to hide, and that's what I had to do."

His eyes searched hers. "I didn't mean for you to feel that way."

"Well, I did." She crossed her arms, shaking her head as frustration rose. "What in the hell are we doing, Gabe?"

He fell silent.

Her chest rose with a painful breath. "Do either of your brothers know about this? Whatever this is? They don't.

Neither do my parents. I guess that's because we're not in a relationship, right?"

Gabe looked away, a muscle flexing in his jaw.

"So, I don't even know why I'm pissed or disappointed, because it's not like we've even talked about what the hell we're doing."

"We're talking now."

Nikki's laugh was harsh. "Yeah, well, it's a little late for that."

"Is it?" His gaze swung back to hers. "How is it too late when we are now just talking about this?"

"Because we're *now* just talking about this!" She drew in a slow, even breath. "Like last night wasn't even a date. It was a dinner to celebrate me getting an apartment, but—"

"How is that not a date?" he fired back. "We went out. We had dinner. I would've picked you up, but it was *you* that was dead set against that."

She opened her mouth. Well, shit. He had a point there.

"And we were getting to the part of the night that really felt like a date before we were interrupted."

"You mean when you asked me to run away before your brother found us?"

His nostrils flared. "Look, I get that I handled that wrong, and yeah, I felt like shit afterward. I was trying to protect you."

"Really? Or were you trying to protect yourself?"

Gabe's jaw hardened. A moment passed. "I guess I was trying to protect both of us."

She stared at him, unsure of how to feel about that.

"I didn't want you to have to deal with Dev. You know him. He would've said something incredibly offensive, because that's how he is," Gabe went on. "But I shouldn't have had you leave. That was wrong, because I'm not trying to hide you."

"You're not?" The knot was back in her throat.

"This situation isn't easy, Nic. You know that." He dragged a hand through his hair as he gave a little shake of his head. "All I know is that—fuck, I can't stop thinking about you. When you're not right in front of me, I'm wondering where you are and what you're doing. And when you are near me, it takes literally everything in me to keep my hands off you. I know that I want you more than I ever wanted anyone in my life."

He drew back like his own words shocked him.

What he said . . . wow. More than anyone in his life? More than Emma? Because if that was the case, that was huge, but that . . . that was all lust. It was sex. It wasn't romance. It sure as hell wasn't love.

Love?

Where did love come into play?

Her shoulders squared. She wasn't kidding herself any longer. Love was involved, because if last night had hurt her heart it was because her heart was open to him.

"You say all of that," she said. "But you haven't even kissed me, Gabe."

"What?" He looked confused.

"Kissed me. On the lips with your lips," she explained, rolling her eyes. "So don't stand there and tell me you—"

He moved so fast she wondered if he had special powers. Before she could even take her next breath, his hands were on her cheeks and he was tilting her head back.

And then his mouth was on hers.

Chapter 26

It was just a kiss—their first kiss—but Nikki knew the moment his mouth touched hers, she'd never been kissed like this.

His lips were on hers and there was nothing soft and sweet about this kiss. Oh no, this kiss branded her within seconds. His mouth moved along hers as his fingers played out across her cheeks.

Everything they'd been arguing about seconds before slipped away, and it was just him finally, *finally* kissing her. Nikki's body, her heart, and every part of her took over. Rising onto the tips of her flats, she wrapped her arms around his neck as she kissed him back.

Gabe shuddered, and Nikki thought that she might've stopped breathing right then and there. Mind reeling and senses spinning, she trembled as the kiss deepened, and when the tip of his tongue rolled over hers, she was lost.

And she'd been right. She'd never been kissed like this— like he was tasting her and owning her. A near-primitive sound rumbled from within him.

He lifted his head, breathing heavy. "You're right. I haven't kissed you. Shouldn't have waited this long."

And then he was kissing her again.

There was a brief second where Nikki worried that this wasn't smart. Her heart, oh God, her heart was in this and she knew what that meant. She . . . she loved him, and everything he said about her didn't mean he felt the same, but she couldn't stop herself.

Nikki wanted this too badly.

She always wanted this.

Gabe slid his hands off her cheeks, down her arms, and to her hips. He lifted her up, and instinct took over. Wrapping her legs around his waist, she held on as Gabe turned, pressing her into the wall behind them. Her stomach dipped like she was at the highest hill of a roller coaster.

His head tilted, deepening the kiss once more as he rocked his hips into hers. Her fingers tangled into the soft edges of his hair as she moaned into his mouth. Her heart was racing, her pulse pounding as her legs tightened around him.

He moved them to the side, knocking into something that was propped up there. A broom? She wasn't sure. It clattered to the floor, and Gabe laughed into the kiss as he pulled her away from the wall. His hands dropped to her rear and squeezed as he started walking. A maddening riot of sensations shot through her as he held her there, devouring her as he took them into the office.

She'd only seen inside it once, knew that there was a table, a few chairs, and a couch. She had a feeling that was where he was taking her, and she was so onboard with that idea.

They fell backward, onto the couch, their lips not breaking contact as they sunk into the soft cushions. Reaching down, he gripped her thighs, his hand opening and closing, and then he lifted her leg up, hooking it around his waist. His mouth was still claiming hers as he rolled his hips, pressing into where she throbbed for him. She tilted her hips, seeking what they both wanted. He answered with a ragged groan.

His lips seared hers as he reached under her shirt, the rough skin of his hand burning up her skin. The pressure of him pushing against her was almost too much, but not ever enough. The grip on her thigh almost hurt as they moved against each other, her hands tangling in his hair, his yanking the cup of her bra aside and closing around her aching breast.

His mouth left hers then, blazing a hot trail down her throat. He reached the collar of her shirt as he plucked at her nipple.

"Gabe." She arched her back, crying out.

He rocked backward, pulling his hand out from her shirt. For a brief, disappointing second, she feared that he was going to stop. "Shirt. Off. Now."

All righty then, he definitely wasn't stopping.

Before she even moved, he was tugging his shirt off over his head and tossing it aside. Her eyes widened as his hands dropped to the button on his jeans.

"Catch up, sweetheart," he said.

Nikki sat up as far as she could and reached for her shirt, but she apparently wasn't moving fast enough because he all but ripped it off her.

Damn.

He caught her before she lay back down, wrapping his hand around the back of her head, holding her in place as his mouth moved over hers once more. His other hand was up to no good, finding the clasp along the back of her bra. He obviously had a lot of experience in that department, because within seconds, he had it unhooked. One-handed. The straps slipped down her arms. He reached between them, hooking his fingers along the center of her bra. He pulled it free, and that, too, hit the floor.

Then he let go of her.

She fell back onto her elbows, her lips swollen as she watched him stare down at her, his intense gaze feeling like a touch.

"I need you. Fuck, Nic. I need you so bad," he said, his eyes burning as they met hers. "I don't have a condom with me, but I'm clean."

Her heart was throwing itself against her chest so fast and hard that she thought she might have a heart attack. "I'm on the pill."

"Thank fuck." He leaned over her, planting a hand by her

head. The muscles in his arm strained. "You want this? If you don't want to go this far, we can stop. Right now. Just tell me."

"Yes. I want this." She didn't hesitate. Not for a damn second, and she'd probably regret the hell out of that later, but not right then. "I want you."

Gabe looked like he murmured some sort of prayer and then he was swinging off the couch. She turned, unable to look away as he shucked off his pants, briefs and all, and then he was standing before her, completely nude. She eyed his erection as she bit down on her lip.

"You keep looking at me like that, this is going to be over before we even get started."

Oh my.

She forced her gaze up to his. "That would be disappointing."

"Exactly." His face was tense. "Stand up."

A fine shiver rolled through her as she did what he demanded. He got ahold of her pants and he had her naked in record time. Seriously. If it were an Olympic sport, he would've gotten a gold medal.

She started to laugh, but then he was kissing her again and guiding her onto her back, settling between her legs. She could feel him, hard against the softest part of her.

Nikki tensed, preparing for him to slam into her, like it had been that night, but that's not what happened.

Gabe kissed her again, but this kiss was . . . it was different. Slow. Sweet. Tender. He kissed her like he cherished her, and he kept kissing her until she felt herself relax.

Then his mouth left hers.

Kissing and nipping at her skin, he made his way down her throat. The edges of his soft hair brushed the swell of her breast, stretching her nerves. He drew her nipple into his mouth as he slipped his free hand between her thighs, and every part of her body flared to life. Pleasure rolled through her as her fingernails dug into his hair. Nikki's gasp turned into a moan as he thrust his finger into her. Her hips nearly came clear off the couch as he moved to her breast, taking it deep into his mouth.

Her body clenched around his hand as hot, tight shudders wrecked her. He was driving her crazy, moving his hand slowly and torturing her with his mouth and tongue.

Nikki groaned his name as she rolled her hips against his hand.

A satisfied smile split his lips as he lifted his head. "Damn. I love hearing you say my name when I've got my finger in you."

Pleasure spiked as he slipped another finger inside.

"God, you're so wet." His thumb smoothed over the tight concentration of nerves, flooding her body with wet heat. "You're ready for me."

"Yes." She grabbed a fistful of hair, dragging his mouth back to hers. Lightning was rushing through her veins. "Now," she said against his mouth. "I want you *now*."

He made that sound again as he withdrew his fingers, and then she felt him again, hard and hot at her core. The arm pushing into the couch shook as he broke the kiss, pressing his forehead against hers. He slowly pushed in.

"Oh, God," she panted, gripping his arms as he inched in, stretching her. The bite of pain mingled with the pleasure, twisting together.

He halted. "You okay?"

"Yeah." She brushed a hunk of his hair back. "It's just been a while. Like a really long time."

Gabe shuddered. "I know it makes me an ass, but you have no idea how badly I want to fuck you after hearing that."

Nikki trembled. "More than before?"

"Didn't think that was possible." He kissed her. "But yeah."

She slid her other hand down his arm, curling her fingers around his forearm. "Then do it."

He lifted his head, and those sea-green eyes were blazing. "Do what, Nic?"

Never in her life had she spoken those words, but she did just then, without an ounce of embarrassment. "Fuck me."

His hips punched forward almost out of reflex. Gabe's eyes drifted shut as he groaned. He pushed in, and she took him, bringing her knees up and hooking her legs around his waist as he sunk all the way in.

For a long moment, neither of them moved. Their bodies were flush, hip to hip, chest to chest. She could feel him throbbing deep inside her, and then he started to move.

His large body trembled as he slowly pulled out and then rocked forward, causing Nikki's back to arch.

"God," he groaned. "You feel . . . God, you feel too good."

So did he. She wanted to tell him that, but she was beyond words at that point, completely lost as he set a slow pace that drove her to the breaking point, but not quite over. His mouth found hers once more. Tilting her hips, she met each deep and even thrust until she couldn't, until the pace quickened and his body was holding hers down.

Gabe's cheek pressed into hers as the couch squeaked under them and knocked into the wall. She could feel him swelling and tightening with each breath she took. Tension built deep inside her as she dug her heels into his back, urging him to move faster, and harder, and he answered.

It felt like every muscle in her body tensed up and the coil spinning deep inside her unfurled at a dizzying rate. There was no slow buildup to the climax. The deep pounding thrusts sent her over the edge.

Crying out as the most intense pleasure rolled over her in tight, hot waves, all she could do was hold on as his hips pounded into her in a tempo that was shattering.

"Gabe—oh God, I can't—" Her head kicked back as Gabe worked an arm under her shoulders, pulling her to him as he ground his hips into her. She couldn't tell if she was having another orgasm or if it was the first one still destroying her. She fell back, eyes closed, body nearly limp.

Her name was rough on his lips as he pulled out at what seemed like the last second, pushing his arousal against her stomach as he came, pulsing against her stomach.

Gabe braced his weight on one arm, his hips still jerking as she felt him kiss her shoulder. A moment passed and then he kissed the corner of her lips.

Nikki took a shallow breath. "That was . . . one hell of a kiss."

GABE STARED UP at the ceiling, listening to the rain beat the roof as he dragged his fingers along Nic's arm. Her warm breath danced along his arm. She was on her back, snug between him and the back of the couch, and he was on his side, barely hanging on to the couch. His arm was under her shoulders and she was currently using his bicep as a pillow, but he didn't care. He'd never been more comfortable in his life.

And sex had never felt like that in his life.

Not even with Emma.

He was a little amazed about how that thought didn't slice through him like a barb-tipped whip. It was just *there*. A thought. A past. Nothing more. Nothing less.

Gabe dragged his gaze from her face. He'd cleaned her up with his shirt, but neither of them were covered. Her breasts rose and fell with deep, even breaths. He loved those plump little nipples. He felt his dick stir to life as his gaze dropped to where her thighs were spread. She was almost bare between her thighs. Just a dusting of hair. He'd already known that. Obviously, but seeing her, all of her, lying next him, completely comfortable, was a whole different thing.

His gaze found his way back to her breasts. The deeper, pinker skin of her nipples made his mouth water.

"Are you staring at my breasts?" she asked, her voice soft. He grinned as his gaze flickered to her face. Her head was still turned away from him, but he could see that her eyes were closed. "Maybe."

"I think you were."

"It wasn't the only thing I was staring at."

She turned her head toward him. Lashes fluttered open, and then he was staring into those beautiful brown eyes. "You're a dirty old man."

"Damn straight." He pressed his dick against her thigh.

Her eyes widened slightly. "Are you hard?"

"Almost." He lifted his hand to her cheek. "I have a beautiful woman lying naked next to me. I'm going to be in a permanent state of hardness."

She laughed softly.

Looking over his shoulder at the wall clock, he sighed. "Do you have to be anywhere?"

"No, but I should probably text my mother," she said, yawning. "I told her I was going to get boxes."

"Want me to grab your phone? I think your purse is somewhere on the floor."

"Not yet," she said. "Because that means you'd have to move, and you're warm, and I'm comfortable."

Good. He didn't want to move either.

Hell, Gabe didn't want to let her go.

That thought seemed like it came out of nowhere, but it really didn't. He pushed it aside. "You hungry?"

She made some sort of noncommittal sound and lifted a shoulder, which jiggled her breasts, and now his dick was rock hard. Great.

Her eyes had drifted shut again. He traced her lower lip. They should probably talk. He was sure they hadn't really settled anything, but how could talking settle things?

He had a feeling that talking would make things worse, because she'd been getting real close to touching on the subject of what they were, and he didn't have an answer for her.

His fucking head was a mess when it came to this woman.

Gabe closed his eyes as an almost keen sense of desperation washed over him. The feeling that there was an expiration date on this—on them—was hard to shake.

He thought about what Dev had said to him the night before. What was he thinking? He should be focused on getting a place in Baton Rouge and building a new life with his son.

Not this—not building a life with Nic.

Gabe never planned to rip William away from his grandparents. That was why he was looking for a place in Baton Rouge. Eventually, he wanted his son living with him full-time, but that was going to take time. More time than three months, and the thing was, there may not ever be enough time for the Rothchilds to give him up.

If the Rothchilds fought him and took him to court, it wouldn't look good if Gabe was dating a much younger woman. Gabe knew that—knew that people went to ugly places to protect the ones they loved. Hell, he'd done some ugly things to protect people.

He wasn't Dev, though. They had the power and money at their fingertips to ensure that there'd be no problems with custody, but he wouldn't do that to his son. He wouldn't do that to Emma's parents who'd lost their own child.

It was a fucked-up situation.

A burn centered over his chest. What he was doing was unfair to Nic. Gabe wanted her, but he knew he wasn't going to get to keep her, because she was going to want more. She deserved more, and he didn't have that in him.

He wondered if he ever truly did, even with Emma.

He'd have to give her up.

His eyes flew open as he felt the flick of her tongue on his thumb. Their gazes connected as she drew his thumb into her mouth, sucking hard enough that it sent a burst of pure lust to his cock.

Fuck.

All thoughts evaporated.

He lifted up on his elbow, his gaze glued to where those lush lips were wrapped around his thumb. "I'm going to fuck you," he said.

Nic's eyes closed as she moaned around his thumb. Fuck. That was the hottest thing he'd seen and heard in a while.

Keeping his hand curled around her chin and his thumb in her mouth, he rolled her onto her stomach. He gripped her hip, urging that sweet ass up in the air.

"Don't move," he said, and once he was sure she was stable on her knees, he gripped his cock and guided himself to the prettiest part of her. He pulled his thumb out of her mouth and curled his arm around her shoulders, effectively keeping her in place.

He remembered how tight she'd been, so when he eased himself into her, he did it slow, giving her time to adjust to his size. Then she twitched that ass of hers, tilting it back on his cock.

He sucked in air. "Thought I told you not to move."

"I can't help it," she said, making a tight, slow circle with her hips. "You feel too good."

Gabe held still as she rocked back, riding his dick. Watching her ass move . . . yeah, this wasn't going to last long. Not at all.

Using his hand, he stilled her hips as he lowered his mouth to her ear. "I'm going to fuck you now. Hard, babe. I'm going to fuck you *hard*."

Nic shuddered.

And that's what he did.

There was no slow buildup. This was no slow seduction. He fucked her hard, slamming into her, driven by the way her back bowed and her soft moans filled the room.

He knew he should slow down. She'd said it had been a while, but he couldn't. His blood pounded and she felt too damn good, clenching and squeezing down on him. He reached around, finding her clit, playing with her as he hammered away.

Her cries grew louder as she thrust her hips back at him, riding him just as hard as he was doing her. The couch was going to knock a damn hole in the wall, but he couldn't stop.

You're going to lose her.

A chill swept down his spine.

Gabe lost all semblance of control when he felt her spasm around him. Pulling his hand away, he pinned her down, one hand on her lower back, the other lifting up her hips. He thrust into her over and over, feeling like he lost a little bit of his mind as his release powered through him.

Feeling like he lost a little bit of himself.

Chapter 27

$\mathcal{N}$ikki had been a nervous wreck when she texted Gabe Sunday morning and asked if he wanted to meet her at the shelter. Part of her had expected him to turn down her offer, but that's not what happened. His response had been immediate and now they stood in front of Ned Rivers, being handed leashes.

Ned was one of the volunteer supervisors at the animal shelter, an older man who'd grown up in the city, and had a bad run at things in his younger years that had included a stint in prison. While doing time, he'd taken part in a program that involved rescue dogs and ever since he'd dedicated his life to second chances.

And that was what this shelter was all about.

Second chances.

Seemed oddly fitting to be there with Gabe.

Right now, Ned was giving Gabe a speculative look. Nikki was confident it had nothing to do with it being Gabe's first time here, but more about who he was. Very few locals didn't know who the de Vincents were.

"Thanks, Ned." Nikki took the leash while the older man eyed Gabe. "Who needs the exercise today?"

"Besides me?" Ned quipped, grinning up at her. "Fusion and Diesel." He slid a glance in Gabe's direction. "They're full-sized pits. You think you can handle them?"

Gabe gave a half grin. "I hope so."

"You'll be fine." Nikki hid a smile as he took the leash from Ned. "Fusion and Diesel are just big babies."

"Their names don't give that impression," he commented.

Ned snorted as he picked up a file off his desk, but he kept his mouth shut. Nikki curled her arm around Gabe's and pulled him back out the front door of the office.

"I don't think the guy likes me," Gabe said as they rounded the outside of the building, drawing closer to the sound of barking dogs.

"He doesn't know you." Nikki slipped her arm free as they neared the high chain-link fence that surrounded the kennel. If the de Vincents weren't so infamous around the country, he would've passed as any normal volunteer dressed down in a pair of loose, gray sweats and a plain shirt.

Goodness, he looked good dressed like that. Silver sunglasses on, hair pulled back at the nape of his neck in a neat bun. Then again, he pretty much just always looked good.

"Thank you for coming," she said, stopping in front of the gate. One of the workers hurried over to unlock it.

"No problem. I was up and don't have much planned."

Nikki smiled at the worker who did a double-take in Gabe's direction. "Not heading into the workshop?"

"Later." He placed a hand on her lower back as they walked through the open gate. "You?"

She lifted a shoulder. "Maybe."

"You should." His hand trailed over her hip, causing her to shiver.

Nikki bit down on her lip as she wandered over to the kennels. "Is there a reason why you think I should?"

"Multitude of reasons."

Stopping to pet a golden retriever, she looked over her shoulder at Gabe. "Does one of those reasons involve a couch?"

Those sunglasses shielded his eyes, but she could feel his heated stare. "It can. But there's also a desk I think was feeling lonely last night."

She laughed as she scratched the retriever under the chin.

After a few moments, she pulled her hand free, and the retriever whined. "You've already had your walk, baby. I'm sorry."

The twinge in her heart as she walked away from the poor dog wasn't anything new. She met the worker at the last two kennels, and within a few moments Diesel and Fusion were on their leads, tails and butts wiggling as they sniffed Gabe's shoes.

"I hope that means they like me." He stared down at them.

"They pretty much like everyone. Pits are friendly dogs," she said, leading them over to the large stretch of grassy area. "They get a bad rap, though."

Gabe was grinning at his black-and-white spotted pit. "Which one is this?"

"That's Diesel."

"He's freaking strong."

Diesel was excitedly pulling at the leash, sniffing every blade of grass, it seemed, while Fusion did his hopping thing, which was how he walked when he was excited.

"I imagine volunteering here has to be hard for you," Gabe commented, drawing her gaze. "I figure you'd adopt all the dogs."

"I wish I could." She brushed a strand of hair back from her face. "If I had a ton of money, I'd love to have my own rescue."

Gabe chuckled. "You sound like Julia. She said the same thing."

"That's because Julia is good people." She grinned. "I want to get a dog, but with an apartment, I'd have to get a small, lazy one. These guys would go nuts inside one."

Gabe was quiet for a moment. "Lucian always wanted one of these when he was growing up."

"Your dad would've had a shit fit—" Her eyes widened. "Sorry. Lawrence would've had a fit."

"It's okay." He grinned. "Lawrence was my father even

if it wasn't by DNA. He's the only father I knew. And you're right. There was no way he'd allow any of us to have a pet."

"Because it would make noise," she commented, thinking back to the day the senator was in the house. "And leave dog hair everywhere."

"We almost had our mother convinced once, though. Actually, it was Madeline. She wanted one of those little dogs. The kind that bites ankles." He knelt beside Diesel and patted him. The dog immediately flopped onto its sides, panting for belly rubs. Gabe obliged. "I think it was a Yorkie or something like that."

From what Nikki remembered of Madeline, she could picture the often-sullen girl carting around that type of dog. She watched Gabe scratch Diesel's belly. "Why did your mom end up not getting her one?"

"Don't know. She and Mom had a weird relationship. Went from her doing everything and anything for Madeline, and then it was like they weren't even speaking to one another." He dragged his fingers to the dog's chest, and Diesel thumped his tail off the grass. "But you know how all of that ended."

She did, and she still couldn't believe it. "I really am sorry that any of you had to go through that."

He tipped his chin up and a faint smile tugged at his lips. "Makes you wonder if the de Vincent curse is real, doesn't it?"

The curse had a thing for women.

It was said that the land the house was built on was tainted. Apparently it was used as a quarantine area during the many deadly flu outbreaks that plagued New Orleans. Legend went that the patriarch of the de Vincents was warned not to build a house there, but he hadn't listened, which angered the spirits of all who'd died on the land. The strange thing about the curse, if one believed in those kinds of things, was that it seemed to really hate women.

Two things happened to the de Vincent women. They either ended up . . . unstable.

Or dead.

And there was a long, very verifiable history of those two things.

"Do you believe in the curse?" she asked, scratching the pit behind its ear as she glanced over at him.

Gabe's hand stilled along the dog's hip and a long moment passed before he answered. "I used to think it was just an interesting story my grandmother would tell us, but sometimes I do wonder if there is some truth in it. Not even counting all the bizarre deaths in our family that span centuries? Just look at what has happened in the last couple of years. Our mother. Emma. Our sister. Julia could've died that night on the rooftop. So maybe the curse is real. Seems like everything—everyone we touch ends up tainted."

"Not everything." She reached over and touched his arm, her chest heavy for him—for his family. "Not me."

He studied her a moment and then smiled. "Not you."

NIKKI WAS PROBABLY the biggest fool alive, but she couldn't keep the grin off her face as she picked up the stack of towels Monday afternoon and started to carry them upstairs.

Devlin had given her Friday off to focus on her move, telling her this before he'd left for Houston. So not only could she get an early start on her move, she didn't have to cook dinner for the rest of the week as he wouldn't be returning until Saturday afternoon.

That also meant that since Devlin wasn't here, there'd be no reason for Sabrina or Parker to be either.

Win. Win.

The goofy grin she'd been rocking since Saturday night wasn't completely due to Devlin's actual thoughtfulness or his absence. A lot of it was due to what went down between her and Gabe. That played a big role in it.

Goodness.

Gabe was . . . he really was insatiable.

Her cheeks flushed as the weekend replayed itself for about the hundredth time. Saturday night had been . . . amazing, but Sunday afternoon and evening? They were a repeat of Saturday and then some. He'd made sure that desk hadn't been lonely, setting her on the edge and feasting on her before he stood her up and turned her around, bending her over. When he'd taken her from behind, she'd never been more turned on in her life nor had she ever been . . . taken that hard before.

She found that she really, really liked it.

Gabe hadn't stopped there. He'd ordered lunch from the diner down the street, like he'd done Saturday night, and picked it up for them, and afterward, he'd pulled her into his lap and they'd had sex again.

The last time . . . it had felt different.

It had been slower, and somehow it was so much more intense. It had felt like they were making love.

And they'd talked—just talked about everything. Her upcoming move and Gabe told her once more she needed to get a dog, which brought up the whole armadillo thing again. Nikki wasn't against getting a dog, but she knew she needed to hold off on that. She didn't want to get a dog and then never be home because she was working and going to school.

And they talked about Lucian moving out, and how it was going to be weird with him not being in the house. Gabe talked more about his sister—what she'd done and what it had meant to him and his brothers. They even talked about who his father could've been, but Gabe really had no clue. After dinner and the last time they'd had sex, they'd just lain together, and it felt so normal, so right.

It felt like something real, something deep. It felt like love.

Stopping in the hallway, she closed her eyes and inhaled deeply. She shouldn't let herself think *that*, but she couldn't help it. Her heart was like a jumping bean in her chest every time she thought about the way he'd kissed her goodbye, like he didn't want to let her go.

And she didn't want to go.

A little niggle of warning squirmed in the pit of her stomach like a snake waking up from slumber. They talked about everything but what *they* were. And while the sex had been amazing, it didn't solve anything.

It didn't answer any of her lingering questions.

Opening her eyes, she wondered where Gabe was. She hadn't seen him. He was probably at the shop, but she'd figured he'd be back soon. He'd always brought her a smoothie around this time.

She hurried down the hall before her arms gave out. Rounding the corner, she almost ran into Julia.

"Hey." The woman immediately reached for the towels. "Let me help you with that."

"You don't have to."

"I know." She took half off the top, smiling. "But I hate seeing people doing things when I'm more than capable of helping. Where are you going with these?"

Yet again, Nikki was reminded of how much Julia was not like Sabrina. "These are actually going to Lucian's apartment."

"Then this worked out perfectly," she replied, walking with Nikki. "How is your mother doing?"

"Really good. She's nearing the end of her treatment, so we're crossing fingers that when they do the scans, it'll show that the cancer is gone."

"I really hope so."

"How're the renovations on the house going?" Nikki asked as they neared Lucian's rooms.

"We're almost done. I think we'll be in there before the holidays, so I'm looking forward to that," she said. "You know, having my parents down and everything. I really do not want them coming here for dinner—" Her eyes widened. "I probably shouldn't have said that."

Nikki laughed. "It's okay. I totally understand why you wouldn't want your parents to spend Thanksgiving at the de Vincent table. It would probably be the most awkward and strained dinner of all time. Trust me. I've seen some of them while the parents were alive."

"I keep forgetting that you know how this family is," Julia said, looking at the closed door to Lucian's rooms. "I don't think people on the outside would understand how they are."

"They wouldn't," she agreed, thinking of Ross. She hadn't told Gabe about running into him, figuring he really didn't need to know that. But people like Ross wouldn't understand the de Vincents. They'd always think and assume the worst.

"And my parents wouldn't. Lucian and Gabe? Sure." Julia shifted the towels. "But Devlin and Sabrina? The senator? No. They'd be like *What in the hell is wrong with these people?*"

Nikki grinned. "I think that's a question many ask themselves daily."

Laughing softly, Julia's gaze made her way back to her. "But you're like family to them, so you understand all of this. You know how the boys seem to always fight for what's best for them, what they really want. That fight makes them do and say stupid things." She paused. "And I'm sure you know that, too. You seem to be really close to Gabe."

Nikki stilled, unsure of how to respond to that. "Gabe has always been . . . kind to me." She promptly thought about the weekend and flushed. He hadn't exactly been *kind* then. "We both like to work with wood."

"I bet you do," Julia said, grinning.

Her eyes widened. "I didn't mean it like—"

"I know." Julia laughed. "Anyway, so yeah, I hope to be out of here by the holidays. I can't wait for my parents to see the new house. I think Lucian is planning on taking them on weird city tours or something."

Relieved at first that the conversation moved back to safer topics, Nikki let her smile fade a little as envy sprung to life. Tours with the parents. Holidays with them. A happy future that included the people you cared about. No matter how she felt for Gabe, she wasn't naive enough to see that in their future.

And that was . . . well, it was just *sad*.

Nikki dropped off the towels and started back downstairs after leaving Julia, but she stopped in the hallway. Her legs just refused to move as the reality of the situation swept over her.

She was in love with Gabe.

That was no surprise. She'd been in love with him since the day he saved her in the pool. That love had driven her to do idiotic things—things that Gabe had taken part in.

But she hadn't chased after him when she returned. She'd steered clear and it was he who came to her, claiming he wanted to be friends. It was he who ruined her date and made the first move. It was Gabe chasing after her.

That had to mean something.

What Julia had just said rose to the surface. *You know how the boys seem to always fight for what's best for them, what they really want.*

Gabe wanted her. He'd proved that time and time again, but it wasn't easy. There were his brothers. Their history. Her parents. Their age gap. None of that mattered to her. She loved him and a little piece of her heart told her that it was quite possible that Gabe felt the same.

After all, it wasn't like he was hurting for female companionship. He could easily go out there and find someone if it was just about sex, and it would be easier for him to do that. There wouldn't be all these complications. He had access to a metric crap-ton of no-strings, stress-free sex.

There was a reason why he'd gone for her, and Nikki

couldn't help but think of what Rosie had said when she'd told her about the little room Gabe had set up for her in the shop. What had Rosie said? That maybe Gabe had spent the last four years hating himself, because he'd wanted her back then, just like he wanted her now.

You didn't want someone that long without having strong feelings for them.

Nikki knew what she needed to do.

She needed to tell Gabe how she felt.

Her legs started moving. She didn't go downstairs. Since her father had left for the day, she gave in to the impulse. She hurried outside, taking the quickest route to the other wing, walking along the porch. She shivered as the wind blew the rain in. Climbing the stairs on the right wing, she made her way to the third floor, to the outside entrance of Gabe's suite.

She hesitated at the doors and then knocked. The door cracked open. It had been left unlocked and unlatched. Her stomach dipped. Gabe had to be home then. She stepped inside the living area part of his apartment. The lights were off and the door to his bedroom was open. She could hear the shower running.

Inching toward the bedroom, she stepped inside the spacious room.

She thought about surprising him by stripping naked and jumping in, but then she rolled her eyes. She didn't exactly have the nerve to do that yet, and besides, if she did that, they'd get nothing discussed.

Nikki looked around his bedroom instead. She actually hadn't been in his apartment since that night. Not once had she cleaned his rooms and he hadn't mentioned it to her since the day in the gym.

Now that she was here she found that very little had changed from what she remembered. It was sparse. A huge bed in the middle. One end table. There was a worn book on the stand, next to what appeared to be a picture frame.

The room was too dark for her to see who the picture was of. There was one large dresser across from the bed, one that Gabe had made himself. The intricate ivy ran the length of the beautiful piece of furniture. Nikki inhaled, catching the fresh, clean scent of his cologne.

Her gaze traveled over the dresser. She almost didn't see it since it blended in so well. She did a double-take and her lips parted.

"No way," she breathed, walking over to the dresser.

She picked up the necklace, immediately recognizing the thin, cheap leather knock-off rope. Her breath caught as she ran her thumb over the medallion she'd carved for him. It was rather simple and kind of crude. Just a circle with a sword and chisel she'd carved into it. For some reason, she'd thought adding the sword was the cleverest thing ever. Kind of dumb now; the whole the-chisel-is-mightier-than-the-sword thought she had going on, but Gabe . . .

After all these years, Gabe had kept it.

Tears pricked at her eyes as she curved her fingers around the medallion. He'd kept the necklace that she'd brought him that night four years ago. He hadn't hidden it. It lay on his dresser, where he could see it every day.

Every day for four years.

More affected by that than she could've ever imagined, she brought the necklace to her chest just as she heard the water turn off in the shower. Unable to even begin to stop the smile racing across her face, she turned toward the bathroom. A few moments passed and then the door opened. Steam rolled out as—*holy shit.*

Sabrina Harrington walked out of Gabe's shower, wearing nothing but a towel around her slender body.

Nikki's mouth dropped open. "What in the hell?"

The woman jolted, her eyes widening. She paled so quickly that for a moment Nikki thought she might actually pass out. "What are you doing in Gabe's room?" Sabrina recovered, snapping out the question.

Was she serious? Asking *her* that question. "What are you doing in his shower?"

Her lips twisted in a smirk as she clutched at where the towel was folded above her breasts. "Why do you think I'm using his shower?"

Nikki laughed—straight up laughed. She couldn't help it, because she knew what Sabrina was insinuating with that comment. "You are so full of shit—like so much shit that you have no space left for a brain."

She drew back, her mouth dropping open. "Excuse me?"

"There is no way in hell Gabe knows you're up here in his shower, you utter freak. If he came in here and found you, he would kick your ass out." Nikki laughed again, mostly out of shock. She couldn't believe this. Taking a shower in Gabe's bathroom was beyond freaking creepy. Like she was pretty sure she'd seen stalkers do this on that one TV channel that focused on crime stories. "Holy crap."

"What do you know?" Sabrina shot back, her free hand curling into a fist.

"I know he can't stand you. Everyone knows that, so don't even stand there and try to act like he even knows you're up here." Nikki held her ground. "And how convenient that you're in here when Dev left for Houston. Were you up here hoping to surprise Gabe? Jesus. What is wrong with you? Seriously."

"And what are you doing up here, you bitch? Cleaning his room and rifling through his stuff?"

Nikki's brows lifted as she started to turn away. She needed to find Gabe stat. This thing with Sabrina had crossed all kinds of lines. "I actually have a reason to be up here. Unlike you, you creepy, sad woman."

"Oh, I know why you're up here. I know all about you and Gabe. He's fucking you, right? Isn't he, *Nicolette*." Sabrina waited until Nikki faced her. "Not that I blame you, but I hope, for your sake, you realize that's all he's doing. Just fucking you." She looked her over with a rather impressive sneer. "After all, that's what your type is good for."

"My type? Whatever. I don't even want to know why you think—"

"Why I think you guys are fucking? Because I heard you two together just last week. You were in one of the extra bedrooms," Sabrina said. "You sound like a whore when you call out his name."

Shock splashed through her. There *had* been someone in the hallway that day. She'd chalked up the door opening to the weird house, but it had been Sabrina. Anger quickly replaced the shock. She'd been watching them? Listening to them?

"At least he's fucking me," she fired back, too damn furious to stop herself. "I bet that just gets to you, doesn't it? You've wanted him for how long and all you get to do is shower in his bathroom like a stalker?"

Sabrina let out a choked-sounding screech. One that sort of unnerved Nikki. It was far past time she got out of this room and found Gabe. Something truly was not right about this woman.

"You know he's in love with another woman, right?" Sabrina said.

"You're talking about Emma? I know all about her."

"I'm talking about the mother of his child," Sabrina said.

Everything inside of Nikki stopped as an icy chill swept down her spine. She thought she hadn't heard her right. The mother of his child? "Gabe doesn't have a kid."

A wide smile broke out across Sabrina's face. "Oh, yes, he does. His name is William and he lives in Baton Rouge with his grandparents."

Nikki's entire body jerked. Baton Rouge. Gabe was looking for a place there—no, no way. Sabrina had to be lying, because after all the things Gabe and she talked about, after everything they'd shared, there was no way he'd never mention that he had a child.

"Didn't know that, did you?" Sabrina sounded smug. "That's because he's only fucking you, Nikki. He's not sharing his life with you."

The venom-laced words were a barb that struck home. She shook her head and backed up, still clutching the necklace in her hand. "You're insane."

"I'm not insane. I'm just right."

"If you think Gabe is going to be okay with this—"

Sabrina shot forward then, gripping Nikki's arm. "If you know what's good for you, you'll keep your mouth shut about this."

She glanced down at where Sabrina held onto her arm. "You are truly out of your mind if you think I'm not going to say something to Gabe—to Devlin. Your fiancé needs to know—"

"You open your mouth about this and I will make sure you never speak again." Sabrina's pale eyes flashed cold. "Do not underestimate me, Nikki. The de Vincents aren't the only ones who know how to make people disappear."

Disbelief washed over Nikki. "Are you seriously threatening me?"

"You say you know everything about Emma?" Sabrina smiled. "Bet you don't know that the brothers killed her attacker, did you? Lucian and Gabe. His name was Chris. They beat him to death."

Nikki's chest turned cold. Not because she was hearing something like that. She'd grown up in the de Vincent home. She knew what they were capable of. What terrified her was that Sabrina might know something that dangerous.

"Let go of me," Nikki said, holding Sabrina's gaze.

"Are you going to keep your mouth shut about this?"

Something occurred to her as she stared at Sabrina. She thought about the day she'd fallen down the outdoor steps. Sabrina had been there. Nikki had even thought about the possibility of it having been Sabrina, but she dismissed it, because Sabrina would've had to be seriously insane to do that. She also thought about the day Gabe's passenger window had been broken out while she sat in the seat. Could Sabrina have been involved in that?

Now it didn't seem so crazy. Sabrina could've seen her carrying the flowers, locked the second-floor doors from that hallway, and then waited for her outside. Could she have been following Gabe—following Nikki and saw where she lived? Nikki had thought it might've been Ross that night she'd spilled champagne on Sabrina, but what if it was Sabrina?

All because she speculated something was going to happen between Nikki and Gabe. Jesus.

"Was it you?" Nikki asked, her unease growing. "Did you push me down the stairs that day I was carrying the flowers?"

Sabrina gave her an icy smile. "If I had done that, I could've killed you. I'm not a bad person."

Her response did nothing to make Nikki feel better. She yanked her arm free. "Stay away from me." She backed out of the bedroom and then turned, hurrying for the inside door.

Sabrina followed her into the living area. "You're going to wish you never stepped foot in Gabe's room."

Nikki already did.

Chapter 28

Gabe walked through the downstairs, the strawberry smoothie in the crook of his arm as he reached into his back pocket for his phone. He'd been all over the damn main floor, looking for Nic. Where in the world was she? He was getting back to the house a little later than normal, but she was usually in the kitchen around this time.

He was just about to call her when the doors to the back staircase swung open and the person he was seeking came rushing out, looking like she'd seen a ghost.

"Are you okay?" he asked, walking over to her.

"Yeah. I think so. I'm actually looking for you." She glanced over her shoulder. "I need to talk to you."

Unease grew inside him. "What's going on?"

She shook her head as she grabbed his arm and pulled him into a nearby room—the one his mother used to watch movies with them in. She closed the door behind them and leaned against it.

The unease gave way to concern. "Okay. You're really starting to worry me." He palmed her cheek, guiding her gaze to his. "Talk to me, sweetheart. What's happening?"

"I'm sorry. It's just that the craziest thing happened." She slipped away from the door, walking over to the couch.

When she turned, that's when he saw something dangling from her left hand. "What's in your hand?"

Nic blinked and then glanced down. "Oh. Oh my God, I didn't even realize I was still holding this." Color burst along her cheeks as her fingers opened.

Gabe went to her, setting the smoothie on the coffee table. "Is that . . . ?" It was. She was holding the necklace she'd given him all those years ago. It *had* been on his dresser. "You were in my bedroom?"

"I went upstairs, looking for you. The porch doors opened when I knocked. I thought you were in there, so I went inside." She stared at the necklace and then lifted her gaze to his. "I heard the shower running in your bathroom."

His brows lifted. The shower had been running in his room? "Yeah, that wasn't me."

"I know." She started to sit down on the couch but stopped. "I found Sabrina in your room. She was in your bathroom taking a shower."

There was no way he heard her right. He stared at her. "What in the *fuck*?"

"That was pretty much my reaction when she stepped out of the bathroom wearing just a towel," Nic replied.

"Is she still up there right now?"

"I don't know. I just left."

He hadn't even seen her car parked outside. Anger burned through him like acid. Turning, he started for the door. He was going to drag that woman's ass out of the house. He was so fucking done with this shit—

"Wait." Nic stepped around the coffee table. "She knows about us."

Gabe turned to her. So fucking angry, he almost didn't process what she said. "What do you mean?"

"She heard us last week, when we were in one of the extra rooms." Nic swallowed.

Hell.

That wasn't the greatest piece of news, but since Dev already speculated the truth and Gabe hadn't done much to deny it, Sabrina knowing about him and Nic only bothered him because of how it could affect Nic. That woman was batshit crazy enough to mess with Nic out of some kind of twisted jealousy.

"I think she's been, I don't know, stalking us in this house." Nic shuddered. "It's creepy."

"Creepy" wasn't even the right word for it.

"She tried to insinuate that you knew she was there, but I knew better. There's something wrong with that woman, Gabe." Nic lifted her chin, meeting his gaze. "I don't know why you haven't said anything to Devlin, but something needs to be said, like yesterday. She even threatened me so I would keep my mouth shut about her being in there. She's out of her mind."

No truer words had ever been spoken. Part of him couldn't even believe Sabrina had escalated to this point. What had she been doing up there? Waiting for him to come home? Did she actually think she had a snowball's chance in hell of seducing him?

"I think . . . I know this sounds crazy, but I think she pushed me that day I fell on the steps," Nic said, shaking her head. "I asked her and what she said in response really wasn't a denial, Gabe."

A chill swept down his spine. "What did she say?"

"That if she had done it, it could've killed me and that she wasn't a bad person," Nic told him. "Not exactly the most reassuring response. I think—God, I think she pushed me, Gabe."

Shit.

"And you know that day your window was broken out? I know this sounds crazy, but what if she was involved in that? I mean, it was exactly where I was sitting."

Gabe fought the urge to pick up something and throw it. Nic could've broken something or worse that day she fell. It was a damn miracle that she hadn't been more seriously injured. The same with the car.

And would it have been because of him? Nothing had started up again between Nic and him at that time, but there'd been that dinner that Nic had spilled the champagne on Sabrina. He'd spent that entire dinner staring at Nic.

Sabrina would've noticed.

"I'm sorry that you had to deal with this," he gritted out. "I'm going to make damn sure you—"

"That's not the only thing she said." Nic dragged her empty hand through her hair as she looked away. "She said—she said you had a child."

Every muscle in Gabe's body locked up. There was no way. Sabrina couldn't know about William. Dev would've never told her that. Unless that woman was legit stalking him—

Holy shit, she had to be.

For Sabrina to know about William, she had to be honest-to-God stalking him. Sickened and furious, Gabe was actually struck speechless. He'd kept his mouth shut about Sabrina this whole time because her infatuation or whatever the fuck with him had been harmless. Something that he already knew that Dev had to be aware of, because everyone in the damn world knew it, but this—this was too much, too far.

"It's not true, right?" Nic asked, inching closer to him, the rope of that necklace still dangling from between her fingers. "You don't have a child."

There was a brief moment where he considered lying and that horrified him straight to the core. He wasn't trying to hide William's existence. He wouldn't do that, but he knew the moment he told Nic, everything would change between them. Not because he didn't think she'd be interested in a man who had a child.

But because *this* was how she was finding out.

That desperate feeling from Saturday night surged back to life as he stared into her beautiful brown eyes. He saw it. Her absolute refusal to believe that Sabrina had been telling the truth.

Gabe couldn't look at her. "I have a son."

No.

No way.

Nikki was too shocked to think anything other than that for several moments, because there was no way Gabe had a child and hadn't mentioned him *once* to her.

"That's not funny, Gabe." Her hand tightened around the necklace.

He still wasn't looking at her. "It's not a joke, Nic."

Her mouth opened, but she didn't have words at the moment. She took a step back, bumping into the coffee table. "You . . . you have a kid—a son? Emma and you?"

His shoulders rose with a deep breath. "Yes. His name is William. He's five years old."

Five years old? That meant—things clicked into place. "When you guys met up? She got pregnant. That's why you've been going to Baton Rouge—why you're looking at getting a place there."

"That would be correct," he replied, his tone so cold and detached that Nikki jolted.

"You . . . you told Sabrina about this—about your son?" Her voice pitched in a way that was humiliating to her.

His head swung in her direction as he finally looked at her. "I never told Sabrina shit. The only people who know are my brothers and maybe your parents. They probably overheard something, but no way in hell did I tell that woman. Neither would Dev."

Nikki wasn't sure what she believed anymore. "Then how did she know when I . . . ?"

"The woman has been stalking me." A strangled-sounding laugh escaped him. "It's the only thing that makes sense. Dear God, she actually has to be doing that."

That did make sense. Nikki had seen the crazy firsthand, but that didn't explain why he wouldn't have told *her*. "You never told me about him."

A muscle flexed along Gabe's jaw as he looked away again.

"How . . . how could he have never come up in conversation? You talked to me about Emma—about what was done to her and what happened to her. You could've told me then." Her heart was pounding so fast she thought she might be sick. "I mean, that's a big deal. Having a kid is a huge deal."

"Yeah, it is." His features were carved out of stone.

"Then why haven't you told me? I mean, we've talked a lot. We've shared a lot—"

"We've hung out. We've had sex. We're passing time. That's what we've done," Gabe snapped. "Why would I've told you about him? I won't even be living here full-time soon."

He hadn't just said all of that.

Oh God, he really hadn't just said that to her.

Nikki stumbled back a step from what felt like an actual slap in the face. Her throat threatened to seal closed as she stared into the face of a man who had become a virtual stranger to her.

Sabrina had been right.

He's only fucking you. He's not sharing his life with you.

Nikki's chest cracked wide open. The truth of those words was right in front of her face. They probably always had been, but she'd been too damn naive to see them.

"Shit." Gabe dragged his hand through his hand. "I—"

"There has only been one other time in my life that I've felt this stupid, this naive, and that was four years ago when I woke up and you called me *Emma*."

His eyes widened slightly.

"You don't remember that? You called me *Emma*." Her lower lip trembled as the edges of the medallion pressed into her palm. "That's when I knew that you were still in love with her."

"No." His voice was rough. "I don't remember that."

"Of course not." She laughed, and it sounded bitter and frail. "You'd think that would've been the thing that would've stuck with me. That would've stopped me from falling in love with you again."

Gabe paled. Blood drained from his face as he stared back at her.

"But how could I fall in love with you when I've *been* in love with you since I was sixteen and you pulled me out of the pool," she said, dragging in a deep breath, but it got stuck in her throat. "That's why I came to find you today. I needed to tell you because I thought—" She cut herself off, because she was such an idiot. "It doesn't matter now. I don't know what you've felt for me. If you've felt anything at all, but you sure as hell don't feel the way I do." Her voice cracked, right along with her heart. "I made a fool out of myself four years ago. And now you've made a fool out of me. There's not going to be a third opportunity."

She opened her hand, letting the necklace she'd given him four years ago fall to the coffee table. She started for the door, desperately trying to keep it together before she lost it.

"Nic—"

"Stay away from me," Nikki warned, throwing up her hand. "If you care about me at all, you'll stay away from me."

Chapter 29

Gabe climbed the stairs to his apartment in a daze, the necklace held tight in his hand.

He'd fucked up.

He knew that to his core. He'd fucked up.

Pushing open the porch doors, he came to a complete stop when he saw Sabrina sitting at the bar. At least she had clothes on, but it was obvious she had just gotten out of the shower. Her wet hair was slicked back and for once, there wasn't an ounce of makeup on her face. Shock gave way to fury.

"Are you fucking serious?" he demanded, stalking toward her.

She held up a hand. "I know you're mad—"

"Get the fuck out of my apartment and this house or I swear to God—"

"Or what?" Her lips parted. "You're going to drag me out of here? You're going to tell Devlin? I don't think so."

"You are out of your fucking mind."

"No. No, I am not." Her cheeks flushed red. "You're only saying that because I'm a woman going after what she wants—what she *deserves*. If I were a man, you'd be applauding me."

"If you were a man, I'd physically kick your ass out of here." He struggled to not lose it. "How in the hell did you know about my son?"

She smirked. "I have my ways."

"Don't give me any of that vague bullshit, Sabrina. Have you been stalking me?"

Sabrina snorted. "You call it stalking, I call it keeping tabs. I mean, really, Gabe, it wasn't hard to find out that Emma had a child. Not when you started going to Baton Rouge nearly every week. All I needed was to look into what you were doing—"

"Did you have someone follow me?"

She lifted a shoulder. "I saw a picture of him and I knew he was your kid. He looks like a de Vincent."

Holy shit, Gabe knew Sabrina was just about capable of anything, but this was fucking surreal. "You better not even think about going near my son."

"I don't care about your son, but you know who probably would? Nikki. She probably would've cared, but it didn't seem like she knew about him."

Gabe flinched.

Smiling, she crossed one slender leg over the other. "I did you a favor. You should be thanking me."

"What?"

"I got rid of Nikki for you. Come on, you couldn't have been serious about her. I did your dirty work again."

All he could do was stare at her. "You told Nikki so she'd stop seeing me?"

"Not like you two were really seeing each other, let's be honest. You were fucking her. That's all. Not like you told your brothers about her or were calling her your girlfriend," she said. "She wasn't perfect Emma."

As much as he hated to admit it, her words struck home. Was that how Nic felt about this—about how he handled things with her? Well, no shit. She did.

Jesus.

Gabe shook his head, focusing. "Did you push Nic that day? Did you push her down the stairs?"

Sabrina tilted her head to the side. "That would be so trashy. I have more class than that."

He didn't believe her for one second. "This all stops now. You stay away from Nic. You stay away from—"

"Or what? I know you're not going to say anything. I mean, you tell your brother, then I'll make sure Nikki has the worst run of luck known to man. You say one word to Devlin, you know I'll do it."

Gabe's hands closed into fists. He knew she would try.

"I'll ruin her life. I'll make it my life mission, and I have—"

Gabe moved so quickly he didn't even give himself time to really think about what he was doing. His hand went around her throat and he put just enough pressure on her so that she knew he wasn't playing around with her. "You so much as look at Nic the wrong way, I won't just stop at destroying you. Do you understand me, Sabrina? I am tired of your shit. I am tired of you messing around in my life. I am tired of you involving yourself where you don't belong. I am beyond fucking tired of it."

Her lip curled. "Oh, do you like it rough, too, like Devlin?" She slipped off the stool. "I bet you fuck just as hard—"

"I don't want you," he said, holding her gaze. "I've never wanted you. Dear God, woman, what have I ever done to give you that impression?"

"You never let yourself want me." She wet her dry lips. "First it was because of Emma and now it's because of *Nikki*—"

"It's never been because of them. It was always because of you," he shot back. "You may be packaged as pretty as they come, but you're fucking ugly and rotten to the damn core. There has never been a single thing about you that is redeemable."

Sabrina flinched.

"You need to get that through your head," he said, shoving her away from him before he did something he just might not regret. "And if you ever—*ever* threaten Nic again, I will kill you. Do you understand? You know that's not a threat."

Sabrina paled and he thought he saw her eyes start to glimmer before she straightened. "I never wanted Devlin."

"Then why in the hell are you marrying him?"

"Because I don't have a choice," she whispered, and then her eyes widened. The rest of the blood appeared to drain from her face.

"What the hell does that mean?"

Sabrina shook her head as she seemed to pull herself together. "I will marry Devlin. And I will do *anything* to make sure that happens."

He stared at her, slowly shaking his head. The woman was unstable. "Get the hell out of here and stay away from me and my son."

Sabrina had enough common sense to hightail her ass out of his apartment, and it wasn't until he slammed the door behind her that he realized what she'd said to him.

I did your dirty work again.

Again?

What in the hell had she meant by that?

SABRINA WASN'T THE only woman who'd gotten the hell out of the house Monday afternoon.

So had Nic.

She'd left, and Gabe guessed it was a good thing that Dev wasn't home for that, but she had come back Tuesday. Not that he approached her, but he knew she was there. He'd caught a glimpse of her that morning, carrying a rag into the sitting room.

Their paths only crossed once on Tuesday. Down in the kitchen. He'd just . . . hell, he found himself in there and there she was, putting the groceries away for the week.

But when Nikki realized he was in the kitchen, silently watching her, she'd left the room. Just up and walked away, leaving the groceries on the counter and in the bags. She hadn't said a word to him and had barely even looked at him.

Gabe had finished putting the groceries away.

Now he was sitting on the foot of his bed, staring at that

necklace he held in his hand. He wanted to talk to her. He wanted to try to explain why he hadn't told her about William.

He wanted to apologize, because what he'd said to her was wrong. She was more than a hookup, more than someone he was just wasting time with. That wasn't what Nic was to him. He didn't even know why he'd said that to her. Or maybe he wasn't being honest with himself.

He said it because he felt guilty—guilty that he'd kept it from her, ashamed that he'd hid William from her. And he'd lashed out at Nic just like his father had lashed out at their mother whenever he'd done something wrong and was cornered.

Gabe was no better.

But damn, he missed her.

He missed the way she smiled. The way her laugh blew all of his concerns and worries out of his mind. He missed the way she could just sit next to him in the shop in silence and be *happy*. How they could work together and how she made him feel, like he was worthy of her attention and time. He missed how he could just talk to her about everything.

Everything except the most important thing about his life.

Shit.

Why hadn't he told her?

The reasons he came up with weren't good enough. Worst of all, his excuses didn't give Nic enough credit. He knew that she would've listened to why he wasn't raising William. He knew she was young and probably wasn't even near the point in her life where she'd be thinking about caring for a child, but she'd said . . .

She'd said she loved him.

That she'd been *in love* with him.

His eyes closed as he pressed his hand—the necklace to his forehead. His chest hurt like someone had taken a dull knife and carved his heart out. Worst part was that he'd wielded that knife.

He knew why it felt that way.

He'd felt that before.

He didn't know how to fix things with Nic. He wasn't even sure he could, if he had it in him. The odds were fucking stacked against them. He'd stacked them himself.

But there was something else he needed to do.

He needed to talk to Dev the moment he was home. This kind of conversation wasn't one you had over the phone. This was a face-to-face discussion and it was long overdue.

This shit with Sabrina had to end.

NIKKI WAVED GOODBYE as Bev dropped off the dry cleaning. Gathering up the numerous plastic-covered suit jackets that all belonged to Devlin, she made her way to his rooms in the right wing.

Devlin was the only one who seemed to get clothing dry-cleaned on the regular. It was rare for Lucian, and Gabe . . . he never wore anything that required dry cleaning, it seemed.

Her chest ached as she drew in a stuttered breath.

She didn't want to be here, in the house where every damn thing was a constant reminder of Gabe. She'd rather be in her bed, under heavy blankets, eating beignets and corn chips until she passed out from a food coma.

The hurt she was feeling now made what she experienced four years ago feel like an unrequited crush. She was absolutely destroyed.

Blinking back fresh tears, she unlocked Devlin's room and quickly hung up his suits. He preferred the plastic to be left on, for whatever reason. She left the room, locking up.

The house was eerily quiet as she made her way back downstairs. Her father was gone and Lucian was with Julia at their house to go over some of the renovations.

She had no idea where Gabe was, but she didn't think he was here. She hadn't seen him since yesterday in the kitchen. He'd walked in and just stared at her, like he was going to say something to her, but Nikki couldn't deal. So she'd left, and thankfully, Gabe had the decency to put away the groceries before they'd gone bad.

There was just nothing Gabe could say to her at this point. He'd said it all, with words and actions.

Grabbing the vacuum, she made her way to the smaller room with the TV, and by small, she meant by de Vincent standards. It was still larger than most living rooms.

Nikki was about to plug in the vacuum when she heard footsteps in the hall. Her stomach dropped as she looked up and stepped back from the outlet, thinking it was Gabe.

She wasn't ready to see him. No way. She didn't think she'd ever be ready—

Parker stepped into the doorway, and her stomach dropped for a whole different reason. Muscles all along her neck tensed up. "What are you doing in here?"

His lips thinned. "Wow. I see the last time I told you that you needed to speak to me with respect went in one ear and out the other."

Nikki hadn't forgotten his threat, and after her showdown with Sabrina, she was worried about how it could affect her parents. But she couldn't imagine that after what Sabrina had done, Gabe wouldn't talk to Devlin.

"I'm not trying to be rude," she said, and that was only partly true. "But how did you get in the house? My father isn't here to let anyone in."

He cocked his head to the side. "If you don't want people roaming into the house, then perhaps you should lock the doors."

People shouldn't be entering homes they didn't live in randomly, but that wasn't the point. Nikki was damn sure all the doors were locked, all twelve billion of them.

"I came to see Devlin," Parker said, stepping into the room.

"He's not home." Unease blossomed in the pit of her

stomach like a noxious weed. How did he not know Devlin wasn't home?

He had to.

Nikki didn't believe him for one second. A shiver coursed down her spine. Why was he here?

"Is that so?" Parker mused, flicking an imaginary piece of lint off his pressed navy-blue dress shirt. "Doesn't look like anyone is here, actually. Anyone but you."

The unease grew as Nikki stepped to the side, so she wasn't standing between the TV and one of the chairs. "Gabe is here."

"Is he?"

She wasn't sure, but she sure as hell hoped someone was here. She nodded.

"Cool. I'll have to pay him a visit." He looked around the room and then his pale-blue-eyed gaze settled on her. "But I'm glad that I've found you, especially now."

She swallowed hard as she glanced at the doorway. Parker was making her nervous, causing instinct to roar to life in her.

"I wanted to visit with you," he said, reaching back and closing the door behind him. "Uninterrupted."

Chapter 30

*N*ikki's heart thundered in her chest as she dropped the cord to the vacuum. It thudded on the carpet quietly.

"My sister really does not like you." Parker undid the button on the left cuff of his shirt. "I mean, she *really* doesn't like you."

"I . . . I kind of guessed that already," she replied.

"Did you? But I don't think you understand what happens when my sister doesn't like someone." Parker rolled up the sleeve to his elbow. "She was telling me that you misunderstood a certain situation recently."

The only situation recently was the one where she was naked in Gabe's bedroom, but she sure as hell didn't misunderstand anything that she saw.

"And she's worried that you're going to say something to her fiancé." He undid the button on his other sleeve. He rolled that up, too. "But I told her that you wouldn't dare do something like that, but she said you already spoke to Gabe."

Her heart lurched into her throat. "She was in his bedroom—"

"Waiting to speak to him about her engagement to his brother." Parker let his arms hang loose as he smiled. "To discuss a party to celebrate it. She wanted to get Gabe's opinion on the type of champagne to order."

Nikki's mouth dropped, and she couldn't not respond. "And she needed to do this after she took a shower in his bathroom? Are you guys serious right now? Is this some kind of joke?"

"She spilled a drink on her shirt and took a shower. Gabe wasn't up there." Parker moved around the coffee table. "But you were."

"Do you think Gabe isn't going to say anything?" she demanded, sort of dumbfounded. "After this?"

"He's not going to say a word," he replied confidently.

She gaped at him. He was as insane as his sister.

"Why were you in Gabe's private quarters, Nikki?" he asked.

"I *work* here. That's why—"

"Now, come on, Nikki, you weren't in his bedroom because of work." His lips pursed. "Well, unless you were planning to do some work on your back. You know, I'm sort of offended."

She gasped. "You're offended?"

"You treat me like you can't stand me. Every time I come near you, you look at me like I'm seconds away from pouncing on you," he said, watching her move around to the other side of the coffee table. He laughed. "You're doing it right now."

"Because you're kind of freaking me out, Parker."

"What have I ever done to you to make you scared of me?" he asked.

Her brows shot up. "Besides right now, when you came into this house knowing you're not supposed to be here? How about that time in the pool house?"

His jaw hardened. "Nothing happened that day in the pool house."

"Because Lucian walked in." Balls of ice formed in her belly. "You wouldn't leave, even though I was standing there in the towel, and you tried to pull it off me—"

"And you had no problem flashing your tits and ass for Gabe every time he came around, so sue me for thinking you had no problem with me seeing them."

Nikki sucked in a sharp breath. "I wasn't showing those parts of my body to anyone when I was seventeen, but even if I was, that's my choice. Just like it's my choice when it comes to who I will share them with now."

"Aw, don't you sound like the cute little feminist." He snorted. "The fact remains, I didn't do shit to you. I've never done anything to you other than invite you to my penthouse."

"Yeah, thanks for that, but I'd rather pluck every hair on my body with a rusty pair of tweezers before I'd even remotely entertain that offer," she snapped.

A hard look crept into his eyes. "You're a little bitch who needs to be put in her place."

Nikki neared the edge of the coffee table. "And what is my place?"

"Not sure yet," he replied.

"You need to leave," she said, keeping her voice level. "You need to leave now."

Parker laughed. "Not sure Devlin will be thrilled with how unwelcome you're making his future brother-in-law feel."

Torn between being a little scared and being so thunderstruck by the fact that Parker and Sabrina thought there was still an engagement after Monday, she almost couldn't formulate a coherent sentence.

"Fine," she decided, walking toward the door. "You don't leave, I'll go to the police and report you as trespassing." Reaching the door, she opened it and stepped out into the hallway, aware that Parker was following her. She turned, not wanting him to be at her back. "I'm giving you ten seconds to—"

"You'd call the cops on me?" He laughed. "That's harsh."

"You've got five seconds." She reached into her back pocket for her phone. "And I will—"

Parker grabbed her arm, his grip tight. "Calling the cops will seriously be a bad idea for you, Nikki."

"Let go of me," she ordered, twisting her arm.

His fingers bit into tissue and bone, causing her to gasp

in pain. "Remember what I said about your parents? I can make sure they don't have a job—"

"I'm really beginning to think your threat means shit when the likelihood of Devlin marrying Sabrina is literally nil." She held his gaze even as her heart threw itself against her ribs. "Now let go of my arm."

His eyes flashed with anger as he yanked her forward, against his chest. "If Devlin ends my sister's engagement because you ran your mouth to him or to Gabe, you're going to wish you kept quiet."

Every part of her body that touched his crawled. She jerked back. "Let go of me right now."

"Or what?" Parker's voice dropped as he yanked her against him again.

"Or I'm going to rip off the hand you're touching her with."

Relief shot through Nikki so fast she thought she might faint as Parker's eyes widened at the sound of Gabe's voice. He let go of her arm, and she stumbled back as Parker turned to the side. Nikki saw Gabe then, stalking down the center of the hallway.

His striking features were all hard lines. Seeing him surfaced mixed emotions in her, but she was happy that someone was here.

"Gabe." Parker's well-practiced smile fell into place. "I was looking—"

Nikki squeaked as Gabe cut off whatever Parker was about to lie about with a very large hand around Parker's neck. He slammed the thinner man against the wall.

"Give me one good reason why I don't choke the life out of you right now," Gabe asked, his voice way too calm. "I doubt you can come up with one, but I'm feeling generous."

Having never seen Gabe like this, Nikki backed into the opposite wall. She suddenly remembered what Sabrina had said about the man who attacked Emma. She'd forgotten that in the mess that had followed.

Parker gagged as Gabe's grip tightened on his throat. "Still waiting for one good reason. Just one."

Nikki saw it in him then. He might be the brother everyone claimed was the most levelheaded, but she saw right then what brewed beneath the surface. She wished that it scared her or that it made her look at him differently.

It didn't.

Parker dug at Gabe's hand, his face turning red.

"Why was he grabbing you, Nic?" Gabe asked in the same flat tone.

She glanced between them, perversely satisfied by the pleading look Parker shot her. "I told him that if he didn't leave, I was going to call the cops."

"And why wouldn't he leave?"

"I don't know. You'd have to ask him."

"I'm sure he'll have an answer I don't want to hear. What was he doing here?"

Nikki crossed her arms. "He said he was here to see Devlin."

He cocked his head to the side. "Bullshit, Parker. You know Dev isn't back in town until Saturday. So why are you really here and how the hell did you get in?"

Parker couldn't really respond, not with Gabe choking him. The man's face had gone from red to a purplish color. Nikki decided to speak up. "I think he came here to tell me to keep my mouth shut about what I saw on Monday."

"Really?" Gabe let go of Parker.

Parker slumped against the wall, coughing as he dragged in air. "Jesus," he bit out, voice hoarse as he rubbed at his throat. "You were choking me."

"No shit." Gabe bent at the waist, getting his face right in his. "Did Sabrina send you to threaten Nic? You're probably not going to answer that question honestly, so don't even bother."

Parker started to look away, but Gabe grabbed a fist-ful of hair and forced the man to look him dead in the eye. "I want both you and your sister to understand some things—I thought I'd made it perfectly clear to Sabrina on Monday, but I'll say it again. Stay away from Nic. Don't look at her. Don't even breathe in her direction. If you or your sister do, that will be it. Do you feel me?"

Parker didn't respond.

Jerking his hand back, Gabe slammed Parker's head into the wall. "One more time. Do you feel me?"

"I feel you," Parker gasped.

"Good. The next thing is a message for Sabrina. Let her know that I will be talking to Dev. That's going to happen the moment he comes home on Saturday. Sabrina fucked up and she's going to live with that. Just like you're going to."

Parker swallowed hard. "If Devlin doesn't marry—"

"I don't give a fuck. At all. Not one single fuck," Gabe said, and when he smiled it was the scariest damn smile Nikki ever saw. "Do you understand me?"

"Yes," Parker groaned.

"Perfect." Gabe let go of Parker's hair and the man leaned against the wall, his chest heaving. "Just one more thing."

Parker lifted his chin.

Smiling, Gabe cocked his arm back. He moved as fast as lightning striking. His fist connected with Parker's jaw and down the man went, folding like a paper sack.

"Oh my." Nikki placed her hand over her mouth.

Gabe towered over Parker. "Get up and get the fuck out of this house before I do worse."

Parker didn't protest. He got up and he ran—the man *ran* down the hall and then he all but tore at the front door to get it open. He didn't look back.

And that just left Gabe and her in the hallway.

"There's something wrong with the Harrington family," she murmured.

"That there is." He sighed, working the knuckles of his hand. "That's the second time I punched a man because of you."

Nikki slowly turned to Gabe. "What?"

"Are you okay?" he asked instead of answering.

"Yeah." She folded her arms across her chest. "I don't know how he got in here. I locked the doors."

"I hate to tell you this, but I just came in through the mudroom. That door wasn't locked."

"What?" Disbelief filled her. "I locked that. I know I did."

Gabe shook his head as he walked ahead. "Did Parker do anything to you?" He went to the front door and threw the lock. "Are you sure he didn't hurt you?"

"No. He scared me, but he didn't hurt me." Now that the adrenaline was fading, a whole different kind of anxiety was rising.

Gabe faced her and then looked down at his hand. "I told him once to stay away from you. He obviously has a problem listening."

"You did?"

"Let me see your arm." He started toward her.

Nikki backed up. "Nothing is wrong with my arm."

"I'd feel better if you'd let me check it."

"Why do you care?" The question burst out of her as she backed up.

"Why do I care?" he repeated slowly. He looked away, biting down on his lip. "Nic, we need to talk—"

"No, we don't, because you're going to say 'Of course I care about you,' and things are going to get really awkward and really painful." She unfolded her arms. "Because you obviously don't care about me in *that* way."

He turned his head back to her. "Nic . . ."

"You know the way. The one that makes you share actual important details about your life." That knot was back in her throat. "Like that you have a son. And you can't deny that. You really can't." Squeezing her eyes shut, she exhaled raggedly as she struggled not to break down. "Thank you for talking to Parker. Punching him. Whatever. But I still don't want to talk to you." She opened her eyes and hated that his face blurred. "I don't want to see you."

NIKKI HAD NEVER been more grateful to have something like a move to occupy her thoughts. She wasn't thinking about Gabe all day or worrying with residual dread every time she thought about Parker or Sabrina.

Today was the first day she hadn't felt like staying in bed and crying like she was eighteen all over again. Un-packing boxes and putting away utensils had a strange way of emptying her head of all thoughts.

It had helped that her parents spent part of the day with her, as did Rosie, who'd just unloaded the last of the towels, leaving them on her bed.

As Rosie came out of the short, narrow hallway, Nikki's gaze fell to the little island that separated the kitchen and living room. Off to the right was a space for a kitchen table.

She hadn't gotten one of those yet.

Her gaze got snagged on the chisel kit Gabe had given her. It lay open from when Rosie was poking around in it, looking for something sharp to open a box with.

She'd brought it with her to the apartment, because she refused to let what happened with Gabe ruin something she enjoyed doing once more.

Seeing the kit hurt, but she'd be damned if she let that stop her.

"You doing okay?" Rosie asked, wiping her palm on her forehead.

"Yeah." She lifted her hands above her head and stretched her back. "Just a little lost in my head."

"Remember what I told you." She adjusted the scarf that was holding her curls out of her face. "Fuck him."

"I remember." Nikki had filled Rosie in on what had happened days ago. She trusted that Rosie wouldn't say a word about Gabe having a kid, but she had left out what

Sabrina had said about the man who'd hurt Emma. That was something Nikki would never repeat, ever. "Fuck him."

Fuck him had become Rosie's new motto.

Rosie draped an arm over Nikki's shoulders. "It'll get easier."

"I know." She swallowed and then smiled. "Been down this road with him before."

Her friend kissed her cheek and then leaned against the island. "I still think there's more to why he never told you about his son. I'm sure that he'll probably explain himself eventually."

"It doesn't matter if he does." Nikki sucked air through the pain piercing her through her chest. "To not tell me something that huge that impacts his future—that would've impacted our future together—tells me that he wasn't even thinking that far ahead."

Rosie said nothing.

"At the end of the day, I was just . . . someone he was passing the time with. He said it himself, Rosie. He's going to leave here."

"Men say stupid things they don't mean all the time."

"And sometimes they say the things they mean." She drew in a breath but it got stuck around the messy ball at the back of her throat. "God, I can't believe I still love him. I'm an idiot."

"You're not an idiot. Pretty sure he's the idiot."

She smiled at her friend. "Thank you so much for helping out today. I really appreciate it."

"No problem. I wish I could stay and help longer, but I'm filling in for Randy today. It's the fall and you know how popular the ghost tours are in the Quarter."

Nikki grinned, sort of wishing she could join her. "Totally okay. You've done so much already."

After Nikki promised to make Rosie the first meal in her new apartment, they said goodbye and then Nikki was alone.

It was too quiet.

She immediately turned on the TV, so thrilled that the cable had been turned on that morning. She needed the background noise.

Placing the remote back, she stopped and stared at the coffee table the remote had been sitting on. Her chest squeezed painfully. A moving truck had showed up that morning, right after the cable guy actually. At first she had no idea what was in it, and it wasn't until the men started bringing in the items that she realized it was the pieces Gabe had promised her.

Her throat burned as she looked away, pressing her lips together.

Nikki sucked in a stuttered breath. Every time she thought about the two of them, about what they shared and then what he said to her, it broke her heart over again.

She wished she hated him.

God, it would be so much easier if she could.

Walking into the kitchen, she pulled out the tub of spaghetti her father had made for her. She nuked it in the microwave and spent the next however many minutes mindlessly eating.

There was still so much she needed to do.

After putting away the books in the small bookshelves, she made her way back to the bedroom to tackle the pile of towels just as night had fallen.

She really did love her apartment. It wasn't huge, probably smaller than the apartment Gabe had at the de Vincent house, but it was perfect for her. She just wished the whole experience wasn't tainted by the sickness in her heart.

Hell, if she was being honest with herself, she wished he was here with her, sharing a bottle of wine in celebration and breaking in the bed.

None of that was going to happen.

Sniffling, she used her shoulder to wipe away the stupid tear coursing down her cheek as she picked up another towel to fold. She'd get over this and this time it wouldn't take her four—

Click.

Her breath caught and everything inside her stilled when she heard the front door of her apartment open.

Chapter 31

The back of Nikki's neck tingled as she dropped the towel she was folding onto her bed. Her body flashed hot and then cold as she turned to the open bedroom door, her heart pounding erratically in her chest.

Someone just walked into her apartment.

Hadn't she locked the door?

She stepped back from the bed and peered out into the hallway. There would only be one person she knew who was arrogant enough to walk into her apartment unannounced, but it couldn't be him. Not after everything.

Still, she held onto the little spark of hope and crept toward the bedroom door, straining to see out in the hall. She heard nothing but the low hum from the TV she'd left on in the living room. All she could see was the arm of her couch and the island that separated the kitchen from the living room.

"Gabe?" she called out, her hands opening and closing at her sides.

A heartbeat passed and then a man stepped into her line of sight. A man that was definitely not Gabe unless he lost weight and height in record time.

And decided that a *black ski mask* was a new fashion accessory.

For a horrifying second, Nikki couldn't move, couldn't even breathe as she stared at the man at the end of the hall. Like an animal petrified in front of oncoming headlights, she was frozen as her body raced to catch up to what her brain was ordering it to do.

The man started down the hallway.

Icy terror exploded in her gut as instinct finally took over. Springing into action, she lurched forward, grabbing the end of the door. She slammed it shut and then turned the pitiful excuse of a lock.

"Shit. Shit." She spun around, looking for her cell phone. Black ski masks were bad, so bad. She shot to the bed, yanking up the towel. No phone.

Something heavy crashed into her bedroom door, jarring the whole wall. A shriek parted her lips as she whipped around. Her phone—Christ, her phone was in the living room!

The man hit the door again. Wood cracked down the center, and Nikki stumbled back. Her chest rose and fell heavily as the center of the door gave way, wood splintering. A gloved hand reached through, finding the lock.

Oh my God, she couldn't believe this was happening. There was a strange man—a strange masked and gloved man in her apartment, and she watched enough *Forensic Files* to know this was going to end badly.

Her wild gaze darted around the bedroom, landing on the glass doors of the balcony. Instinct told her she wouldn't make it in time, not with the doors being locked and the bar in place.

Weapon—she needed a weapon.

Spinning around, she grabbed the lamp, the only truly heavy thing she had in her bedroom. The door swung open and she whirled around, ripping the plug out of the wall.

"Stay back!" she yelled, holding the lamp like a baseball bat.

The man started toward her.

Shit.

There wasn't a part of Nikki that hesitated. She swung

that lamp with every intention of knocking the dude's head off. Except that's not what happened.

Nikki swung at nothing but air as the man ducked low and charged her. His shoulder hit her stomach hard, doubling her over. A startled gasp of pain parted her lips as he reached up, yanking the lamp from her hands and tossing it to the floor. The lamp crashed into the carpet as Nikki straightened. She darted to the side, going for the hallway.

She didn't make it.

He got her around the waist. One second she was standing on the floor and the next she was falling through the air. She hit the bed *hard*, knocking the air out of her lungs. She was startled just for a second, and it cost her.

Twisting at the waist, her scream was muffled as he came over her, slamming a hand over her mouth as he straddled her hips, effectively locking her legs down.

Panic froze her muscles as the man leaned down, lowering his head toward hers. His eyes . . .

His hand pressed on her mouth, bruising her lips as his other hand dropped to her shoulder and then slid down, over her breast.

He squeezed painfully, eliciting a sharp cry that didn't reach her ears.

A whole new horror exploded as she screamed against his hand. This man—*oh my God.*

Pure terror fueled the adrenaline pumping through her veins. Bucking her hips, she tried to throw his weight off, but he pressed down. Pain burned through her chest, but she ignored it as she swung her hand as hard as she could, slamming her fist into the side of his head.

The man's head jerked back and his grip on her mouth loosened. She swung again, connecting with his jaw. A burst of pain lit up her knuckles. He fell back just enough for her to sit up, pulling one leg free. She twisted, reaching for the edge of the bed.

A hand dug into her hair, jerking her head back. Fiery

pain pricked along her scalp as he flipped her onto her back.

"Stupid bitch," he grunted in a voice that raised the hairs along her body.

That voice. That voice. She knew that—

His fist slammed into her jaw. The burst of pain was raw and startling. Then the fire spread across her face. A metallic taste filled her mouth. Blood. *Blood*. He hit her again.

Another burst of pain radiated from her eye—her left eye—darkening her vision as she collapsed onto the bed. Thoughts were . . . they didn't make sense all of a sudden. Nikki tried to sit up, but her head felt weird, too heavy.

It hurt.

"Stay down." A hand slammed into her stomach, winding her. Something . . . something felt like it cracked. A rib?

She went down, stunned and lost in a sea of startling pain and disbelief. *Why is this happening?* The question cycled over and over. Precious seconds wasted as he grabbed her leg with one hand, dragging her to the edge of the bed. He got between her legs as the ceiling above blinked in and out.

Why is this happening?

Minutes ago she was folding laundry, trying desperately not to cry, not to lose herself to the rioting emotions, to the knowledge that she'd made her bed with Gabe and she was going to have to sleep in it. It was just minutes ago. . . .

Fingers dug into the skin of her stomach, curling around the band on her leggings. She felt them being tugged.

Rage, hot and suffocating rage mixed with the terror, pushed her past the pain, past the confusion of what was happening. Her thoughts cleared.

She lifted her hips and maybe the guy thought she was helping him, because he shifted back, letting go of her leg. Nikki kicked out with everything she had in her, slamming her foot into his stomach.

He grunted, falling backward onto his ass.

She wasted no time.

Scrambling off the bed, her feet hit the carpet and she started running. Her movements were sluggish and jerky, slowing her down as she reached the hallway.

Make it to the door. Scream. Someone will hear you. Scream. Nikki screamed—screamed as loud as she could, but it sounded weak.

Weight crashed into her back, taking her down. Her chin snapped off the floor, sending a bolt of pain down her spine. She didn't stop—didn't let herself cave for a second to the pain. Not even when he slammed a fist into her back, delivering a kidney shot.

"Fuck this." He flipped her roughly, slamming the back of her head to the floor.

She drew in another breath to scream, but his hand clamped down on her throat, stealing her breath before she realized she'd taken her last one.

Nothing could've prepared her for that feeling hitting every single nerve. Her body heaved as she tried to get air, but the hand around her throat was letting up.

She was going to die. She knew in that moment, he was going to kill her. Her entire life flashed in front of her. She saw her parents. She saw Rosie and Bev. She saw Gabe.

No.

No way was she going out like this.

Her arms flailed and she went for the only exposed area of skin she could see. The skin around his eyes. She went nails first, digging into his right eye as her lungs spasmed.

He howled, letting go of her throat to grab her hand, but she didn't let go. He yanked back, but her fingers got stuck in the ski mask. He twisted his head, scrambling back on his hands. The mask got tangled for a second and then slipped free as Nikki wrenched in the opposite direction, dragging in deep gulps of air as blood and spit dripped from her mouth.

Rising to her knees, she realized the mask was in her

hand. Wheezing, she pushed to her feet as he kicked out at her, missing her and slamming his boot into the wall. Stumbling forward, she looked over her shoulder.

"Parker," she gasped, dropping the mask.

His head whipped around. Blood streamed down the side of his face—a face contorted in pain and anger. He lurched to his feet. "Told her we should've played it the same way we did with his other bitch, but she wouldn't listen. Said two car accidents would look suspicious. Should've taken you out that first night I followed you."

Understanding filled her and was quickly followed by horror. "Emma? You caused Emma's accident?" Her words came out weird sounding, mushy, but Parker seemed to understand them, because he let out a roar that sent a bolt of primal fear down her spine.

Nikki spun, forcing her legs to move as fast as they could. The hallway seemed endless. Some part of her, some part focused fully on survival, knew she wouldn't make it to the door if she tried. *It* knew that if he got her down one more time, she wasn't getting back up.

Her conscience clicked off as she made it to the kitchen island. Survival was in control, guiding her hand to where the chisel kit sat, open. She grabbed the biggest one and turned.

Nikki didn't know how it happened, just that it did.

She was holding onto the chisel so tightly with both hands that when his chest knocked into her fist, she still didn't let go. Not even when his eyes widened with shock. Not even when his hands and fingers hit at her face, scratching at her as they slipped away. Not even when she felt the warm rush of liquid drenching *her* hands. Not even when his knees gave out and he fell forward, tearing free from the chisel.

He fell forward, face-first, and his body . . . it twitched a couple of times and then went still.

Nikki still held onto the chisel.

Several seconds passed as she stood there and then the strangest damn thing happened. The logical part of her brain churned on.

She needed to call the police. Yes. That's what she needed to do.

Shuffling into the living room, her body moved without thought as she found her phone on the coffee table. She picked it up. The phone was slippery in her hands.

Numb.

She was so numb.

Nikki called 911 and she didn't know exactly what she said to them, but they told her police were on the way and she thought they might've asked for her to stay on the line, but she needed to call Gabe.

She figured that he and his brothers needed to know that Parker was in her apartment and that he was dead. That she really believed that Parker had admitted to having something to do with Emma's car accident. That was important since this . . . this would involve the de Vincents. There would be police. Questions. Scandal.

Devlin was going to be so . . . disappointed.

She didn't know what Gabe would think.

In the back of her mind, she knew she wasn't thinking right as she called Gabe. She wasn't really thinking at all as she inched backward, the phone ringing in her ear. Her back hit the wall and she slid down it.

The phone rang and rang, and Gabe didn't answer.

Still holding the chisel, she pressed the phone to her chest as she stared into the hallway, watching the blood slowly seep across the tile.

Chapter 32

Gabe reached for his phone in his pocket for what felt like the hundredth time since he saw that Nic was calling him.

He was shocked to see her name come up on his screen. He'd figured that after their last conversation, she'd rather punch him repeatedly in the nuts than call him.

What could she want?

Probably wanted him to take back the furniture he'd sent over earlier. She could hate him now all she liked, but that stuff was hers. They belonged with her.

He heard his phone ring again, but he reached inside his pocket, silencing it without looking at who it was.

Whatever it was, it was going to have to wait until the drama in his house died down enough he could sneak off and see what she wanted. Dev had come home early, and the first thing Gabe did was hunt him down.

Dev tossed back a third glass of bourbon. "I knew."

"Excuse me?" Gabe said, surprised. He'd just sat there telling Dev everything about Sabrina, and that was how his brother was going to respond?

"I knew that she was chasing after you. I also knew she was batshit crazy when she wanted to be." Dev walked around his desk and grabbed the bottle of bourbon, pouring himself another drink. "I, however, hoped she would grow tired of chasing you. I'd hoped that she would be . . . smarter than this."

He gaped at his brother. "Are you fucking serious?"

Dev walked back to his chair. He sat, placing his glass on the desk. "Do I look like I'm joking?"

He almost came out of his seat. "You knew she was on me, fucking with my life—"

"I didn't know that. The last part," Dev interrupted. "If I had, things would've changed. I would've put a stop to it."

"Would you have?"

His brother's cold gaze focused on his. "Yes. Family first. Family always."

"Then what are you going to do about it?" Gabe demanded. "You can't plan to still marry her."

"Of course not. It's over. Most likely would've been even if you hadn't told me or if Nikki kept quiet." He picked up his glass. "I don't want the Harrington empire *that* badly."

Gabe sat back as he dragged a hand over his head. He was so fucking relieved he could practically kiss his brother. "Well, I'm sorry that your fiancée—"

"Don't be. I never loved her. I barely tolerated her."

"What was it then?" Curiosity filled him. "If you knew that she's been trying to fuck me for about a decade, why did you stay with her? You couldn't have wanted her company that badly."

"I labored under the false belief that I could handle her." He swished his drink around. "That I would be able to keep an eye on her more easily if I was married to her."

"That doesn't make sense."

Dev lifted a shoulder. "There were things she knew. Things I haven't exactly been honest with you about."

Understanding flared. "You're talking about Christopher Fitzpatrick. You said—"

"I never told her what had happened to him," Dev interceded. "She knew. Whether it was Emma who told her or not, I don't know. Keeping her close so she didn't jeopardize my family was paramount."

"Holy shit." Gabe was shocked and awed as he stared at

his brother, seeing him for what felt like the first time in years. "You were with her to protect—"

"I was with her because I chose to be. And I choose not to be with her anymore. It's as simple as that."

Gabe slowly shook his head. When they were younger, Dev always . . . he always took the brunt of the punishment when the brothers got in trouble. Hell, sometimes it was almost like he volunteered for it. He was always with their father, *always*, and often Gabe wondered why, because the man was not kind to Dev, but it wasn't until Gabe grew older that he realized why Dev willingly stayed by Lawrence's side.

It kept the man from paying too much attention to Gabe, to Lucian, to Madeline. Dev had protected them back then.

And he was still doing it.

Jesus.

Gabe cleared his throat. "Is it really over, though? You think Sabrina is going to take the breakup even moderately well?"

"She will." He stared into his glass. "I can be very convincing."

He studied his brother. "Sometimes you scare me."

A rare, real smile appeared. "Sometimes I scare myself."

Gabe's brows lifted.

"By the way," Dev said, taking a drink. "What are you going to do about Nikki?"

The change of subject was swift. "What do you mean?"

"You know what I mean. You've been with her."

Gabe's eyes narrowed. "Like I told you last time, she's not up for discussion."

He lifted a shoulder. "I hope you're thinking about the . . . long-reaching complications of progressing forward with Nikki. She's nearly ten years your junior, just out of college, and she works for our family."

"I've thought about it, Dev."

"I know I've said this before, but it bears repeating. What do you think will happen if the Rothchilds decide to take you to court for custody?" he asked. "You and your twenty-two-year-old girlfriend. I'm sure that wouldn't look ideal to a judge."

"Nic may be ten years younger, but she's responsible, mature, and a better fucking adult than half of us," he said, his chest squeezing because what he said was true and he still shit all over her. "William is my son. I would like to see any judge rule against me if it comes to it."

Dev dragged a finger along the rim of his glass. "Then we should make sure that it doesn't come to that."

He shot Dev a look. "Nic would be . . . I would trust her with William. No questions asked." The moment the words left his mouth he knew he spoke the truth. That was a bitter pill to swallow, considering that realization was about a day late and a dollar short.

He'd hurt her again, but this time he knew the wounds of his words and lack thereof cut far deeper than anything that happened four years ago.

"Should've figured she'd eventually get her little claws in you." A faint, humorless smile appeared on Dev's face. "If only Lawrence was alive to see this."

"I'm not quite sure what to say to that."

"He would've had a lot of things to say."

"I'm sure he would."

"Except he wouldn't have stopped at just thinking those things," Dev continued. "Why do you think I didn't like Nikki running around in those fucking bathing suits? Wasn't because of you." A muscle throbbed along his jaw. "It was because of *Father*."

Nothing could've stunned him more. "What?"

"You never noticed the way he'd watch her?" His lip curled in disgust. "I did. I saw it."

Gabe blinked slowly. "What are you talking about?"

He didn't answer for a long moment. "You didn't know

him, Gabe. Not like I did. Only I knew what that fucking bastard was capable of. What he got away with."

Everything inside him froze as he stared at his brother. His insides turned cold. "Did he—?" He cut himself off. No. Nic would've mentioned something, especially after he talked to her about Emma. But that knowledge did nothing to assuage him, especially considering she never told him about Parker in the pool house, not until he asked. "What did he do?"

"What didn't he do would be the better question." He threw back the rest of the drink, his lips thinning as he bared his teeth. "I don't think I've ever been happier than I was when I learned he wasn't my father. That his fucking blood didn't course inside of me." His gaze drifted from Gabe. "Trust me, Gabe, you and I are the lucky ones."

He gripped the arms of the chair. What did Dev know? One question clambered to the surface. One that he couldn't stop himself from asking. "Did you do it? Did you kill him?"

Dev's gaze slid back to Gabe. He didn't answer.

A long moment passed, and then Gabe leaned back in his chair. Pinching the bridge of his nose, he cursed under his breath. Truth be told, he didn't want Dev to answer that question. Wasn't even sure why he asked it.

Gabe dropped his hand to the arm of the chair. "You know, Sabrina said something else. She said she was doing my dirty work again. I have no idea what she meant by that, but it sounded like she'd done something else before."

Dev's gaze sharpened. "I don't think—"

The office door swung open. Gabe looked over his shoulder as Lucian charged in. The fact Lucian did this without knocking set off warning bells. His pale face didn't help either.

Dev's instinct must've been screaming the same thing as Gabe's, because he leaned forward and asked, "Do I even want to know?"

Their younger brother looked at Gabe, slowly shaking his head as he clenched his phone. "It's Nikki."

Ice drenched Gabe's skin. He was moving before he knew it, reaching into his pocket and pulling out his cellphone. He saw a missed call, and his heart stopped. It hadn't been Nic calling him again. It had been from *Troy*. His head whipped in Lucian's direction. He was standing, but he couldn't feel the floor underneath his feet.

"Care to elaborate?" Dev asked, sounding calm—too calm when it felt like the entire room was shifting under Gabe's feet.

"I just got off the phone with Troy. He said Nikki was attacked at her apartment—"

That was all Gabe heard—all he needed to hear in that moment. "Is she okay?"

Lucian opened his mouth. "I don't . . . I don't know."

His entire word stopped as a horrible sense of déjà vu washed over Gabe, rocking him straight to the core. No way. Not Nic. He couldn't lose—

He cut himself off, not even giving that horrific thought a chance to breathe and take on a life. "Where is she?"

"At University Hospital," Lucian answered.

Gabe started for the door.

"Wait. You haven't heard it all." Lucian turned to Dev. "It was Parker Harrington."

NIKKI WINCED AS the young doctor shone the light into her left eye.

"Sorry about that." He tilted his head and then sat back, snapping off the light. "You're definitely going to be bruised and swollen in this eye, but there doesn't appear to be any serious damage to the eye or the socket."

She started to nod, but then wisely decided against it since it felt like her entire body was one giant throbbing bruise.

"We should get your X-rays back soon, but I think they're

just going to confirm what we already know. You have a contusion along the left side of your ribcage, but I don't think any of the ribs are broken. You're going to be sore, probably for a week or two, but you're a very lucky young woman."

She *was* lucky.

Nikki knew that all the way down to her aching bones. Parker was . . . God, he was going to kill her. Not only that, he was—

She sucked in a sharp breath.

The doctor smiled faintly. "We want to keep you for a few hours, probably through the rest of the night just in case you have a concussion. You took some pretty significant hits to the head."

Her gaze flickered over the doctor's shoulder, to the doorway. Her stomach dropped. A uniformed cop stood there. Troy had been in here earlier, but she hadn't seen him since she'd been wheeled off for X-rays.

He better not have called her parents.

"We're going to give you something for the pain in a bit," the doctor was saying. She wished she could remember his name. "It's going to make you a little sleepy, so I don't want you to worry if you feel like dozing off, okay?"

"Okay." Her voice sounded hoarse and each time she talked, it hurt. A scary reminder of how closely she'd come to having her life choked out of her.

And she didn't even want to think about why, but there was no stopping it. It was all she could think about.

Parker had threatened her—threatened her parents' jobs—and he'd warned her about Sabrina, but he was *Parker.* He'd scared her the day Gabe had punched him, but she never, ever in a million years thought that something like this would happen.

But as she'd sat in the apartment, waiting for the cops to show up, her brain slowly clicked things together, and maybe she was wrong, but she doubted it.

Her gaze drifted back to the cop. With her rapidly swelling left eye, she couldn't make out the cop's features. They were blurry. As she stared at his back, she thought of . . . Sabrina.

Parker had come after her because of his sister.

She never thought they were capable of something like this, but Parker was Sabrina's brother. *Was.* Parker . . . wasn't anything anymore.

Oh, God.

Her lower lip trembled, and that felt like crap, because it was split and it freaking hurt. She was surprised he hadn't knocked any of her teeth out.

"Are you sure there's no one you want us to call for you?" the doctor asked, drawing her attention.

"I've called my friend." That wasn't exactly true, but she planned on calling Rosie whenever it got close enough to the time they were going to release her.

The doctor stared at her a moment and then nodded. "All righty then. A nurse will be in shortly to get some pain meds in you."

"Thank you," she said, and then watched him walk out of the curtained room.

And then she was alone with the exception of the cop. Why was he here? Probably because Troy didn't believe for one second that she had no idea whatsoever why Parker wanted to hurt her.

But if she said why, then she'd have to explain what she saw and that, well, that dragged the de Vincents into it. Part of her wasn't even sure why she sought to protect them. Perhaps it was something ingrained in her because of her parents. Either way, she wasn't saying anything to any cop.

Closing her one good eye, she tried to get comfortable on the bed, but every time she moved, her body protested. The blanket was thin, and she was . . . so damn cold.

She drew in a stuttered breath as tears crawled up the back of her throat.

She killed a man.

And she . . . she didn't know how to feel about that, because even though she was glad to be alive, killing someone was . . .

She felt detached from all of this. Like she was above her own body, tethered by thin, fragile strings that could snap at any given moment. She had no idea what would happen when they did break.

The nurse came in, asking Nikki how she felt as she administrated whatever pain meds. She felt it when it hit her system, washing over the back of her skull and pooling in her mouth.

Nikki closed her eyes and waited for whatever they gave her to take the pain away, along with the memory of Parker's eyes, wide with shock.

Chapter 33

Gabe was aware of Lucian following him as he stalked down the hallway of the hospital, heading for where he'd been told Nic was being kept. His heart lodged somewhere in the vicinity of his throat, he rounded the corner and came face-to-face with Troy.

"There you are," Troy said. "We need to talk."

"It can wait." He sidestepped Troy.

"No." Troy grabbed his arm, halting him. "It can't."

Gabe looked down at Troy's arm. "You know I respect the fuck out of you and think of you as a brother, but if you don't let me go, things are going to turn ugly as fuck."

Troy didn't let go. "Look, I know you want to go see her, and you will. She's right down that hall, living and breathing, but you've got to give me a couple of minutes."

"Gabe." Lucian was there, placing a hand on his shoulder.

His eyes met Lucian's. "She called me and I didn't answer."

"But you're here now and you'll see her." Lucian squeezed Gabe's shoulder. "Give Troy a couple of minutes."

Cursing, he turned to the detective. "Make it fucking quick."

"It was Parker Harrington," he said, keeping his voice low. "He broke into her apartment—"

"I know this," seethed Gabe.

"But what we don't know is why he would do that. You know I'm no fan of Parker's, but beating the shit out of a girl and trying to kill her? That seems out of character for him."

Gabe couldn't feel the floor again as Troy's words coursed off him. If it wasn't for Lucian's hand on his shoulder, he would've done something crazy. He knew it.

"Where is Parker?" Gabe asked, thinking they better have him locked up real damn good to keep him away from the piece of shit.

Troy glanced between the brothers and when he spoke, his voice was low. "Parker's dead."

"What?" Lucian exclaimed.

Everything in Gabe stilled.

"Nikki took him out. With a *chisel*," Troy said, and Gabe's mind went absolutely blank—blank with fucking rage. "The damn patrolman had to pry the chisel out of her hands when he got there." Troy looked down the hall. "She got the son of a bitch right in the chest."

"Jesus." Gabe turned, shrugging off Lucian's hand as he thrust his fingers through his hair.

"It was self-defense," Lucian said.

Troy cocked his head to the side. "We know. That shit is obvious, but we don't know why, and Nikki ain't talking."

"What do you mean she isn't talking?" Gabe demanded.

"She's saying she has no idea why Parker would want to hurt her, and I'm thinking that's bullshit." Troy met his stare head-on. "I'm willing to bet she isn't telling the whole story, and the only reason I can fathom she'd be doing that is because it has something to do with one of you. And since Parker's sister is Dev's goddamn fiancée, it's not a big leap of logic."

Gabe stiffened. Fucking Sabrina. He turned to his brother. Their eyes met, and he knew right then Lucian was on the same wavelength.

Lucian stepped to the side. "I need to call Dev."

"Oh, no you don't." Troy turned to Lucian.

Done with this conversation, he ignored Troy calling out

his name as he stalked down the hall. Her room was easy to find, because of the police officer standing guard. The man's gaze moved over his shoulder, and Troy must've signaled him, because the officer stepped aside.

Walking into the hospital room was like moving through quicksand. The sensation of having been right here before nearly took his knees out from under him. It didn't matter that Troy had said she was breathing and alive.

Breathing and alive didn't mean shit.

Gabe knew this.

Drawing in a shallow breath, he tugged the curtain aside and then he saw her—well, he saw her back.

Nic was curled on her side, facing away from the door. He saw one IV bag and the bare minimum of monitors. That was good, all things considered.

But she looked so small in the bed, too small.

Gabe made his way around the narrow bed, his gaze desperate to see those beautiful brown eyes. Then he really saw her.

His heart fucking broke right then.

Knowing what Troy had said about what Parker had done to her couldn't have possibly prepared him for what he saw. There didn't appear to be more than a few inches of her face that wasn't battered. Her lip was red and angry. Bright red bruises were forming along her jaw, turning purple around the edges. Her fucking left eye was swollen shut, blue, and purple. There were scratches on the one cheek he could see.

His knees weakened on him.

Gabe wished Parker was alive for several reasons. One of them being that Nic wouldn't have had to do something like that. She was too damn good to carry that kind of weight. But the most selfish reason? He wanted to beat that motherfucker to death, paying him back for every bruise, every second of pain she felt.

He sat down in the empty chair in front of her, wondering

where in the hell her parents were. Resting his elbows on his knees, he dragged his hand down his face.

Goddamn, she didn't deserve this. No one did, but she really didn't deserve this.

His eyes . . . his damn eyes felt damp.

He should've seen this coming. The mindset that Sabrina and her brother were harmless annoyances was proven false the moment he realized just how much Sabrina had known about him. He should've anticipated one of them going after Nikki. Neither Sabrina nor Parker ever believed that Gabe would be the one to tell Dev. He *knew* this, so he should've been there for her.

God.

Nic shivered, catching his attention. Gabe exhaled heavily, glancing down at the blanket. It had slipped to her waist. Carefully, he leaned over and tugged it up to her shoulders.

She stirred, wincing. His gaze flickered over her. What else was wrong with her? What couldn't he see? A shudder worked its way through him.

Nic moved again and then one eye opened. Awareness crept over her features. "Gabe?"

"I'm so sorry." His voice was thick. "So fucking sorry."

Her brow knitted as she tried to sit up. "What . . . ?" She sucked in a sharp breath.

He reached for her, but froze, unsure of where to touch her that wouldn't hurt her. "How can I help you?"

Nic's lips thinned as she eased onto her back. "What are you doing here?"

The question surprised him. "Where else would I be?"

She didn't answer as she looked away. Her neck. Holy fuck. He saw the bruises on her neck, bruises that looked an awful lot like fingers.

"Jesus," he growled.

Nic's hand stilled. "Do I look that bad?"

He realized he was clenching his fists. "You look beautiful."

A hoarse, choked laugh left her. "I think . . . you're having problems with your vision."

"I'm seeing just fine." His hands opened and closed. "Where are your parents?"

Her one eye closed. "I haven't called them yet."

"Nic."

"I don't want them to see me like this. They'd freak out . . . and my mom doesn't need this right now."

Gabe couldn't believe she was worrying about upsetting her parents. "Babe, they're going to have to see you eventually."

"I know." She swallowed and then winced. "But they don't have to see me right now."

"You called me," he said after a moment, voice rough. "I didn't answer. I was talking—"

"It's okay. It doesn't matter."

"It matters, Nic."

Nic was quiet for a moment. "I called you afterward. I wasn't thinking straight. I thought Devlin . . . should know."

She hadn't been calling him for help, and God, that cut him deep. When she needed him the most, he'd created a situation where he couldn't be there—where she wouldn't even think about coming to him.

That wasn't something he would easily forgive himself for.

Nic lifted a hand, prodding gingerly at her lip. "Ow."

A wry smile twisted his lips and he leaned over, gently catching her wrist and pulling her hand away. "Don't poke at it."

Her gaze met his and then darted away. A moment passed and then he let go of her wrist. God, he wanted to gather her in his arms and never let go.

"Do you know if they've . . . um, if they've removed the body yet?" she asked.

"I don't know, but I can find out."

Her lip trembled. "There was a lot of blood. It probably ruined—"

"I'll take care of it." And he would. She would never have to see any of that again. "I don't want you to worry about that. I'll make sure everything is the way it was before."

"Thank you," she whispered.

"You don't need to thank me. I should've . . ."

"You should've what?"

Been there. He should've been there to protect her. He should've handled things differently with her. He should've told her about William, and he should've . . . he should've let himself feel what he was feeling instead of being a closed-off jackass who had been terrified of feeling what he was beginning to feel for her.

He should've let himself love her.

The outcome could've been different. Easily. Instead of going to a hospital room, it would be a morgue and a funeral. Like with Emma, he wouldn't have gotten a third chance to make things right.

And he needed to make things right.

It was funny how in moments like this you realized what mattered the most and how everything else was fucking background noise.

Nic broke the silence. "I'm going to . . . I'm going to call Rosie and I'll go home with her. I can't go back there until it's cleaned up."

"You'll come home with me," he said, frowning. "And you'll stay as long as you need to."

"I don't think . . . that's smart."

"Why the hell not?"

She stared at him a moment and then looked away. He needed to tell her what he'd been thinking and feeling, but now was not the time.

Gabe picked up Nic's hand. Her knuckles were red, swollen. There was dried blood under her fingernails, between her fingers. Seeing all of this pissed him off, but there was no denying that his girl was a fighter.

His girl.

Those two words felt just as right as they did the first time he thought them, but this time, he let himself welcome them, *feel* them.

"Are you up for telling me what happened?" he asked after a moment.

"I didn't even know it was him at first," she said, her voice soft. "He was wearing a ski mask and he came at me. I was trapped in the bedroom and he . . ." A shudder rolled through her.

Every muscle went rigid as he folded both hands over hers. Troy hadn't mentioned any type of . . . of sexual assault, but a whole new wave of fury and horror was building inside him. "He what, sweetheart?"

"I think he was trying to, you know, rape me." Her eyes were closed, and thank fuck for that, because he was sure there was no hiding the murderous rage he could feel brimming to the surface. "I fought back and I guess he decided to give up on that and tried to . . . end it."

He gently squeezed her hand. "Did he say anything to you?"

"Yeah, he did." Her inhale was shaky. "He said something I don't even know how to tell you."

"You can tell me anything." He kissed her knuckles, and her one good eye flew open.

A long moment passed. "He pretty much said he was there because of Sabrina. She's . . . she's dangerously obsessed with you. I don't know why he'd do what he's done for her, but Gabe, he said . . ."

His gut churned. "He said what, Nic?"

Nic let out a shaky breath. "He said that he wanted to play it like he had before, but Sabrina said two car accidents would be suspicious."

Gabe stilled.

"I think . . . God, I think he was talking about Emma.

I know that sounds insane, but they're obviously insane. I don't know how Emma had a car accident, but Gabe, I think that's something that needs to be looked at."

He couldn't even feel the hand he was holding. He didn't see Nic or hear the steady beeps of the monitor. When he drew in a breath, he didn't catch that overpowering disinfectant smell that cloaked hospitals. He was there, in the room with Nic, but he also wasn't.

Did Sabrina and Parker have something to do with Emma's accident?

It was possible. From what he knew of the accident, Emma had appeared to lose control of her vehicle less than a handful of miles from her parents' house. She'd been leaving to pick William up from them. Her car had struck a tree. Could someone—that someone being Parker—have run her off the road?

It was more than possible.

I did your dirty work again.

Sabrina practically admitted it herself.

His entire being felt like it shifted, but he knew he hadn't moved—hadn't even blinked. The ever-present rage resurfaced, and damn, it was like his skin was on fire.

"Gabe," Nic whispered.

He heard her, but he also didn't. He was stuck on what she'd said. Emma's death hadn't been an accident. It had been murder, because that woman was obsessed with him. He couldn't process it, couldn't think around it.

"I'm sorry," Nic said softly. "I'm so sorry."

His entire body jerked at her quietly spoken apology and her bruised, battered face came back into focus. Nic lay on that hospital bed. Not Emma. They took Emma away from their son, but they hadn't succeeded in taking Nic from him.

Lifting her hand to his mouth once more, he kissed her palm and closed his eyes. He'd lost a piece of Emma the night she'd been assaulted and then he'd lost her the night he retaliated. They'd come together once in the last five years, and that gave him his son, but Gabe had long since accepted before he learned what had happened to Emma that it was over between them. Why Sabrina would've gone after her, after all this time, was beyond his level of understanding.

"Are you okay?" she asked.

Was he? Fuck no. Anger compounded with helplessness was a dangerous mess, but he pulled it together. He had to. For her. Again, her concern shook him to his core. She shouldn't be worrying about him right now.

"I'm okay." His eyes opened. "I'm okay, sweetheart."

She was quiet for a moment. "I didn't tell Troy or the cops anything about what . . . Sabrina or Parker had said to me."

He lifted her hand to his forehead. "Dev will be appreciative of that, but I don't give a fuck if you told them. You didn't have to lie to avoid a scandal. You shouldn't even be worrying about that."

She was quiet for a moment. "What's going to happen?"

"I don't know." Whatever was going to happen wouldn't be pretty. "I talked to Dev today. He came home early. Told him everything."

"Really?"

"Yeah. He's ending it with her."

A harsh laugh parted her lips. "So, if . . . Sabrina got Parker to silence me it was all over nothing? Or was it just out of anger or was it jealousy?"

He'd underestimated Sabrina. Could've been just out of jealousy, but it did leave the question of why would Parker risk so much for his sister?

"It . . . it didn't even matter," she said. "Because you told Devlin anyway. Parker did all that for nothing. He died—"

"I don't give a fuck about him. He deserved what he got. I just wish you never had to find yourself in that situation.

That you didn't have to fight—" His damn voice cracked. He couldn't finish.

"Gabe?"

He shook his head, still holding onto her hand. "You shouldn't have to deal with any of this."

"It's okay," she said quietly. "It'll be okay."

"Are you trying to comfort me?"

"I don't know. I guess?"

Gabe shook his head in wonder. "You're . . . I honestly don't know what to say."

She tried to pull her hand free, but he held on. He was never letting go. "I think you've already said enough."

He deserved that.

A long moment passed as she lifted her gaze from where he held her hand. "Why are you here?"

"We need to talk. Not now." He lowered his mouth, kissing the top of her battered hand once more, silencing her protests. "But we're going to talk later."

Chapter 34

Gabe stayed with Nic until she dozed off, and it took a hell of a lot out of him to leave her even at that point. But he needed to speak to his brothers.

He found them in one of the private rooms down the hall, Dev standing in the corner of the small room, arms folded across his chest. Lucian was seated on the couch. Beside him was Julia. Luckily, Troy wasn't there. He closed the door behind him as Julia rose.

"Is she okay?" she asked, concern clear in her gaze and the set of her lips.

"She's roughed up real bad, but she'll be okay." At least physically. His voice was gruff when he spoke again. "She's resting right now."

Lucian exhaled heavily as he leaned back on the uncomfortable couch. "Jesus." He dragged his hands down his face as Julia sat down once more, touching his arm. "Where are Livie and Richard?"

"She doesn't want them to see her like this," he explained. "And we've got to respect that." His gaze found Dev's. "Agreed?"

"Agreed," he murmured and then spoke louder. "You talked to her about Parker?"

Gabe couldn't sit as he came to stand in the middle of the room. "I did. He went after her because of Sabrina, but that's not all."

"It's not?" Lucian lowered his hands and reached over, picking up Julia's.

"Not even fucking remotely all," he bit out.

Dev's gaze slid to the couch. "Perhaps Julia should—"

"No," Lucian cut him off as he looked over his shoulder. "Julia is a part of this family, not just the good parts but also the fucked-up parts. She stays."

Dev snapped his mouth shut and wisely kept it shut.

There was a part of Gabe that would've preferred that Julia didn't hear this, but it had nothing to do with trust. "Parker insinuated that he and Sabrina had something to do with Emma's accident."

Lucian paled, and it seemed he was at a loss for words, but it wasn't his reaction that shocked Gabe. It was his older brother's reaction. Mainly because Dev never had a reaction to anything.

But he did now.

Blood drained from his face as he lurched forward a step and then seemed to catch himself, unfolding his arms. "Are you sure?" he asked in a voice that Gabe barely recognized. "What were you told?"

Gabe repeated what Nic told him. "It makes sense. Especially when you take into consideration what Sabrina said to me herself."

"Good God," whispered Julia.

Dev held Gabe's gaze for a moment and then looked away, his lips pressed into a hard line. A muscle flexed in his jaw.

"We need to find Sabrina," Gabe said.

His brother gave him a curt nod. "I will pay a visit to Stefan first and then the Harringtons' home. No one is going to shield her from us."

Gabe drew in a shallow breath. "She will answer for this."

"She will do more than that."

"You need to take the bed, Nikki. Seriously." Rosie stood in front of an old chess table that had been converted into a coffee table.

Her friend's apartment contained a strange assortment of things. Beaded curtains separated the living room from the bedroom. Posters of haunted places in New Orleans dotted the walls next to paintings that looked like they belonged in a museum. Human-shaped candles lined bookshelves that were nearly overflowing with true accounts of hauntings and, oddly enough, cookbooks. There were normal-looking candles sitting in front of a surprisingly large TV.

Nikki gingerly sat down on the couch. "The couch will be fine." She tugged at the hospital wristband, sighing when the thing wouldn't budge. What did they seal these things with? Gorilla Glue? "Thank you for picking me up."

"If you say thank you one more time, I'll scream." Rosie sat beside her, concern etched into her face. She glanced at Nikki's cell phone. "You really need to call your parents."

"I will." She sighed, pushing a strand of hair back from her face. "I have time. I mean, I doubt they're going to say my name when this hits the news."

"Hon, it's already hit the news," Rosie told her. "It was all over the local news this morning. Parker *Harrington*? That's a big deal."

Her stomach twisted. "But they didn't say my name, right?"

"No. Bizarrely, they were speculating it was a domestic situation between him and a woman he was seeing."

"God." She leaned back in hopes it took the weight off her ribs. "I just don't want my parents to freak out."

"They're going to freak out. Not trying to stress you out, but their daughter was almost murdered and looks like she went toe-to-toe in a cage match."

Nikki flinched. "That's not helping."

"I know it's not, but it's not like you're going to take a nap and wake up looking like nothing happened. Your parents are going to be upset when they realize you've waited this long to see them."

She knew this. "I'll call them in a little bit."

"Okay." Rosie rose, walking to where the curtains were letting the morning light stream in from the glass doors of the balcony. Nikki's phone rang just then. From where she sat, she saw who it was and Rosie guessed it. "Is that Gabe?"

"Yeah," she whispered. That was the third time Gabe had called. "I texted him and told him I was coming here."

"But he wanted you to go home with him?" She closed the curtains, and the room darkened.

When Gabe had finally left her side in the early morning hours to check in with his brothers, Nikki had put her escape plan in motion. Luck had finally been on her side. Rosie answered her call and she was released from the hospital all before Gabe returned.

"He did, but that wouldn't be the smartest decision." Nikki smoothed her hand over her knees, concentrating on taking deep breaths.

"I'm sure he took all of that into consideration when he made the offer."

Nikki couldn't help but think about how he'd held her hand, kissing it. The way his eyes had appeared damp and how he'd been so reluctant to leave her side. He'd said they needed to talk, but she knew that whatever he was feeling or thinking was greatly skewed by what just happened.

"It doesn't matter." She closed her one good eye. "I just want to sleep. Okay?"

"All right. I'll leave it alone if you get your ass in my bed and sleep there." When Nikki opened her mouth to protest, Rosie lifted a hand. "I'm already awake and if you sleep out here, you're not going to get any rest. I'm also not a shitty friend. You're taking the bed. So get up and get your ass in there."

A weak smile tugged at her lips. "You're not a shitty friend." Pushing herself up, she ignored the spike of pain. "I'll get in bed."

And that's what she did. Not only that, she was able to change into a pair of sleep shorts and a loose tee shirt that fit well enough to be comfortable. At this point, she'd wear anything to not be in the clothing she was in.

She didn't want to see the leggings or shirt ever again, and Rosie apparently sensed that because as Nikki got comfortable, she removed the clothes from the bedroom.

It took a while for her to settle in, finally giving up and lying prone on her back. The room was so quiet she wondered if Rosie was still in the apartment. The silence, though, it dragged on her nerves, and when she closed her eyes, she heard Parker's ragged breathing, she felt him on her, and she saw those shocked eyes.

Nikki pressed her lips together, ignoring the ache it caused. Emotion crawled up her throat. Tears burned the back of her eyes. She didn't want to cry. Besides the fact it was going to sting the hell out of her swollen eye, she feared that if she started she wouldn't stop. Not anytime soon. Too much had happened. Too much and she didn't know how she was going to deal with this.

With *any* of this.

"ARE YOU SURE her friend lives here?" Dev asked as they walked up metal stairs to a second-floor apartment over what appeared to be a voodoo shop. "Or a priestess ready to raise the dead?"

Gabe ignored the comment. "You didn't have to come."

"Yes, I do." Dev adjusted the black sunglasses he was wearing. "Nikki got hurt because of my relationship with Sabrina."

The responsibility fell on both of them. Gabe should've said something about Sabrina earlier, and Dev should've shut that shit down with her years ago.

None of that mattered at that point.

Gabe stopped in front of the door that had what appeared

to be some kind of wooden Celtic cross hanging from it. The craftsmanship caught his eye, but that was weird as shit, so whatever.

He hoped this was the right place. It had taken some investigating, requiring him to call Bev, because he knew Nic was friends with her daughter. It was Bree who told him where Rosie lived.

He knocked on the door while Dev joined him on the landing. A second later the door inched open. Jackpot. It had to be Rosie since she fit Bree's description to a tee. She peeked out, her hair held back with a purple scarf with . . . *skulls* all over it?

Yep, they were skulls.

"Figured you'd find your way here." She looked over his shoulder and frowned. "Surprised to see *that* one here."

Dev stepped to the side. "Excuse me?"

The woman ignored him. "You here for Nikki?"

"Yes. You going to let me in?"

She blocked the door. "Depends. Are you finally going to do right by my friend?"

"Who is this woman?" Dev demanded.

"First name Nonya, last name Your Business," she snapped, her gaze not leaving Gabe's face.

Despite everything, Gabe was fighting a laugh. "I'm going to try to."

"Trying isn't good enough, bud. Not anymore," Rosie shot back, surprising Gabe. "You trying is pretty much like me trying not to eat the last cupcake in the fridge. It's not real successful."

"Okay. I'm going to do right by her. That's why I'm here," Gabe said again. "You going to let me in?"

She appeared to think it over and then she stepped back, opening the door. "She's in the bedroom."

Gabe walked in. "Thank you."

"Don't make me regret this," she said, voice low. "Because you will not like it if I regret this."

He smiled then, unable to help himself. "I won't."

"Good."

Gabe stepped around the somewhat scary woman when he heard Dev ask, "Is that really a beaded curtain?"

"You got a problem with that?" she fired back. "Are they not up to your taste or class?"

"I'm pretty sure that most people over the age of twelve find them to be tasteless."

"Behave," he said to Dev, leaving him in the room with Nikki's friend.

He parted the beads and stepped into the dark room. It took a moment for his eyes to adjust, but he found her lying in the center of the bed.

When he got back to the hospital room and saw that she was gone, he was caught between wanting to curse and laugh. If she was putting effort into doing exactly the opposite of what he wanted, then that was a good sign.

Walking over to the bed, he sat down. Even in the darkness of the room, he could see that the bruises looked worse than before. His jaw locked down as he reached out, carefully catching a strand of her hair. He brushed it back from her face.

"Nikki," he said.

Her brows knitted and then her right eye opened. She focused on him, and he saw the sleep clearing from her face.

"Good morning." He smiled.

She stared at him for a moment. "Where is Rosie?"

"Out in the living room."

"How did you . . . find me?"

"Took a little investigating," he replied. "You didn't think I'd come looking for you when I saw that you left? When you didn't answer my calls?"

"I thought . . ." She looked away. "I figured you'd give me some space."

"That's not what you need right now."

"How do you know?"

"Because I do," he replied, and saw her shoulders tense. "Sometimes giving space isn't always the right thing to do. And what you need right now is me to be there for you. I'm here."

"I'm not Emma."

"I know that."

She exhaled heavily. "I know you feel guilty and you're probably thinking all these things, but none of it's real, you know? None of it's going to be there a week or a month from now, so can we please not do this?"

"Like I said before, we need to talk and right now is not a good time for that, but I'll tell you this. You have no idea what I'm thinking or if it's real," he said, placing his hand on the other side of her legs. "All I know is that I fucked up with you. I should've told you about William and I sure as hell shouldn't have said the things I did. I know damn well you'd be amazing with him. You would accept him. He'd accept you. I spent the last couple of days regretting the hell out of that, wondering if I could fix this, wondering if I was even worth it. But seeing you in that hospital bed—seeing you now? Knowing you could've died, and here I was, once again, waiting on third and fourth chances to appear without me working for them while paying attention to stupid shit. I realized none of that mattered when it came to you and me. None of it."

Nikki didn't move. He wondered if she was even breathing.

"I'm here because there's no other place I should be. I'm here because you need me," he said, kissing the top of her head. "And I'm here because I realized something before you were hurt."

"What?" she whispered.

"That's something we'll discuss later, okay? Right now, I just want to get you home and I just want to hold you so that I know without a doubt you're okay—that you're going to be okay."

She didn't respond and then her face crumpled. "Oh, God."

"Sweetheart." He shifted closer, reaching for her.

She tried to sit up as she pressed her hands over her face. Everything about the way she moved, the way she tried to hide her tears fucking slaughtered him.

Gabe reacted. He climbed right into the bed with her, gathering her up in his arms as carefully as he could without hurting her. But then, the way her shoulders shook with sobs, he doubted she could feel him.

But he was there.

He wrapped his arms around her, holding her as she pressed into his chest, her fingers opening and closing around nothing but air. He held her, trying to soothe her with words that didn't make much sense. Then he just held her, letting her get it all out, because that was the best thing for her. It had to be.

At some point, he was aware of Rosie checking in on them, but she didn't say anything and she left, leaving them alone.

He didn't know how much time passed before the sobs slowed and the raw sounds ended. She sniffled as she drew back, putting a little bit of space between them. "Sorry." Her voice sounded worse than before. "I didn't mean to cry all over you."

"It's okay." He kept his arms around her, his hold loose. "I make a good tissue."

Her laugh was shaky. "It just . . . hit me all at once."

"Understandable."

She carefully wiped at her eyes. "You really . . . you really want me to come back to your house?"

"I do, and we should probably leave soon, if you're up for it," Gabe said, letting himself grin just then. "Dev is in the other room with your friend."

"What?" She looked thunderstruck. "You left Rosie with him?"

He bit back a grin. "I don't think you need to worry about your friend. I'm more worried for Dev."

She leaned over, peering toward the beaded curtains. "That's not good."

"Probably not," he agreed. "Come home with me, Nikki. Let me be there for you. Let me start to fix this."

Nikki's gaze drifted back to him, and for a moment he feared she would say no, and then he was going to beg. He was also prepared to pick her up and carry her out of there.

"Okay," she said, slipping free from his hold "All right."

Chapter 35

Gabe watched Richard step out into the living area, leaving his daughter inside his bedroom with her mother. The man looked like he'd aged about a decade between the time he'd gone into the room and now. Gabe felt like that himself. The last twenty-four hours hadn't been easy.

He'd gotten Nic here, and she didn't fight him when he took her straight up to his apartment. She'd fallen asleep after managing to get a half a bowl of soup in her, but she hadn't slept long.

Nightmares plagued her, and there was nothing Gabe could do but hold her through them, reminding her that she wasn't back in that apartment and reminding himself that she was still very much alive.

This morning she'd finally been ready to call her parents. She had to be, because Richard was going to show up to work tomorrow. The visit hadn't been easy.

He hated seeing Livie cry.

He also hated seeing how much it affected Nic.

"Would you like something to drink?" he asked.

"Yes." Richard cleared his throat, still staring at the closed door. "A drink would be nice."

"She'll be okay." Gabe walked to the small bar near the private, eat-in kitchen. "She's strong. Just like Livie."

The older man nodded. Several moments passed. "And what will happen to Sabrina?"

Sabrina was, not surprisingly, currently missing in action, and not of their doing. "Dev has people looking for her. It will be handled."

"In the typical de Vincent fashion?"

Gabe poured two scotches. Richard had worked for their family for a very long time. "Do you really want to know the answer to that?"

"That's my only child," Richard said, facing Gabe. "My Nicolette is a good girl. She has a good heart. She's going to make other people's lives better one day. I want that woman to pay for what happened to my girl."

Gabe inclined his head as he handed the drink to Richard. "We want the same things."

The older man took his drink and downed half of it in one swallow. He set the glass on the bar. "I've looked after you since you were in diapers and I know a lot about your family—a lot about you."

"You do."

"I've always respected you, thought of you and your brothers as sons of mine." He placed his hands on the bar as his steady gaze held Gabe's. "You all always have your reasons for doing what gets done. I understand that, and even when you three have done things that go against everything I believe in, I still cared for you all like you were my own."

Gabe's shoulders stiffened. Richard knew a lot. He'd seen a lot. Even more than Livie.

"And I know you boys respect me and my wife, so I expect a straight answer to this question," he continued. "You have my daughter in your bedroom, in your bed, and I know you two have been spending a lot of time together. Not like before. I want to know what your intentions are."

Gabe didn't hesitate and he didn't lie. "I love her."

The older man's jaw tightened. "You just learned that the woman you loved for the last ten or so years had died and hid a son from you—"

"I know what you're getting at. I understand why you

would think about Emma, but what I feel for Nic has nothing to do with Emma. There will always be a part of me that loves her." He took a deep breath. "But the part that loves Nic is bigger."

Surprise flickered across Richard's face and then he picked up the glass, finishing off the scotch. "You're ten years older than her."

"Doesn't feel that way. Maybe one day it will, when I'm your age, but not now. And correct me if I'm wrong, but aren't you eight years older than Livie?"

"When we got together, things were different."

"When you two got together, she was barely eighteen, right?"

"As I said, things were—"

"You loved each other," Gabe corrected. "That's all that mattered. And now look at you two, married for how long?"

Richard arched a brow. "And what about William?"

"I will take her to meet him, when she's ready, and we'll go from there," he explained. "Look, I don't have everything figured out. I haven't even told Nic how I feel yet, but I'm telling you. I love her. I'm in love with her, so all I can tell you is that we'll figure everything out."

"You haven't told my daughter that you love her?"

"Not yet." He glanced at the closed door. "My timing has been off."

"There's no wrong time to tell someone you love them."

Gabe felt his heart lodge in his throat as he stared at the man he considered more like a father than a butler. He knew that when her parents came to see her, he was going to have this conversation with her father. The man wasn't going to *not* question why Nic was in his bed. The thing was, he wasn't sure how Richard would take to the news.

He'd actually prepared himself to stand there and let Richard take a swing at him, if Nic's father felt like he needed that.

"What are you saying?" he heard himself ask.

"What I'm saying is that I suppose my girl could do worse than a de Vincent falling in love with her."

A slow grin tugged at his lips. "You think Livie will feel the same, with the curse and all?"

"You're not the brother I worry about when it comes to the curse," Richard replied. "You're the brother I worry about least."

NIKKI SAT IN the chair out on the porch that overlooked the pool. A soft, thin blanket was draped over her legs, warding off the cool breeze rolling over the land and lifting the wisps of hair off her neck.

Beside her sat a glass of sweet tea and an untouched book Julia had lent her. Nikki wanted nothing more than to lose herself in a good read, but the last few days consumed her thoughts.

Seeing her parents react to how she looked was something that was going to stay with her for a long time. Hell, not like she was going to forget the attack anytime soon, but for some reason, seeing her father nearly break down when he got a look at her absolutely destroyed her.

Her parents were the strongest people she knew.

Nikki was glad she did see them. It wasn't until her mom wrapped her arms around her that she realized just how badly she'd needed her momma in that moment. Nothing made you feel like everything was going to be okay like a hug from your mom.

What didn't make her feel all that okay was her mom asking her why she was in Gabe's *bed*. That had been awkward to say the least, because she wasn't sure how to answer it. She wasn't even sure what was going on between them.

Gabe had worked with the landlord and her apartment was currently being restored. It wasn't just a quick cleanup job. The subfloors had to be pulled up because the blood had . . .

Nikki reached for her glass of tea. Her hand trembled, causing the ice to shake as she took a drink.

In other words, it was going to be a couple of days before she could get back into her apartment. Gabe, along with Rosie, had grabbed several days' worth of clothing for her.

She would've loved to have been a fly on the wall for that trip.

Setting the tea aside, she tugged the blanket up to her shoulders and closed her eyes. The swelling had started to go down in her left eye, so it was beginning to function like a normal eyeball, thank God. Her rib still ached, usually when standing up or lying down at first, but it was getting better.

Life was trucking along even though no one had a clue where Sabrina was, and it wasn't because the brothers had helped her disappear in that creepy, not-really-missing kind of way.

Sabrina had bailed.

That meant she was still out there, and that was terrifying. The woman wasn't working with all the appropriate tools in the shed. And that made Nikki think of the rumored de Vincent curse. Women died, went missing, or lost their minds.

When she thought about Sabrina, about the de Vincents' sister, and their mother, it really made her begin to wonder if there was some truth behind it.

Or if they really just had mega bad luck.

Nikki should probably be worried since she was a woman living temporarily in the de Vincent house, but so was Julia. Then again, Julia was almost murdered by Daniel.

And Nikki was almost killed by Parker.

Maybe she should be worried.

She still had a hard time thinking about what Sabrina and Parker had been capable of. The fact that they'd been following her—following Gabe this entire time left her more than just a little disturbed. She no longer doubted for a second that Sabrina had been responsible for her fall down the stairs or the broken-out window. The latter had probably been Parker, and all those times she felt like she was being watched she had most likely been right. She had no idea what they thought to accomplish with the whole breaking-out-the-car-window thing, but maybe they just wanted to scare her or maybe it was just an act of jealous rage. She didn't know.

What they had done to her, tried to do to her, had been horrible, but what they'd done to Emma and her son had been a million times worse.

Nikki simply could not understand how someone could be so evil—how whatever Sabrina had felt for Gabe had twisted into something so dark and ugly.

It was likely that she'd never understand.

Opening her eyes to the sound of approaching footsteps, she wasn't surprised when she saw Gabe round the corner of the porch.

Barefoot.

"Hey," he said, coming near but stopping about a foot from her. "You need a refill?"

"No, but thanks."

Gabe had been waiting on her hand and foot since she'd been sequestered away in his rooms. Admittedly, she kind of liked it. Who wouldn't?

"It's getting kind of chilly out here," he said, looking over the railing. The breeze caught the loose strands of his hair, tossing them across his face. "You want to head inside?"

That's not what Nikki wanted to do.

She was ready for this talk he'd promised, beyond ready, because she had to know where they stood. Over the last couple of days, Gabe had acted like the doting boyfriend, caring for her, sleeping beside her, and waking up along with her if she had a nightmare. He'd been perfect.

But they hadn't kissed. There'd been no touching of the

naughty and fun kind. There'd been no further talks. They were in a holding pattern.

Nikki had already lost her heart to Gabe. Twice now. She needed to know if there was going to be a third time, because Nikki was done chasing Gabe.

"What I want is for us to talk," she said, staring up at him. "You said we would, and I think it's time we do."

Gabe was so still for a moment that a kernel of dread took root in her chest. "Yeah, it's time to have that conversation."

She drew in a shallow breath. "Then talk."

"I've been playing this conversation over and over in my head, wanting to get it perfect, you know? Because I think you deserve that." He leaned back against the railing, his hands folding over the vines. "So I mentally tallied up all the times I fucked up, starting back at that morning when I woke up and called you by the wrong name."

Nothing used to hurt Nikki more than remembering that moment, but over the last couple of weeks, she'd come to realize that was a blip on the radar of things that could send you careening headfirst into years of intensive therapy.

"And I discovered that my list was rather lengthy," he said, his tone wry and self-deprecating. "So much so that I don't even know how we've made it to this point."

She wondered that herself and then she usually stopped thinking about that when she did because it made her wonder if she was being a doormat for her heart.

"But the most inexcusable thing I did was not tell you about William and how I responded when you questioned me about him. I was caught off guard. My defenses went up. That's no excuse," he said. "I shouldn't have reacted the way I did."

"Why didn't you tell me? What's the real reason if it wasn't because you didn't think it was my business?"

He looked away, his chest rising with a heavy breath.

"Honest? I was embarrassed. Not that I have a son. God no. But that I have a son who is being raised by his grandparents. I have a son that I didn't know about for five years. A son that I'm still not raising and who's living a few hours from me. It's not an easy thing to share."

"I get that. I really do, but you didn't know he existed until his grandparents called you. You can't blame yourself for not being there for him."

"Are you seriously defending me right now?" He sounded shocked.

"I still think you're an asshole for how you treated me," she said, meaning it. "But I'm just telling it how it is. She kept William from you, for whatever reason. That's not your fault."

"But I'm not with him now."

"Because you're giving his grandparents time to deal with it. Look, I'm not saying you're handling this perfectly, but you're doing the best you can in a messed-up situation."

He was quiet for a long moment. "You know, I'll never know why she didn't tell me about him. Like what is so fucked-up about me that she didn't want me to know I have a son?"

"Don't do that to yourself." She scooted forward, ignoring the ache in her ribs. "You're not perfect and your family is a little weird, but whatever reason she kept him a secret from you is on her, not you."

When Gabe didn't continue, she pressed on. "I've known you since I was a kid. I know you, Gabe. There isn't anything that would make me think that you'd be a bad father. That there'd be any reason why I wouldn't want you in a child's life."

"Even if you knew that I helped murder someone?"

Her stomach knotted. "I already know."

"What?" He paled.

"Sabrina told me when she told me about William. I just didn't get a chance to bring it up and I thought, well . . ."

"Well what?"

She exhaled roughly. "I know what happened to Emma. Maybe it makes me a bad person, but he got what he deserved. I mean, am I supposed to feel bad for someone who did that?"

He said nothing.

"And I . . ." She drew in a deep breath. "I killed Parker."

"That's different. You were defending yourself."

"And you were defending the woman you loved."

"It's not the same thing."

She met his gaze. "If she decided to keep you out of William's life because of what happened with her attacker, then that's her choice. I can't blame her for it. I can only say what I would do if it were me."

An intensity filled his stare. "And what would you have done?"

"I would've wanted to help you."

He let out a choked-sounding laugh. "You would."

"I would," she insisted. "I hate the fact that I . . . that I killed someone, but I did it to survive, and if I hadn't, I wouldn't be here. I know what happened with that guy isn't the same, but it sure as hell gives you a new perspective on things."

Gabe nodded slowly as she watched him. She got it, why he'd kept such a big secret from her. She still didn't like it. Could she forgive him?

Was he worth forgiving?

In her heart of hearts, she already knew the answer to that question.

One side of his lips kicked up. "You know, I kind of pictured this conversation happening under different circumstances. Maybe a candlelight dinner or after we fucked each other senseless."

Her stomach twisted in the most pleasant way at the last part.

He pushed away from the railing. "But a wise man that

you know fairly well told me that there's no wrong time to tell someone that you love them."

Nikki stared at him, unsure if she heard him correctly or not. "What?" she whispered.

His grin turned shy, almost boyish. "I love you, Nic."

"Since when?" she blurted out.

He laughed, long and deep. "I don't know. I think maybe it was when you told me to clean my own rooms."

She drew back. "That's when?"

"Well, yeah, that and maybe it was the first time you came while saying my name."

"Maybe you should stop giving examples."

Laughing, he reached between them, gently cupping her cheeks. "I don't know the exact moment, but I know it happened. Maybe it was all at once. Maybe it was a slow thing. I don't know, but what I do know is that it's real. What I feel for you is not just lust—even though I feel a lot of that, don't get me wrong. It's deeper. It's heavier. It makes me think about things I never thought I would think about again."

Her heart was thundering in her chest. "Like what?"

His gaze searched hers. "Like moving in together. Maybe getting a pet fish and then we'll go and adopt one of those dogs you work with. Small steps and then bigger ones. Like going out and finding the biggest, most obnoxious ring that still won't be big enough to put on your finger. Like starting a family, one with William and you, and maybe another kid or two."

She sucked in a soft gasp. She couldn't believe what she was hearing, but every instinct was telling her that he was being for real.

"So, yeah, I love you, Nic." He dragged a thumb along her lip, careful not to hit the still-healing part. "And if you don't love me anymore, I'm going to spend however long it takes making you fall in love with me again. And I have a lot of time on my hands. I'm a de Vincent. I get what—"

"I love you, you idiot," she said, laughing as stupid tears filled her eyes. "I mean, if I didn't I wouldn't still be here. I didn't—"

Gabe's lips met hers, and the kiss was soft and sweet and careful. The kind of kiss she dreamt about when she was younger, because it was a kiss of a man in love. She could tell the difference. Sounded crazy, but it was true.

She gripped his arms, blinking back tears as he lifted his mouth from hers. When she was younger, she'd dreamt of this moment, might've even prayed for it a time or two, and the reality was so much more beautiful and raw than she could've prepared for. Emotion swirled inside her, messy and bright and consuming.

Her voice shook as she said, "I love you, Gabe."

"I will never grow tired of hearing you say that. Never." Gabe then got an arm under her legs and the next thing she knew he was lifting her into his arms, blanket and all. He cradled her to his chest as he carried her inside. "And I'm going to spend the next couple of hours proving just that to you."

Chapter 36

*N*ikki had never been more grateful than she was at that very moment that Gabe had stayed the night at her place. It didn't have anything to do with what happened in her apartment over a month ago. Though Gabe had stayed with her several nights after she returned to her apartment. He'd been with her for what turned out to be her first full night in this apartment.

If she hadn't loved him then, she would've fallen in love that night, when she couldn't get comfortable in her new place and he was there to distract her. When she woke in the middle of the night, afraid that someone was breaking into her place, he was there to get out of bed, check all the locks and door, and then hold her until she finally fell back asleep.

And that night had rinsed and repeated several nights until the trauma of living through what Parker had tried to do subsided just enough that she'd slept through the night.

The gratefulness didn't have anything to do with the fact they had to get up somewhat early, because they had to hit the road.

It had everything in that moment to do with how Gabe had woken her up about thirty minutes ago, first with his hand between her thighs and then his mouth, and now, as the last of the release was rolling through her, she decided she could wake up every morning like this.

Her grip tightened on the silky strands of his hair as she tugged that wonderful mouth of his to hers. She could taste herself on his lips as she kissed him.

"Hey," he said, brushing his lips over hers.

"Morning." She rolled him onto his back and straddled him, trailing a path of short kisses down his throat and over his chest.

His hands tightened on her hips. "Did you sleep well?"

"Perfect." Her tongue flicked over his nipple. "How about you?"

"Like a babe." He groaned as she reached between their bodies, gripping his hard length. "You know, you fell asleep on me last night."

"Did not." She lifted her hips, settling herself on his erection.

"Yeah, you did." He slid his hands around, cupping the cheeks of her ass. "You passed straight out on my chest."

She grinned. "It was the wine."

"Just the wine?"

"And maybe the orgasms," she admitted.

"It was definitely the orgasms." His words ended on a groan as she sunk down his length, seating herself fully. "I liked it, though."

"Yeah?" She started rocking her hips back and forth.

"Yeah." He dragged one hand up the center of her back, tangling it in her hair. "I like your weight on me. I think that's why I always sleep better when I'm with you." He brought her mouth to his. "I like this better, though."

Her laugh was caught by his kiss, and there really was no room left for words. Their bodies moved in a rhythm that was slow at first and then faster, until the only sounds left in the room were their soft pants and moans. The tension built deep inside her as she ground down on him.

"I love you," Gabe said against her mouth.

Those three little words sent her spiraling over the edge. Whatever semblance of control and rhythm were lost. Her chest was flush to his as he wrapped one arm around her back, the other around her waist as he anchored her in, taking over. He thrust into her, hitting every spot that drove her crazy. Startling pleasure shot through her veins. She flew apart again, shattering into a million little pieces. This time, Gabe followed her off the edge, kicking his head back as he spent himself deep inside her and let out the sexiest sound she'd ever heard.

Nikki collapsed on top of him, her heart rate slowing down as her body still twitched. "I think . . . I'm going to fall asleep on you again."

He chuckled as he smoothed hair out of her face. "I normally wouldn't have a problem with that, but we're going to have to get up soon."

They did, but at that moment, her muscles felt like they were made of soup, and Gabe wasn't moving yet. His one arm was still draped over her and his other hand was resting on the side of her head.

Nikki closed her eyes.

Things hadn't been exactly easy the last month. Her parents fully accepted her relationship with Gabe, but her mother had called upon Gabe unbeknownst to her until after the fact. They had a *private* conversation, one that Gabe skated around addressing whenever Nikki asked, but she was pretty sure that her mom might've threatened him at some point.

Lucian and Julia hadn't batted an eye when Gabe asked them to join them for dinner the first time. Probably had to do with the fact that they'd suspected something was going on, and when she'd been set up in Gabe's bedroom after the attack, it was probably a good indication that they were more than just friends.

And Devlin was just . . . well, he was Devlin.

Nikki actually hadn't seen him much since the day he showed up with Gabe at Rosie's apartment. Even when she returned to working at the de Vincent house, he rarely ate dinner at home and seemed only to be there in the evening. She had no idea how he was handling everything, but she guessed he had a lot on his mind.

Like where in the hell was Sabrina?

No one had seen her. Heard from her. Nothing. Her family reported her missing, and all that did was compound the scandal now circling the Harringtons and de Vincents. The magazines and gossip websites were having a field day with everything, as was Ross Haid. After all, you had a murderous son and missing daughter of one wealthy family who had been engaged to another massively wealthy family whose name was synonymous with scandal.

But she and Gabe . . . they were doing just fine, all things considered. They were together. For real. No hiding. She'd had so many fantasies of the two of them being together, but none of them, not a single one, even touched what it was like in real life. A tired, happy smile tugged at her lips.

"What are you thinking about?" he asked.

"Us," she admitted. "I was thinking about how many times I dreamt about this and how it being real is so much better than the dreams."

The arm around her clenched and he was quiet for a moment. "Sometimes I still think I don't deserve you."

She lifted her head so she could see him. "You deserve me, Gabe. You prove that every day."

"I'm going to keep proving it."

"I know," she whispered.

"We should probably get up and get on the road soon," Gabe said, but he tightened his arm around her waist, pulling her closer. "It's not a long drive, but I'd rather not get stuck in traffic."

She kissed his chest. "We should."

Nikki was ready to get the day started, because today was a huge day. One of the biggest of Nikki's life, because it was a step toward her future—*their* future.

Nikki was meeting Gabe's son today.

"Are you nervous?" he asked, brushing the hair back from her face.

"A little," she admitted.

"You shouldn't be." Gabe sat up, holding her so they were eye level. His gaze met hers.

"You think?" she asked.

"I know this." And then Gabriel de Vincent said the words she'd spent the better part of her life dreaming for; the same three words she'd never grow tired of hearing. "I love you."

GRAVEL CRUNCHED UNDER the tires as Gabe inched into the parking space toward the back of the lot. They were a few minutes early. He turned off the engine and then looked over at Nic. Her gaze met his, and without really thinking about it, he reached over and picked up her hand.

"I'm still nervous," she said, threading her fingers through his, and he already knew this. The fact she changed her clothing five times before settling on a pair of dark jeans and a chenille blouse before they left was evidence of that. "But I got this."

He drew her hand to his mouth and kissed the top of it. "I know you do."

She rewarded him with a huge smile, a breathtaking one. "Are you nervous?"

Gabe almost lied and told her no, but that wasn't how it was between them. They were honest, even when it was uncomfortable. "I am. I always am when I get to see him."

Even when he saw William last weekend, which he had. He figured it was best that he spent some time with his son before he introduced him to Nic. The Rothchilds knew he was bringing Nic with him today. They hadn't been resistant to the plan, but they also hadn't been wholly thrilled about it. But it wasn't personal. They didn't feel that way because of Nic or her age or her relationship with Gabe.

They didn't feel that way because Gabe was involved with someone who was going to be a part of their grandson's future.

They felt that way because of Emma.

The pain of losing their daughter was still evident in their eyes and every time he spoke to them.

Gabe had to tell them about Sabrina, even though he didn't want to put that kind of knowledge in their heads. He didn't want them to have to carry that or experience the helplessness turn into the kind of rage that could ruin a person, but with Sabrina still out there, the Rothchilds needed to be on guard just in case she attempted anything that involved his son.

Hopefully her whereabouts would be discovered and she'd become a nonissue, but Gabe wasn't taking any chances by leaving the Rothchilds out of what was happening.

"It's okay for you to be nervous. As long as you know he loves you, Gabe." Nic squeezed his hand and then leaned across the seat, curling her other hand around the nape of his neck. She brought his mouth to hers, and she kissed him softly. "As long as you know I love you."

"Mmm," he murmured against her lips. "We better get out of this car before we end up engaging in inappropriate behaviors."

Nic laughed as she drew away. "Let's go."

They climbed out, and walked to the front of the car. Gabe took her hand in his and they made their way through the cars and entered the park. He knew where the Rothchilds would be meeting them, by the playground area. His boy was an active little man and Gabe knew from experience that he'd run from the swings to the seahorses to the jungle gyms.

"There they are," he said as they crested a small hill. The Rothchilds were sitting on a bench while William hung from one of those metal bar contraptions.

They must've said something, because William quickly untangled himself and turned from his grandparents, spotting them before Gabe could say a word. The little boy's face broke out into a wide smile. Some of Gabe's fear began to fade. William recognized him. It was a stupid fear, one he had every time he saw his son. Would William forget him in the days that passed between visits? It was a fear that probably wasn't going to go away until things became more permanent, but William recognized *him*. That . . . that was good.

"Oh my word," Nic whispered under her breath, but he could hear the thickness to her words. "He looks like you, Gabe."

"He does, doesn't he?" Pride filled his voice. "He's going to be a little heartbreaker."

Nic laughed. "Yes—yes, he is."

She squeezed his hand as William took off toward them, racing around the merry-go-round, his little arms and legs pumping. Gabe felt the rest of his fear evaporate. Not only did William recognize him, he appeared ecstatic to see him, and that—yeah, that about broke Gabe in all the best ways. Nic slipped her hand free, just in time, too. Gabe lowered himself to one knee as William all but launched himself at his father. The little guy threw his arms around Gabe, and even though his weight was slight, he almost bowled him over.

"Hey, little man, it's so good to see you." His voice was hoarse as sandpaper. "Real good."

William could hug. Gabe already knew that. It was a full-bodied hug, one without reservations. The kind of hug a son gave to his father. The kind of hug that could bring fresh tears to the eyes of a full-grown man.

Then William pulled back and lifted his head, his blue-green eyes filled with curiosity as they fixed on Nic.

She grinned down at him, wiggling her fingers. "Hello."

"Hi." A tentative smile tugged at his son's mouth.

Next month, don't miss these exciting new love stories only from Avon Books

The Duke Buys a Bride by Sophie Jordan
The last thing Marcus, the Duke of Autenberry, expects to see after sleeping off a night's drunken shenanigans is a woman being auctioned in the village square. Before he can think about the ramifications, he buys her, thinking he's winning the girl her freedom. Instead, he discovers he's bought a wife . . .

A Duke by Default by Alyssa Cole
New York City socialite and perpetual hot mess Portia Hobbs is tired of disappointing her family, friends and—most importantly—herself. But an apprenticeship with Scottish swordmaker Tavish McKenzie is a chance to use her expertise and discover what she's capable of. Turns out, she excels at aggravating her gruff, but sexy, silver fox boss . . .

The Protector by HelenKay Dimon
Salvation, Pennsylvania, was advertised as a modern Utopia: a commune to live with other like-minded young people. Cate Pendleton's sister was one of them. Now she's dead—and Cate won't rest until she finds out who killed her. Stonewalled at every turn, she approaches a DC fixer, Damon Knox, a mysterious man with a secretive past. But Cate soon discovers that she not only needs Damon, she wants him . . .

And don't miss the final installment
in the de Vincent series

MOONLIGHT SCANDALS

Coming February 2019
From Avon Books

Acknowledgments

I want to thank Kevan Lyon for being the amazing agent that she is, always there to support whatever story idea comes to mind and working with me every step of the way. I cannot thank Taryn Fagerness enough for getting my books to as many countries and readers as possible. Because of you, I have an entire wall of books representing so many different languages. Thank you to my editor, Tessa Woodward, who decided to bring the de Vincent brothers to life, and to Shailyn Tavella, along with the wonderful team at HarperCollins/Avon Books. Thanks to Kristin Dwyer, who has worked tirelessly to get this book into as many hands as possible.

A huge thank-you to Stephanie Brown for helping keep my life on track and making me laugh. Without Sarah Maas, Laura Kaye, Andrea Joan, Stacey Morgan, Lesa Rodrigues, Sophie Jordan, Cora Carmack, Jay Crownover, KA Tucker, and countless other amazing friends I would've probably lost my mind by now. THANK YOU.

A special thanks to all the members in JLAnders who make me feel all kinds of special. And none of this would be possible without you, the reader. Because of you, I get to write another book, bring another world to life. Thank you.

"William, I want you to meet someone very special to me." Gabe kept an arm around his son's narrow waist as he looked up at Nic. Their gazes met, and Gabe felt this swelling in his chest he'd never really experienced before. "I know you're going to love her just as much as I do."